The new Zebra Regency Romance logo that you see on the cover is a photograph of an actual regency "tuzzy-muzzy." The fashionable regency lady often wore a tuzzy-muzzy tied with a satin or velvet riband around her wrist to carry a fragrant nosegay. Usually made of gold or silver, tuzzy-muzzies varied in design from the elegantly simple to the exquisitely ornate. The Zebra Regency Romance tuzzy-muzzy is made of alabaster with a silver filigree, edging.

A DELICATE DILEMMA

Demetra opened the door to the front parlour, walked into the room, and was pulled into her husband's arms.

It was little more than twenty-four hours since she had left Frank. She had seen him only this afternoon. There was really no call to cling to him as if they had just been reunited after months apart. So Demetra thought later. At the time, she did not think at all, not for a very long while. Indeed, she could not have said when she would have come to her senses, had Frank not at last ended the kiss. He raised one hand to smooth a wayward curl back from her face and said softly, "Come home, Demetra. Nothing can be serious enough to keep us apart."

Demetra stared up at him, suffused with longing. Why did he have to do this to her now, when she was about to uncover the nature of the entire plot? Her plan was admittedly risky. If it were awry, their separation was Frank's only protection . . .

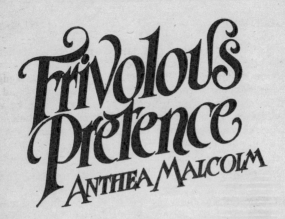

Frivolous Pretence

Anthea Malcolm

ZEBRA BOOKS
KENSINGTON PUBLISHING CORP.

ZEBRA BOOKS

are published by

Kensington Publishing Corp.
475 Park Avenue South
New York, NY 10016

First printing: February, 1990

Printed in the United States of America

For Doug, again.

And with thanks to Dick, Julianne, and Kory

Now, a consort is a wife; little conducive to harmony in the present day, and seldom visited by a man of fashion, unless she happens to be his friend's or his neighbour's.

George Coleman, *The Heir at Law*, 1797

Her fame by the filth of the Green Bag invaded,
If guilty, why e'en let the Queen be degraded;
But this I must say (without treason or slander),
What's sauce for the GOOSE is fit sauce for the GANDER!

The Morning Chronicle, October 2, 1820

Chapter 1

Tuesday, October 3, 1820

"Demetra!" Unable to believe that his wife had once again betrayed him, Frank Hawksley flung open the door and strode into the oak-paneled library.

"Oh, hullo, darling." Demetra was perched on top of a tall ladder, a book held carefully in both hands, a dust rag lying forgotten on one of the rungs. "Listen to this—

> *Tell me no more of constancy,*
> *that frivolous pretence,*
> *Of cold age, narrow jealousie,*
> *disease and want of sence.*"

Demetra closed the book and looked at her husband, her eyes dancing. "Lord Rochester did have a way of making the most appalling sentiments sound clever, didn't he?" she observed. "Though I daresay half the ton would agree with him. More than half, if one counts those who wouldn't admit it in public. Especially these days."

Now that he was actually before her, listening to the familiar, lilting voice, staring up into the warm gray-green eyes, Frank felt his resolve weakening. He was not a man given

7

to prevarication—indeed, many of his fellow Whigs said his greatest fault was his inability to hold his tongue—but in this case he could barely voice his suspicions to himself, let alone to his wife.

"Frank?" Demetra said, wondering at his silence. "Aren't you going to tell me what happened today? How was Brougham's speech? How's the betting running at Brooks's? Don't you know I've been on tenterhooks since you left for the House this morning?"

Though she was smiling, Demetra spoke no more than the truth. She always found politics interesting, but the events taking place in the House of Lords were nothing short of extraordinary. The long estrangement between the Prince Regent (now, since his father's death in January, King George IV) and his wife, Queen Caroline, had come to a head. The King wanted a divorce and the Queen was being tried before the Lords on charges of carrying on *a most unbecoming and disgusting intimacy* with her courier, Bartolomeo Bergami. The trial had been in progress since August, but today the defense had begun its case with an opening speech by the Queen's Attorney-General, the dynamic if controversial Henry Brougham.

"Brougham's speech was very good," Frank said at last. "Demetra—"

"*Good?*" Demetra exclaimed. "I thought the man was supposed to be brilliant. The Queen needs more than 'good.'"

"It was an excellent speech, even by Brougham's standards. And a long one. He'll continue tomorrow. Demetra—" Frank took a step forward, then checked himself. "Do you think you might come down?" he said impatiently. "This isn't the easiest way to carry on a conversation."

"Speak for yourself," Demetra retorted. "I rather like being able to look down on you for a change. Besides, you're quite indecently handsome from this angle, love."

She expected him to laugh and say, "And not from any other?" When his face remained serious she gathered up the book and dust rag and nimbly descended the ladder. Demetra was small and slight and moved gracefully, but the ladder was as old and worn as everything else in the Hawksleys' newly acquired London house, and it swayed dangerously as she reached the bottom rungs. Frank quickly steadied the ladder and held out a hand to her, but he released her as soon as she was standing on solid ground.

Demetra looked at him quizzically. She had not been jesting when she called him indecently handsome. Frank might not boast good looks in the classical tradition, but he was an undeniably attractive man. It was not his features, which were regular but rather harsh, nor his manner, which was perfectly correct but gave the impression that he was more than a trifle impatient with social amenities. No, it was an energy, a presence, which had caught her eye as she sat in the attic above the House of Commons seven years ago and which had held her ever since. That, and the fact that when he smiled he could make her forget almost anything else.

But there was no trace of a smile on his face now. Hoping to lighten her husband's mood and expression, Demetra said, "Don't tell me. The King says if Parliament won't give him a divorce, he'll break away from England and form his own country."

That did draw a faint smile from Frank, though it was a pallid imitation of his usual grin. Demetra placed the book and rag on a table which at least did not look in imminent danger of collapse and brushed the worst of the dust from her faded blue merino dress. "Now," she said, moving to a reasonably clean leather armchair, "perhaps you'd best tell me about it."

Frank remained where he had been standing and regarded his wife. In the plain dress, her titian hair confined at her neck with a ribbon and tumbling down her back, she looked more like the nineteen-year-old who had eloped with him to Gretna Green than a matron of six-and-twenty. Somehow she had gotten a smudge on her nose. Frank subdued the urge to wipe it away and tried not to think about the kiss that inevitably would have followed.

He walked to the chair opposite hers, but remained standing, gripping its back. "Have you seen your brother since you arrived in town?" he asked abruptly.

"I saw both my brothers when I took the children to see Mama and Papa," Demetra said, surprised, "and my sisters too, for that matter."

"Did you talk to them?"

Demetra's brows rose. "Of course I talked to them. My family's accused me of a lot of things through the years, Frank, but never of holding my tongue."

Demetra's family was old, wealthy, and staunchly Tory. It was perhaps not surprising that the rebellious Demetra had fallen in love with a young man of no particular birth or fortune whose political views even many Whigs considered extreme. In the first months after her elopement, Demetra's parents had not spoken to her, and Demetra had been equally determined not to speak to them. At last she had begun to pay them an occasional visit, though Frank refused to cross their doorstep.

And then, two years after their marriage, Frank had resigned his seat in the House of Commons and they had retired north to his father's sheep farm in Durham. Demetra's mind quickly skipped over these unpleasant events, as one might ignore the pain of a wound which continues to fester.

She had seen little of her family during the five years she and Frank had spent in the country. But now they were back in London, thanks to the unexpected deaths, in quick succession, of Frank's cousin and uncle, which had made her husband Baron Chester and left him with this house in Park Street, an estate in Surrey, and—if not a great deal of money—more money than they had seen in their entire married life. During Demetra's recent visit to her parents' house, her mother had given her to understand that Frank's elevation to a barony made him far more palatable to his in-laws.

But it had done nothing to make her family more palatable to

Frank. In fact, he and Demetra had had a spirited quarrel about her visit last week. If she wanted to reestablish relations with the family who had virtually driven her away, it was quite her own affair, Frank had claimed, but there was no call to drag the children into the midst of the conflict. Demetra had won in the end, Frank not being willing to stop her and the children from leaving the house, but now, as he questioned her about the visit, his face was remarkably grim.

"What did you talk about?"

"Good heavens, I don't remember. Sophy's début, Edwina's dresses, Lewis's new horse—"

"What about your elder brother?"

Demetra grinned. "As I recall, Quentin and I mostly ignored each other. A matter of prudence."

"Did you discuss the trial?"

It was a reasonable question. One could scarcely go anywhere these days without discussing Queen Caroline's trial. Scandal involving the royal family would always attract attention, of course, but the trial had gone beyond that and become a matter of political debate. As the ruling party, the Tories (such as Demetra's father and brother) supported the King. The Whigs, at least the radical Whigs (such as Frank), seeing a splendid chance to score a victory against the Tories, supported the Queen. In fact, it was because of the trial that Frank had had to return to London and take up his newly acquired seat in the Lords sooner than expected, leaving Demetra to settle affairs in Durham. During the three-week recess between the prosecution and the defense, Frank had returned to the country and escorted Demetra and the children to town. They had arrived only the previous week.

"As it happens, I took the greatest care not to talk about the trial," Demetra said. "I was on my very best behavior. It may come as a surprise to you, my sweet, but there are times when I think it best not to speak my mind."

"You didn't discuss the trial with St. George?"

"With Quentin? Certainly not. I told you, we were trying

11

not to quarrel. Frank, what on earth is this about?"

He lowered his gaze to the floor, unable to meet her sharp eyes. "Have you seen St. George since then?"

"I ran into him in Oxford Street, the morning I went to see about the new upholstery for the drawing room chairs. I must say, I was rather surprised to find him abroad so early, but no, I did not discuss the trial with him or do anything more than exchange commonplaces."

Frank ran a hand through his thick, close-cropped dark brown hair. "You're sure? Sometimes you can let something slip, without realizing—"

"I'm very sure." Demetra fixed her husband with a hard stare, forcing him to meet her gaze. "Frank. *What is this about?*"

Frank raised his head and looked her full in the face. "Nicholas saw St. George in Wardour Street this morning."

"Wardour Street?"

"Outside the Contessa Montalto's lodgings."

Demetra looked at him blankly, about to ask who the Contessa Montalto was and why Quentin shouldn't be outside her lodgings. He had, after all, recently returned from Italy and might very well be acquainted with a contessa. In fact, knowing her brother, he might very well be much more than acquainted.

But before Demetra could voice any of this, memory returned. Like everything else these days, it had to do with the trial. As Queen Caroline had for some years been living in Italy and had allegedly committed adultery with an Italian, a number of Italians had been brought to London to testify at the trial. Most of them were testifying for the Tories. The Contessa Montalto was an exception. Frank had mentioned her to Demetra only a few days before. The contessa, he had said, had recently arrived in England and the Whigs expected great things of her.

"I thought you told me her whereabouts in London was a secret," Demetra said, recalling the rest of her conversation with her husband.

"It was," Frank returned evenly. "Only a handful of us knew where she was staying. Nicholas asked if I'd told anyone."

"But you didn't, did you?" Demetra said reasonably. "Except me, of course."

Frank was silent but this time he did not look away. Demetra stared into the dark eyes, which could be gentle and tender or amused or blazing with anger, and saw none of these usual expressions. Instead they held the question he could not bring himself to put into words.

"Frank," she said, torn between shock, indignation, and a kind of desperate amusement, "you can't seriously think I'd be so idiotish as to tell Quentin something like that?"

His silence was answer enough. Demetra, never one to turn away from the unpleasant, said it for him. "How silly of me. Why shouldn't you think it? It's the logical explanation after all. Nearly everyone is convinced I did the same thing five years ago."

It was almost a relief to be able to say it, almost a relief to think back to the events of that summer and not ignore them as she had taught herself to do.

1815. The year of Waterloo. The year their first child was born. The year Frank's colleagues became convinced that Demetra had betrayed their confidence to her Tory brother. The year Frank resigned his seat in the Commons, supposedly because of his father's failing health, though Demetra was convinced she was at the root of it.

It wouldn't have been so bad if she had not been certain that, for all his fierce defense of her, Frank did not truly believe her protestations of innocence. He could perhaps not be blamed for having moments of doubt, but his lack of faith hurt Demetra more than she cared to admit.

When Frank's sudden inheritance of his uncle's barony gave him a seat in the House of Lords and the chance to leave his self-imposed exile in Durham and return to the political life

13

he loved, Demetra had hoped that they could finally put the past behind them. Now it was only too clear that they could not.

Frank watched the expressions flitting across his wife's face. He wanted to tell her not to be a fool, to say that of course he believed her, he had always believed her, he had never suffered a moment's doubt. But even if he did so, it would be of little use. Demetra had the damnable knack of always being able to tell when he was lying.

Five years ago, when he first faced the possibility that his wife had betrayed him, Frank had tried to suppress his doubts. When he could not do so, he told himself that the past didn't matter, that it was the future which was important and if the future was to be preserved the best course was to act as though the events of 1815 had never happened.

In Durham he had not hesitated to talk to Demetra about sheep. When he had brought her to London only last week, he realized that their life would be intolerable if he could not speak to her as openly about politics. Whatever she had done five years ago, he had thought he could trust her now. And so he had not hesitated to tell her about the Contessa Montalto.

"I didn't say that," Frank said at last, into the silence.

"No, but you thought it." Demetra sprang to her feet and faced him, five feet two inches of fury. "You thought it five years ago and you're thinking it now."

"Five years ago I—"

"Five years ago you defended me as an honourable man should, and all the time you were thinking—"

"How can you know what I was thinking?" Frank had been holding his temper in check, but he could never do so for long.

"You didn't do a very good job of hiding it," she maintained, and then made haste to regain the offensive. "If you believed me, why did you refuse to talk about it?"

"I thought it best—"

"To ignore the fact that your wife had betrayed you."

"Demetra, you aren't making this easy."

14

"*I'm* not making this easy! What the devil do you think you're doing? If you expect me to make a tearful confession you are going to be sadly disappointed. I had nothing to confess five years ago and I certainly have nothing to confess now. I didn't say anything to Quentin. Do you believe me?"

Frank drew a breath. "If that's what you say, of course I believe you."

"Like you believed me five years ago?"

He started to speak, then bit back the words. "What more can I say?" he said quietly.

"Nothing." Demetra turned away from him and walked to the fireplace, then turned back to face him, her own voice more controlled. "Did you tell Nicholas I'm the only one you talked to about the contessa?"

"He asked me."

"And you're not a liar. Does Nicholas think I told Quentin?"

"Nicholas isn't one to jump to conclusions." Nicholas was also a gentleman, and so of course he had not voiced his suspicions, though he had not been able to conceal them from Frank, any more than Frank could conceal his from Demetra.

"And the others?" Demetra asked.

"I don't know what the others think."

"But you can guess as well as I can," Demetra said. "Frank, we both know why you resigned five years ago."

Frank stiffened, his hands tightening on the chair back. "Of course we do," he said in a measured tone. "Father was ill, the farm needed attention—"

"Yes, but that wasn't the reason, at least not the only reason. If it was, why did you refuse to stand for Parliament again, after your father died and the farm was put in order?"

"That has nothing to do with you, Demetra," Frank said firmly.

"And the trial has nothing to do with Queen Caroline," Demetra retorted. "I think we both hoped that if we ignored it we could put it behind us, but now it's clear that we can't. You

15

resigned because of me, because the Whig leaders thought I wasn't to be trusted. Did they force you to give up your seat?"

"Of course not."

"Did they hint that it would be best if you did?"

"Demetra, I can't see what good is served by dredging up the past."

"A great deal of good when the past is the same as the present. I thought perhaps it would all be forgotten by now, but because of this latest trouble it's going to be worse than ever, isn't it? Now that you're a peer you can't resign your seat, but you'll have precious little chance to do anything if your own party doesn't trust you. And don't tell me you'd just as soon go back to Durham and raise sheep, because I know perfectly well it's not true."

"I thought you were happy in Durham," Frank protested.

"Of course I was happy. I'm always happy when I'm with you. That's not the point. It's not me we're talking about. It's you."

"Did I ever say I was unhappy?"

"Frank, if you're trying to convince me that you were happy escorting me to the local assemblies and talking pigs with the squire—"

"Dogs." Frank grinned unexpectedly. "The squire has dogs, Demetra. It's the vicar who raises pigs."

"Well it's the same thing, Frank. Just as dull. Don't deny you're glad to be back in Parliament."

"I won't deny it. But—"

"But you won't truly be happy as long as your friends don't fully trust you. And I won't truly be happy as long as you don't fully trust me."

"We've been over that."

"Yes." Demetra walked to the window and stared out into the tangled remains of the late Baron Chester's garden. Frank was being pigheaded. He was one of the most pigheaded people she knew—though, in fairness, she was not exactly compliant herself. She had followed Frank's lead once. After several

16

fruitless quarrels, she had more or less accepted his decision to ignore the summer of 1815. The succeeding years had not been as glorious as the first years of their marriage. They had not been unhappy, but the problem had not gone away and this fresh crisis meant they could no longer ignore it. If their marriage and Frank's career were to survive—and Demetra had no intention of giving up on either one—something of a fairly drastic nature was called for. She was not entirely sure how the thing was to be managed, but it was clear what her first step should be.

It would not be particularly pleasant, but she would be a very poor-spirited creature if she let such a paltry consideration stand in her way. Frank would dislike it excessively, of course, but that had never stopped her in the past.

Demetra turned back from the window. "The house is in terrible condition," she said. "There are an army of workmen about. It's certainly no place for the children. For all our sakes, I think it would be best if I took them away for a time."

"Don't be a fool, Demetra," Frank said sharply. "If you imagine things will be improved by your going back to Durham—"

"I have no intention of going back to Durham, Frank."

"Then where the devil will you go?"

Demetra lifted her chin. "Why, to my parents' house. Where else?"

Chapter 2

"I have no desire to be reminded that I am a grandmother, Demetra." Catherine Thane, Countess Buckleigh, handed her daughter a cup of fragrant tea. "And in any case it's rather late for you to pretend concern for my maternal feelings. They were never very strong, and five children were enough to do away with them altogether."

Demetra raised her cup, inhaling the subtle smoky scent of the tea, so unlike the harsh brew they were accustomed to drink in Durham. "If it's inconvenient, Mama—"

"I didn't say it was inconvenient, Demetra, I said it was odd. Your children seem sturdy little things, and I daresay life on a sheepfarm has quite inured them to physical discomfort."

"There's nothing uncomfortable about sheep, Mama, except sometimes the price of wool. Unless, of course, you object to the bleating and the smell when they're wet."

"Don't throw country crudeness at me, Demetra, it's an affectation. Old Chester was careless, but I can't believe his house is not habitable."

"It's dirty, Mama, and needs ever so much work, and the children will only be in the way. And there isn't a proper staff, only Robbins, who's been with Frank for years and is doubling

18

as a butler, and Mrs. Burbage, who sees to the meals, and Mary Rose, who has her hands full with Colin and Annie. But if you don't like it, we can go to a hotel."

Lady Buckleigh looked hard at her daughter. It was not an idle threat. The girl was quite capable of setting herself and her children up in a hotel, where they would be the objects of endless speculation. Or taking lodgings in an unsavory part of town. Lady Buckleigh did not for a moment believe that the condition of the late Baron Chester's house was sufficient reason for her daughter to remove herself from her husband's protection. Was there at last a strain in that improbable marriage? "Have you quarreled with your husband, Demetra?"

"Quarreled with Frank? All the time."

"Don't be clever. People will say you've left him."

"People may say what they choose, there's nothing further from the truth," Demetra retorted with a flash of temper. Then she returned to the sweetness of manner she had adopted for this crucial visit to her mother. "I never thought you cared for what people might say, Mama."

"I don't care for it, Demetra, but I respect it. There's all the difference between the two, as you would be wise to learn." Lady Buckleigh regarded her eldest child with something approaching exasperation. Demetra was no beauty. Her hair was thick, curly, and indecently red, a throwback to some ancestor on her father's side. Her features were pleasing enough, but with no special distinction, and her pale skin was disfigured by freckles which ran all over her nose and spattered her cheeks. She had a kind of raffish charm, but she was willful and had never learned to curb her tongue, and two children and seven years of marriage had not tempered her impudence.

Lady Buckleigh tried a different tack. "I can't help but think that coming into the title is the best thing that could have happened to your husband, Demetra. He'll mingle with a different sort of people, and even among the Whigs some gentility is bound to rub off. I don't suppose," she added,

19

struck by a sudden thought, "that you intend to have him move in here too?"

"I wouldn't dream of it, Mama, and be assured neither would Frank. He'll do very well in one or two rooms while the house is being done over, and he'll be glad to have us out of his hair."

"You can't have your old room back, you know. It's Edwina's now."

"No matter," Demetra said with a happy smile. Her objective had been won. "I can share with Sophy, if you like. Or sleep in the nursery with Colin and Annie."

"You can have the yellow room," Lady Buckleigh said repressively. Demetra was going to make it difficult, but Lady Buckleigh was not without affection for her errant daughter and could not entirely suppress a feeling of triumph that Demetra had seen fit, at last, to return to her family. "When do you propose to come?"

"Today, if I may."

"And when will you bring the children?"

"They're already here, Mama."

Lady Buckleigh had not expected such an imminent invasion. Demetra must have been very sure of her welcome. But then, Demetra had never questioned that events would fall out exactly as she wished. "They're remarkably quiet. Where did you hide them?"

"I left them in the kitchen with Mary Rose. She came with us from Durham and they're used to her. They'll be no trouble," Demetra added hastily, with an assurance she did not quite feel. "If you could send one of the footmen to Park Street for our boxes—I've scarcely had time to unpack since I arrived in town, and they're all ready."

It occurred to Lady Buckleigh that Demetra was the most efficient of her three daughters. Not like Edwina, who was inclined to indolence, nor like Sophy, who had a memory like a sieve. In this, at least, Demetra took after her mother. It was not the virtue Lady Buckleigh had been most anxious to instill, but it was a legacy of sorts. "And your maid?" she asked, knowing the answer she would be given.

"Oh, I do without," Demetra said calmly. "Will you give me another cup of tea?"

As Lady Buckleigh complied with this request, she gave some thought to the problem of her daughter's clothes. Demetra's dress was dated and shabby and, while perhaps it would do in Durham, was hardly fit to be seen in London. Not on the Baroness Chester. Was money going to be a problem? How much had the old man left? Reflecting that her daughter was not only going to disrupt the house but prove to be an expense as well, Lady Buckleigh passed Demetra her cup, refilled her own, and prepared to launch a discreet inquiry into the state of the Hawksleys' domestic economy.

But before the countess could begin, her youngest daughter burst into the room. "Mama, where do you think we have been?" She stopped short, suddenly abashed by Demetra's presence. Save for a brief meeting the week before, Sophy had not set eyes on Demetra since the age of thirteen and she was not sure what line she was expected to take with the sister who was spoken of seldom and then in disapproving tones. "Demetra," she said, "how nice of you to call."

Coming from the forthright Sophy, it was a ridiculous statement. Demetra smiled and held out her hand. "Come sit by me, Sophy. I'm not dangerous, and Mama assures me that Frank's title makes me almost respectable."

Sophy grinned and sat awkwardly on the sofa beside her sister. She was, to her mother's despair, a giant of a girl, with unruly sandy hair and brusque manners more suited to the country than the drawing room. She was barely eighteen, but Lady Buckleigh, judging that what could now pass as refreshing high spirits would in one or two years' time mark her as a hopeless misfit on the Marriage Mart, had brought her to London in the spring and allowed her to make a quiet début.

Sophy had not been a success. Her figure, fortunately, was well developed—indeed, her breasts were likely to attract more notice than was seemly—and when she was carefully dressed she might almost be accounted handsome, but she did not take the marriage game seriously and she treated incipient suitors with a bluff camaraderie that forestalled romance and drove out all thoughts of marriage, even to an earl's daughter.

Demetra looked at Sophy with affection. Of her four brothers and sisters, Sophy had always been her favorite. She had been an endearingly unconventional little girl and—despite, Demetra was sure, their mother's best efforts—she had not grown into a conformable young lady.

Sophy's moment of shyness had passed, and she returned to her first question. "Mama, where do you think we have been?"

"I've been to London to look at the queen," Demetra quoted softly.

Sophy's face fell. "How did you know?"

"Sophy, you didn't!" The image of the daughter of one of England's staunchest Tory families calling on the reprobate Queen Caroline sent Demetra off into a fit of the giggles.

"Sophy, don't exaggerate," Lady Buckleigh said reprovingly. "Demetra, the Queen is not a subject for laughter."

"Oh, I quite agree, Mama, I think she has been treated most shabbily." Demetra knew that the Whigs were exploiting the Queen for their own ends, just as the Tories were vilifying her for theirs, but in politics she was a committed Whig, and in the matter of the argument between husband and wife, she was firmly on the side of the woman.

"She has brought it on herself," Lady Buckleigh announced. "On the best construction, her behavior has been imprudent. I can only conclude that Caroline of Brunswick is a victim of her own vanity or her own stupidity. In any event, she's not a fit subject for the drawing room."

"I don't know why, Mama," Sophy said. "It's all people were talking about last night at the Swinfords'. Lady Nelliston was saying that when the Queen was in Geneva she went to a ball in a dress that bared her—"

"Sophy!"

"Both of them. They say she did it in Italy too. I don't know why you should be upset, it was a Greek fashion, if one can judge by the statues they left."

"The Greeks are not English," her mother said, "and neither, thank God, are the Italians. And you have no business listening to a woman like Lady Nelliston."

"Then why do you take me to visit at houses where she is present?" Sophy asked, not unreasonably. "She was only talking of fashions, and you're forever after me to think more about my clothes, so I thought the conversation was quite unexceptionable, and I must say I thought it very interesting. Though not very comfortable," she added, glancing down at her own swelling breasts, "I mean, they would bounce about so." She exploded in laughter. "So don't worry, Mama, I shall stay well covered."

Lady Buckleigh stared at Sophy with disfavor. The countess was not a prude, but she believed in at least the appearance of decorous behavior. She poured her youngest daughter a cup of tea, relying on the calming efficacy of this ritual. "I trust you do not talk like this outside of our own walls, Sophy."

"Why ever not, Mama? Everyone else does."

That was all too true. Bawdy talk was in the air. Even the Archbishop of Canterbury had taken to telling risqué stories, and every publication was full of the Queen's scandalous behavior up and down the Italian peninsula and even into the Holy Land. The Home Secretary, Lord Sidmouth, had forbidden his daughters to read the newspapers, a useless exercise, Lady Buckleigh thought, for the girls would do so anyway, and far better to have it in the open than to let it fester in secret where the shameful thoughts would only grow and make them unmindful of where their duty lay.

"I hadn't realized how provincial we'd become in Durham," Demetra said. "Everyone's furious with Parliament, but no one gives a fig for who is king or queen." This was not strictly true, but Demetra was well aware that the gossip that seemed of consuming importance in the capital lost much of its force when translated two hundred and seventy miles north.

"Well, I think it's interesting," Sophy persisted. "We did see the Queen, you know, in a carriage in Pall Mall. She's rather fat, but so is the King, and she's dreadfully painted, but they say he is too, so I don't see a particle of difference between them."

"What were you doing in Pall Mall?" Lady Buckleigh inquired. "I thought you'd gone to Weyridge's."

"Oh. Well, we did, but then Edwina wanted to walk and somehow that's where we got to." Sophy looked confused. Edwina never wanted to walk anywhere, and it was only when they came upon Elliot Marsden that she had indicated she was in no particular hurry to return home. Sophy had been quite willing to comply, for she knew that their mother did not approve of Edwina's friendship with Mr. Marsden, and she had dawdled conveniently behind while the couple conversed.

"I see." Lady Buckleigh did not for a moment believe the story. She looked with distaste at the tepid liquid in the bottom of her cup. "Ring for a fresh pot of tea, Sophy. Did Edwina return home with you?"

"Of course, Mama, what else would she have done?" Sophy rose and walked to the bell rope.

"Yes, Mama, what else would I have done?" Echoing her sister's words, Lady Edwina Thane entered the room and sat down gracefully on a stiff-backed chair. "I've already ordered fresh tea, Sophy, you needn't bother to ring. Hullo, Demetra."

Edwina, five years Demetra's junior, was a dark beauty like their mother, with an admirable figure, an innate elegance, and an instinctive understanding of what was owed to the name of Thane. But Demetra sensed undercurrents in Edwina's manner that did not accord with what she remembered of her sister, and she looked at her with some curiosity. "We were talking about the Queen," Demetra said.

"Everyone's talking about the Queen. She's quite ugly, you know," Edwina informed them, "and from all reports she never washes, and she has the grossest appetites. All the

24

appetites. One wonders how she can possibly be guilty of half the things of which she stands accused. I find it hard to imagine a man—"

"Edwina!" Her mother's voice cut her off. "Ah, fresh tea. Thank you, Manningtree."

There was silence until the butler withdrew.

"I doubt that she is guilty of any behavior worse than that of the people one meets every day," Demetra said when the door had closed behind Manningtree.

"She is guilty of imprudence," Lady Buckleigh insisted as she busied herself with the teapot, "and of flagrant disregard for the look of things. Appearance," she finished majestically, "is all."

"But that's just it," Demetra said. "She *wants* to be noticed. I'm sure she's never forgiven her husband for the way she was treated in England. He lay drunk on the floor on her wedding night, he gave her jewels to his mistress and made her take the woman as her lady-in-waiting, he exiled her from the court and kept her from her own daughter, and then he accused her of adultery and of bearing a child out of wedlock. No wonder she left the country. How was she supposed to feel about him? Why not pay him back by embarrassing him in all the capitals of Europe?"

"There are better ways of managing a husband," Lady Buckleigh proclaimed.

"It's hard to manage anybody when you're in exile."

"She would never have been exiled had she chosen to behave with circumspection. Any clever woman can give the appearance of seemly conduct," Lady Buckleigh said.

"Demetra's on the side of the Queen," Sophy announced, as though this were an act of great daring.

"That's a matter of course," Lady Buckleigh said, "considering where her husband sits."

"It's not at all a matter of course," Demetra insisted hotly. "I'm on the side of justice, and the Queen has not had a fair hearing."

25

Edwina was amused. "And you, Mama, where do you stand?"

"With the King, that goes without saying. Though he has no right to cast stones. In the matter of his marriage, he's behaved disgracefully. They should be separated, of course, and the Queen should be sent back to the Continent—it makes little difference how she behaves among foreigners—but I do not believe in divorce."

"The King certainly has no right to one," Demetra said, "but if I were the Queen, I might be tempted to let my marriage be dissolved."

Lady Buckleigh looked at her eldest daughter in sudden alarm. She had been outraged by Demetra's marriage, but its dissolution would be infinitely worse. The radical Whigs were known to be careless in these matters, but that was no excuse for Demetra to be contemplating another imprudent act. "There are ways of handling these things," the countess said, "that are agreeable to both parties."

Demetra smiled and picked up her cup. She could read her mother well, and she had not missed that flash of alarm. It would do no harm to have Mama believe that she was having second thoughts about her marriage.

"The behavior of the mob is execrable."

It was the voice Demetra had been waiting to hear ever since she arrived at Buckleigh House. She turned to see her brother Quentin, Viscount St. George, walk slowly into the room, followed by her younger brother Lewis.

Whatever her feelings about Quentin, Demetra had to admit he was pleasant to look upon. He was a handsome man of twenty-five, not much above average in height but well formed and fashionably dressed. Like Edwina, he was dark, but his countenance showed nothing of his sister's softness. His face was long, with a broad, high forehead and sharply drawn features. His lips, thin but well shaped, gave a hint at once of sensuality and malice. His eyes seemed perpetually narrowed, as though to ward off intrusion by those who would pry into his thoughts, and his bearing betrayed the arrogance of a man who was heir to a comfortable fortune and an earldom. He was very successful with women.

St. George took a stand against the mantel. "I have been attacked," he announced.

"Oh, Quentin, how thrilling!" Sophy leaned forward eagerly. "Whatever did you do to provoke it?"

"Don't be spiteful, Sophy," Lewis said. He was the youngest of the Thane children, and Sophy was the only one of his sisters to whom he dared stand up. "I was there, and it really happened. We'd been at White's and we came out into Piccadilly and there were ever so many people about, on their way to demonstrate for the Queen. They had signs and banners and were shouting all manner of obscenities about the King's supporters, and one of them made a rude gesture and another tore at Quentin's cravat and I pushed him away and then some other men started pushing back and then—" He paused. It had been an heroic moment for Lewis, but it had had no sequel and he was not sure how to properly round off his story.

"And then Quentin lifted an eyebrow and they cowered in terror," Edwina suggested dryly.

"No, I lifted my stick," St. George returned in the same tone. "Lewis," he said generously, "was quite fierce."

The young man blushed with pride. He was just seventeen and had only recently been admitted to his brother's company on terms of some equality.

"The country is rotting," St. George went on in a derisive tone that did not quite mask the outrage underneath. "I come home after months on the Continent and find the rabble in control. Barricades in front of the House, gunboats on the river, windows smashed, people pulled out of carriages. Thornton passed the Lievens' house today and saw a large scrawl on the wall outside their stables—*The Queen forever. The King in the river.* You'd think the Government would see fit to make the streets safe for decent men to walk abroad." He turned to his mother. "Would you mind if I rang for brandy?"

"Not in the drawing room, Quentin." Lady Buckleigh had satisfied herself that neither of her sons had been in any real danger. "You may have a cup of tea."

St. George waved the offer away. "No matter, I'll be off soon. I just wanted to deliver Lewis home."

"I'd like some tea, Mother." Lewis took a chair near Demetra. He was an awkward boy, with hands and feet that were not yet under control, but he had fine features and clear skin and glossy dark hair, and Demetra judged that he would one day rival his elder brother in good looks as he promised to do in height.

St. George became aware of his eldest sister's presence, and he made her a mocking bow. "I hadn't expected to see you again so soon, Demetra."

"Why ever not, Quentin? Surely I may visit my family."

"You've shown scant interest in your family."

"They've shown scant interest in me. But that's all changed now," Demetra continued hastily, seeing her mother's frown. "There's no use worrying over the past, like a dog with an old bone. You may not approve of me, Quentin, but you can't deny our bond."

"That's an appalling bit of sentimentality."

Demetra giggled. "Yes, it is rather, isn't it? Think of it this way, Quen. We shared the same roof for eighteen years. Surely you can tolerate my company now and then. I'm quite prepared to tolerate yours." Her smile robbed the words of apparent offense, but they carried the sting of childhood rivalries.

"I have never been able to understand," Lady Buckleigh said, "why my children quarrel so much more than anyone else's." It was quite true. Demetra and Quentin, who was a year her junior, had been squabbling from nursery days. Then it was Quentin and Edwina. And Sophy and Lewis, also a year apart, bickered constantly.

"We don't, Mama," Edwina said, "we only do it more openly."

"People should keep their feelings decently hidden. It's the

28

secret of all civilized social intercourse and the only thing that makes family life supportable."

"Then you haven't attended Parliamentary debates, Mother," St. George said.

"Nor do I care to. There's quite enough of that sort of thing in the papers." Lady Buckleigh set down her cup, got to her feet, and moved toward the door. "I have some things to see to." She paused in the doorway and looked back at her offspring. Her expression was unreadable. "Demetra will be staying with us for a while," she said, "and she's brought the children."

After Lady Buckleigh's announcement, there was dead silence in the room. Demetra observed her brothers and sisters with amusement. They had clearly not expected this. Edwina, she could swear, was wondering whether her elder sister would want her room back. Quentin was regarding her as though she were a problem he had to solve. Sophy and Lewis seemed perplexed. This evidence of Demetra's return to their parents' favor was clearly outside their understanding.

It was Sophy who broke the silence. "How splendid!" she exclaimed. "We'll have ever such interesting talks."

"Why?" Lewis asked bluntly. "I thought you had a house."

"We do," Demetra said, "but it's in dreadful condition and needs a great deal of work, so I'm going to live here until it's put to rights."

St. George eyed his sister speculatively. "Have you left Hawksley?"

Demetra lifted her chin a fraction. "No, Quentin, I have not."

"How stupid of me. There are ways of handling these things, aren't there? And Mother doesn't believe in divorce."

"Don't be beastly, Quentin," Sophy said. "Demetra didn't say anything about a divorce."

"Not even," Demetra said, "about a separation."

"I don't see what all the dust-up is about," Lewis

29

complained. "Married people aren't supposed to live in each other's pockets. Mama—Mother and Father scarcely ever dine together." He had slouched over to the fireplace and assumed a careless pose next to St. George.

"The secret of their amicability," Edwina murmured.

"If I were married to a woman like Mother," Lewis went on, greatly daring, "I think I would want a little separation in my life."

"But you don't have to marry a woman like Mama, Lewis," Sophy said. "You can pick out a nice conformable girl who will hang on your every word."

Lewis blushed, more at the notion of being married at all than at this image of domestic felicity.

"Will your husband be glad of a little separation, Demetra?" St. George inquired.

"Don't be idiotish, Quentin," Sophy burst out, "Demetra's not at all like Mama."

"Ah, you don't know our sister like I do, Sophy. Demetra inherited Mother's most commanding traits."

"Dubious praise, Quentin," Demetra said, "though it's probably the nicest thing you've ever said to me. I'd rather have inherited her looks."

"Yes, she's still a handsome woman, isn't she? You see what you have to look forward to, Edwina. Yours is the beauty that will endure."

Edwina did not look at her brother. "I daresay Demetra's will prove quite as durable," she said with little show of interest.

"Will your husband come here?" Sophy wanted to know.

Demetra had not thought that far. Frank had met her parents and her elder brother before they were married, and it was not an experience she was eager to repeat. The others had never seen him, but she could imagine the stories they must have heard. "Of course he'll come," she said, with a certainty she did not feel. "He'll want to see the children, and I doubt that even Mama will deny the house to Baron Chester." She grinned. "But I'm not sure you'll be allowed to meet him."

Sophy laughed. "You're bamming me!"

"*I'll* be willing to shake his hand," Lewis said with utter seriousness. It was a declaration of independence from Quentin, whose strictures against Frank Hawksley had been familiar sounds these past seven years.

"Thank you, Lewis," Demetra said, oddly touched by this sign of her younger brother's support.

"Where will you sleep?" Sophy asked.

"Mama says I'm to have the yellow room, and the children of course will be in the nursery. And speaking of the nursery, I must go up and have a look at it and see what needs to be done. Come with me, Sophy, or I may get lost. It's been years since I've been in such a grand house."

The others were quiet after Demetra and Sophy left the room. Lewis looked from Quentin to Edwina. "Well, I'm glad she's here," he said defiantly. "I always liked her."

"You scarcely knew her," St. George said.

"I was twelve when she left London," Lewis said with dignity. "I remember." And with that Lewis, too, left the room, closing the door carefully behind him.

"Poor Lewis," Edwina said.

"Oh, Lewis is right enough." St. George's thoughts were clearly elsewhere. "Do you mind very much?"

"Why should I mind?"

"Demetra has a way of making her presence felt. And her brats will be all over the house."

Edwina was not sure this was such a bad thing. Demetra had brought an air of excitement and restlessness to Bruton Street that accorded with Edwina's own disquiet. "No," she told him, "I don't mind at all. And you?"

"Oh, it's all one to me," St. George said. "But it's not like Demetra. I wonder what the devil she's about."

Demetra was perched on one of the nursery beds, her arms

31

clasped around her knees, while Sophy poked about the room, remembering old hiding places and old toys. Demetra answered her chatter absently. She was thinking about Quentin.

Her brother was clever and not too nice about how he obtained his ends. It was not chance that he had appeared in Wardour Street outside the Contessa Montalto's lodgings. Where Quentin was concerned, Demetra did not believe in coincidence. He was up to something. He had to be stopped.

That much had been clear to Demetra when Frank confronted her in the library two hours earlier. She had come to Buckleigh House to keep Quentin under observation and find out precisely what his game was. If he thought there was some strain in her marriage, so much the better. It would put him off his guard and make it easier to discover what he was about. And when she had proof of his schemes, she would go to the Whigs and expose him. If she was able to do that, surely the Whigs would no longer suspect her of disloyalty. Nor would they then suspect Frank. And their marriage, now foundering on Frank's mistrust, would be reclaimed.

Demetra set herself to think through the problem. How had Quentin learned where the contessa was being kept? If she knew that, she would know where to begin. Someone obviously must have told him. But Frank said there were few men who knew, and none of them had any use for her brother. Quentin might have approached their wives or mistresses, but the contessa had only been in England a few days, and even Quentin would scarcely have had time to tumble them into bed.

"Demetra?"

Sophy had spoken her sister's name twice before Demetra realized she was being addressed. "I'm sorry," she said with a rueful smile, "I was just remembering. I swear, when I'm up here I feel like I'm twelve years old."

"You almost look it." Sophy's voice held a touch of envy. "It's one of the advantages of being small. If I hadn't grown so big, I don't think Mama would have been half as eager to bring me out."

"Don't you like being out?"

"Not really," Sophy said frankly. "Mama says I'm not trying, and I suppose that's the way it looks to her, for I make a point of not remembering all the things she tells me about how I should walk and talk and what I should do with my eyes and hands. There's no use trying to remember, for I always do it wrong anyway. I'm not very good at being a girl." She laughed. "*That* kind of girl. You know what I mean."

Demetra grinned. "I know exactly what you mean. You're being molded."

"But it won't work. It didn't with you, did it?"

"No, but I had to leave home, and that's a drastic remedy. I don't advise it unless you have a good excuse. I was out of my head with love."

Sophy looked at her curiously. "He must have been a very special man."

"He was. He is. And I still am. Does that answer your questions?"

"I didn't mean to pry."

"Of course not," Demetra said. "And I don't mind. Tell me about your Season."

"Oh, it's much like anyone else's, I suppose. Except that I'm not taking very well. I'm very hearty with the boys, which makes them think of their sisters, and I'm not pretty enough or conformable enough to interest the men. That's the way I planned it, of course. I knew I could defeat Mama." She sat down at the other end of the bed. "I don't know why Mama is so anxious to marry me off, unless it's because she's afraid I'll turn out like Edwina and not want to marry anyone at all."

"Edwina? I can't believe it. She's had men dangling after her since she was sixteen, and she's loved every minute of it."

"Oh, it's not men she doesn't like, it's the idea of being tied to any single one of them. Of course Mama expected her to marry Tony, but something happened between them last year and he went off to America and hasn't come back."

"Did Edwina mind very much?" Demetra asked.

"I don't think Edwina minded at all. It's hard to be enthusiastic about marrying your cousin, and I think she was relieved when it was over. But ever since then she's been difficult. She's taken to making clever remarks and doesn't listen to Mama like she used to. And in a funny way," Sophy added, "she seems more human. Even Lewis says so, and he's so full of himself he doesn't notice very much else."

"Perhaps it's because he's trying to become a man," Demetra suggested.

"Exactly. And he doesn't know whether to model himself on Quentin or Papa or Manningtree. I told him he should concentrate on Manningtree—he's by far the grandest of the lot."

Demetra laughed. "When does he go to university?"

"That's the problem. Not for another year. I don't think he did very well at Harrow, so he's having a year of study at home, or he will as soon as Mama finds another tutor. Lewis hates it, of course, and escapes with Quentin whenever he can, and Mama encourages it because she thinks Quentin will give him a bit of polish and teach him how to go on."

It was, Demetra decided, a very good thing she had returned to Buckleigh House, and not just because of her problem with Quentin. Her sisters and her youngest brother stood in crying need of elder-sisterly guidance. She would have to watch out for Lewis—Quentin was not the model Demetra would have chosen for him—and she would have to do something about Sophy, lest their mother trap the girl into an unfortunate alliance. And she would have to get to know Edwina, whose flippant manner seemed to conceal a gnawing discontent. As for her elder brother, she could start by learning what Sophy knew. "Why did Quentin come back to England?"

"I don't know," Sophy said. "We didn't really expect him. He'd done something rather beastly a year ago. Did you know?"

"A friend wrote us about it," Demetra said cautiously. "I

34

don't know the details."

"It was a man called Murray. A publisher, and a dreadful radical, though he didn't deserve what happened. Quentin disapproved of his politics. He took Edwina's bracelet and made it look as if Murray had stolen it. Mama tried to pass it off as a sort of prank, but Papa was furious and made Quentin write a full confession and then he sent him away. Quentin seemed to like it abroad, though, and he wrote about staying in Rome until the winter. The next thing we knew, he was back in Bruton Street."

So it had been a sudden return. That accorded with what Demetra suspected. "And what does he do with himself, now that he's back. Does he plan to set up his own establishment?"

"I don't think he can be bothered, and Mama seems to want to keep him under her eye. She wants him to get married, and she's pushing Beatrix Thornton under his nose. She thinks marriage is the answer to everyone's problems," Sophy added mournfully.

Demetra laughed. "Perhaps she wants you all off her hands."

"Or off her conscience. But it won't work with Quentin." Sophy looked around, as though to be sure they were truly alone, and moved closer to Demetra. "He's got a new mistress, and I think it's serious, because he seems to have brought her with him from Italy."

"However do you know?" Demetra asked, trying to keep the rising excitement from her voice.

"Lewis told me. He'd gone walking early one morning and came upon Quentin in Oxford Street, talking to a woman. She was dark and rather pretty and Lewis said she sounded foreign. Quentin was furious when he found Lewis was there, but he tried to pass it off, and he made Lewis promise to keep it quiet—you know the sort of thing, *we men must have our pleasures* and *it won't do to upset Mother*—and ever since, Quentin's been taking Lewis about, just to make sure he understands. But everyone knows Quentin has women, so why

35

should he want to keep this one quiet?"

Demetra stared at her sister. She felt at once appalled and elated. Was that how Quentin had learned of the Contessa Montalto's whereabouts, because she was his mistress and had told him? Could she have been his mistress before she approached the Whigs and offered to testify for the Queen? And if so, was her offer to provide evidence for the Queen part of one of Quentin's plots? Did he plan to have her change her story in the witness-box and condemn Queen Caroline instead of exonerating her? It was precisely the sort of scheme her brother might have concocted.

If that was the case, Quentin posed a serious threat to the Queen and to the Whigs who were supporting her. For a moment Demetra considered returning to Park Street and telling Frank of her suspicions. But she was not sure Frank would believe her. And even if he did, he would more than likely storm over to Buckleigh House and confront Quentin and make a mull of everything. No, she would need proof before she took her suspicions to anyone. And in case anything further went wrong, it was best that Frank was as distanced from her as possible.

What a dreadful coil. She must think carefully. After Quentin's appearance outside the contessa's lodgings, the Whigs would move her to new quarters, that went without saying. And if the contessa was in league with Quentin, she would want to let him know of the change in her direction as soon as possible. Where would they meet? In Oxford Street again? It was an appropriately innocuous setting. And, Demetra remembered, she herself had met Quentin in Oxford Street a few days before, at an hour when she would not have expected him to be abroad. Yes, that must be where he met with the contessa.

But it would be hard for them to manage, for the Whigs did not want the contessa seen in public before her appearance at the trial. Perhaps the woman Lewis had seen was a companion or a maid who carried messages between the contessa and

Quentin. Or perhaps—this was a new possibility—the contessa was innocent and it was the maid Quentin had seduced and was paying, in one way or another, for information.

But in either case, the unknown woman would want to get a message to him about the change the Whigs were sure to have made in the Contessa Montalto's lodgings. And the message was likely to be delivered in Oxford Street tomorrow morning. Demetra was going to be there.

"Demetra?" Sophy said again.

"What? Oh, I have no idea why Quentin would want to keep this particular *chère amie* a secret. But then, Quentin's always up to something, isn't he?"

Chapter 3

Tuesday, October 3–Wednesday, October 4

It was nearly nine when Frank left his house that evening and walked the few blocks to Green Street for the meeting of the four men who were responsible for the Contessa Montalto.

Nicholas Warwick had found Frank and the others in the House of Lords that afternoon, just after adjournment, when the halls were filled with the buzz of talk about Brougham's speech and the mood of the Whigs had turned suddenly jubilant. When Nicholas told his colleagues about his glimpse of the Viscount St. George outside the contessa's lodgings, Berresford had exploded. Kenrick had intervened and proposed they meet that evening, when they might have a better idea of what had occurred and what needed to be done.

Kenrick, Lord Braithwood, was Frank's closest friend. It was Kenrick who had encouraged Frank to try for a seat in the Commons, who had introduced him to like-minded Whigs and put him up for membership at Brooks's, who had stood by him five years ago and tried to persuade him not to leave Parliament. On Frank's recent return to London, Kenrick had once again offered his support. But even Kenrick might pause at this new evidence of his friend's unreliability.

Frank climbed the familiar steps of Kenrick's house, rang

the bell, and was shown into the library. Rowena, Kenrick's wife, was with him, but the others had not yet arrived. They greeted Frank warmly and Rowena, who was always direct, put into words what they must both be thinking. "How did Demetra take it?"

"Badly. She denies that she said anything to her brother, deliberately or inadvertently."

Rowena studied his face. "And you believe her."

"I have to believe her." Frank knew it was no kind of answer.

"Nonsense," Rowena said. "If that's what she said, that's the way it was. I'll call on her tomorrow."

"You'll find her in Bruton Street. She's gone back to her parents." Then he felt ashamed, for Rowena had meant only to be kind. He tried to explain. "We had a stupid quarrel."

"All quarrels are stupid," Rowena said, "but that makes them no less painful. Where are the children?"

"With her. She says the house is unfit to live in and she'll stay away until the workmen are through. That's not the reason, of course."

"Of course it is not. She's gone home to find out what her brother is up to."

"Or to try to keep him out of trouble." Frank thought this was the likelier explanation. "But either way, why wouldn't she tell me?"

"Because you have a wicked tongue, Frank, and you set her back up. And because you were worried and upset and when you're like that you get pigheaded and there's no reasoning with you." She looked at his ravaged face and took pity on him. "Have you dined?"

He shook his head. "I don't want anything." He had drunk a good deal in the four hours since Demetra had left the house, but he had not been able to face the prospect of food.

She nodded. "Coffee, I think. I'll have it sent in."

The two men watched her leave the room, a slender, vibrant woman with red-gold hair. She had four grown daughters and

39

six grandchildren, but she looked not much above half her age. Kenrick was her second husband. He was ten years her junior and tongues had wagged at the match, but Frank knew that it was a happy one and that Kenrick, after nearly two years of marriage, could still not quite believe his good fortune.

Frank threw himself into a chair and stretched out his long legs. "I'm sorry." He made a vague gesture, as though he would encompass it all—his own bad temper, the suspicion that had fallen on Demetra and consequently on himself, the suspicion that had fallen on her five years ago, and the trouble Kenrick had then taken to defend the young and outspoken Frank Hawksley.

"Don't be," Kenrick said. "Nothing's certain, and nothing's proved. If St. George is up to something, we're better off being forewarned." He sat down and crossed legs that were even longer than Frank's. He was an unusually tall man, very thin, with a long narrow face and long, elegant hands. His eyes were dark and penetrating, but they held a glint of humor. "I've always expected Berresford's passion for secrecy would get us into trouble."

Frank smiled and they sat in companionable silence until the simultaneous arrival of the coffee tray and the other two visitors, Nicholas Warwick and the Earl of Berresford.

Beyond the four men and the Queen's longtime legal advisers, Henry Brougham and Thomas Denman, no one was supposed to know the whereabouts of the Contessa Montalto before she appeared in the witness-box. Berresford—who had found the contessa and brought her to the attention of the defense—had insisted on secrecy. He was afraid the Tories might try to subvert her.

"I warned you this would happen." Arthur Berresford gave his colleagues an accusing look, ignoring the presence of the butler, who was setting out the cups.

"You did," Kenrick agreed. "That will be all, Tuttle. We'll help ourselves. But the prosecution knows the contessa is to be a witness," he continued when the butler had left the room.

40

"We had to expect there might be some attempt to find her."

"It shouldn't have happened." Arthur glanced briefly at Frank. "The contessa is my responsibility."

Frank and Nicholas exchanged glances. Neither had Kenrick's patience when it came to dealing with Arthur Berresford. Berresford was ambitious, but neither his money nor his birth had earned him the place he felt he deserved in his party's councils. He had no clearly defined political position. His father had adhered to the conservative wing of the Whig party, so Arthur allied himself with its more liberal members. He was attracted to novel and showy ideas and flirted with grandiose schemes of reform. But he was inconsistent in his enthusiasms, and though he spoke well, he had little skill in reasoned discourse. The party considered him unreliable.

Though vain and self-indulgent, Arthur was not lacking in wit. He knew his reputation, and he longed to change it. The contessa had given him a way to do so. Her testimony would confound everything the Government's investigating body, the Milan Commission, had charged against the Queen.

"We've never denied she's your responsibility, Berresford," Kenrick said. "Your meeting with the contessa was a fortunate accident. The Queen's supporters will be grateful."

Arthur was pleased by this last statement, though he preferred to think of his encounter with the contessa as a matter of skill rather than chance. Three weeks ago, when the House recessed at the close of the prosecution's case, Arthur had sent his wife to the country to visit their daughters while he went off to Paris for what he felt was some well-deserved relaxation. He met the contessa at an embassy reception and was immediately attracted by her luxuriant beauty. The earl was fond of women, and he swore he would find his way into her bed.

But when he learned that the Princess of Wales, now the disputed Queen of England, had once spent a night with her entourage under the Montalto roof, he put aside his amorous pursuits. The contessa had a story to tell that would help Her

Majesty's case. He would bring her to England.

The contessa had been reluctant to come, but he urged it as her duty, and little more than a week after they met, he brought her to London and installed her in rooms in Wardour Street.

Arthur had no use for the Queen's Attorney-General, Brougham, whom he considered an upstart, so he went to Kenrick Braithwood, who had radical leanings but was a fellow peer. Kenrick agreed to meet the contessa, but he brought with him two colleagues, Nicholas Warwick and Frank Hawksley. The issue of the contessa's credibility was too important, he said, to rely on the judgment of one man. Arthur was forced to acquiesce.

After this interview, Kenrick went to Brougham. The contessa, Kenrick said, would make a credible witness, and as nearly as he could judge, her story held together. Brougham, who had as little use for Arthur as Arthur had for him, was skeptical and insisted that she be interrogated when Arthur was not present. Which was why Nicholas, who sat in the House of Commons, had been sent to speak with the contessa this morning, when all the peers were gathered in the House of Lords to hear Brougham open the Queen's defense, and why Nicholas had happened upon the Viscount St. George.

There was an interval while coffee was poured. Arthur requested brandy. Kenrick asked him how the contessa found her new lodgings.

"She understands the need for caution, but she's not happy about the move—the rooms are not to her liking."

"It was the best I could find at short notice," Nicholas said.

"No blame attaches to you," Arthur said. "I told her it was temporary. I'll look out for something better. Wardour Street was more convenient than—"

"Don't say it." Frank set down his cup. "I don't want to know her whereabouts and there is no need for you to tell me."

There was a strained silence at this reminder of the reason for their meeting.

"My wife denies saying anything to her brother," Frank went on, "or to anyone else."

"As does mine," Kenrick said, making it clear that Frank should not be the only suspect member of the group.

"And mine," Nicholas said.

Arthur surveyed his colleagues. "I have never discussed the contessa with my wife. So," he went on, "we seem to be at an impasse. Unless—" He hesitated. "Brougham?"

"Impossible. Even if he wanted to sabotage his own case, he'd find other ways of doing it." Nicholas was normally an even-tempered man, but Arthur set him on edge.

"It makes no difference how it happened," Kenrick said. "The Viscount St. George may have been in Wardour Street on some unrelated business, but if that was not the case, if he was, in fact, attempting to see the Contessa Montalto, the important thing is that it not be allowed to happen again. The fewer people who know her direction, the better. Let's keep it with Warwick and Berresford. Like Hawksley, I have no need to know."

This reminded Arthur of another grievance. He turned to Nicholas. "You visited the contessa this morning."

"At Brougham's request," Nicholas said. "He wanted to know how she would hold up under cross-examination."

"And?" Arthur's tone made this an accusation.

"I think I can satisfy him. You know the story. The contessa only met the Queen once, over a year ago, just before the Conte Montalto died. The conte was a sick man, and the couple led a retired life—a penance, I would think, for the contessa. She is not the kind of woman to enjoy being immured in the country."

There was a murmur of agreement.

"The Queen was traveling, and an axle broke on her carriage. It was late, there was heavy rain, and the party took refuge on the Montalto estate. All this is quite straightforward. The real issue is the nature of the conversation between the contessa and the Queen, and how the Queen was led to share

43

such intimate confidences with a stranger." Nicholas smiled. "The contessa is a complicated woman, but whatever else she may be, she has the gift of eliciting confidences. I told her far more about myself than I intended."

He leaned forward, his manner intent once more. "But the thrust of her evidence is clear, and she will not be shaken from it. The Queen's apparent intimacy with Bergami was deliberate sham, a calculated lie, intended to punish her husband. Nothing, she told the contessa, was sufficient to make up for the humiliations he had heaped upon her, and she left England six years ago vowing to make his name a mockery throughout Europe, no matter what it cost her. There was much more in this vein—the contessa said they talked for several hours. She also said that the Queen seemed a very good-natured woman and she felt quite sorry for her. Which has the ring of truth."

"Quite." Arthur had been pacing up and down before the fireplace. "It refutes the outrages reported by the Milan Commission. All the perjured statements and bought testimony they sent back in the Green Bag. But"—he stopped suddenly and faced the others—"I fail to see why your interrogation was necessary, Warwick. Brougham has access to the Queen. He must know she would corroborate the contessa's story."

"She doesn't know the contessa is here. If she did, she might insist on seeing her, and Brougham thinks it better that they do not meet. The contessa can then swear truthfully that she has had no contact with Her Majesty since that first meeting, and no one can accuse her of tailoring her story to the Queen's wish."

Arthur frowned. It was reasonable enough, but he felt his prerogatives had been abused. "When will Brougham call her to testify?"

"I imagine sometime next week. He hasn't finished his opening address. And he does not want to disrupt the order of the first witnesses. He'll let us know." Nicholas paused. "I'll not need to see the contessa again."

"Nor will I nor Hawksley." Kenrick stood up. "She's in your hands, Berresford. Do whatever is needed to make her comfortable. Change her lodging if you like, but don't tell us. We trust your discretion."

Arthur appeared mollified, and the talk turned to Brougham's speech and how it might have influenced those members of the House who had still not taken a firm position on the Bill of Pains and Penalties brought against the Queen. On the last division, only forty-one of the peers had voted to rescind the bill. It was the need to increase this number—the Government's majority stood at 165—that accounted for Kenrick's tolerance of Arthur Berresford. Berresford was cousin to the Duke of Waterford, who counted himself a moderate Whig, and if Waterford came over to the Queen's side, so would several of his followers, including his brother-in-law, the Marquis of Dinsdale.

Frank watched Berresford now, a faultlessly dressed man with thick dark hair and heavy brows. He was accounted handsome, though his soft mouth and heavy jaw gave him somewhat the look of a petulant boy. Frank had little use for Berresford, though he kept his feelings hidden for the sake of Berresford's wife, whose parents were neighbors of the Hawksleys in Durham.

They had not discussed Demetra tonight—Kenrick had seen to that—but Frank knew that Berresford believed she had lied about talking to her brother. And Kenrick and Nicholas? They were old friends, and they would be fair, but they could not help suspecting Demetra. It was ironic, Frank thought. Five years ago he was happily married and awaiting the birth of his first child, while Kenrick was a bachelor not quite as content with his state as he let on and Nicholas was a widower recovering from a disastrous marriage. Now Kenrick and Nicholas were contentedly married, while Frank's relationship with Demetra was in a shambles.

Frank excused himself abruptly and left the house. He stood on the steps for a moment, grateful for the dark and the quiet and the cold clear air, then began the walk to Park Street, thinking about Demetra. When he had proposed to marry this beautiful, headstrong girl against the wishes of her family, his friends had warned him about the Thanes. There was strong family loyalty among them, they said, and Demetra would be no exception. But Demetra had left her family and seemed content to do so. She had even abandoned her title, claiming she preferred to be addressed as Mrs. Hawksley. Her mother had not entered their house until Demetra became desperately ill after Colin's birth. In Durham, Demetra had scarcely talked of her family at all, though she made no secret of writing occasional letters. But three days after her arrival in London, she had taken Colin and Annie to Bruton Street. Frank had been annoyed. What was it his wife had said? *You're being pigheaded, Frank. Family come before politics.*

How far would Demetra's loyalty take her? She had been furious when she heard of St. George's trouble last year, but she had seemed to see her brother as less malicious than misguided. *If I'd been around,* she had said, *he never would have done it. He wouldn't have dared.*

Demetra had been surprised when he confronted her this afternoon. If she had said anything about the contessa to St. George, it had been inadvertent. But as soon as she learned that her brother was in another scrape, she had determined to rescue him. Even if she had to leave her husband to do it. Frank swore, drawing a curious glance from a couple crossing Upper Brook Street, and consigned all families to the flames of hell, save his own. He missed his wife.

"Frank," Demetra murmured sleepily, and reached out to feel his comforting presence. Her hand met nothing but a smooth, cool expanse of sheet. Sitting up in bed and brushing

46

the tangled hair from her eyes, she realized she was in neither the rustic simplicity of Hawksley Manor nor the moth-eaten decay of the Park Street house. The quilt, the canopy, the bed curtains, and the window curtains were all patterned in perfectly matched pale yellow. She was home—if Buckleigh House could be called her home—she had left Frank, and she had to act quickly to save her marriage, her husband's career, and perhaps the outcome of the Queen's trial from her brother's designs.

Wide awake, Demetra flung back the bedclothes, crossed the thick Wilton carpet—woven in cream and the exact same shade of yellow as the drapery—and drew aside one of the window curtains. The morning was gray, but there was no sign of rain. She glanced at the clock. Not much past eight. Still, Quentin did not number laziness among his sins. She would have to act quickly. There was no time to be lost.

She went to the wardrobe and chose a simply gray dress and a slate-colored pelisse, which she had hastily made up the previous spring when they were in mourning for Frank's uncle. She pinned up her hair, tucked any telltale russet strands beneath a cap, and covered the cap with a plain straw bonnet to which she had added black ribbons that same spring. She would, she hoped, pass for a governess on a morning errand. She doubted that Quentin ever paid attention to governesses.

Demetra quietly made her way along the corridor and down the broad main staircase to the hall, where she found Manningtree giving instructions to a handsome young footman whose name, Demetra thought, was Stephen. Manningtree took far too much pride in his work to betray any surprise at seeing Lady Demetra—Lady Chester—up and bent on an errand at such an early hour. But he was rather taken aback when, instead of ordering one of her mother's carriages, she asked him to hire a hackney coach.

"A—hackney, my lady?" Manningtree's well-modulated

voice faltered over the unfamiliar word.

"A hackney, Manningtree."

The butler nodded. "A hackney for Lady Chester, Stephen."

"As soon as possible," Demetra said. "I shall be back downstairs in a quarter hour." She gave a regal smile and ascended the staircase with the dignity suitable to a baroness. On reaching the first-floor landing, she cast a quick glance over her shoulder to be sure she was out of the butler's view and hurried up the remaining two flights to the nursery at a much faster pace.

Colin and Annie had been in good spirits when she tucked them in the night before, thinking their sudden removal from Park Street a great lark and finding the nursery suite very large and grand. This morning, as Demetra had feared, the novelty was beginning to wear off. Colin demanded that she tell Mary Rose that it was perfectly all right for them to explore the house, since they had been able to go everywhere in the Other London House and it wasn't nearly as big. Annie wanted to know when they were going to see Daddy.

Demetra said that she thought Daddy would visit them as soon as he was able and tried to explain that, unlike the Other London House, this one did not belong to them and so they had to be very careful not to bother Grandmama and Grandpapa and their aunts and uncles.

Colin considered this and went straight to the flaw in the argument. "If this isn't our house, why are we here instead of home with Daddy?"

Demetra bit her lip. "Remember what I said to you yesterday, about how workmen need to come and fix the house before it's comfortable for us?"

"Why is Daddy still there?" Annie demanded.

Demetra reached out absently to adjust her daughter's sash. "Someone has to be there to talk to the workmen, darling. Besides, it's time you got to know your grandparents."

Colin was generally a reasonable child, but he looked outraged at this last. "Grandmama only saw us for five minutes yesterday," he informed his mother. "And Grandpapa didn't see us at all."

Demetra considered a moment. "Annie, could you be a love and get Mary Rose for me?" And while Annie ran into the adjoining room where Mary Rose was having a cup of tea, Demetra put an arm around her son and drew him toward the window. "I'm afraid things are rather complicated just now, darling, and it's easier for me if we stay here. You can be a tremendous help by trying to keep Annie happy. It's a bit hard for a three-year-old to understand."

Colin stared at her with eyes that were the twin of her own, set under Frank's straight dark brows. "Oh," he said. "All right. Of course."

Demetra kissed him. How had she and Frank ever managed to produce such a reasonable, tactful child? "Thank you, darling. Thank you very much."

When Demetra returned to the ground floor, Manningtree informed her that the hackney—he still seemed to have difficulty with the word—was waiting. She thanked him and was about to give him a message for her mother, when she realized that she was six-and-twenty and no longer obliged to explain her actions to anyone. She swept out the door and down the front steps to the waiting carriage.

"Pull up in the nearest side street," she instructed the driver. "So that I can see Bruton Street through the window. When a certain young man comes into view—he may be driving a curricle or walking or even on horseback—I will signal you. I want you to follow the young man. I expect him to head for Oxford Street, though I cannot be certain. It is most important that you maintain a discreet distance. Is that clear?"

"Perfectly clear, ma'am," the driver said, his expression wooden.

He must think it was a lovers' quarrel. So much the better. Demetra settled herself in the none-too-comfortable carriage and bent her mind to the task of outwitting her brother.

Forty-five minutes later, she decided it had been a grave

mistake not to bring a book. On further reflection, she realized this would have been impractical, for she would not have been able to read and watch the street at the same time and would very likely have missed Quentin. Still, it was vexatious. She had nothing to occupy her but her thoughts, and these had a tiresome habit of drifting to Frank.

How was he managing in her absence? Perfectly well, no doubt. He had always been resourceful, and he had been on his own in London for nearly two months before she arrived. In any case it wasn't her domestic management she wanted him to miss. But she very much hoped that he had missed her when he woke up this morning, as much as she had missed him when she did. In fact, she hoped he had missed her when he went to bed last night. *She* would have missed *him* then, Demetra decided, with a mental apology to her husband, had she not had so much else on her mind.

She had told Colin and Annie that Frank would come to see them soon, but she could not be certain that he would actually bring himself to call at Buckleigh House. Ever since their elopement, he had been adamant in his refusal to have anything to do with her family. Would he be stubborn enough to let that keep him from the children? He had been so happy to have them with him in London, surely a few nights of dining alone would soften his resistance. But perhaps he wouldn't be dining alone. Frank had a number of friends in London. Kenrick and Rowena Braithwood, Nicholas and Livia Warwick, Arthur and Helen Berresford—

Well, the Berresfords did not quite belong in that category. Frank had too little use for Arthur to count him a friend, but as for Helen—

Demetra leaned her chin on her hand and contemplated the only woman she had ever considered a serious rival for Frank's affections. Frank might say he had been over his passion for Helen long before he met Demetra. Frank might even believe that was the case. But though Demetra did not doubt that her husband loved her, she knew Helen still meant something to him. Demetra could understand this, from the security of Frank's arms she could even accept it, but she had never been able to meet Helen Berresford without feeling a wave of jealousy.

Somehow the thought of Frank dining with Helen, sitting in her drawing room, dancing with her, seemed worse now than it had these past two months when Demetra had been in Durham and Frank in London. Was that because in Durham she had at least had Frank's letters to reassure her, whereas now she had nothing but the memory of yesterday's quarrel?

Demetra shifted her position on the carriage seat, which was growing more uncomfortable by the minute, and drew the collar of her pelisse more closely around her throat. It was a decidedly crisp morning. She regretted not having rung for coffee before she left Buckleigh House. Quentin, she thought with all the jealousy of an elder sibling, was probably even now comfortably ensconced before a crackling fire in the breakfast parlor, enjoying a leisurely meal.

But in this, at least, Demetra wronged her brother, for even as the thought crossed her mind a smart curricle driven by a handsome pair of dapple grays came into view. Demetra had never seen the carriage or pair, but she had no difficulty recognizing the driver. She rapped sharply on the roof of her own carriage, and the hackney driver obediently pulled back into Bruton Street.

Now that they were directly behind the curricle, Demetra could not see Quentin and she had to trust that her driver was keeping him in sight as they turned into New Bond Street and made their way to Oxford Street, where the driver turned again and at last drew up his horses. Demetra glanced at the shops which lined both sides of the street. If her memory served correctly, they were not far from the spot where she had happened across her brother a few days before.

A moment later, Quentin himself sauntered into view—he must have left his curricle up ahead, out of Demetra's line of sight. His goal seemed to be a shop identifying itself as Norby's

Ribbon Warehouse. Even at this early hour several customers—chiefly servants executing commissions, Demetra
suspected—could be seen through the windows. As Demetra
watched, a young woman hurried out the door, a parcel in one
hand, and collided with a surprised Quentin.

Or was he surprised, Demetra wondered, as Quentin and the
woman exchanged what appeared to be words of apology. This
woman fit the description of the woman Lewis had seen with
Quentin.

When the brief exchange was concluded, Quentin went into
the shop and the young woman moved on down the street.
Demetra rapped on the roof of the carriage, signaling the
hackney driver to start forward. After they had gone a block or
so down the street, past the spot where Quentin had left his
curricle and out of view of the ribbon shop, Demetra rapped on
the roof again. As soon as the hackney came to a standstill, she
sprang to the ground and pressed a generous sum into the
driver's hand, saying she had no further need of his services.

The young woman was in plain view on the opposite side of
the street, only a few yards ahead, walking briskly but no more
briskly than the other pedestrians. Demetra crossed the street
and fell in step behind her quarry, keeping the woman in sight
but trying not to get too close.

The woman turned north into Titchfield Street. Whether
she was the contessa herself or merely that lady's maid, she was
a hardy walker. Demetra had never thought to be so grateful
for her long tramps in the Durham countryside. But after going
some distance, Demetra's quarry slowed her pace and at last
stopped altogether. The woman glanced about, seeming
confused.

Oh, poison, Demetra thought. She's lost.

After a few moments of indecision, the young woman turned
west on New Cavendish Street and made her way, not quite as
briskly but without further mishap, to a small house just off
New Portland Street, where she rapped at the door and was
admitted.

Demetra stood watching on the opposite side of the street, scarcely able to believe that it had been so simple. She had found the Contessa Montalto's new lodgings. That is, she had found them if all her surmises were correct, and Demetra, not given to false modesty, was certain that they were. The first part of her plan had succeeded. Now she had to decide on the second.

Chapter 4

Wednesday, October 4

Demetra returned to Bruton Street in another hackney. She had very nearly called on the contessa there and then but, upon reflection, decided she should plan her strategy more carefully first. Even Demetra's powers of invention could not, as yet, hit upon a suitable way to sound out the contessa about her relationship with Quentin. Still, Demetra was quite satisfied with her morning's work and she arrived at Buckleigh House in good spirits, in time to have lunch with the children.

After a pleasant hour in the nursery—marred only by Annie again asking when Daddy would come see them—Demetra returned to her room and put on her best pelisse (in point of fact, her only other pelisse) and a chip hat trimmed with green ribbons which brought out the green in her eyes. She was engaged to go shopping with her mother and sisters. Lady Buckleigh had proposed the expedition on the previous evening, in a tone which made the suggestion not subject to debate. It seemed a singularly silly way to spend the afternoon when she ought to be furthering her investigation of the Contessa Montalto, but living in Buckleigh House entailed certain concessions. Besides, Mama was right. Demetra's wardrobe was in desperate need of refurbishment.

"This is quite an adventure," Demetra announced, when the four of them were settled in her mother's barouche. "It must be more than five years since I've been to a dressmaker."

"Did you really make your own clothes in Durham?" Sophy asked.

"Yes, and the children's too, not to mention Frank's shirts. I draw the line at coats and breeches."

"And you always said you hated sewing." Edwina had noted that while Demetra's clothes were out of fashion they did have a certain style.

"Well, I did, until I realized it could actually be of use."

Demetra had grown used to economizing, but she could not deny that it was pleasant to enter Madame Dessart's elegant establishment, knowing she could spend more in one afternoon than she had spent in an entire year in Durham. Lady Buckleigh had insisted on purchasing a wardrobe for her daughter, and Demetra had given in, practicality winning out over pride.

Madame Dessart received them herself. The Thane family were valued customers. Madame had dressed Lady Demetra before her marriage, and had since dressed Lady Edwina, who set off almost every gown to advantage, and Lady Sophy, who presented more of an artistic challenge, but as great a financial reward.

But though Madame Dessart remembered Demetra Thane as a strong-minded girl, she was unprepared for quite how strong-minded a woman she had become. Lady Chester said firmly that Lady Edwina might be able to carry off masses of puffing, piping, fringe, rouleaux, languettes, and various other trimmings, but she herself was so short she would be quite overpowered. To Madame Dessart's further surprise, Lady Edwina, who had hitherto been looking rather bored, said she quite agreed with her sister, and began to offer her own suggestions for simplifying the designs Madame brought forward.

Sophy was delighted. After a visit to the milliner's, which

went along similar lines, she was unable to hold her tongue.

"I've never had so much fun shopping," she said when they were back in the carriage. "I knew you'd stir things up, Demetra."

Demetra kept a straight face and avoided her mother's eye. Lady Buckleigh was silent. Demetra did not think her mother, whose taste was very good, could have any objection to her ordering of her gowns and hats, but Mama might not be best pleased by the alliance which had sprung up, however briefly, between her elder daughters.

The shopping expedition had taken longer than anticipated and it was past four when the barouche pulled up in Bruton Street. Demetra was at the front door before her mother and sisters had even left the carriage. She had told Colin and Annie she would return by four, and this was no time to go back on promises. As Demetra rang for admittance, she heard a masculine voice addressing her mother and sisters. She turned to the street and saw a fashionably dressed young man walking down the sidewalk, his eyes fixed on Edwina, who had just descended from the carriage. Glad she had made her escape in time, Demetra turned back to the door just as Stephen opened it. The footman's face wore an odd look of anticipation which was explained when Demetra stepped into the hall and found herself face to face with her husband.

Without looking round, Demetra knew that Stephen was observing her and Frank with great interest. She had no doubt that her sudden arrival in Bruton Street had been a subject of avid speculation below stairs on the previous evening, as it no doubt would soon be in many London drawing rooms.

"Frank," Demetra said with a brilliant smile, and she walked forward, both hands extended. "How splendid. I'm so glad you had time to call. The children will be thrilled."

Frank had the sense to take her hands, though his eyes told her he did not relish putting on a performance for the servants. That was only to be expected. Frank didn't relish putting on performances for anyone. It was a decidedly awkward quality for a politician and precisely why, no matter what difficulties they were facing at the moment, she was just the sort of wife he needed.

"Well, well. They do say if you live long enough you'll see everything. So you've finally condescended to cross our threshold, have you, Hawksley?"

Demetra, Frank, and Stephen all turned to the stairs, which St. George was descending at a leisurely pace.

Frank met his brother-in-law's eyes and put his arm around Demetra. "Your servant, St. George. I've come to see my children. And my wife."

"How very wise of you. Not that you'll be able to stop the talk, of course, but I'm sure any little gesture will help."

"Talk?" Frank inquired softly, in a tone that dared St. George to elaborate.

"Talk," St. George echoed pleasantly, as he reached the bottom step and crossed the hall toward them. "Didn't mean to imply there was anything in it, old fellow. But you know the sort of thing people will say."

"No, St. George," Frank returned coldly, "I can't say I do."

"You mustn't tease Frank, Quentin," Demetra cut in hastily. "He has the most disgusting lack of interest in gossip imaginable, which is most vexatious, because what else is one to talk about in the country? Or in London, for that matter?"

"What else indeed?" St. George agreed, his eyes still on Frank.

Demetra was not at all sure she could cope with both Frank and Quentin for any continued length of time, but at this point the bell sounded and Stephen opened the door to admit Lady Buckleigh, Edwina, and Sophy.

There was a moment of silence as the three ladies took in the scene before them. Then Lady Buckleigh moved forward, her face wearing an expression that might almost have been called warm.

"Chester," the countess said—Mama would remember to use Frank's title, Demetra thought—"how very good of you to call. It's been far too long since we have seen you."

It was a parody of understatement. Quentin raised his brows, Sophy choked, and even Edwina looked amused. Demetra glanced quickly at her husband. Frank, she thought, do *please* try to be sensible. Frank looked surprised, but to Demetra's relief, he made a creditable bow in her mother's direction. "Thank you, Lady Buckleigh. You are very kind."

"Not at all. I trust we shall see more of you, now that you are situated in town. I don't believe you are acquainted with my younger daughters. Lady Edwina and Lady Sophy."

Frank bowed once again. Edwina and Sophy looked at their sister's impossible husband with curiosity. Edwina reflected that it was just like Demetra to capture a man who was not only unsuitable but oddly attractive. Sophy thought he had a rather forbidding face, but she had decided she liked him the moment she walked into the hall and saw him glaring at Quentin.

Concluding that her husband had already endured more than enough of her family for one afternoon, Demetra took his arm and turned to her mother. "Please excuse us, Mama. Frank's a very busy man and he called to see the children."

Children, in Lady Buckleigh's view, took second place to mothers-in-law, but she allowed this to pass—to the surprise of her offspring, Demetra included—and merely asked Frank to take a cup of tea in the small drawing room when he finished his visit to the nursery.

Demetra and Frank ascended two flights of stairs in silence, their arms still linked, as neither felt any inclination to alter this position. But as they left the second floor behind and started up the narrower stairs to the nursery, Frank said in lowered tones, "What the devil was that about?"

Demetra smiled. "Well, love, I think that Mama has decided, now that you're a baron, her wisest course is to make the best of a bad bargain and see what can be done with you. Besides, shocking as my marriage was, my divorce would be even worse. She's terrified that we'll follow the King and Queen's example."

Frank stopped, released her arm, and swung her around to face him. "Does she have cause to be?"

"Don't be silly, darling." Demetra looked calmly up at him. "I brought the children here so that we would be out of the way while the house was done up. That's what I told Mama. That's what I've told everyone."

"Except me."

"I said precisely the same thing to you, Frank. I just elaborated on it." Demetra pulled away from him and started up the stairs again. "At all events, I'm excessively glad I did come here, for they need my help much more than you do. As far as I can make out, Mama wants to marry off both Edwina and Sophy before they have a chance to follow in my footsteps, only Edwina is proving surprisingly sensible and doesn't want to marry the men Mama thinks suitable, and Sophy doesn't want to marry anyone at all. And Lewis is just at the age where boys tumble into scrapes and need someone sympathetic to help them out, and of course Mama isn't in the least sympathetic, and Papa's never paid much heed to any of us—"

"And St. George?" Frank inquired. "Does he need your help too?"

"Oh, I daresay," Demetra said lightly. "I'll have to find out, won't I? Here we are. The third door on the right, love. I think it would be best if you had some time alone with Colin and Annie."

Frank left the house an hour later in no very certain temper. He had stopped in the drawing room to take his leave of Lady Buckleigh, though he declined refreshment, pleading the press of business. Demetra, who was in the room along with her sisters, insisted on walking to the door with him, keeping up a bright, cheerful facade all the while. Their quarrel the previous day had been bad enough. This, Frank thought as he drove down Bruton Street, was exasperating beyond belief.

He and Demetra had always quarreled, even in the first

idyllic days of their marriage. These last five years in Durham their quarrels had perhaps been sharper and the making up less sweet. But it had never occurred to Frank that Demetra would actually leave him and return to the family she had run away from to become his wife.

I daresay. I'll have to find out, won't I? Demetra's words had confirmed Frank's suspicions. She had returned to Buckleigh House in order to rescue her brother from whatever bit of folly he was engaged on. Frank had a sister of his own. He could understand sibling loyalty. But how far was Demetra willing to go? What would she do if it proved she could protect her brother only at the expense of the Whigs? Frank was afraid of the answer to this last question. If Demetra chose her brother over her husband and his colleagues, Frank was not sure their marriage could survive the strain.

In this grim humor, Frank reached Park Street. Robbins, who had been Frank's batman in their long ago days on the Peninsula and was now serving as both valet and butler, greeted him at the front door with the information that a lady had called and was awaiting his return.

"A lady?" Frank repeated.

"Yes, sir," said Robbins, taking Frank's hat. "She didn't give her name."

Frank looked at him in surprise.

"She did not seem eager to volunteer the information," Robbins elaborated.

"And you were tactful enough not to ask."

"Precisely, sir. I've shown her into the parlor. Mrs. Burbage brought her some tea. Will you be wanting anything else?"

"No. Thank you. And Robbins—"

"Yes, sir?"

"This isn't what appearances might suggest."

Robbins gave a grin which belonged to a comrade in arms rather than a valet. "I didn't think it was, sir."

Frank returned the grin and started down the hall. He was

puzzled. He could think of no lady who would call on him in such secrecy. Could this have anything to do with Demetra? He quickened his pace and pulled open the door to the parlor.

His visitor was standing by the window, but she turned at his entrance. "Frank!" she exclaimed. "Thank God! I am in the most dreadful predicament!"

Frank shut the door. "Then you'd best sit down and tell me about it, Helen," he said calmly.

Helen Ransom, Countess of Berresford, flung back the veil which she had added to her dark blue satin bonnet expressly for this visit—veils were no longer fashionable, but Helen had wanted some disguise—and regarded him with exquisitely anguished blue eyes. She was a remarkably pretty woman, somewhat above the average in height, with a graceful figure, and a pink and white complexion not marred by a single freckle. Her richly embroidered cambric round dress and pelisse of ethereal blue *gros-de-Naples*, were in the very latest style, and her golden curls had been elegantly coiffed by a talented French maid.

She did not appear pleased by Frank's prosaic response, but after a moment's hesitation she moved to a sofa which had been hastily draped with a length of flowered chintz to hide the worn spots in the upholstery.

Frank drew up a walnut Queen Anne chair, which had been salvaged from one of the bedrooms. "Now," he said, "what has you so overset?"

Helen was silent for a moment. She picked up a half-empty teacup from the sofa table, but did not drink. At last she met Frank's eyes and exclaimed, "This is all so awkward! Your man tells me Demetra is away."

Frank crossed his legs. "Yes," he said casually, "she's gone to stay with her parents for a bit while the house is put in order. If you call in Bruton Street, I daresay you will find her at home."

Helen looked surprised. "But I don't wish to speak with

Demetra, Frank. It's you I came to see. I need your help quite desperately!"

"Well then. Here I am. I'm sorry I kept you waiting, but I don't see where the awkwardness lies."

Helen set down the teacup and regarded him with what might almost have been called impatience. "Frank, I know you have always been careless of appearances, but even you must realize that it was bad enough for me to call when your wife is from home. For me to insist on waiting to see you— Only think of the conclusion your butler would have drawn had I given him my name!"

"Whereas your refusal to do so instantly calmed all his suspicions," Frank said dryly.

Helen's eyes widened. "I thought you at least would show me some sympathy," she said, her lower lip beginning to tremble. "I have no one else to turn to."

Frank reached forward and took her hand. "I'm sorry, Helen," he said in a far gentler tone. "I'm in a dreadful temper, but I've no call to take it out on you. Of course I shall do whatever I can to assist you."

Frank had known Helen since they were both in the nursery. They had grown up on neighboring estates, tolerating each other as one might tolerate a cousin with whom one has little in common. Until the summer after Frank left Oxford, when they had suddenly found they had eyes for nothing but each other.

It was an unsuitable match for a number of reasons—not the least being lack of fortune on both sides—and Helen's parents had made haste to pack her off to an aunt in London. Frank's father, recognizing his son's restlessness and dissatisfaction with life on the family sheep farm, had bought him a commission, and Frank had gone off to the Peninsula. It had been there, a year later, that he learned of Helen's marriage to the Earl of Berresford. The news had caused him several anguished weeks, but he had recovered long before he met Demetra.

Not that Helen was not a beauty, as much now as she had been at seventeen. But she seemed sadly pale beside his vibrant Demetra, and her fragile helplessness made Frank think longingly of his exasperating but never helpless wife.

And yet— He could not deny that he still felt something for Helen. He had a brotherly affection for her that went back to the days before there had been anything romantic between them, but it was more than that. She had been his first love, and looking at her now, he was reminded of all that she had once meant to him.

"What's the problem, Helen?" Frank said.

Helen lifted a lace-edged handkerchief and dabbed at her eyes. "I—it's—I cannot possibly tell you, Frank!"

"If you can't tell me about it, there's not much I can do to help you," he pointed out.

"But if you knew— You will be dreadfully shocked."

Frank smiled. "I doubt that, Helen. I don't shock easily."

"You only say that," Helen returned with sudden asperity, "because you think I am still a silly chit of seventeen who is not up to snuff. But I have spent a great many years in London—more than you have, Frank—and I am every bit as worldly as Emily Cowper or Madame de Lieven or—or anyone else." She wound her handkerchief through her fingers. "You see, Frank, I—that is—I never meant it to happen, but—well—there are these letters."

"Letters?"

"Yes, and I know you will say it was imprudent of me to have written them, which of course it was, though naturally I never dreamed they would fall into the wrong hands, and it's no good scolding me now that the damage has been done, so pray do not scowl, Frank, for I do not think I can bear it!"

"I have no intention of scolding you, but I still do not entirely understand. You wrote letters to someone—someone for whom you cared—and now you are worried that the wrong person may be in possession of them?"

"I know the wrong person is in possession of them, for he was so obliging as to write and inform me of the fact, and he threatens to— Oh, Frank!" Helen looked him full in the face at last. "Arthur must never find out. He would utterly cast me off. You're the only person I can trust. You will get the letters back for me, won't you?"

Chapter 5

"I'll do whatever I can." Frank spoke promptly, but he could not entirely keep the surprise from his voice.

"I knew you would be shocked!" Helen sounded almost triumphant. "You mustn't hate me, Frank, I couldn't bear it if you did, though I know you must feel a strong sense of—"

"Of course I don't hate you."

"I was sure I could depend upon you to be sympathetic, for no matter how you disregard the forms, you have always been far more gentlemanly than—than many other gentlemen, so I felt certain you would not condemn me, even though you must be dreadfully disappointed—"

"Nonsense," Frank assured her.

His words did not have quite the intended effect. "Nonsense?" Helen sat up a trifle straighter and her eyes opened wide. "Francis Hawksley, do you mean to say you *expected* me to—"

"No, no," Frank said quickly. "That is—I—I have no right to pass judgment on you, Helen."

"But you expected more of me. No, don't deny it, Frank, I know you must have, for would you not be sorely disappointed if you learned that Demetra had—"

"Demetra wouldn't—" Frank checked himself, but not quite soon enough.

"You see!" The handkerchief returned to Helen's eyes. "You have a higher opinion of Demetra's character than of mine. You consider me a creature sunk beneath reproach."

"I didn't say anything of the sort." Frank's voice was tinged with impatience. "I merely meant—" Damnation. Why did Helen have to drag Demetra into this? It cut a trifle too close to the bone. Not that he suspected Demetra of infidelity. Not of amorous infidelity at least. But there was more than one kind of betrayal.

"I know what you meant, Frank," Helen said sadly.

Frank regarded his old love with mounting exasperation. What he had meant, and what he could not possibly say, was that any woman married to Arthur Berresford could not be blamed for giving her husband a taste of his own medicine.

Helen took his silence—as she had taken everything he had said—as a sign of disapproval. "Before you judge too harshly, Frank, I beg you will try to understand my position. If you knew the mortification I have endured these past years, and yet I never once went beyond the line—not that there weren't times when I might have, for though you may not credit it, I still receive the most flattering attentions from a number of gentlemen—yet I never dreamed—until—do you remember when you met Arthur and me in Paris last year?"

Used from long practice to keeping up with Helen's train of thought, Frank followed this abrupt turn in the conversation with admirable promptitude. He remembered the meeting very well. In a rare journey away from Durham, Frank had gone to France on business for his ailing uncle and had encountered Helen and her husband quite by chance and been asked to dine with them. Arthur Berresford, Frank recalled, had spent most of the evening carrying on a very indiscreet flirtation with the beautiful wife of a British diplomat. Helen had looked less acutely miserable than resigned and long-suffering.

"I daresay you may have noticed that Arthur's behavior was

not—not such as to make a wife comfortable. Of course," Helen added, her tone suddenly bitter, "it never is, but in Paris he was worse than ever and with Lydia Sutherland of all people, I've always considered her dreadfully common. Not that I deliberately planned to be revenged on Arthur, but I'm sure that influenced me when I met Gareth and then he was so dreadfully impetuous and I quite forgot—oh, dear, Frank, I really should not be telling you any of this, and I beg you will forget it, all except the part about the letters. I should have asked Gareth to return them, but I was certain he could be trusted and I still am, so how this dreadful creature ever came to be in possession of them—"

"Helen," said Frank, catching hold of this last. "Who is the dreadful creature?"

Helen reached inside her reticule and with trembling hands abstracted a sheet of paper, much creased, as if it had been folded over and over in agitation. After hesitating a moment, she handed the paper to Frank. The note was unsigned and written in a bold, slanted hand. The writer had come into possession of correspondence which he believed Lady Berresford would not wish to come to her husband's attention. If she would meet him—or send someone to meet him—between four and five the following afternoon by the lodge in Green Park, he was sure they could come to a mutually satisfactory arrangement. He could be known by his moustache and by his blue-and-gold-striped waistcoat.

Frank read the note once, then folded it neatly in two. "I'll go, of course," he said matter-of-factly. "May I keep this? It could help."

Helen nodded and bit her lip. "I—I know a great deal of money is going to be required, Frank. Fortunately, it is just past quarter-day and I still have most of my allowance—though I would have a good deal more if I hadn't ordered those new dresses and let Mrs. Bell talk me into that wretched sultana turban, which makes me look at least thirty-five—and then I am quite prepared to sell some of my jewels. It will be awkward, but I suppose I can have copies made, though considering the amount of attention Arthur pays to me, I doubt he would notice if I ceased wearing jewelry altogether. Only I wonder, Frank, if you know where I might go—?"

"I expect I could find out," Frank said, pocketing the letter, "but there's no need to be hasty. Fortunately my uncle left me quite comfortably situated. Let me settle with our friend in the blue-and-gold waistcoat and we'll sort things out when the letters are safely back in your possession."

Helen was not accustomed to think overly much of others, but she was moved to protest. Frank had a family to support, and his uncle's fortune could not be so very large—

"Quite large enough for dealing with your ordinary blackmailer," Frank assured her. "Don't distress yourself, my girl. I can't imagine the business will take long. I should have the letters by late tomorrow afternoon and we can arrange a suitable time for me to return them to you." He paused, then added quietly, "No one who knew your situation could judge you harshly, Helen."

"That," said Helen, her voice far more crisp than previously, "is arrant nonsense, Frank. You know society always judges more harshly of women in these matters, and even were it not for society, there is Arthur to consider and no one—not even you, Frank—can make me believe that Arthur would show me one particle of sympathy."

For once Frank knew Helen was not exaggerating. Arthur Berresford might disregard his own marriage vows, but Frank could not see him imitating Peter Cowper or William Lamb or any number of other men in the beau monde who turned a blind eye to their wives' infidelity.

"Frank," Helen continued, with some hesitation, "you must know that Arthur wants a son very much—indeed, I think that was the sole reason he married me—and though we have three perfectly healthy and quite delightful girls, and there is no reason"—she colored slightly—"that is, I am not of an age where there could not be more children, I sometimes think if he had the least excuse Arthur might—might seek to divorce me."

Frank started to tell Helen not to be ridiculous, then considered Arthur Berresford and held his tongue. "Berresford won't hear a whisper of this," he said instead. "My word on it."

Annie ran her spoon around the inside of her dish to be sure she hadn't missed any of the almond custard. "Cards?"

"I discovered I was good at them when I was quite young, and one tends to like things one's good at." Sophy was slouched in her chair, elbows on the nursery table. The posture would have horrified her mother, but it made it easier to make eye contact with her small niece.

"Did you play cards with Mummy?" Colin asked, curious about his mother's life before she'd been his mother.

"Sometimes," said Sophy. "And," she added with a touch of pride, "I taught your Uncle Lewis."

After Frank's departure, Sophy had volunteered to come up to the nursery with Demetra and sit with the children while they ate dinner. Demetra was delighted that they were getting on so well—Annie could be counted on to take to almost anyone, but Colin was more reserved with strangers—and relieved that Sophy had distracted the children from questions about Daddy and home.

"Could you teach us to play cards?" Colin asked.

Sophy looked surprised. She did not have much experience of small children and Colin and Annie did not fit her image of five-and three-year-olds, but she was intrigued by her new role as aunt and wanted to do the right thing. "I suppose there are some games we could try," she said cautiously, "if you like."

"Tomorrow?" Annie suggested, licking her spoon.

Sophy grinned. "Tomorrow would be splendid. I can spend the morning with you. If it's all right with Demetra."

"Of course. In fact, it would be a tremendous help, for I

have some errands and I shall need to take Mary Rose with me."

Demetra smiled at Mary Rose, who was also seated at the nursery table. This was the first the girl had heard of the next day's outing, but she did not show the least sign of surprise. Mary Rose was eminently trustworthy. Which was fortunate, as Demetra's proposed errand involved calling on the Contessa Montalto.

Annie, who had finished her custard and as much of the less interesting parts of the meal as she cared to consume, had begun to clamber down from her chair when there was a knock at the door, followed by Edwina's low-pitched voice asking if she could come in.

"Mama's ordered dinner for seven-thirty so we'll have plenty of time to get ready for her soirée this evening," Edwina explained as she entered the nursery. "I thought I should warn you."

Sophy looked at her sister in surprise—even before she made her début, Edwina had seemed determined to put as much distance as possible between herself and anything as childish as the nursery—but Demetra grinned and thanked her for the warning.

Edwina did not seem certain what to do next. There was a brief, awkward silence, broken by Annie, who had been sitting still far too long. "What's your name?" she asked, approaching the newcomer.

Colin looked at his mother. Annie was utterly fearless with strangers, and while this had generally been all right in Durham, Colin had a feeling that it might not do for London.

But Edwina, though somewhat uncertain, did not seem to take it amiss. "I'm Edwina Th—your Aunt Edwina," she said.

"You met Aunt Edwina last week, remember, darling?" Demetra prompted.

Annie was silent for a moment, thinking back over the confusing new images of the past week. Then she smiled. "I remember. You can have my place." Annie gestured to her

70

vacated chair, then climbed on her mother's lap.

After a moment's hesitation, Edwina advanced into the room and drew out Annie's chair. Mary Rose made haste to clear away the dirty dishes.

"I haven't been up here in ages," Edwina said, looking from the white-painted walls to the faded flower print curtains to the toys piled hastily to one side before dinner. "I must say it looks remarkably nice, considering it survived all five of us."

"Probably because we weren't here very often," Demetra pointed out. The Thane children had spent most of their time at Buckleigh Place in Berkshire.

"Actually we did a lot of damage when we were here," Sophy said. "There are still stains from the time Lewis used the table as a canvas. Remember, Nurse was furious—though actually it was Hannah who had all the work of cleaning it up."

Colin set down his cup of milk. "We know Hannah," he said. "We played with her children."

Sophy and Edwina looked at Demetra in inquiry. "I took the children to visit Hannah a few days after we arrived in London," Demetra explained. "I should have mentioned it earlier. She asked to be remembered to all of you."

"Even Quentin?" Edwina asked dryly.

"Quentin went to Harrow the year Hannah came," Sophy reminded her. "She didn't have to put up with him. Much. Though even that was probably more than enough. Dear Hannah. I think she was the nicest of all our nursery maids."

Edwina was not given to looking back on childhood with nostalgia, but she admitted that Hannah had been remarkably understanding.

Though Demetra had been eleven and officially advanced to the jurisdiction of a governess when the sixteen-year-old Hannah came to the Thane nursery, the two girls had become friends. The friendship had lasted even after Demetra eloped with Frank and Hannah married a young man who worked in a draper's shop in London. It had been much less of a strain taking Colin and Annie to Hannah's crowded, noisy house,

Demetra reflected, than taking them to see her own family.

Which reminded her of her mother's soirée that evening. It should provide a good opportunity to observe Quentin. Not to mention Edwina. Edwina's visit to the nursery suggested that she might be feeling the want of companionship. Yet, though she had been in Buckleigh House for more than twenty-four hours, Demetra knew little more about the state of Edwina's mind and heart than she had learned from Sophy on the first evening. She would have to see what could be done tonight.

Though Frank assumed an air of calm as he saw Helen to the door, her visit left him shaken. It was not so much Helen's predicament which troubled him—that was serious, and would be expensive, but he should be able to extricate her from it—as this evidence of the extent to which a marriage could disintegrate. True, the Berresfords had never been what Frank would call a model couple. But Helen at least had entered into the contract determined to be a model wife, and if rumor was to be believed, she had once fancied herself very much in love with Berresford.

Unable to face the prospect of dining alone, Frank left for Brooks's. Of course, he and Demetra were nothing like Helen and Arthur Berresford. And yet he could not rid himself of the sense that if they continued to live apart, they would grow apart. After the trouble five years ago, they had been able to sustain their marriage on the trivialities of everyday life: leaky roofs and childhood illnesses and unpaid bills. If they no longer had that to hold them together . . .

It couldn't happen to them. By God it wouldn't! Frank left his club shortly after ten and headed not for Park Street but for Buckleigh House. Bruton Street was crowded with carriages and there were lights shining through chinks in the curtains all across the front of the house. His in-laws must be entertaining. Frank grinned. This was going to be interesting.

The footman, the same footman who had been on duty when

he'd called that afternoon, was understandably bewildered by the arrival of an uninvited guest who was also a member of the family.

"I have no wish to trouble Lord and Lady Buckleigh," Frank said. "I desire a few moments' conversation with my wife—"

"Oh, I say, you must be Chester. Awfully glad to meet you at last."

A dark-haired young man, still in the throes of adolescence, had emerged from one of the rooms down the hall. "I was out when you called this afternoon," he explained, approaching Frank and the footman. "I'm Lewis Thane." He extended his hand.

Frank shook hands and found himself returning his brother-in-law's smile. There was something very likable about young Thane, despite the fact that he bore a disturbing resemblance to St. George.

"I suppose you've come to see Demetra," Lewis continued. "She's upstairs with half the rest of the world. I'm supposed to be studying, but no one should have to face Latin and Greek after ten o'clock. I'll take you up."

"Thank you. But I'd prefer not to disturb your parents and their guests." A scheme was beginning to form in Frank's mind. "Is there somewhere we could speak privately?"

Lewis nodded, surprised at the request, but pleased at being spoken to in a man-to-man fashion. He led the way to the front parlor and looked at his brother-in-law expectantly.

"I wonder," said Frank, "if you would be so good as to ask Demetra to come downstairs for a few moments."

"Of course," Lewis said, wondering at the need for secrecy.

"Tell her," Frank continued, beginning to enjoy himself, "that there's a surprise waiting for her. But don't mention my name."

He was still uncertain about enlisting young Thane's aid, but Lewis, fresh from his books, was ripe for anything that smacked of conspiracy and intrigue. "Yes, sir," he said with enthusiasm, and without further questions went to perform this office. But he paused at the door, hesitated, and then turned back impulsively. "I'm glad you're here, sir. I'm glad Demetra's back. Families ought to be together, don't you think?"

It was said with disarmingly naive candor. Frank struggled for an answer that was honest without being crushing. "Ideally, I suppose they should."

Lewis, a straightforward young man, took this remark at face value. "Personally, I don't see why there's been so much fuss. We all used to get on perfectly well together. At least as well as most brothers and sisters. Of course Sophy and I and even Edwina are years younger, but Demetra and Quentin used to be thick as thieves."

"Were they?" Frank asked before he could stop himself.

"Lord, yes. Quentin don't like to admit it now, but Demetra was always helping him out of scrapes. When Quentin took out Papa's new curricle—I've never seen such a dust-up— Demetra said he'd been in the library with her the whole afternoon. Papa knew she was lying, but there wasn't anything he could do about it. It saved Quentin a beating at the very least. Sophy's never done as much for me." Recalled to his mission, Lewis straightened his shoulders. "I'll send her down directly, sir. Demetra, I mean, not Sophy."

Lewis left the room, blissfully unaware of the havoc he had just wreaked on his brother-in-law's emotions.

"I always feel the most insignificant child at this sort of thing," Sophy whispered to Demetra. From their vantage point in a small alcove, separated from the rest of the gold drawing room by a trio of handsome pillars of Siena marble, the sisters had an excellent view of the guests. The company, chiefly composed of Lord Buckleigh's colleagues and their wives, moved through the drawing rooms, sampling light refreshments and discussing, with some vehemence, the day's events in the House of Lords. Demetra knew most of those present.

They had been shadowy, seldom glimpsed presences in her childhood, and many of them had been at her come-out ball and at the variety of entertainments to which her mother had taken her during her first and second Seasons. In the seven years since her marriage to Frank, she had seen almost nothing of them.

"Of course," Sophy continued, "Mama always makes sure there are at least a few young people present. Mostly young men. That's what makes the evening really ghastly. She always works it so there aren't enough young women to go round. See, Hugh Thornton's been reduced to talking to his own sister."

Demetra vaguely recognized Hugh, a stocky young man who'd been friends with Quentin since childhood. Beside Hugh stood an elegant young woman with a long, finely bred face and masses of gold hair, elaborately arranged with a cluster of artificial white roses.

"Good heavens," Demetra said, "is that Beatrix Thornton?"

"Yes." Sophy looked at Beatrix without interest. "She's turned out quite pretty, hasn't she? Not a match for Edwina, of course, but then few people are."

"So that's what Mama has in mind for Quentin," Demetra said thoughtfully. "What does Quentin think of her?"

"I don't think he's totally averse to the idea, but he's not in a hurry to get married. He has Other Interests."

In more ways than one, Demetra thought. Sophy, who considered the Thorntons a dull lot, continued to scan the guests. "There's the Earl of Deavers by the fireplace. Poor man, I shouldn't think he's having a very exciting time of it. He doesn't take politics too seriously."

Demetra followed Sophy's gaze and saw a pleasant though unremarkable-looking man in his late twenties, dressed with considerable expense and reasonable taste. He was listening, with an expression of dutiful boredom, to a conversation between Lord Sidmouth and Lord Stafford. "But Mama thinks he's an eligible parti for you?" Demetra asked.

"Oh, not for me. I don't think Mama expects me to land an earl. She prides herself on being a realist, you know. It's Edwina she'd like to see Countess of Deavers."

Demetra ran her eye over the earl again and realized he was the young man who had stopped to speak with Mama and the girls in Bruton Street that afternoon. He looked nice enough but a trifle bland for the restless Edwina. And it sounded as if he was not what Edwina wanted. What did she want?

"Where do you suppose Edwina's gotten to?" Demetra asked. "I haven't seen her since the guests started to arrive."

"Nor have I, but I expect she's with Elliot," Sophy said candidly.

"Elliot?" Demetra tried to think if there was a Lord Elliot or a Mr. Elliot whom she should remember.

"Elliot Marsden," Sophy explained. "He's a barrister and he was Aunt Aurelia's protégé and now Papa's rather taken him under his wing. I'll explain it all later, it's quite Gothic really. But anyway, Elliot came down to Buckleigh Place last Christmas and Papa helped him stand for Parliament at the General Election in March and he dines here quite a bit, which Edwina likes and Mama doesn't, if you see what I mean."

"I think I begin to. I'd like to meet Mr. Marsden. If you don't think Edwina will mind."

"If we don't go talk to them, someone worse will," Sophy pointed out. "More important, if we don't go talk to someone, Mama will bear down on us with an eligible bachelor in tow."

The two sisters made their way to the other end of the gold drawing room with surprising speed. They passed their mother just beyond the entrance to the small drawing room, but fortunately she was busy talking to the Duke of Wellington and Mrs. Arbuthnot.

Edwina was standing by the windows at the far end of the room, her gown of amaranth terry velvet beautifully set off by the dark rose curtains. It was the sort of detail Edwina thought of. The gentleman at her side had his back turned, so it was not until she and Sophy were almost upon them that Demetra had

76

a good look at Elliot Marsden. He was a man in his early thirties, with a strong, rather square face, attractive dark gray eyes, and an air which suggested one would not easily grow bored with him. Demetra was confirmed in this opinion when, after Sophy had performed the necessary introductions, Elliot said he had heard Lord Chester speak in the Upper House and been most impressed.

When Demetra had thanked Elliot warmly, Sophy asked if he had been in the Lords today and heard the rest of Mr. Brougham's speech.

"Yes, it was splendid. I imagine it accounts for the number of long faces here tonight."

"And do you share their concern, Mr. Marsden?" Demetra asked.

Elliot regarded her for a moment. "Quite frankly, Lady Chester, I am coming more and more to believe that it would be best for all concerned if the wretched bill was abandoned altogether."

"Mr. Marsden is much more moderate than Papa," Edwina explained. "In fact, it won't do to spread it about, but he quite admires Mr. Canning."

Demetra smiled. George Canning, while holding a Cabinet seat, was not quite accepted by the other Tories, particularly the more extreme Tories, such as her father. Demetra considered Canning almost tolerable. He had even withdrawn to Paris rather than be forced to support the Government against the Queen. Elliot Marsden rose in Demetra's estimation.

"I don't think Papa would agree with you about abandoning the bill," Sophy said. "Or Quentin. Not that it matters much what Quentin thinks. I mean, after the scandal last summer no one really trusts him, do they?"

Elliot looked diplomatically impassive, but Edwina gave a dry smile. Sophy had come close to the truth. Demetra knew that their father was still angry with Quentin because of the events the previous summer. Now she realized that she had seen Lord Buckleigh's attitude echoed in the way the Tory leaders present this evening treated her brother. And Quentin, in general far too arrogant to give a fig for the opinion of others, seemed to be going out of his way to be ingratiating. Was he hoping that his scheme with the Contessa Montalto would rehabilitate his reputation with the Tories, just as Demetra was hoping to rehabilitate her own and Frank's reputations with the Whigs by foiling Quentin's plans?

"I say, this looks much the most interesting group in the room, even if it does include my sisters."

"I thought you weren't supposed to be here, Lewis," Edwina said in her most elder-sisterly tone.

"Mama said I didn't have to put in an appearance, not that I couldn't." Lewis took up a position between Demetra and Sophy. "Dressed all right, ain't I? Don't need knee breeches for a soirée, even Mother would agree. Besides, I've a message to deliver. There's a surprise waiting for you in the front parlor, Demetra."

"What sort of surprise?" Demetra inquired.

"Can't say. I'm sworn to secrecy."

"When Lewis says things like that, you'd best keep your eye out for frogs," Sophy advised.

"I wouldn't do anything like that to Demetra!" Lewis was indignant. "I *like* her!"

Amid the general laughter which followed, Demetra excused herself and went to discover the nature of her surprise. She might have given the matter more thought had her mind not been occupied with Elliot Marsden, who seemed a much more appropriate match for Edwina than did the Earl of Deavers. There were one or two obstacles, such as Mama's opposition and the fact that Edwina might not yet realize Marsden was what she wanted, but Demetra did not think it would be too difficult to bring Edwina's affairs to a satisfactory resolution.

Quentin was another matter. All she had learned this evening was that he was going to some lengths to restore himself to favor. She would have to hope that her scheme for meeting the Contessa Montalto tomorrow morning met with better results. Demetra opened the door to the front parlor, walked into the room, and was pulled into her husband's arms.

It was little more than twenty-four hours since she had left Frank. She had seen him only this afternoon. There was really no call to cling to him as if they had just been reunited after months apart. So Demetra thought later. At the time, she did not think at all, not for a very long while. Indeed, she could not have said when she would have come to her senses, had Frank not at last ended the kiss. He raised one hand to smooth a wayward curl back from her face and said softly, "Come home, Demetra. Nothing can be this serious, not serious enough to keep us apart."

Demetra stared up at him, suffused with a longing that was more than physical—though the physical element could not be denied. Damn him, why did he have to do this to her now, when she was about to meet the Contessa Montalto and hopefully learn the nature of Quentin's plot? If she told Frank everything, assuming he believed her, assuming she could keep him from marching upstairs and confronting Quentin, assuming she could persuade him to go along with her plan, could she risk going from Frank's house—from Frank's bed— straight to the contessa's lodgings? Her plan was admittedly risky. If it went awry, their separation was Frank's only protection.

With a strength of will which her mother would have admired, Demetra wrenched herself from Frank's arms.

"I can't," she said, retreating to the opposite side of the room. "Not yet. Please, Frank, I need more time."

"Time for what?" Frank followed her across the room, though he did not attempt to touch her again. "Listen, Demetra, whatever it is you're doing, you can do it from Park Street. I'm willing to compromise. I won't say a word, no matter how often you visit your family, no matter how often you bring the children to see them, only—"

"But that's just it, Frank. I can't do what needs to be done

79

from Park Street. I told you this afternoon, my sisters and Lewis need me, they are in the most dreadful—"

"Damn it, Demetra, I will not be bamboozled with—"

"I wouldn't dream of trying to bamboozle you, Frank. It's perfectly true, though I don't think the situation is at all hopeless. In fact, I just met a man who will be perfect for Edwina. His name is Elliot Marsden and he sits in the Commons. Do you know him? He said some remarkably handsome things about one of your speeches."

"Marsden? Yes, I've heard of him. Nicholas says he's a good man, for a Tory, but that doesn't—"

"I'm so glad. I'd rather Edwina married a Whig, of course, but it really would be a bit much for two Thane daughters to go over to the Opposition, don't you think?"

"I can't say I've given the matter much thought. What I would like to know—"

"So if she had to choose a Tory, it looks as if she's done remarkably well. Not that I wouldn't help if the man she really wanted was a rabid conservative, but—"

"Demetra—" Frank took another step forward and checked himself only a few feet away from her. She was wearing a familiar dress of moss green sarcenet, but the length of white lace draped across her arms must have been borrowed from one of her sisters, as must the pearl bandeau which surmounted her hair. One of the maids must have drawn Demetra's unruly hair into this intricate arrangement of curls and plaits. The overall effect was subtly but unmistakably different from the Demetra to whom Frank was accustomed. She looked like a woman who belonged in this house, at this gathering, and Frank was once again struck by the thought that if she remained in Bruton Street for any length of time, she would become totally estranged from their way of life. "If only you would take me into your confidence—"

"Into my confidence?" Demetra affected a look of surprise and sought refuge in smoothing her dress, which had become sadly rumpled during that unsettling embrace. She did not want to walk away again, but if she looked at him for too long at such close quarters, she would be lost. "Well, dearest, I would have, but I didn't honestly think you were much interested in Edwina's affairs. And then too, arranging marriages is a very delicate operation and requires a good deal of tact, which isn't exactly your forte—"

He might have taken her in his arms again and the conversation would have had a very different ending. He must have known that—he knew her disgustingly well—but instead he said quietly, "I've seen what happens to couples who begin to live separate lives. I don't want it to happen to us."

Demetra raised her eyes and forced herself to look at him. "The King and Queen, for instance?" she asked dryly. "Don't distress yourself, darling. If I wanted to take lovers, I would hardly do it under Mama's nose, would I? And speaking of Mama, if you haven't anything more to say, I really should return to the guests."

It took another surpreme effort of will, but Demetra swept past him and back into the hall.

Chapter 6

Demetra looked at the small clock on her dressing table. Ten o'clock. Time to leave for her call on the Contessa Montalto. Time to stop thinking about her husband. After her second night in Bruton Street, she missed him more than ever.

She stood up and walked to the cheval glass. She was wearing the plain gray dress that her mother abhorred, and her hair was covered by a white cap. "Disguise enough," she said. Her features were neat and pleasant to look upon, but in no way memorable. What people saw, when they remarked her, was her hair—a thick, dark coppery red, it framed her delicate face in a mass of unruly curls. It was all they saw. No one would connect the prim little figure in the glass with Lady Buckleigh's errant daughter.

Mary Rose laughed. She was standing near the window, waiting for her mistress to be ready. "And who am I?"

"My helper. Assistant to the assistant. I'm Miss—Miss Newley. Miss Catherine Newley." It amused her to appropriate her mother's name. "With Madame Forestière's establishment." Demetra donned the dark gray pelisse she had worn when she followed Quentin to Oxford Street the day before. "Madame, of course, would not go out herself, even for a person as exalted as—as the lady I am about to pay a visit."

Mary Rose nodded. She was a girl of quick parts. "Who is too indolent or too indisposed to visit the shops. Poor lady. She must be dreadfully bored."

Demetra grinned. "I'm counting on it." She picked up a paper-wrapped package. "You'll have to carry the parcel. It's a length of plum-colored velvet Mama said I might have. Miss Newley, of course, carries nothing at all." Demetra hesitated over her bonnets, then selected a large-brimmed Leghorn that shadowed her face. "Perhaps a trifle fashionable, but Miss Newley should be allowed her little touch of vanity."

Lady Chester's departure caused no particular comment among the servants at Buckleigh House, nor did her request for a hackney. She directed the driver to Oxford Street and then, following the route she had taken the day before, asked him to turn up Titchfield. As the hackney approached New Cavendish Street, Demetra rapped on the roof and brought the carriage to a halt. "We should arrive on foot," she told her companion, and she stepped down from the carriage, told the driver to wait, and walked toward the house into which the woman she had followed the day before had vanished. Mary Rose, the paper-wrapped parcel carried carefully in her arms and the light of adventure in her eyes, kept pace by her mistress's side.

Demetra had had scant time to prepare for her meeting with the contessa, but she had been thinking furiously how she was to bring it about. She would have to gain admittance to the house—after the sighting of Quentin in Wardour Street, there was sure to be increased vigilance at the door—and she would have to gain admittance to the contessa's chambers. And then—well, and then she would have to use her wits.

"The lady will be closely guarded," Demetra said. "Visitors, I suspect, will not be welcome. But a respectable woman, bound on a respectable errand—"

"With a respectable young woman at her side."

"Exactly. And an excessively pretty one, too." Demetra glanced briefly at Mary Rose, whose dark hair escaped the confines of her cap. She had the freshness and high color of a country girl and innocent dark eyes that did not betray the intelligence within. "You're to wait below while I pay my visit and find out everything you can about the lady and her maid. I'm sure there's a maid, and I'm as interested in her as in the lady."

Mary Rose nodded. "But if the man who answers the door slams it in our face?"

"Why then, you'll throw yourself into the doorway and have a fit."

"I should have thought of that," Mary Rose said with admiration in her eyes. She had unbounded faith in Mrs. Hawksley's powers of invention.

Demetra was less confident, but no trace of this appeared in her demeanor. The important thing is not to hesitate, she told herself as she approached the house where she hoped to find the contessa or at least the woman her brother had met yesterday morning. She ascended the steps briskly and rang the bell with determination.

No one came. Demetra was acutely conscious of the footfalls of the people who passed behind her, the creak of cartwheels, the cry of a child in the distance. She lifted her hand to ring again, then let it drop as she heard the faint sound of raised voices within. She straightened her back and pursed her lips. Miss Newley would not like to be kept waiting.

After an eternity, the door was opened a grudging six inches and a pair of suspicious eyes under squinting brows peered at her through the opening. "I'm from Madame Forestière," Demetra said firmly, as though this statement alone would cause the door to be flung wide to receive her. "At Lord Berresford's most particular request."

The door opened another six inches. The eyes belonged to a tall, portly man with a large nose and a soft, indeterminate chin. His coat was wrinkled around the shoulders as though it had been hastily donned, and his neckcloth had seen service for several days. "He said nothing about you," he grumbled.

The man's eyes betrayed his uncertainty and Demetra had a moment of exultation. The contessa was here.

But still the man hesitated. He closed the door a fraction and looked behind him till a faint moan from the doorstep drew his attention once more. "If I could just sit down for a moment," said Mary Rose in her lilting country voice, and she raised her dark eyes to the man in the doorway and laid a well-shaped hand on his arm.

The doorkeeper—he could not be dignified by the name of butler—wavered no longer. The door flew open and he put his arm around Mary Rose and helped her to a chair which, other than a small table, was the only furniture in the narrow hall.

"Abominable girl," Miss Newley said under her breath. Then, in a decisive voice, "Give me the parcel, I'll go up alone." She turned to the man, whose truculence and uncertainty had returned. "Pray take me to her ladyship."

"Here now," he said, drawing himself up to his full height, "I don't know as I can."

"Send her up, Pawley. I will see her."

The pleasant contralto voice held a note of command and, oddly, a touch of agitation. "Come, come, do not waste time." The woman standing at the top of the stairs beckoned to Demetra. "I will see you at once. Pawley, see to the young woman, she looks ill."

"If I might have a cup of tea?" said Mary Rose in a timorous voice.

The woman threw up her hands in an expressive gesture. "Ah, tea, tea, it is the cure for everything that ails the English. Give her tea, Pawley, take her away and give her tea. Come," she said once more to Demetra, who by this time was halfway up the stairs. The woman vanished inside a door which led to a room at the front of the house.

In the dim light of the stairs, Demetra had had only an impression of an ample figure, an imperious presence, and a heavy perfume dominated by the scent of musk. In the sitting room above, its curtains half-drawn to screen the sun, Demetra felt the full force of the contessa's beauty. She was an exotic, un-English woman, though she had a finely textured, cream-colored complexion that an Englishwoman might have envied. There was no delicacy in her features, but this passed for naught. Her face was dominated by her eyes, large and deep-set under dark, high-arched brows. The lids were unusually full and gave a sleepy, heavy-eyed cast to her countenance, accentuated, Demetra was sure, by the skillful application of blacking. There was a hint of color too in the cheeks and on the softly curved mouth with its full lower lip.

She was not as large as Demetra had supposed. She had a splendid bosom, but her legs were rather short and her hips were slim. Yet even in repose, as she faced Demetra across the room with a hint of speculation in those enormous eyes, she exuded a vitality that magnified her presence.

Demetra had no doubt that she was face to face with the Contessa Montalto. This was certainly not the woman Quentin had met in Oxford Street yesterday morning. Quentin had met the maid. Was the maid his only accomplice or was the contessa his creature as well? Demetra looked round, but could see no evidence of the young woman's presence. Where was she?

Demetra still held the parcel of plum-colored velvet in her arms. How long could she play out the farce of Miss Newley? How introduce the name of St. George and learn, from the play of expression on that magnificent woman's face, whether or not she was his conspirator? She was certainly not his lover. Quentin had no use for women who were stronger than he.

"I know no Madame Forestière," the contessa said in her faintly accented English.

"No," Demetra agreed, "it was a sudden wish of Lord Berresford." She looked at the contessa's gown—a round high dress of violet-colored *gros-de-Naples*, ornamented at the border with irregular puffs of jonquil-colored satin—and had a sudden inspiration. "He thought you might need something more sober for . . ." She let the thought trail off.

"Ah." The contessa tossed her head in comprehension. But she continued to regard Demetra with that look of speculation.

Demetra moved to a table and laid the parcel down, as though she would display the glowing folds of velvet to her customer. Her story, she was sure, had been accepted, but she did not understand the contessa's look and she dared not prolong this charade.

Demetra had intended to present herself as Quentin's mistress, fiercely jealous of his attentions to the foreign woman she had seen with him yesterday morning, but in the contessa's vivid presence her own drab appearance made the story unlikely. Then she remembered the look on the doorkeeper's face as he helped Mary Rose to a chair. Of course. Mary Rose was quite pretty enough to attract a gentleman's attention. Miss Newley had been outraged by Viscount St. George's seduction and abandonment of Mary Rose, and she had sought out the contessa's lodgings in hope of tracing the man who had ruined one of her girls. Pleased with her story, Demetra raised her eyes to the contessa's face and prepared to speak, but the contessa waved her words aside.

"Enough of these dresses, I have no time to think of them." She indicated the parcel. "Leave it be. Sit down, sit down, I must talk to you."

Bewildered by this unexpected outburst, Demetra complied. The contessa did not, however, immediately address her but walked instead to the window, lifted the curtain, and stared down into the street. After a few moments she tossed her head as though she had come to a decision and turned toward Demetra. "The people who brought me here," she began, "they show me much generosity. But they are"—she made a gesture with her hands—"how shall I say it? They are tender with me, as though I am a flower that will wilt in their cold English climate. That is no way to treat a woman, not a real woman."

She moved toward Demetra and took a chair at last. "You, you work for your living, you will understand. I do not like to

87

be told I must not go out, but they would keep me indoors until—ah, never mind that." Her voice was now decisive. "I must go out. There is a message to be sent and someone I must see, and I would leave without Mr. Pawley, that dragon they keep to watch me, knowing I am gone. It is only for a few hours. You must help me."

Demetra did not try to hide her bewilderment at this astonishing volte-face. The contessa seemed hardly surprised at Miss Newley's response and hastened to reassure her. "You will not lose by this, I swear by Our Lady," she went on, crossing herself hastily. She stripped off one of her rings, a dark gold of antique design set with a red stone that might have been a ruby or might have been a garnet, and pressed it into Demetra's hand. "No one will know you are involved, I take it all on myself. And, *se piace a Dio,*" she added under her breath, "I shall be back before they know."

She still held Demetra's hand between her own, holding the fingers closed over the bulky ring which cut into Demetra's palm. "Say that you will do it," she said, her voice soft but compelling, "say that you will help."

Demetra nodded dumbly, withdrew her hand, and slipped the ring into her reticule. The contessa would expect her to take it. *Se piace a Dio* indeed, she thought, this was a stroke of incredible luck or the most appalling thing she had ever done. "When do you wish to leave?" she said in her efficient Miss Newley voice.

"Now, at once. Give me five minutes only, I will leave a note for my maid." The contessa went to a small writing desk and scribbled two lines, then disappeared into an inner room.

Demetra opened the door into the corridor and peered over the railing. The chair near the foot of the stairs was empty. There was no sign of Mary Rose, nor of the contessa's dragon, Mr. Pawley. Good. Mary Rose had had half the young men around Hawksley Manor at her feet. She would have no trouble keeping Pawley in the kitchen.

Demetra went back into the contessa's rooms just as that

lady emerged from the inner chamber wearing a hooded cloak of dark blue merino and carrying a large urn-shaped reticule with a steel clasp. "No, give those to me," Demetra said. "The hall is empty now, but if Pawley comes out, it must look as though you have come after me to give me further instructions." She moved to the table and unwrapped the parcel of plum velvet.

The contessa nodded with approval. She removed the cloak and brought it to Demetra, running her hand over the rich glowing material in the parcel. "It is nice," she said, with a tinge of regret in her voice, "I should like that."

Demetra rewrapped the parcel, praying that Pawley would not notice it was larger than it had been on their arrival. "My girl is not in the hall," she said. "She must be having tea in the kitchen. Ring for Pawley. I'll ask him to take me to her. That's when you must slip out. Go left, then turn right at Titchfield Street. I left a hackney waiting. Tell the driver you are with the two women who were his passengers. We'll join you in a few minutes."

No questions or demurs. The contessa was a splendid conspirator. She moved quickly to the bell rope and tugged it firmly, then flung open the door and walked out onto the landing. Demetra followed, the parcel in her arms, and only then realized the contessa still carried her reticule. Too late. She could hear the sound of a door below and footsteps coming down the hall. Demetra ran down the stairs quickly, praying that Mary Rose would stay in the kitchen. The contessa's voice floated after her. "Pawley! The lady is leaving. See her out."

Demetra remembered to turn at the bottom of the stairs and sketch a curtsy to her valued customer. Then she turned to the doorkeeper. "Where is the young woman I left with you? Has she recovered from her faintness?"

"Aye, missus," he said, not pleased with the strident note in her voice. "She's below. I'll fetch her."

"No," Demetra said, "I'll see for myself." She moved toward the back of the hall, where a green baize door indicated the entrance to the nether portion of the house. Pawley was forced to go with her, and Demetra talked loudly to him all the way down the stairs to the kitchen, hoping to drown out any sound of the contessa's departure.

Five minutes later they were back in the hall. The parcel was now in Mary Rose's arms, and Pawley was hovering solicitously over her. Demetra, who was somewhat ahead of them, could see that the bolt had been drawn. She turned abruptly. "Girl, pay your respects to this gentleman for his kindness to you." Then, head held high, she walked toward the door. By the time Pawley reached her, the bolt was once more in place.

They found the contessa waiting in the hackney. She had drawn back into a corner of the carriage, a prudent move for she would have attracted considerable notice, if not for her exotic appearance and expensive and fashionable dress, then for the fact of her being abroad without hat or outer garment. She greeted Demetra with relief, remarked on the vileness of the English weather, and donned the cloak Demetra drew out of the parcel. Her impatience was palpable. She glanced briefly at Mary Rose, dismissed her, and turned to Demetra. Again that speculative look. "I must find someone to take a message. And then I must find a place to stay quiet for the afternoon. You understand?"

"I know a place," Demetra said, thinking furiously. The contessa was using her because she had no other choice. She had to learn what the contessa was about, but the contessa would be reluctant to trust a woman sent by Lord Berresford, the very man she was trying to evade. "And I can take the message for you. I don't like seeing women kept under lock and key." That was certainly true. Demetra had never been able to bear being confined. She looked straight at the contessa, and her sincerity shone from her eyes.

The contessa held her eyes for a moment, then sighed and relaxed against the worn squabs of the carriage. "It is well."

Demetra signaled the driver and gave directions to an

address in Pancras Street, off the Tottenham Court Road. She would take the contessa to Hannah. She knew her former nursery maid could be trusted.

Nothing more was said until the carriage pulled up in Pancras Street. Then the contessa opened her reticule and withdrew an envelope which she handed to Demetra. "It is urgent," she said, "and for her eyes only."

Demetra glanced down at the envelope on which was inscribed an adress in St. James's Square. She gave a small start of surprise. Above the address was written the name of Lady Berresford.

Shortly after four that afternoon, Frank left the House of Lords in Westminster and made his way to Great George Street, where Evan, the groom he had acquired when he came to London, was waiting with his curricle. Frank had had a bad day. In his last two months in London, he had grown used to being alone in the big four-poster bed in his uncle's house, secure in the knowledge that Demetra would soon fill the empty space beside him. The night she left him he had drunk himself into insensibility, but last night he had lain awake, angry and apprehensive. Damnable woman! Why did she refuse to come back to him?

He knew Demetra had some loyalty to her siblings, but he had been shocked by young Thane's words. What was it the cub had said? *Demetra and Quentin used to be thick as thieves.* Why had Demetra lied to him about her relationship with St. George?

Last night when he had kissed her, she had clung to him with all the longing he felt for her. Surely that had not been feigned. But the moment had not lasted. She had withdrawn from him as surely as she had left his house. Perhaps it was more than her appearance that had changed. Perhaps—oh, God, he could not do without her—perhaps she was tired of being Demetra Hawksley and wanted to become Demetra Thane once again.

Frank pulled back as a carriage cut close in front of him making the turn for Westminster Bridge. He was too preoccupied to curse the driver. He crossed the road, threading his way through the mass of vehicles in St. Margaret's Street and turned into Great George Street.

There was also the problem of Helen. Her sudden appearance the evening before had aroused feelings that were not present when he met Lady Berresford in company. He remembered other clandestine meetings, when they had been young and cared for each other more than all the world and she had been his Nell. For a moment he had been thrown back in time, caught by her loveliness and vulnerability and need of him. For a moment only. Helen, too, was an exasperating woman, and he had no fondness for helpless females. Still, he had been moved by her plight and angered by the behavior of a husband who could drive his decorous wife into the arms of another man.

Frank strode purposefully toward the carriage which would take him to the meeting with Helen's blackmailer. If he could not make Helen happy, at least he would make her safe.

He took the ribbons from Evan and turned into Whitehall, threading his way through the crowd of vehicles and pedestrians that thronged the street, letting the residue of the day's testimony wash over him. It was a wearying business. *How did Bergami conduct himself? In the common way in which a servant would. How did her Royal Highness conduct herself towards him? In the manner that a mistress would conduct herself. Did you observe any impropriety of conduct between the Princess and Bergami? Never.* Lady Charlotte Lindsay, who had once been Lady of the Bedchamber to the Queen, had been testifying, the fifth witness called by the defense that day. And then the King's Solicitor-General had begun his cross-examination. *Lady Charlotte had said she walked out several times with the Queen. Was it five or six? Could she swear that it was not four? Had her Royal Highness walked arm in arm with Bergami? Could she swear that she did not? Did she recollect seeing*

Bergami in the Queen's bedroom? Yes, because we dined in the bedroom and Bergami used to wait upon us as servant.

And on and on. Since the beginning of the trial, Frank had disbelieved half of what was said and distrusted nearly all the rest. He did not doubt that the Queen had behaved imprudently. From all accounts Caroline of Brunswick had been an impulsive, free-spirited girl, made angry and vengeful by the shabby treatment she had received in the English court. But what did it matter if she pretended to take a lover? What did it matter if it were not pretense, and she took her pleasures where she could? The same could be said of half the married women in London. Even Helen—

Frank's thoughts came abruptly back to his present errand. Without thinking, he had led his pair around Charing Cross and into Haymarket. He pulled up, cursing, at the confluence of carriages and a coal wagon which blocked the road. He drew out his watch. Half past the hour. The appointment was between four and five and he had near a mile to go.

Down Piccadilly and then at last the oasis of Green Park. Across the park he could see the massive pile of the Queen's Palace, but old Queen Charlotte was now dead and Caroline was not being allowed to take her place. He drove past the shining ribbon of the reservoir, swans hovering motionless on its surface. The lodge was at the farther end of the park. Frank pulled up a short distance away and left the horses in Evan's care. He preferred to make this encounter on foot.

The day had been fine, and a large number of people were strolling along the paths. Frank joined the throng, dodged some small boys chasing a dog, and subdued his urge to stride rapidly toward his destination. Whoever the man he was to meet, it would do Helen no good if their meeting attracted attention.

As he neared the lodge, he moved slightly off the path and surveyed the passersby. Helen's blackmailer was to be marked by his mustache and a waistcoat striped in blue and gold. Frank looked around in apparent idle curiosity. Then he froze, struck by the familiarity of a figure standing not a dozen paces away. It had been ten years or more since he had seen that assured, arrogant stance. He smiled involuntarily, then cursed. At any other time—

He was about to move away when the man turned and met his eyes and he was caught in the moment of mutual recognition. "York!" he called, and "Hawksley! By all that's holy!" said the other.

They walked rapidly toward each other and clasped hands, the consciousness of shared memories in their faces. They had last met at Torres Vedras at the end of a particularly bloody skirmish and Ian York had gone to considerable risk to get Frank off the field. Whatever his faults—and he had many— York was a man of desperate courage.

For a moment Frank forgot Helen and her blackmailer in the pleasure of seeing again the man who had refused to let him bleed to death. York had not changed, though his face had weathered and its lines had deepened. He had the same glossy black hair, the mocking eyes, the ready smile. "You've sold out?" Frank said. "When? Where have you been?"

"After Waterloo. I stayed abroad, it suited me. And you?"

"Raising sheep in Durham. Don't laugh, York, it's hard work. Listen, we have to talk, but not now. Have dinner with me tonight. Come to Brooks's at eight. Do you know it? Top of St. James's Street."

"Eight o'clock." Ian moved off a few feet, then looked back over his shoulder. Hawksley had not moved from the spot where they had met. Ian retraced his steps. "This is a bit awkward," he said with a rueful smile, "but I have an appointment. It's with a lady, and she may not want to be noticed. Do you suppose—"

Frank grinned. "I might have known." York had two passions, cards and women. Frank wanted to oblige his friend, but he had his own appointment to consider. He looked around, searching for the man with the mustache.

Oh, damn his soul to heaven, the mustache. York had taken

to wearing a mustache. And he sported a blue-and-gold-striped waistcoat.

The light went out of Frank's eyes. "She's not coming, York. Your appointment is with me."

"The devil it is." Ian stared into his friend's eyes, as though looking for the jest, and saw that he was quite serious. "I hadn't counted on this."

"No," Frank said pleasantly, "I don't suppose you had. But you're a gambler, York. You've lost." He grasped Ian firmly by the wrist. "I want those letters now, no questions asked. Then we can talk."

There was no mistaking the force behind his words. Ian York was a well-made man, but Frank stood half a head taller than he, his shoulders were broader, and his eyes had gone suddenly murderous. Ian lifted his shoulders a fraction and allowed his smile to return. "You can have what I have, Hawksley," he said in a light voice, "though I've pockets to let."

The passion went out of Frank and he released Ian's wrist. Ian massaged his arm. "You've got a damnable grip."

"Round your throat, next time. Give them to me."

Ian reached into a pocket, extracted two thin sheets of paper, and handed them to Frank. "Is this what you're after?"

Frank opened the sheets. The letter began *My dearest own* and was unmistakably in Helen's hand. Frank folded the pages quickly and put them in his pocket, feeling he had made an unpardonable intrusion on Helen's life. He looked up quickly, his brow drawn. "And the others?"

Ian spread his hands wide and the mocking light was back in his eyes. "That's all, I swear it." He moved away as Frank made a threatening gesture.

"Where are they? Do you know?"

"I do and I don't. It's been a damnable business, Hawksley," Ian said in a conversational tone that maddened Frank. "They were mine by rights."

Frank was stunned. It had not occurred to him that York could be the man Helen referred to as Gareth.

95

Ian laughed. "No, no, not in that way. I—I acquired them. And they were taken from me. I have a fair idea where they are now. You can help me get them back."

"You're going to help *me* get them back. They're not yours."

"Ah, yes, the lovely Helen."

Frank's look turned dangerous. "You are never to approach that lady again. If you do, I shall kill you."

Ian threw up his hands. "All right, all right. It was a woman with me too." And he said no more till Frank had led him to his curricle and sent Evan to walk home on foot. Then he directed Frank to Great Portland Street.

Once the horses had been set in motion, Frank allowed himself to relax. The situation had its comic side. He had often enough rescued York from the folly of his excesses, and they had a fondness for each other. He did not think York was playing him false now. "Blackmail's a filthy game, you used to have better taste."

"It was quite by chance," Ian said after a moment. "I was in Siena and I'd been playing cards, you see, quite as usual, and this young fool, Lovell his name was, joined the table. He'd drunk too much and had no business being there, so I took him away. He was feeling sorry for himself and wanted to tell me about it, which is how I learned about the letters." He shook his head. "It was in strictest confidence, of course, and I never should have let it go any further, but women make me talkative, you know, especially after— Anyway, I told Bianca, and she had the idea that we might use the letters. They were no good to Lovell, and we were living on tick. She got me to introduce the boy to her, and one night when she was solacing him I went to his rooms and took the letters."

"A woman." Frank's voice was grim. He had been bedeviled by women these past two days.

"A magnificent creature! Her breasts, her thighs . . ." Ian's voice trailed off in memory.

"The letters."

"The letters, yes. Well, Bianca and I could not quite agree to

96

whom they belonged, so we decided to come to England together. We'd got as far as Choisy-le-Roi, but by then we hadn't much of the ready. I left Bianca at an inn and went on to Paris to repair our fortunes. Then the most damnable luck. I fell afoul of the law and was detained for several days, and by the time I'd got back to Choisy she had flown. Resourceful woman," he added, with nothing but admiration in his voice. "I was sure she'd gone on to England, but she'd have had to find a man to take her. She had no money. I made inquiries in Paris, the kinds of places she was likely to have been, and I finally got a name, but it took me near a week. Following them here was easy."

"The letters," Frank repeated.

"Bianca had insisted on keeping them when I went to Paris. But I'd managed to hold one back—that's the one I gave you— and as soon as I knew Bianca was here, I wrote to Lady Ber— Well, you know what I did."

Frank shook his head. York had always been muddle-headed where women were concerned. "How do you know your Bianca hasn't already sold the letters?"

"But she hasn't, has she?" Ian said with perfect logic. "Or you wouldn't be asking me about them. We're in time."

If York was right, they were well in time and the whole dirty business could be concluded this afternoon. "Don't mistake me, York, I mean to have the letters and I will allow no application to Lady Berresford. I could turn you and your friend over to the magistrate, and I will should you play me false."

"Ah, to have come so far."

Frank grinned. "And to so little effect. Yes. I'll stuff your pockets with enough to take you back to France and beyond. Take your woman and take my advice. Stay there. Don't come back till my memory grows less tender."

Ian smiled and they sat in companionable silence till they were in Great Portland Street. Then Ian directed Frank to the turning into New Cavendish Street and they pulled up a short distance beyond.

"You've not been here before?" Frank asked as they stood on the steps before the house Ian had pointed out.

"No."

"But you're sure this is the place?"

Ian shrugged. "In this world, Hawksley, one can be sure of nothing." And he rang the bell.

There was no reply and they were forced to ring again. Still no one came. Impatient, Frank tried the door and, to his surprise, found it open. He strode into the narrow hall and looked about. Ian pushed past him and made for the stairs. Only then did Frank look up and see the frightened face of a young woman staring down at them. Her hair was dark and bound in an unflattering braid round her head, and her dress suggested that she was employed as a servant. Her face bore signs of recent distress.

"Where is your mistress?" Ian demanded as he ran up the stairs.

The young woman stared at him.

"Your mistress," he insisted. "The contessa."

Frank halted halfway up the stairs. "The contessa?"

Ian turned round and looked at him as though the matter were obvious. "The Contessa Montalto."

"Oh, my God," said Frank Hawksley.

Chapter 7

Of all the places in London that Frank should not have been, the residence—the second and very secret residence—of the Contessa Montalto was high on the list. Frank had made a point of staying ignorant of the contessa's lodgings. But St. George could have followed the contessa and told Demetra, and Demetra could have told her husband. That's how Berresford's mind would work. And Berresford's tongue. For a wild moment Frank thought the events of the past twenty-four hours—the reported sighting of St. George in Wardour Street, Helen's blackmail letter, his encounter with York, his own presence in this house—were part of a monstrous plot to ruin him with the Whigs.

No, he could not believe it. Berresford was far from subtle, and Helen was genuinely afraid of him. Frank did not understand Demetra, but he thought he could read Helen well. She had never been able to dissemble. And if that was the case—

Well, if that was the case, Berresford had brought to London a woman who was prepared to blackmail his own wife.

Frank threw back his head and gave a shout of laughter. Then he raced up the stairs, grabbed the young woman by the wrist, and dragged her into the front room that opened off the landing.

Once inside, he loosed the woman's wrist and she scuttled across the room, staring at him as though he had gone mad. Frank had a moment of compunction, but brushed it aside. The maid—for that was who she must be, though she had been out when Frank was taken to meet the contessa in Wardour Street—was likely to be her mistress's confederate. Nonetheless, he subdued his urge to roar at her. "We mean you no harm," he said. "We seek your mistress. Is she here?"

The young woman shook her head.

"Where is she? Where is the Contessa Montalto?"

"*Non so, non so,*" she whispered rapidly. They were the first words she had spoken.

Curse it, the girl was Italian.

"She says she doesn't know," Ian said.

Frank moved toward the young woman. "You understand English. Do you speak it?"

"Yes, yes, I know the English tongue." The words were spoken carefully, in a light, clear voice.

Ian came up then and smiled at her, and the terror left her face and her body visibly relaxed. "What is your name?" he asked, and his voice was caressing.

She turned to him in relief. "Marta, *signore.*"

"And you serve the contessa?"

She nodded.

"For how long?"

She hesitated. "A long time. For many months," she said at last.

"I think not," Ian said, still in that gentle, caressing voice. He moved closer and his eyes willed her own to meet them.

"No," she said as though mesmerized. "It is perhaps not so long."

Ian nodded in satisfaction. "And where has your mistress gone this afternoon?"

"I do not know," she said.

Frank made a move toward her and she backed away. "*Giuro*," she said, crossing herself rapidly. "It is a thing that has never before happened. But there is a note. I will get it for you."

She darted toward an inner door. Ian followed, but Frank was before him. He took the letter from Marta's hand. It was in Italian, and it was unsigned. Frank knew Spanish well, but he did not trust himself to decipher the other tongue. "What does it say?" he asked Marta.

"It says she must go out and she will be back before it is night. I am not to worry."

"This is her hand?"

Marta nodded. "I am sure."

Ian took the letter, then handed it back to the girl. "She's right. It's perfectly simple. The contessa could never bear sitting home by herself. She's merely gone out for amusement. We'll wait." And he walked out of the inner room and flung himself on a sofa that stood near the windows overlooking the street.

"No, no," Marta said, looking after him in distress.

"Marta," Frank said quietly, "isn't the door below kept locked?"

"Yes, it is so."

"And who answers the door when a caller arrives?"

"The man Pawley," she said. "But he is not here. When I see the note, I send him to go to Lord Berresford."

"When?"

"A half hour. Perhaps more."

The devil. Berresford could be here at any moment, and there was no way Frank could possibly explain being in the Contessa Montalto's lodgings.

York, who had overheard this last exchange, must have reached the same conclusion. When Frank returned to the front room, his companion was on his feet and moving toward the door.

Frank turned to Marta and pressed some coins in her hand.

"I'm sorry we frightened you. My friend was anxious to see the contessa, but it's of no moment. He'll return at a more convenient time. And don't be alarmed," he added. "We're a civilized nation. No harm will come to your lady."

The two men hastened outside and walked rapidly toward Frank's curricle. Frank gave the office to his pair and turned the carriage down Titchfield Street. "The contessa is an enterprising woman," he remarked.

Ian leaned back and crossed his legs. "I thought you'd appreciate the irony. To take as her protector the husband of the woman she intends to—"

"Quite." If York believed the contessa was Berresford's mistress, so much the better. Frank had no desire to make him privy to Berresford's real intentions in bringing the contessa to England. "When did you find out?"

"When I looked for her in Paris. There's no mistaking Bianca. And no forgetting her either. Several people remembered that she was much in the company of the English Lord Berresford. They told me the same thing in Boulogne, and again at Dover. When I got to London, I followed him to her lodgings."

Frank laughed at the simplicity of it. "So your Bianca—she *is* the Contessa Montalto, isn't she? There's no mistake about that?"

"She's the contessa. Italy's not like the English ton, Hawksley. There are lots of old families with good titles but with worthless land and no money. She could have withered away, a starving little black widow making her obeisance to the church. She had a taste for other things."

As did you, Frank thought. York was the third son of an impoverished Irish baron. Frank raised his hand in a gesture of peace. "I make no judgment, York. If your Bianca chooses to take money from Berresford, it's no concern of mine. But when it comes to blackmailing his wife—"

"I'll go back tonight—" Ian began.

"You'll not go back, York. This is my game, and frankly I

don't trust you."

"But you told the girl—"

"I told the girl to pay attention to you when she tells Berresford of the two strange men who burst in on her this afternoon. Berresford doesn't know you. He does know me."

"Ah." Ian's face had a knowing look.

Frank noted this with exasperation. York thought he was Helen's lover. Well, let it be. Perhaps it would keep York from speculating about any role the contessa might be playing in the trial.

"I repeat, York, this is my game," Frank said. "Stay clear, or I vow you'll regret it."

Ian made a gesture of protest. "You forget, Hawksley. I have an interest in the woman."

"Even though she's tricked you in the matter of the letters? Even though she's found another man?"

"Berresford's a temporary expedient. I don't doubt she'll do well out of him, but she'll not stay with him long. And I want her back."

"For God's sake, why?"

Ian laughed. "You don't understand. There are things between us. . . . Let's just say that we do well together, and we need each other. The rest is a matter of necessity. We have to live."

A relationship built on purposeful inconstancy was beyond Frank's comprehension. But he could not dislike Ian York, nor could he wholly condemn him. He was not sure what his next move should be. He dared not return to New Cavendish Street, and in any case, when Berresford learned of the contessa's disappearance, he was bound to move her again, perhaps this very evening. Provided, of course, that she returned, but Frank could see no reason why she should not. The contessa was unlikely to throw over Berresford's generosity for the sake of blackmail money from his wife when, with a little luck, she could have both. Frank was certain that the enterprising Bianca had escaped her warders this afternoon for the sole

103

purpose of delivering a message to Helen. And to Helen he must go as quickly as possible, to return the single letter he had taken from York and to warn her to expect a second demand from a second blackmailer.

They had crossed Oxford Street before Frank spoke again. "Where do you stay, York?"

"New Bond Street, at the Black Horse."

Frank reined in his pair. "Then I leave you here. It's not far." He gripped the other man's arm. "Do nothing till you hear from me. When it's over, you may do with her as you like."

Ian leaped down. "Why, Hawksley," he said with a drawl, "I have a mind to the cards. I fancy I'll be much occupied." And he gave a mocking salute and disappeared into the crowd.

Frank looked after him in exasperation. He could not bring him before a magistrate, and York, he was sure, would not willingly leave London without his errant mistress. Frank dared do nothing that would jeopardize the contessa's appearance in defense of the Queen. Whatever the state of her morals, she had been privy to confidences that would do much to explain—and excuse—Her Majesty's behavior.

He set the horses once more in motion. Ian York was not a man to be trusted, but there were the ties of past friendship and he had no other choice.

It was past eleven when Demetra brought the Contessa Montalto to Hannah's house in Pancras Street. Demetra sent Mary Rose to inquire if Hannah was at home and to inform her that her dear friend Catherine Newley had a favor to beg of her. "If my friend is not at home," Demetra told the contessa while they waited in the carriage, "I shall contrive something else." She smiled to show that she quite entered into the spirit of the adventure.

Hannah was at home and came running out the door, delighted to see her dear Catherine and prettily overawed by the elegant woman who accompanied her. Hannah was a clever, sensible woman with an abundance of good humor, and not by a gesture did she betray her knowledge that Demetra was other than the woman she claimed to be. Before they reached the door of the house, everything had been arranged—a fire to be laid in the spare room, and hot water for washing, and the kettle to go on, and the cake just come from the oven. For of course they must take refreshment, and then—there was an awkward pause while Demetra produced a name—Mrs. Long would be allowed to rest as long as she cared to and they would fetch her a carriage when she was ready to leave.

This suited Demetra very well. While Hannah showed the contessa the comforts of the spare room and Mary Rose went down to the kitchen to keep Hannah's children at bay, Demetra murmured something about using the convenience and disappeared into Hannah's bedroom.

She fumbled in her reticule and drew out the letter the contessa had given her in the carriage. Without a trace of compunction, she broke the seal and unfolded the single sheet of heavy paper. *Lady Berresford,* it began. *I have some letters which you wrote last autumn in Paris. I must give them to someone, and I prefer that it be you. I am sure we can come to terms. I shall be in a hired coach at the north end of the reservoir in Hyde Park. You will know it by a handkerchief on the ground nearby. Between six and seven o'clock. It must be tonight. I cannot wait long.*

Demetra read the letter twice before she could credit what it said. It was blackmail. The Contessa Montalto was blackmailing the wife of the man who had brought her to England. What incredible brass. But Helen? Surely Helen would never— Yet a husband like Arthur Berresford might sorely tempt a wife to stray. Demetra had an unexpected flash of pity for Helen. Whoever the man to whom the letters had been written, Demetra hoped he had given Helen some moments that would be worth the pain she was about to undergo.

Demetra dared not destroy the contessa's note. If Helen did not answer the contessa's summons, the woman might send her letters to Berresford. But the contessa would not do so before she was put in the witness-box. She was playing a dangerous game, and maybe two.

This was more than Quentin's mischief. Or could her brother know about the letters? Demetra paced the room, trying to think it through. No, if Quentin had access to the letters, he would use them to threaten Lord Berresford, not his wife. This was a matter of the contessa's greed.

Demetra found Hannah's writing case and resealed the note. She had not bargained on this new complication. Whether Quentin was involved with her or not, the contessa was not a woman to be trusted. What on earth was she to do with this new information? Demetra dared not keep it to herself. Very well. She would deliver the note to Helen, but then she would go to Frank. He might not believe her, but she would take him to the meeting by the reservoir and let him see for himself.

Demetra felt almost lighthearted. It would be an enormous relief to tell Frank everything, why she had had to go back to her parents' house, what she had learned there, how she had discovered the games the contessa was playing. It would go a long way to restoring his trust in her, and if there was still the matter of why that trust had been so feeble, well, she would deal with that when the time came.

By the time Demetra rejoined Hannah and the contessa, all knowledge of the contessa's perfidy was erased from her face. The three women spent a pleasant half-hour in the parlor while Demetra, still playing Catherine Newley, talked of fashion and the vagaries of her customers, all the time wondering how they were to expose the contessa and retrieve Helen's letters while keeping Lord Berresford ignorant of his wife's inconstancy.

By the time Demetra rose to take her leave, she had the beginnings of a plan. She would need to speak privately to Hannah before she left. While Mary Rose was summoned from the kitchen, Demetra drew the contessa aside. "Be easy in your mind," she told her, "I will execute your commission immediately."

The contessa grasped her hands fervently. "The Lady give you grace. You have a good heart."

For a moment Demetra forgot that the Contessa Montalto was a blackmailer. She found herself warming to the woman. This odd sense of fellowship lasted until she reached the front door, where Hannah and Mary Rose were waiting for her. There, with that instinctive knowledge of Demetra's thoughts that she had always shown, Hannah proposed to escort her visitors to their waiting carriage, and Demetra had her chance.

It took but a few moments. "Mrs. Long has some letters," Demetra said in a rapid undertone. "She will not take them with her when she goes to her appointment, I am sure of it. She'll leave them here, then contrive some excuse to return for them. I must have those letters, Hannah. They will be well hidden, but find them. Replace them with blank sheets. She will be in a hurry when she returns and will not suspect."

Hannah, bless her, asked no questions. They reached the waiting hackney and embraced while Mary Rose, who had been walking properly behind, caught up with them.

Demetra hoped she had read the contessa aright. She would have the letters on her person, for she would not have left them in her lodgings where a search by her maid or by Berresford himself might discover them. But she would not want to risk having the letters on her person when she went to her meeting with Helen or the messenger Helen might send. Today they would only discuss terms. The transfer of the letters would take place at a later time.

Demetra directed the hackney to St. James's Square and climbed in beside Mary Rose. It was the first chance they had had to talk alone since their arrival in New Cavendish Street. Mary Rose had learned nothing there save that Marta, the contessa's maid, had been sent out on an errand, Pawley's feet gave him trouble, and no one of Quentin's description had been seen anywhere near the house.

When they reached Berresford House, Demetra sent Mary Rose to the front door to deliver the contessa's note.

Then she drove Mary Rose to Bruton Street so she could see to Colin and Annie—Demetra could not hope to impose on Sophy's good nature for the entire day—and went on to Park Street to wait for Frank to return home from the House.

The door was opened by a young footman, very much on his dignity, who did not seem inclined to believe that the drab woman on the doorstep was his mistress, Lady Chester. Robbins came to her rescue. "It's his first day," he said when the footman had been dispatched on an errand. "I didn't like to hire him without your knowing, but we need the help, and when you went away . . ."

Demetra felt obscurely guilty. It was not only Frank who was discommoded by her absence. "You did exactly right," she said, "and I'm sure he'll do splendidly. I came by to talk to Frank and to see how the workmen are getting on. The children send their love. We should all be home in a few days."

Demetra ran up the stairs to see what progress had been made in the drawing room. A few days. Maybe sooner. Maybe even tonight. She could not bear to be separated from Frank any longer, not with this discord between them.

The afternoon passed in an agony of slowness. Demetra busied herself with talking to the carpenters and painters and packing useless bits of old Lord Chester's effects to take up to the attic. By five, there was still no sign of Frank. Demetra gave up all pretense of occupation and began to pace the floor. At a quarter to six she could wait no longer. If Frank would not come, then she must go herself. Something might be learned by observing the meeting. And she had no intention of letting this particular drama unfold without her.

It was nearly a quarter to six when Frank was shown into Helen's sitting room. After she expressed polite surprise and inquired whether her guest would take refreshment, after Frank as courteously declined and the footman withdrew, Helen turned to him with a face so distraught that he knew he had come too late.

"You've had another letter," he said flatly.

"Yes, I think I am going mad! One of the footmen brought it to me not an hour ago, and it was excessively awkward because Cecily Armstrong was here and she's such a quidnunc, without any notion of what is owing to another person's privacy, and she insisted I open it and I did and then had to pretend it was a note from my dressmaker, but I don't think she believed me at all for my heart was quaking and I was speaking entirely at random— Frank, how did you know?"

"There are two blackmailers," he said in a cheerful voice, "but they've had a falling-out."

"Oh, my God!" she whispered.

At this, Frank sat down beside her on the couch and took her hands. "It's not so bad, Helen," he said in a gentler voice. "I've dealt with the one. The other is a woman."

"A woman?" She was utterly bewildered. "Oh, Frank, I can't believe it. What would a woman know about blackmail?"

"Nonetheless," he said, disengaging her hands. He reached into a pocket. "I've retrieved one of your letters. It is one of them, isn't it?"

Helen took the pages with nerveless fingers and hastily unfolded them. Then as suddenly she folded them up again. "Yes," she said. Her voice was hoarse, as though she was having trouble speaking. "It's the first one I wrote. There were nine. I supposed Gareth would have kept them, but I didn't dream he would be so careless, though he was very young and inexperienced in these things. I was inexperienced myself or I would never have been so foolish as to write them in the first place, though writing made it seem—" She was struck by another thought. "Frank, you haven't—you didn't—"

"No, only a glance to see that it was in your hand. I do remember your hand, you know."

She colored and smiled, and Frank was tempted to take her hands again. He got to his feet. "Helen, burn it. Now."

She was startled, but did as she was bid. A fire was burning against the chill of the October day, and she fed the pages in one by one. Then Frank took the poker and crushed the remains so nothing but a fine ash remained.

"All right, Helen. Now give me the second blackmailer's note."

She had placed it in the book she had been pretending to read when he was announced. Frank read it hastily, then looked up. "When did this arrive?"

"Not long past noon. Frank, I didn't know what to do. I didn't know where to find you. Well, of course I knew you were at the House, but I couldn't go there, could I? Besides, you would have been excessively displeased if I'd interrupted you at work, at least Arthur always is, though I've never understood why men's problems are considered so much more important than women's. Everyone knows about the Queen, but if anyone finds out about me— I've been in agony all afternoon, waiting to go meet the odious creature, though I scarcely think I can face him, and especially if he is a woman for you know women are never as sympathetic, at least they aren't to me. So you will go with me, Frank, won't you?"

"You stay home. I'll deal better with her myself."

"Oh, yes, of course, for we shouldn't be seen together, should we? People would be bound to talk. I'm so grateful to you. My peace is entirely cut up and I shan't draw a quiet breath until this thing is at an end."

He drew out his watch. "I'll leave now. And I'll take the note, Helen, it's not safe for you to have it here. Now for God's sake, compose yourself. You have to face your husband."

"I've had a lot of practice at pretense," she said with unaccustomed bitterness.

Frank looked at her with pity, but his voice was brisk. "I'll come by tomorrow, after the House rises. The business will not be concluded today, but I should have it well in hand."

Then, though he was longing to be on his way, he waited while Helen rang for the footman to show him out.

It was a quarter past six when Frank entered Hyde Park and

turned north on the path bordering Park Lane. The reservoir was less than a quarter mile away. He left his horses standing in the shelter of some nearby trees and approached the north end of the reservoir on foot.

It was still light and, though the fashionable hour was somewhat past, there were a number of strollers and a sufficient number of carriages that he did not at first distinguish the black hackney with the scrap of linen that seemed to have fallen by its side. It was, Helen's letter had said, to be the blackmailer's signal. Frank wondered how many men had stopped to retrieve the handkerchief and return it to the carriage's occupant and how often the contessa had been obliged to throw it once more to the ground.

But it was in keeping with what he had seen of the contessa that she would choose such a dramatic gesture. Frank picked up the lace-edged square and approached the carriage. "Madam," he said, "is this yours?"

"I am most grateful to you, sir." The hood of her cloak covered her hair and shadowed her face, and had he not been expecting it, he would not have immediately recognized her. But her voice gave her away. He could not easily forget that faintly accented, rich contralto.

As she leaned forward to take the handkerchief from his hand, she gave a start of recognition. So she remembered him. "I believe we have a matter of business to discuss," he said. He pressed some coins in the driver's hand and desired him to walk apart, then climbed into the carriage and sat facing her. "Now, contessa."

"Now, Lord Chester." She threw back her hood and regarded him with her enormous eyes, a smile playing about her lips. "I had not expected it to be you. But perhaps it is well that we are already acquainted."

"Well or no, we need not pretend that we are not." Frank leaned back and crossed his legs. "I am here as an emissary."

"Of course." The maddening smile was still on her lips. It said, as clearly as words, that she had the advantage and was

111

enjoying it.

Frank felt a flash of anger, but he pushed it aside. He made an effort to keep his voice light. "I believe you have something to exchange."

"How very droll you English are. I have some letters, and you would like to buy them. All that remains is that we agree on a price."

"Very well." Frank leaned forward, hands on his knees. "But I never buy without inspecting the merchandise."

"Of course." She opened her reticule, drew out a letter, and held it out to him. Then, with a gesture that was almost flirtatious, she drew it back. "I must warn you, Lord Chester, that this is the only one I carry on my person. There are others, and they are in a place quite safe that you will not readily discover. If you behave like a gentleman in this, you may have them. If you do not, I will give them to Lord Berresford."

Frank drew a deep breath and held out his hand for the letter. It was a twin of the one he had taken from Ian York—Helen's characteristic flowing hand, this one beginning with *My beloved* and closing with *Your adoring Helen*. He folded the pages deliberately. "Yes, this is what I would buy."

The contessa held out her hand, and Frank reluctantly handed the letter back. "Good, you play the gentleman with me. I can trust your word and you can trust mine. I want five thousand pounds."

Frank leaned back and folded his arms. "That's a great deal of money." It was more than Frank had seen in his last five years on the farm in Durham.

"A lady's reputation is a thing of value."

Even with his uncle's death, Frank could not be accounted a wealthy man. "You will want to conclude this business quickly, as do I. It will be difficult to raise that amount in a short time."

"Do not play with me, Lord Chester. I could have asked twice that amount, but I am a reasonable woman."

He leaned forward once more. "Three."

112

She laughed.

"Come, I am serious. I can't raise five thousand. And though Lord Berresford is a wealthy man, his wife has no money of her own."

"A clever woman would find a way."

"No doubt. But Lady Berresford is a—a softer woman."

"A mouse."

"And Lord Berresford will have been generous to you when he brought you to England. A clever woman would have seen to that."

She smiled. "Very well. You are right, I would have this business done quickly. Forty-five hundred."

"Four."

She hesitated. A spasm of annoyance crossed her face. Then she shrugged. "Four."

Frank drew out his wallet, heavy with the notes he had taken to his meeting with Helen's first blackmailer. "Five hundred now, and I take the letter you showed me. The balance when I receive the others."

The contessa counted the notes rapidly and put them in her reticule. "It is a pleasure to do business with you, Lord Chester," she said, handing Frank the letter. "I think it is better if you do not come to me, and I do not know when I will be free again. Give me your direction. I will send you word when we may meet."

Frank gave her the address in Park Street and prepared to leave the carriage.

"One moment, Lord Chester." She leaned forward and laid a hand on his arm. He was aware of musky perfume and soft flesh, and vagrant thoughts that had nothing to do with blackmail crossed his mind. "You must not judge me," she went on. "I do this because I must. It has nothing to do with the reason Lord Berresford brought me to London."

Frank nodded and jumped down from the carriage. He had received her message. There was no way he could expose the Contessa Montalto to his colleagues without putting Helen at risk.

It had been six o'clock when Demetra reached the park and stationed herself near the reservoir in the shelter of the trees. She had traded her neat gray pelisse for a black cloak and had pulled up its hood to obscure her features. She did not want to attract attention, and certainly not the contessa's.

There were other carriages drawn up on the verge, but Demetra had recognized the contessa's at once, a hackney coach with a telltale handkerchief on the ground beside it. There was no sign of Helen and no one else approached. Demetra schooled herself to patience—it was not her strongest virtue—and willed herself to invisibility.

It was perhaps a quarter of an hour later, with her feet grown cold and an ache in her back, that her attention was caught by a handsome landau, its top raised to screen its occupant, which slowed down as it approached the reservoir. Helen at last. But the landau did not stop, and when it had gone past, Demetra was startled by the sight of her husband walking up the path in the direction of the contessa's carriage. She smiled in relief, wondering what strange chance had brought him here just when she needed him. She would wait until he was well past the carriage and then—

It was not until Frank had picked up the handkerchief and entered the carriage that Demetra understood why he was there. Her insides turned over. Helen had been too frightened to keep the appointment herself. She had sent a messenger. The one person she could trust with her secret. She had sent her lover.

Chapter 8

Thursday, October 5–Friday, October 6

When? Demetra thought, stunned, sickened, enraged. When had it begun? What had the contessa said in her letter? *Last autumn in Paris.* Frank had been in France then, visiting his uncle, and had seen the Berresfords in Paris. Demetra recalled with outrage the letter he had written about that meeting. He had even made a point of the sad state of the Berresfords' marriage and how lucky they were in their own.

Helen must have written letters to Frank during that time abroad, letters which had fallen into the contessa's hands. Had the affair stopped when Frank returned to England? He had been alone in London these past two months. Was Helen the reason he had not urged Demetra to join him sooner? And last night—last night when he had pleaded so ardently with her to come home and she had nearly given in—had he come straight from Helen's arms to Buckleigh House? Somehow that seemed worst of all.

A wave of nausea engulfed her. She grasped hold of a tree and fought for control. Frank was closing the door of the hackney and nodding to the driver. If she knew her husband— and however wrong she had been about his marital fidelity, Demetra still felt competent to predict Frank's behavior

115

toward a blackmailer—he would attempt to follow the contessa. And that must not happen, for if he saw her go into Hannah's house, he would at once make the connection to Demetra. There would be plenty of time to be angry and hurt in the future. Now she must prevent Frank from discovering the contessa's destination. She would have to improvise, for this was a set of circumstances she had certainly not foreseen.

Demetra waited until the hackney started forward, then moved onto the path and walked toward Frank. After a few steps, she allowed her eyes to focus on him and began to hurry forward.

"Frank!"

He turned at the sound of her voice. "Demetra," he said swiftly, "I can't talk now—"

"Yes, but darling—oh!"

Demetra gave a cry of pain as she fell headlong onto the ground.

"Demetra!" Frank was at her side while the other passersby were still looking around to see what had happened.

"It's all right." Demetra managed to put just the slightest tremor in her voice. "I don't want to make you late for your appointment. If you could just help me up—"

Frank gave her his hand. Demetra took it. The drawback of this scheme was that it necessitated touching him, but at least she was wearing gloves. She clambered to her feet, gasped, and staggered. Frank caught her in his arms. Demetra forced herself not to stiffen. She would never get through this if she allowed herself to think about her shattering discovery.

"I'm sorry," she said, "it seems to be rather worse than I thought. I hate to inconvenience you, darling—"

"Don't talk nonsense. Is it your ankle? Do you think it's broken?"

"I'm sure it isn't." She wasn't about to let Frank examine her ankle, which was not only unbroken but would show no signs of swelling or any other injury. "If you could just lend me your arm for a bit—"

116

"I can do better than that. My carriage is not far off. I'll drive you back to Buckleigh House. Can you walk a short distance or shall I carry you?"

Frank's face and voice were filled with concern. But then he would show such care for an injured stranger. A wronged wife should rank as high. "Don't be idiotish, Frank," Demetra said crisply. "I'm perfectly capable of walking. Besides, you'd probably drop me." He had dropped her once. Well, to be fair, he'd tripped on the carpet. On the way to bed. It was a happy memory, but now it brought on another wave of nausea. Demetra gripped Frank's arm.

"What brings you here?" she demanded, as they began to move slowly forward. It was best to ask first, before he had a chance to inquire about her own presence in the park. Besides, she had to admit to a wholly vindictive desire to see him squirm.

"Merely a reluctance to return to my empty house," Frank said easily. He had clearly become an accomplished liar. How despicable of him to use her absence as an excuse, to attempt to make her feel guilty for leaving him alone. Alone indeed!

"Well, I'm excessively glad to see you," Demetra said, "and not just because you came to my rescue. I've been in Park Street you see"—best to admit to that, for Robbins was certain to tell him of her visit—"and I waited for you for an age, and then when I'd given you up I thought I'd come to the park because Edwina and Sophy said they would be walking this afternoon and I meant to return to Buckleigh House with them, but now that I've found you we can talk after all."

There, that wouldn't hold up under close examination, but with any luck Frank would be too busy worrying about his own story to question hers.

Frank was smiling at her. Had she not been so recently and so rudely disillusioned, she could have sworn he was pleased to see her.

"It's about the drawing room chairs," Demetra said swiftly, determined to forestall any questions. "I know we'd decided on

117

cream-colored fabric, but I keep thinking about how dirty it will get, for you know how hard it is to get the children's hands really clean, and it would seem dreadfully unfair to forbid them to play in the drawing room, besides being shockingly difficult, and in any case wouldn't it be easier simply to change the color? And if we wait until tomorrow to talk, you won't be finished in the House until four, so I won't be able to do anything until Saturday and then very likely they won't start on the commission until Monday—"

"Demetra." Frank regarded her with amusement. "I've no objection to talking now. If you can manage."

"It's my ankle that's hurt, not my head." Demetra reminded herself to limp.

"We can talk on the way to Bruton Street. But we'd best find your sisters before we leave the park. They'll be wondering what's become of you."

"No, for they don't expect me. I merely happened to know that they meant to walk in the park this afternoon and I thought I'd see if I could find them for I didn't fancy being on my own any more than you did."

This barb failed to draw even a hint of a reaction from Frank. "Do you mean to tell me you came out on your own?" he demanded.

"Of course I came out on my own. Good heavens, Frank, you sound like Mama. I went out on my own dozens of times—well several times—the first week I was in London. Why should it be any different because I'm living in Bruton Street?"

"No reason at all." His face relaxed. "I'm sorry I snapped at you. I'm rather preoccupied at the moment."

"Adultery is a preoccupying business," Demetra could not resist retorting. "I mean the Queen's of course," she added hastily, forcing herself to smile. "Her alleged adultery, I should say. Not to mention the King's, which one could say is at the root of the whole business."

"One could at that," Frank agreed. "Here we are." Frank

helped her into the carriage with the greatest solicitude. "Now what alternative do you have to cream?" he asked, giving his pair their office, but holding them to a sedate pace so her ankle would not be jostled.

Demetra drew a breath. "Well, I was thinking of crimson, but that would be quite overpowering, and then there's rose, but it does tend to remind me of the small drawing room at Buckleigh House, so perhaps—"

Demetra kept up a flow of chatter about the chairs all the way to Bruton Street and allowed Frank to convince her that they were better off with the cream pattern they had originally selected. When they reached Buckleigh House, she accompanied Frank to the nursery, and apologized to the children for having missed their dinner. She could not hope to deceive Colin, but even he did not seem to realize how wretched his mother was. She should be grateful for small mercies.

It was past seven before Frank left, and even then Demetra could not allow her feelings free rein. Grateful that she had excused herself from dinner, Demetra asked Stephen to procure her a hackney and directed the driver to Pancras Street.

As Demetra had expected, Hannah said the contessa had returned—the pretext was a missing brooch—and that on her subsequent departure she was found to have also retrieved a packet of papers from beneath the mattress in the spare bedchamber. Hannah was well acquainted with the hiding place, having located it during the contessa's absence. And thanks to Hannah's diligence, the packet the contessa departed with was not the one she had hidden.

"I was going to substitute blank sheets, like you suggested, Demetra, but there weren't many letters, so I just copied them. This way it may be longer before she realizes she doesn't have the originals." She looked at Demetra speculatively. "I didn't like reading someone's private papers, but I assume you have your reasons."

Demetra merely nodded and put the letters in her reticule.

119

On the drive home she cursed the darkness which kept her from reading them, but when she was at last in the privacy of the yellow bedroom, she felt suddenly hesitant. She sat down on the edge of the bed and stared at the innocuous-looking bundle of papers, then grasped the first letter and jerked it open.

Helen's hand was beautiful and flowing except for frequent moments when she had apparently been overcome by emotion. The contents themselves proved to be the sort of high-flown nonsense which would make one smile—were it not addressed to one's husband. Had Frank appeared, Demetra could not have answered for the consequences.

The indignant fury she had been forced to hold in check welled to the surface with full force. She was too angry to cry. She tugged off her half boots, snapping the laces, and flung them to the ground, but they made only a discreetly muffled thud against the thick carpet. She reached for a pillow and threw it across the room, but it hit the floor with an even less dramatic plop. Demetra stared balefully at the boots and pillow. Even inanimate objects were against her.

Past memories flooded her mind, images of Frank and Helen sitting together, talking together, laughing together over some private joke from the days before Demetra had known either of them. Every pang of jealousy she had felt in the past—and shrugged off as inconsequential—came back with redoubled force. Every compliment Frank had paid to Helen, every smile Helen had given Frank, suddenly became a sign post Demetra had been blind to overlook. It was a wonder she had not seen it sooner.

Had Frank been secretly relieved when she removed to Buckleigh House? Had Helen visited him in Park Street? Had she been in their room, in their bed? It was too painful to bear, yet the images would not go away. She was furious. She was wretched. She was—

She was veering dangerously close to self-pity. Demetra forced her hands, which were clenched tightly around her body, to relax, and tried to moderate her breathing. It was bad enough to face the pity of others. It was insupportable to face one's own. Even anger, while satisfying, was not in the least constructive.

What was she to do next? Step aside nobly and allow the affair to run its course? Certainly not, it wasn't even worth considering. Leave Frank? Well, she had already done that, at least temporarily, but as for anything more permanent—

No. However angry she was with Frank—and she was still angry, unconstructive though it might be—she was not prepared to give him up, and certainly not to Helen Berresford, who was clearly the wrong woman for him, even were she not already married, and—

Married. Oh, Lord, in all this she had scarcely given a thought to Arthur Berresford. Not only could these wretched letters ruin Helen's marriage, they could just as effectively destroy Frank's career. Arthur Berresford might not be respected by all his fellow Whigs, but his fortune, his title (he controlled several rotten boroughs), and his family connections (he was a first cousin of the Duke of Waterford) made him a formidable power. If he turned all that power against Frank, as he assuredly would if he learned Frank was his wife's lover . . .

Oh, Frank, Demetra thought, you do have the most confounded talent for landing in the briers with your own party.

Well, in addition to rescuing Frank from Quentin's designs, she would have to rescue him from Helen. At least the letters were now safely in her own possession. For a panicked moment, Demetra thought that the copies the contessa possessed could be as damaging as the originals, but then she realized that, while Hannah's hand might briefly fool the contessa, close inspection would show it not to be Helen's.

There was no need now to rush to Frank with the news that the contessa was a blackmailer. But for all the revelations the day had brought, it had not told Demetra any more about the

121

link between the contessa and her brother. She would have to come up with a fresh plan, but first she had to decide what to do about Frank and Helen.

And what to do with the letters. Demetra's first impulse was to burn them at once, but if she did so, Frank might never believe they were truly destroyed. She would have to return them and she would have to do so in person. Any other method was too risky. Helen could not be trusted not to make a mull of things, so it would have to be Frank. When he called tomorrow to see Colin and Annie, she would give him the letters and say, *Don't ask any questions and I won't either.*

Not that there weren't questions she'd like answered. Such as whether or not Frank and Helen's affair was a thing of the past or still very much in the present. It was this question which led Demetra to order her mother's barouche the next morning and direct the driver to St. James's Square.

Demetra had not seen Helen since the affair with Frank had begun. Now, as she waited in a ground-floor anteroom at Berresford House while a footman inquired if her ladyship was at home, Demetra wondered how Helen would behave toward her. She did not think Helen possessed Frank's ability to dissemble. There was, Demetra realized, a good chance Helen would say she was not at home and avoid seeing her altogether.

But before a great deal of time had elapsed, the footman returned and conducted Demetra down the length of the entrance hall, into the staircase hall, and up the circular stairs to the first floor. Berresford House had always been imposing, but since Demetra's last visit Arthur Berresford had commissioned William Porden to remodel and generally embellish the building. The results were opulent, if in dubious taste. Demetra made a mental note to avoid the least hint of gilding in the alterations to the Park Street house.

Helen's sitting room was hung with pale blue damask, less grandiose than the more public portions of the house, but equally ornate. "Demetra," she said, her features carefully schooled into her social mask, "how nice to see you. Thank you, Thomas, that will be all. Have some tea sent in."

There was, Demetra decided regretfully as she shook hands with her hostess, no denying that Helen was a beauty. Moreover, her dress, of palest gray India muslin with a deep frill of Mechlin lace at the neck, must have been recently ordered from one of London's smartest modistes. For a moment Demetra dwelled on how many corners she had cut making her green kerseymere pelisse because that was the autumn Colin had come down with the measles.

But she was being nonsensical. Whatever had drawn Frank to Helen, it was not the superior state of the other woman's wardrobe.

"This is a surprise," Helen said, sitting gracefully on a delicate Grecian sofa. "I mean, you have not called in some time—not that you could have, of course, for you were in Durham, and I myself was in the country—during the recess, I mean, naturally I was in town before that—and then you must be shockingly busy putting your new house to rights, how are the repairs progressing?"

"Dreadfully slowly. Frank and I just had the most exhausting discussion about the upholstery for the drawing room chairs." Demetra moved to a gilt armchair, which looked similar to one she had seen recently in Ackermann's *Repository*. Helen bought new chairs instead of reupholstering old ones.

"I know how difficult it is to agree on colors," Helen said. "We had a wretched time when our house was being done over. I would have preferred pastels, but Arthur thought crimson more imposing and I suppose he is right, but one does get tired of seeing it every day, only of course we aren't in the reception rooms every day, unless we are entertaining a great deal, which we frequently are. Are you going to the Braithwoods' ball on Monday?"

Helen was not as skilled a dissembler as Frank. She did not appear guilty precisely, but she obviously felt ill at ease. As well she might. But was it because she had once been Frank's mistress or because she was currently Frank's mistress? Careful, Demetra told herself, don't lose your temper. She had come to Berresford House on impulse. It now occurred to her that there was not a great deal she could say.

"Helen, I know you have always been very—very fond of Frank." That was putting it blandly. But Helen should take her meaning.

"Well, naturally. We grew up together. Although," Helen added thoughtfully, "when I was quite small I thought him rather horrid. One tends to think boys horrid at that age, doesn't one?"

"I—I expect so." Helen was either more obtuse or possessed more guile than Demetra had credited. "But now that you are older—I mean, now that you are no longer children"—good heavens, this was difficult!—"Helen, to be perfectly blunt, you know Frank's position with the Whigs is not as secure as it might be. It would be ruinous if he came to blows with anyone as powerful as—as your husband. For instance," she added quickly.

For a moment Helen regarded Demetra in puzzlement. Then Demetra saw sudden recognition in her eyes. "You have learned of my visit!" Helen stood up and walked to the fireplace, toying nervously with the end of her cashmere shawl. "Well, indeed, Demetra, I know it was dreadfully wrong of me to have called when you were not at home, but I didn't know that you weren't, and while you may think I should have left as soon as I discovered that was the case, I had something very—very particular to discuss with Frank, though it is of no significance really and I did not stay so very long, and there is no reason Arthur should learn of it unless you tell him, and you won't, will you?"

She turned and looked at Demetra, her eyes filled with anxiety. Demetra stared at her for a moment, quite taken aback. Helen had called in Park Street? Demetra's heart plummeted. The affair was not over then. Or, Demetra thought with sudden hope, had Helen merely called to discuss the blackmail attempt with her former lover?

"Of course I won't say anything to Lord Berresford," Demetra said. "I'm only suggesting that it might be best to use some discretion if you call on Frank again."

"Well, naturally I will behave with discretion, Demetra, I always do. In fact, I find it rather odd for you to be advising me on that score, for you cannot deny that you—oh, dear, I did not mean—really, Demetra, I have much more to fear from talk than Frank does and I will always—"

She broke off, from embarrassment, Demetra thought. It was only when Helen said, "Come in," that Demetra realized there had been a light knock at the door.

"Ah, your pardon, Lady Berresford, I did not realize you were engaged."

The voice was musical and hauntingly familiar. Her mind still on Helen, Demetra turned to the doorway. The possessor of the musical voice was standing with one hand on the doorknob, an expression of charming confusion on her handsome face.

It was the Contessa Montalto.

It was really not surprising, Demetra thought, as Helen introduced them. Arthur Berresford must have learned of his prize witness's disappearance yesterday and decided she was safest under his own roof. Did Helen know her guest was also her blackmailer? Demetra thought not. In fact, Helen seemed positively relieved that the contessa had interrupted her talk with Demetra.

And the contessa? Demetra wondered, shaking hands and looking that lady directly in the eye. Did she realize Lady Chester and Catherine Newley were one and the same?

Something flickered in the contessa's eyes. Not recognition, more a sense that Lady Chester looked vaguely familiar but she could not recall where or even if they had met. It was fortunate Demetra had had little time to dress her hair that morning. It spilled beneath and around her bonnet in a riot of curls, creating a picture very different from that of the neat, prim

Miss Newley.

By the time Demetra left, after drinking a cup of tea and spending twenty minutes exchanging pleasantries with the ladies, she was certain the contessa had not recognized her.

She was safe. For the moment. But what the devil was she to do next?

Frank pulled away from Westminster and headed for St. James's Square as rapidly as traffic would allow. He was in remarkably good spirits. Today's evidence had, he judged, favored the Queen, though there was the matter of a letter which Lady Charlotte Lindsay had supposedly received from her brother, advising her to resign her position as the Queen's lady-in-waiting because of the rumors circulating about Her Majesty. Lady Charlotte had been ordered to search for the letter, but there was a story going about that it and other of her correspondence had been sold to the Government by Lady Charlotte's spendthrift husband.

Frank shook his head. Sad to what depths a marriage could sink. Still, his meeting with Demetra in the park yesterday had left him more hopeful about salvaging his own. Though he had been frustrated in his attempt to follow the contessa, he had been delighted that Demetra seemed to desire his company. He suspected her chatter about the drawing room chairs had been simply an excuse to spend time with him without admitting that she wanted to do so.

When he had extricated Helen from her blackmailer, he would be able to focus his attention on resolving his problems with his wife. As soon as he left Berresford House he would visit Colin and Annie. Perhaps he would see Demetra and they could talk about something other than furniture. His meeting with Helen should not take long.

But when the footman ushered him into Lady Berresford's sitting room, Frank found Helen taking tea with the Contessa Montalto.

For a moment Frank feared that the contessa had called on Helen to make her blackmail threat directly, but when Helen introduced the contessa with every appearance of cordiality, and explained, "Arthur has decided that it is best for her to stay with us for a time," Frank realized that it was Helen's husband who had brought the contessa to Berresford House. He could read Helen well, and he was certain she had no idea she was entertaining the woman who was blackmailing her. A glance at the contessa's faintly amused expression confirmed him in this opinion. Breathing more easily, Frank seated himself and accepted a cup of tea.

"Lady Berresford has most kindly procured a card of invitation for me to a ball given by Lord and Lady—how do you say it?" The contessa turned to Helen with a pretty look of inquiry.

"Braithwood," Helen supplied. "You go there, do you not, Frank?"

Frank nodded. The ball which Kenrick and Rowena were giving on Monday would be a glittering event in Whig society. It would also be an excellent opportunity to pay the contessa and retrieve Helen's letters. It would be difficult for the contessa to go out on her own again, and Frank did not want to risk making the trade in Berresford House. There was nothing better than a crowd to ensure real privacy. The matter could be settled before the contessa's appearance in the witness box. "I shall look forward to seeing you there, contessa," he said. "May I hope that you will save me a dance?"

The contessa smiled, inclined her head, and for the briefest moment met Frank's eyes, her own showing perfect understanding. She was, he had to admit, remarkably able and intelligent. They had settled the entire matter in a mere two minutes, and Helen was none the wiser.

Frank stayed a short while longer for appearance's sake and then excused himself. Helen in turn excused herself to the contessa, saying she would see Lord Chester to the door.

"Of course, I should have rung for Thomas to see you out,"

Helen said, having pulled Frank into the vast, but quite empty drawing room, "but I could not think of any other excuse, and as she is Italian I think it very likely she will not have the least idea how oddly I am behaving. Did it work, Frank? Did you see that—that woman?"

Silently, Frank handed her the single letter he had purchased from the contessa. "I should have the others for you by Tuesday," he told her.

"Oh, Frank, thank heaven!" Helen exclaimed. "I have been in such a state today! First Arthur told me about the contessa being a witness and then he insisted on moving her here and I had no sooner given orders about the rooms than I was informed that she had just dismissed her maid for thieving or some such thing, so now I shall have to share Minot with her, and I know it is poor-spirited of me to object, but there's no denying it will make a difference, and then Demetra called—"

"Demetra called here?" Frank's voice was suddenly sharp.

"Yes, and it was the oddest thing. Frank, you did *not* tell her that I called in Park Street, did you?"

Frank's brows drew together. What the devil had Demetra been about? And how could she have learned of Helen's call? "I told her nothing of the sort."

"Well, I am persuaded she knows of it, Frank. She very nearly accused me of compromising your reputation, which I think quite hard, because my reputation would be much more badly damaged than yours if anyone learned of that call, which I was trying to explain to her, only then the contessa interrupted us— Frank, are you listening to me?"

Bloody hell. The contessa. Had Demetra discovered that the woman had been moved to Berresford House? Had her call on Helen been a pretext to see the contessa? Even if it had not, people like Arthur Berresford would interpret it as just that.

"Helen, I'm sorry. I'm sorry Demetra distressed you. You mustn't take anything she said too seriously. I'm afraid I must leave at once. There's something I have to take care of without further delay."

128

Twenty minutes later, Frank walked into the entrance hall of Buckleigh House and informed Stephen that he wanted to see his wife. The past three days had taught Stephen that Lord Chester was not a man to be argued with. Lady Chester was in the old sitting room with Lady Edwina and Lady Sophia. He would take Lord Chester there directly.

"There's no need," Frank said brusquely. "I know the way."

Frank's recent visits to Bruton Street had given him a rough sense of the geography of Buckleigh House. He ran up the stairs, made his way to the old sitting room, opened the door, and looked past Edwina, who was reading *La Belle Assemblée*, and Sophy, who was playing patience. "Demetra," he said curtly, "we have to talk. Now."

Chapter 9

"Frank," said Demetra, burying her anger and fear beneath a bright smile, "you've come at a capital time. You can sit with the children while they have dinner. If you want to talk first, we'd best go someplace where we can be private. I'm sure Edwina and Sophy will understand if you don't take time to do the civil."

"Of course." Sophy grinned cheerfully at him. "He's one of the family."

Frank recollected his manners enough to nod to his two sisters-in-law, then followed Demetra through a door into an adjoining room.

"That was adroitly managed," Demetra said dryly, moving past the pianoforte—the room was intended for the young women of the family to practice their music—to a chair near the fireplace. "I daresay Sophy and Edwina are speculating madly about us and one can hardly blame them. I shudder to think what sort of impression you made on the servants. Couldn't you—?"

"Demetra," said Frank purposefully, stationing himself before the fireplace, where his wife had little choice but to look at him, "if you choose to live under your parents' roof rather

130

than at my house—our house—there is very little I can do about it. Under the circumstances you may say I have no right to question your actions. But when those actions include calling upon the Contessa Montalto—"

"Calling upon the Contessa Montalto?" Demetra repeated incredulously. "Frank, I've done no such thing! I hadn't even met the woman until this afternoon."

"When you called at Berresford House."

"Yes, but I hadn't the least notion that the contessa was staying with Berresford and Helen."

"Then why did you go there?"

"To call on Helen, of course."

"Call on Helen?" It was Frank's turn to be incredulous.

"Yes, why shouldn't I?" Demetra looked straight at him. "I understand you do it all the time."

The tartness in this reply was lost on the exasperated Frank. "Demetra, you don't even like Helen."

"I never said that. We don't have a great deal in common, but I've known her for years. It's perfectly natural that I should pay her a visit now that I'm in town."

Frank leaned his shoulders against the carved mantle and eyed his wife with misgivings. "And is it also perfectly natural," he inquired, "that I found Helen in an appalling state of nerves as a result of your visit?"

Demetra regarded her husband. She had expected that Helen would tell Frank of her visit, but not that Frank would be brazen enough to confront her with it. "Well, Frank," she said, after a moment, "I hate to be uncharitable, but you know perfectly well that Helen's nerves are *frequently* in an appalling state."

"You needn't compound matters by insulting Helen," Frank snapped.

"I wasn't insulting Helen, merely stating a fact. Do you disagree?"

"Demetra, Helen's nerves are not the issue here."

"But, Frank, you just accused me of leaving them in an

appalling state."

"You won't deny you did more than comment on the weather."

"Well, I should hope I did. My conversational resources would have to be sadly depleted before I was reduced to talking about the weather."

"Cut the line, Demetra," Frank advised, folding his arms in front of him. "You know what I'm talking about."

"But that's just it, Frank, I don't," Demetra insisted at her most wide-eyed. "What on earth did Helen tell you?"

Frank hesitated. He was not certain that Demetra knew of Helen's visit to Park Street, and if Helen was mistaken, there was no point in drawing the visit to Demetra's attention. He did not for a moment believe that Demetra had called at Berresford House out of friendship for Helen. The fact that she was obviously lying about her visit was even more disturbing than the fact that she had made the visit in the first place. "The important thing," he said, "is that as long as the Contessa Montalto is residing with the Berresfords, whenever you visit the house it will appear as if—"

"As if I'm spying on Quentin's behalf," Demetra finished for him. "Is that what you think, Frank?"

"So," Frank continued, "I'm sure we can both agree that it will be best if you do not call at Berresford House in the next few weeks." He wanted to say more. He wanted to demand that she tell him the truth, but that would be quite useless, so he sought for another grievance. "And however angry you may be with me, I'll thank you not to take it out on Helen."

"Frank, you must know I never pick on anyone weaker than myself." Demetra tried to collect her thoughts. She had become sidetracked into a quarrel and was putting off returning the letters. She would have to turn the conversation into calmer channels.

But before she could speak, Frank said, not at all calmly, "That's exactly what I mean."

"What is?"

132

"Saying spiteful things about Helen."

"I was not being spiteful!"

"For the love of heaven, Demetra, you're more generous than this! You must realize that if you were in an unfortunate situation such as Helen's—"

"Unfortunate? She has an enormous house—several enormous houses—plenty of servants, more clothes and jewels than she can possibly wear, and you to act as her champion. Which is more than I can say for myself."

"Demetra, I know you've never been able to be rational about Helen—"

"*I've* never been able to be rational!" Demetra sprang to her feet, all thought of calmer channels gone. "I'm a good deal more rational about her than you are. I'm not blinded by infatuation!"

"I'm not in the least infatuated with Helen," Frank said impatiently. But even as he spoke he could not but recall, with a stab of guilt, the long dormant feelings Helen had recently stirred.

Demetra looked at Frank and felt as if the wind had been knocked out of her. It was true then. This had been no brief dalliance, born of the boredom and isolation of foreign travel. They were lovers still. If not in deed, then in thought, which was just as bad.

And that brought her back to the letters. She should get them now, before Frank stormed out of the house. But if she did so, she would not be able to leave it at that. In her present mood she would call Frank all the things he deserved to be called. And perhaps more besides. And as for Frank—God knew what he would say to her. Was that what she really feared? That he would say he loved Helen and always had and Demetra had only been a poor second choice?

Perhaps she was a coward, but she couldn't face it. Not now. Demetra glanced at the small watch pinned to the bosom of her dress. "It's almost time for the children's dinner. Under the circumstances I hardly think it would be wise for both of us to

133

sit with them. Even if we could contrive to hold our tongues, they are astonishingly good at picking up undercurrents. Why don't you go. Tell them I'll be up later in the evening."

Frank remained where he was standing. "And if it makes you feel any better," Demetra added, "I'll avoid Berresford House until after the contessa's testimony."

"My thanks, madam." Frank crossed to the door, then stopped suddenly and looked back over his shoulder. "Where the devil did you get that dress?"

She was wearing a gown which had arrived from Madame Dessart that morning, a mulberry lustring over an ivory habit shirt with a high neck edged by a narrow frill of lace. "You needn't worry. Mama paid for it."

"If you want new clothes, we are perfectly well able to pay for them ourselves."

"You wouldn't say so if you saw the dressmaker's bill."

"Send it to me. I'll be happy to discharge it."

"There's no need for such an extravagant gesture, Frank. Mama's already taken care of it."

It was at this point, when he was goaded beyond endurance, that Frank recalled his wife's injury on the previous day. "Is your ankle better?" he demanded, his tone far from solicitous.

"Very nearly. I should be quite recovered by Monday. Are you still taking me to the Braithwoods' ball?"

"I don't know," said Frank. "Are you still coming with me?"

"Of course, darling." Demetra raised her brows. "We're still married, aren't we?"

The hour in his children's company calmed Frank's temper but did little to improve his humor. Since the day she had left Park Street, he had been unable to get a straight answer from Demetra. Everything she said, whether it concerned her siblings or the drawing room chairs or even Helen, seemed a pretense designed to keep them from discussing the real issues at hand. He had no doubt that her visit to Berresford House had something to do with St. George. And that meant her efforts to rescue her brother were more active than he had at first supposed. She was now meddling where she could do real damage.

Frank thought again of how Demetra had looked, standing by the piano—which, no doubt, she had often played as a girl—wearing the shiny new dress. She was coming to look and act more and more like a Thane and less and less like his wife.

On this depressing note, Frank arrived at Kenrick and Rowena's house in Green Street, where he had been invited to dine. After the cold grandeur of Buckleigh House, it was a relief to step into the warmth and informality of the Braithwoods' drawing room. The only other guests were Rowena's daughter, Philippa, and her husband, Henry Ashton. Philippa was nursing her daughter, Belinda, though this did not prevent her from entering with spirit into the discussion of the trial.

"Frank, you're just in time," Kenrick said. "Philippa and Henry are assuring us that our side is as conniving and unscrupulous as the prosecution."

"Poor Kenrick," Philippa said affectionately. "Tell us the truth, Frank, are we making things dreadfully uncomfortable for you?"

Frank smiled. He liked Philippa and Henry. Both were talented novelists and both were equally sharp-eyed in the articles they had been writing about the trial for *The Phoenix*. "Oh, Kenrick and I wouldn't have it any other way," Frank assured her. "We're both staunch proponents of a free press. Besides, you say all the things we'd like to be saying ourselves."

Philippa laughed. She was not a great beauty like Rowena, but she had her own charm. "If journalists don't play devil's advocate, who will? You know Henry and I have been on the Queen's side from the beginning."

"While some of our party are still making up their minds," said Frank. It was the more radical Whigs who had first rallied to the Queen's support.

"You can see their dilemma," said Henry, an intense young man with strong convictions and a biting wit. "They wouldn't mind if the trial brought down the Tories, but the way the mob's been carrying on, they're afraid it could bring down far more."

"When one thinks of all the things the average Londoner has to be upset about," said Philippa, "it's ironic that it took the Queen's trial to stir them to action. All finished, darling?"

This last was addressed to Belinda, who gave a contented gurgle and patted her mother's breast. Like Philippa, Demetra had nursed her children herself. As Philippa put the baby against her shoulder and burped her, Frank had a sudden image of Demetra at Hawksley Manor, a child in her arms, the firelight glinting off her hair.

"She's falling asleep already," Philippa said with satisfaction. "Could you ring for Prudence, Henry?"

Frank told himself he was being a fool and a romantic. The nurse came and took Belinda upstairs. Dinner was announced and they moved to the dining room, discussing the specifics of the day's testimony. The company was pleasant, the food good, the conversation entertaining and often insightful, and there were moments when Frank was actually able to forget about Helen and the contessa and almost able to forget about Demetra.

But perhaps the conversation was too exclusively political. No one had said a word about Demetra or even asked after the children. This omission was more troubling than any words. Was Demetra's behavior poisoning not only his marriage but his friendships as well?

He should at least, Frank told himself as the first course was removed, take comfort from the fact that the Queen's side appeared to be prevailing. The others at the table were optimistic.

"The worst the prosecution could come up with today," Philippa said between bites of vol-au-vent of chicken, "was

136

getting poor Charlotte Lindsay to admit that Bergami asked for a drink and the Queen gave him one."

"But Philippa," Henry protested, in mock outrage, "consider the circumstances. Lady Charlotte said she thought Bergami had drunk *directly* from the bottle and then *returned* it to Her Majesty. That might be permissable in an ordinary aristocratic lover, but in a courier? It threatens the entire concept of social order."

"Unfortunately," said Kenrick, helping himself to more of the grilled mushrooms, "that's how many of my esteemed colleagues see it."

"It's quite true," said Rowena. "If only the woman had taken a lover of her own station, she wouldn't come under nearly so much censure."

"But that would have defeated her purpose, Mama," Philippa pointed out. "I'm quite convinced she's spent the last six years trying to embarrass the Regent—I mean the King—as much as possible. And she's been successful, though it seems sad that she should waste so much of her time on her husband. He's not worth the effort."

"I imagine the Ministers feel the same way." Frank took a sip of Bordeaux. "Not only did His Majesty saddle them with a ridiculous case, he returned to Windsor and left them to fight it, and now it looks as if they won't be able to win."

"I hate to put a damper on things," said Henry, "but according to Granville we shouldn't be overconfident. He says the Lords are the stupidest and most obstinate group of men in the country. For a viscount and a Tory he's remarkably perceptive."

Kenrick grinned. "Granville has a point. Still we've one or two more cards to play."

Frank shifted uncomfortably in his chair. Kenrick, he knew, was thinking of the Contessa Montalto. He did not like to see his friend place such confidence in this witness. For Helen's sake he could not risk the least mention of the contessa's blackmail scheme, but he could talk to Kenrick in general terms about the contessa's reliability. He had told Kenrick he would like a word with him in private, so when the meal came to an end, Henry accompanied the ladies to the drawing room, and Kenrick and Frank adjourned to the study.

"I see you've moved the contessa again," Frank said conversationally, when they had reached the privacy of this apartment.

Kenrick had gone to stir up the fire. He set down the poker and surveyed his friend. "Ah. How did you find out?"

"I called at Berresford House and found her in residence."

"I'm sorry you were surprised," Kenrick said, settling himself in a chair across from Frank's. "I was going to tell you tonight. I'd have told you yesterday, but—"

"But Berresford doesn't trust me," Frank supplied cheerfully.

"But you weren't anywhere to be found. Nicholas and I were both at Brooks's with Berresford when he got the message."

"Message?"

"From the contessa's maid. Informing us that her mistress had disappeared."

Frank managed a very creditable look of surprise. "Disappeared?"

"She left a note saying she'd return, but that didn't exactly reassure us. Berresford nearly had a fit right there in the club. Fortunately the contessa did return, not long after we got to her lodgings."

"And her explanation?" Frank was genuinely curious.

"Merely that she could not bear to spend another hour confined to such close quarters."

"Do you believe her?"

Kenrick shrugged. "If she was going to lie, I'd have expected her to come up with something better."

Frank rather thought he would have too.

"But it's a bit more complicated, I'm afraid," Kenrick continued. "According to Pawley, just before the contessa disappeared she had a visit from a woman who claimed to be a dressmaker sent by Berresford. Berresford denies that he sent her."

"And the contessa?"

"She admits that the woman helped her slip out of the house, but she's rather vague about the subsequent details."

"Did Pawley describe the dressmaker?"

"He said she was a sharp-tongued busybody of no particular looks and indeterminate age. She had a very pretty assistant who said her name was Sally and who seems to have made a much stronger impression on Pawley than her mistress did."

"What was the dressmaker's name?"

"She didn't give it, at least not to Pawley. She said she was from Madame something or other—all Pawley can remember was that the name was French. The contessa claims to know neither the woman's name nor her employer's, which I find hard to believe, but one can't argue with her."

"No." Frank leaned back in his chair and looked straight at Kenrick. "Do you think St. George sent the dressmaker?"

"It's possible."

"A lot of things are possible. It's possible there are two unconnected people trying to spy on the contessa. But I don't think it's likely." Frank had no doubt that the contessa had made use of this mysterious dressmaker to slip from her lodgings and make her blackmail threat. But had the dressmaker learned anything about the letters, anything she might tell St. George? And was it mere coincidence that Demetra had visited Berresford House the very next day?

"Whoever the dressmaker was," Kenrick said, "I think the contessa is too shrewd a woman to have revealed anything of substance to her."

"But Berresford feels the contessa will be safer under his roof?"

"He says it's more important we keep an eye on her than keep her whereabouts in London a secret. Which is pretty sound thinking for Berresford. I'm not sure he's the ideal person to have charge of the contessa, but I don't think we need fear her coming under Tory influence while she's in his house."

"No," Frank agreed. Unless, of course, one counted Demetra, whose political allegiance was disturbingly ambiguous at present. "Kenrick," he said aloud, "are you quite sure—are you confident the contessa's testimony is entirely reliable?"

Kenrick laughed. "These days I'm not confident of much of anything. But Nicholas went over her evidence pretty exhaustively"—Kenrick, ever diplomatic, gave no indication that this was the same occasion on which Nicholas had seen St. George outside the contessa's lodgings—"and if her evidence can stand up to Nicholas, it ought to be able to stand up to the prosecution."

Frank took some comfort from this. He could not be entirely easy about the situation, but he dared say no more.

They rejoined the others in the drawing room in time for the tea tray. Frank was reluctant to return to the solitude of Park Street, and it was near midnight before he at last took himself off.

His cheerful manner on taking his leave did nothing to deceive his hosts. Kenrick saw his guest to the door and returned to the drawing room to find the Hawksleys' domestic difficulties inevitably under discussion.

"Poor Frank," Philippa was saying, "it must be beastly for him. And for Demetra. Of course I never knew either of them too well, for I was only in my second Season when they went to live in the North, but they always seemed so happy. In fact, they were the sort of couple who used to make me feel quite lonely and wistful before I met you, darling," she added, perching on the arm of Henry's chair. "I never could believe all that nonsense just before Frank resigned from the Commons."

"Nonsense?" Henry, who had not moved much in political circles before his marriage to Philippa, cocked an inquiring eyebrow at his wife.

"Arrant nonsense," Philippa said firmly. "I'm not sure I know all the details, but Mama or Kenrick can correct me if I get it wrong. There was a by-election for one of the London boroughs, you see, and the Whig candidate was a man Frank had served with on the Peninsula. As I understand it, there'd been something in his past—he hadn't behaved honorably in the field, whatever that means. Frank was one of the few people who knew about it and the Whigs asked him to keep it quiet."

"Lord Holland appealed to him personally," Kenrick supplied. "Frank had no objections. He said the battlefields of Spain and the halls of Westminster require very different sorts of courage."

"But," Philippa continued, "on the day of the election Lord St. George and some of his friends were seen telling any elector who would listen about the man's cowardly behavior. No one ever knew how St. George learned of the story, but some people assumed Demetra must have told him."

"A number of people, I'm afraid," said Rowena, who was entertaining Belinda. "It looked especially bad because she'd just gotten back on speaking terms with her family for the first time since her elopement."

"Mama!" Philippa exclaimed. "You're never saying you believed the rumors?"

"I'm not saying anything of the kind. Of course, one can never know for sure, but like you I'm inclined to think it was all nonsense. Here, I think Belinda wants one of her parents."

"I imagine," Henry said, taking his daughter from Rowena, "that there were some people only too glad of any excuse to discredit Hawksley."

"Very true," Philippa agreed. "How did you know?"

Henry grinned. "The man thinks too much like I do."

"And has considerably less tact, I'm afraid." Kenrick took a sip of brandy.

"Was he forced to give up his seat?" Philippa asked bluntly.

"Nothing as obvious as that, my dear." Kenrick's tone was dry. "Frank denied that Demetra had said anything to St.

George and very nearly came to blows with several of his colleagues in the process. Then he and Demetra went back to Durham. Not long after, Frank wrote to tell me he'd decided to resign his seat. The excuse was his father's health. I tried to talk him out of it, but it was no use. Frank can be damnably stubborn."

"It must have put a horrid strain on their marriage," Philippa said. "Though that doesn't explain why they should suddenly be having problems five years later. They seemed quite happy when they dined here only last week."

Kenrick and Rowena exchanged glances. But though the Contessa Montalto had been moved to more public lodgings, the suspicion that Demetra had once again passed information to her brother was still a secret.

Philippa and Henry asked no awkward questions, but much later, in the privacy of their bed, Philippa said, "It may be just my imagination, but I had the most distinct feeling that Mama and Kenrick know something about Frank and Demetra that they aren't telling us."

"If it was imagination, then our imaginations run along the same lines."

"Well, we know that's true in any event. The thing is, these days I tend to think anything that's secret has to do with the trial."

"Which it usually does. Though how the trial could have caused Hawksley's wife to leave him—"

"I know, I can't think how either. Which doesn't mean there isn't a connection." Philippa sighed. "You don't suppose this could ever happen to us, do you? They once seemed quite as happy as we are."

"Of course it couldn't happen to us. You don't have any brothers."

In the darkened bedchamber, Philippa frowned at him. "You're supposed to say, *No one's ever been as happy as we are.*"

"Am I? It's not exactly up to my literary standard—or yours—but no one ever has, of course. Is that better?"

"It'll do." Philippa snuggled against him. But much as she loved Henry, the Hawksleys continued to intrude on her thoughts. "It wouldn't do to meddle," she said, emerging from a highly satisfactory kiss, "but I think I shall make a point of going to see Demetra. I imagine she could use a friend just now."

It was, Demetra thought when one of the maids brought her chocolate the next morning, most frustrating, not to mention unfair. She had felt able to cope with Quentin before she learned of Frank's affair. And she might be able to cope with Frank's affair and those damnable letters if it were not for Quentin's perfidy. But the two together were almost too much, even for her.

Almost. She wasn't giving up. But the letters and the chain of events that would be set in motion when she returned them would have to wait until matters with Quentin were resolved. There was no real harm in the delay. The contessa might try to sell Frank the forged copies, but Frank would not be fool enough to buy the letters without verifying Helen's hand. Frank and Helen would suffer more than a little anxiety if they learned the letters had disappeared, but that was no more—in fact, it was rather less—than they deserved.

The only problem was that Demetra was anxious about leaving the letters in her room. If Quentin became suspicious, there was a chance that he would search her things. After a few moments of thought, she decided to transfer the letters to the nursery. Quentin never went to the nursery.

Demetra finished her chocolate and dressed. There was no sense in dwelling on the fact that Frank was having an affair with Helen, or that, far from making any progress toward winning him back, she had managed to quarrel with him quite thoroughly yesterday. Well, actually it was Frank who had quarreled with her, but she had certainly quarreled back, so it amounted to the same thing. There was equally no sense in dwelling on the fact that she still did not know the nature of the Contessa Montalto's connection to her brother, and that, having promised Frank that she would avoid Berresford House, she was not in the best position to discover more.

No, she ought to put all her energy toward devising a new strategy. Several new strategies. The atmosphere of Buckleigh House, Demetra decided on her way up to the nursery, was not conducive to forming a plan of action. She proposed a walk in the park to the delighted Colin and Annie. By the time Demetra had breakfasted and preparations were complete, Sophy had been added to the party. Demetra managed a quick visit to the now empty nursery to conceal the letters, and then the four of them piled into one of the Buckleigh carriages for the short drive to Hyde Park.

The Grosvenor Gate and the area around the reservoir now had very unpleasant associations for Demetra, so at her suggestion they walked along the bank of the Serpentine. Annie ran down the path, shrieking happily and calling for Aunt Sophy to follow her. Sophy had no sooner picked up her skirt and given chase, then Colin darted off in another direction, insisting Aunt Sophy follow him.

There were few people abroad at this hour and Demetra, absorbed in watching Sophy and the children, was surprised to hear a voice behind her say, "Lady Chester?"

She turned in time to see a gentleman sweep a gray silk hat from his glossy dark hair. He performed the gesture with a panache which accorded with his dashing style of dress and the dramatic mustache he sported. Demetra was sure she had never met him.

"You're quite right," the gentleman said, advancing toward her, "we have not been introduced. But I am a friend of your husband's. We were together on the Peninsula. Major Ian York, at your service, my lady, and I beg you will excuse my presumption."

He did not appear in much doubt that she would do so. Women, Demetra suspected, tended to excuse Major York a great deal. York, the name sounded familiar. Yes, of course. Frank did not like to discuss his military experiences—which had left him convinced of the idiocy of war—but he had told her about Ian York.

"I could hardly fail to acknowledge the man who is responsible for saving my husband's life," Demetra said warmly, extending her hand. "My children and I owe you our thanks, Major York. I'm sorry Frank isn't with us. He's in the House now. Perhaps you could call on him this evening—"

"You are too kind, my lady. But as it happens, my business is with you."

"Business?"

"I believe we have an acquaintance in common. The Contessa Montalto."

Demetra was now an expert at responding to the unexpected. "The Contessa Montalto?" she repeated, faltering slightly over the name. "I don't believe I—"

"Very well done, Lady Chester," Major York said. "I understand your reticence and I applaud your loyalty to your friend. But you must allow me to explain the circumstances. You see, the contessa and I have had a most foolish quarrel and I am anxious for a reconciliation. Two days ago I—er—happened across her in this park, and I followed her to a small house in Pancras Street. Unfortunately, the contessa must have caught a glimpse of me and—I am afraid our quarrel still rankles with her—she managed to give me the slip. Sometime later a most charming young woman with quite glorious titian hair arrived at this same house. By then I realized I had lost the contessa, so I decided to follow the young woman when she left, in the hope that I could learn something. And having followed her to her home, I made certain inquiries and learned that she was none other than Lady Chester and that Lady Chester was the wife of my old friend Hawksley."

"How very enterprising of you," Demetra said dryly.

"Yes, it was rather, wasn't it?" Major York gave an engaging grin, then made a remarkably convincing transition back to wounded lover. "Lady Chester, I place myself at your mercy. I have no other way to contact the contessa and I cannot rest until we have sorted out our differences."

Demetra stared at him. She had wondered how the contessa came to be in possession of Helen's letters to Frank. Major York provided a link between Frank and the contessa. If Frank had met York in Paris last year, York could have stolen the letters from him. Had York and the contessa been in the blackmail scheme together and then had a falling-out? Did York know anything about St. George? Demetra mulled over this last. If she acceded to Major York's request and arranged a meeting with the contessa, a meeting which she herself could observe or overhear, she might be able to discover what game the contessa was playing.

But it would be difficult to bring York and the contessa together, for she was certain the contessa never left Berresford House unattended. Demetra was hesitating, not sure how much to promise or how much to admit, when she heard her daughter's voice asking loudly, "What's your name?"

Demetra turned and saw Annie apparently exchanging greetings with a chance-met woman. The woman had bent down to speak to Annie, so all Demetra could see was a simple straw hat, ornamented with pink roses, and a few wisps of light brown hair. A small brown-and-white dog was sniffing at Annie's feet.

"Mummy," said Annie, running toward her mother, "this is Fippa."

It was Kenrick's stepdaughter, Philippa Ashton. Demetra had known her slightly before she and Frank moved to Durham, and when they had dined with the Braithwoods last week before all the trouble began—was it really only a week since her world had caved in?—Demetra and Philippa had had a long and enjoyable talk. Demetra remembered thinking she had made a friend. That was back when she had time to think about such trivialities as friends.

"And this," said Annie, gesturing to the dog who had

bounded after her and was investigating Major York's boots, "is Herm'a."

"Hermia!" Philippa followed Annie, calling her pet to order sharply. Hermia paid no attention. Philippa repeated the command, flashing a smile of apology at Major York. Hermia reluctantly retreated to her mistress's side. Annie looked up at Major York and asked him what his name was.

Demetra hastened through introductions. She was beginning to have an idea of how to bring Major York and the contessa together, but she needed to talk to Philippa first. "I'm so glad we met, Major," she said, her tone polite but dismissive. "I trust I shall see you again before you leave London. What is your direction?"

"I'm at the Black Horse in New Bond Street, Lady Chester. I shall look forward to hearing from you. Mrs. Ashton, Miss Hawksley, it's been a pleasure meeting you. And Hermia." He gave a smile which one could not help finding attractive.

Demetra and Philippa returned the smile, Annie grinned, and Hermia barked enthusiastically.

"I'm so glad I ran into you," Philippa said, when Major York had moved out of sight. "I was planning to call at Buckleigh House later today."

Rowena Braithwood and Livia Warwick had both left cards in Bruton Street, but Demetra had been from home at the time. She had not actually received a visit from a Whig lady since her removal to her parents' house. Demetra sent Philippa a look of gratitude, but at this point they were rejoined by Sophy and Colin and some moments were spent on introductions. Then Sophy, sensing that Demetra and her friend would like to talk, took the children on ahead. Hermia, liking their more rapid pace, followed.

"Look," Philippa said quietly, "I don't want to be impertinent, but if there's anything I can do to help—"

"As a matter of fact," said Demetra, "there is. Could you have your mother send Major York a card for her ball? I know it's short notice, but he's only just arrived in town."

"I'm sure Mama won't mind. One more among so many can't be a problem. And any man who tolerates Hermia earns my instant and eternal gratitude."

Demetra smiled. "There is one more thing."

"Yes?"

"I'd rather Frank didn't know Major York has been invited. I'm hoping to surprise him. Frank, I mean."

Philippa was silent for a moment, regarding Demetra with her clear, candid brown eyes. "All right," she said at last. "I daresay you know what you're doing."

"I hope so," said Demetra.

Chapter 10

To Demetra's surprise, Sophy said nothing at all about the man with the mustache, and neither did Colin, who was normally a curious boy. Though they had been occupied with their chase, she was sure they must have noticed him.

But when they reached home and saw the children settled in the nursery, Sophy followed Demetra into her room and flung herself on the bed. "I do not understand," she said, "why I never meet such interesting-looking men when I'm out with Mama. I think it was quite shabby of you, Demetra, to not present him to me."

Demetra, who was in the process of removing her walking shoes, looked up in astonishment. "Sophy, you're susceptible!"

"Well, of course I'm susceptible. A well-made man with curly black hair and the devil in his eyes? I'm sure he's had amazing adventures and seen horrible sights and undergone desperate privations and has snapped his fingers at all of them. He has a merry face, but there's just the slightest hint of untold suffering behind it all."

"You're bamming me." Demetra put her shoes away and found a pair of soft slippers.

149

"I suppose so. But only a little. And I do wish you'd introduced him."

"I couldn't. I don't know him."

Sophy sat upright on the bed. "You introduced Mrs. Ashton to him."

"She's married."

"And you talked to him for the longest time."

Demetra laughed. "In Durham we talk to everybody."

"In London," Sophy said mournfully, "we don't talk to anybody at all."

Demetra considered her sister thoughtfully. Perhaps she'd been misled by Sophy's forthright manner and her contemptuous dismissal of the social round. Perhaps an enthusiasm for cards was her escape from things closer to the heart. Sophy was eighteen. Demetra had not been much older when she fell passionately in love with Frank.

As if in answer to her thoughts, Sophy looked up and grinned. "It's not what you think, Demetra. I've not gone all spooney over him. But the men who are old enough to know things worth talking about won't take me seriously and the rest are witless addlepates who don't know anything at all. Your friend at least looked interesting."

"He's not my friend. He's—" Demetra hesitated. She could hardly tell Sophy the real story. "He's a friend of Frank's. His name is Major York and that's all I know about him, and I shall probably never see him again."

"Oh, very well." Sophy got up from the bed and went to the door. "But if you do," she added, "and if I'm with you, promise me that I shall meet him."

Demetra smiled. "I promise."

Sophy left the room, but in a moment she was back. "If Frank has any other interesting friends," she said, "pray do think of me."

At six-thirty that evening, Demetra entered the drawing

150

room to join her family. They were to dine at the Countess Lieven's, and Demetra was wearing a new gown, a round dress of glacé silk which Madame Dessart had pronounced woefully plain. The hem was scalloped but had no other decoration, and the bodice, which fitted her admirably, was ornamented with nothing more than a narrow band of pleated crêpe. But the sleeves, cut very short, were covered lavishly with blond, and the color, a deep peacock blue, contrasted vividly with her hair. Demetra felt herself to be in more than tolerable good looks. Though she was loath to admit it, she was quite luxuriating in the unaccustomed feel of fine silk and a well-cut gown.

"You were right about the color," Lady Buckleigh said. "It becomes you."

"A smasher." Lewis momentarily forgot his pique at not being included in the evening's entertainment.

"Quite fine, 'Metra," St. George said in his drawling voice. "I shan't mind taking you down to dinner."

"I hope it won't come to that, Quentin," Demetra said. "I don't approve of giving married women access to all the eligible young men. They ought to be content with other women's husbands."

"I'm sure to be sitting by someone's husband," Sophy said. "I can't see what good it is to go out in society before I'm married and allowed to flirt with them."

"You're there to be seen," St. George informed her. "Think of the young men across the table who'll spill their wine because they're sitting in rapt contemplation of your charms."

Lady Buckleigh looked at her son. "You're being vulgar, Quentin."

"The only men who'll notice my charms are the servants who pass behind me," Sophy said, looking down at her bodice. It was cut very low, showing to advantage what her mother considered her greatest asset, and its color, a pale peach, merged imperceptibly with her skin.

"As are you, Sophy," her mother said.

151

"Are servants vulgar?"

"Only when one sleeps with them," St. George said.

"Do we have to talk about that damned trial?" Lord Buckleigh had come into the room. He was a solidly built man of not above middle height, beginning to run to flesh. The lines on his face suggested a permanent state of discontent and he was known to be of uncertain temper. This last—and a reluctance to admit the validity of any position but his own—had kept him from the center of his party's power, but he was respected nonetheless and his opinions were not without weight. "Sophy," he said, nodding to his youngest daughter, and then, "Demetra." He walked over and kissed her on the forehead. Lord Buckleigh was not a demonstrative man, but he had missed his eldest daughter.

He failed to acknowledge his wife, but she did not take it as a slight. They had lived together nearly thirty years and had long dispensed with these courtesies.

Lord Buckleigh pulled out his watch. "What are we waiting for?"

"For Edwina, Father," St. George said.

"There's time, Horace." Lady Buckleigh did not want a scene.

"What happened today, Father?" Lewis did not care whether there was a scene or not, but he had an avid interest in the trial.

Lord Buckleigh made a dismissive gesture. "Servants. Gell's and then Craven's."

"Gell and Craven are the Queen's chamberlains, right, Father?" Lewis was apt to get confused by the many players in this drama.

"Or they were when she left the country six years ago." Quentin had taken up his favorite stand in front of the fireplace, from which position he could look down on the members of his family. "If I remember rightly, they were rumored to be her lovers."

Lord Buckleigh frowned. He had no use for the Queen, but

he was a fair man and he did not like careless gossip. "Lushington—he's one of the Queen's lawyers—had Gell's man, Carrington, on the stand and asked him about a conversation he claims to have had with the Queen's servant, Majochi, about the Baron Ompteda. Gifford quite properly objected."

"The King's Attorney-General?" Lewis asked.

Lord Buckleigh nodded. "Gifford objected," he said again. "He pointed out that Majochi had not been questioned about the conversation, and Lushington therefore had no right to bring it in evidence, but that fool Erskine—"

"Papa," said Sophy, "he used to be Lord chancellor."

"He's still a fool, and a dangerous one at that. Clear enough what the defense were up to. Slandering Ompteda with stories of forged keys and picked locks and stealing papers and fabricating charges against the character of the Queen. Good God, the man was an envoy to the Vatican. Of course the judges ruled against Lushington and said the question could not be put, so Majochi was called in again, over Gifford's objections, and he said—"

"Non mi ricordo." Lewis sat back, looking very pleased at his wit. Demetra and Sophy laughed, but Lady Buckleigh's smile was strained and St. George did not smile at all. Majochi had been the first witness for the prosecution, and his inability to remember anything under Brougham's cross-examination had seriously undermined his credibility. His persistent response to Brougham's questions, *non mi ricordo*, became a popular catchphrase throughout London, and the King's witnesses became known as *non mi ricordos*.

Lord Buckleigh was not pleased with his younger son, but he wanted to be fair. "He did. But he also denied everything that rascal Carrington said. And before that," he continued, putting this particular failure behind him, "they had the same argument about admissibility of evidence when they asked Craven's man some very improper questions. They were trying to impeach the testimony of Louisa Dumont. Erskine got into

153

it again, and Liverpool said—" He broke off, looking uncomfortable.

"You might as well tell us, Papa," Sophy said. "Demetra's married, and I'm sure to hear it in the drawing room after dinner. Madame de Lieven knows everything that goes on."

"We cannot prevent your hearing things, Sophy," said her mother, "but you should not betray such indecent curiosity about them."

At this point Edwina entered the room and put an end to talk of the trial. As they rose and prepared to leave the room, Demetra studied her sister. Edwina was wearing a dress of white watered silk and three white plumes in her hair and looked indecently beautiful. Poor Sophy. No wonder she hated going about. In all charity, Demetra thought, she should get Edwina married as soon as possible.

Demetra had not expected to accompany her family to the Lieven dinner and was surprised to learn that her mother had received a note from the countess to indicate that Lady Chester would be most welcome. But she had not been ten minutes in the Lieven drawing room before she understood. Demetra had left Frank on Tuesday. Today was Saturday, and it appeared that half the ton had been apprised of her move to Bruton Street and were speculating on the reason. In his two months in London, Frank had got himself talked of, as much for his force and energy as for his unconventional opinions. He was an effective speaker, cruder than Brougham, they said, but nearly as eloquent. So when his wife returned to her impeccably Tory family, the ton wanted to know why.

Demetra parried questions with the practiced ease that her interviews with her mother had given her. It would have been worse had it not been for the trial. When she was pressed hard on her own sleeping arrangements, she quickly turned the conversation to those of the Queen.

"I'd always thought it would be quite simple to carry on a

liaison." Sophy had just rescued Demetra from a particularly persistent inquisition and taken her to a small bench at the end of the room. "Any girl who can evade her governess should be able to outwit her husband."

"Perhaps," Demetra said. "But she'd find it difficult to outwit her maid."

"Are you talking about Dumont?" Mr. Henning, a fair-haired young man with a ready smile had approached them. Sophy rather liked Mr. Henning. He was quite taken with Edwina and showed no amorous interest in her younger sister. "You mean the *femme de chambre*, the one who kept insinuating that it looked like two people had been sleeping in the Queen's bed?"

Mr. Henning grinned. "Yes, and the one who swore she herself always slept alone in her own bedchamber. That isn't what Keppel Craven's valet said today."

"Oh, then that's what Papa meant— Mr. Henning, just what did Lord Liverpool say?" .

Mr. Henning looked around. Half a dozen people had joined them. "The Prime Minister said it was quite possible. For her to have slept alone. He said, *a person might have had criminal intercourse with her without having slept with her*. It caused quite the biggest laugh of the day."

The group standing around the bench erupted in laughter of its own. Demetra joined in, then glanced at Sophy, conscious of her role as elder sister. But Sophy did not look in the least uncomfortable. Society had changed during her years in Durham. Or perhaps it was only that the trial had loosened everyone's tongue.

"Oh, I say," Mr. Henning said, "look at Madame Frias." A handsome dark-haired woman had stripped off her gloves and was showing off her hand and arm, as a man might hold out his snuffbox to be admired. Then she pulled up her petticoats to show off trim ankles and delicate feet. "*Les Espagnoles ont aussi des jolies pieds,*" she said to the group of gentlemen standing around her. This was met with good-natured laughter.

155

"She's Spanish," Mr. Henning said. "They tend to be exuberant."

Demetra smiled. She glanced at her mother, who was standing a few feet from the group surrounding Madame Frias. Lady Buckleigh gave a slight shrug. Demetra understood the gesture completely. One must expect such things of foreigners, and besides, Madame Frias's husband was an ambassador.

Demetra was sent down to dinner with an unprepossessing man, well past his first youth, with soulful eyes, a large nose, and a fund of wicked stories that kept her entertained throughout the endless courses. He was some kind of assistant to Count Lieven, who was the Russian ambassador, and he knew everyone who was there. Demetra began to enjoy herself and for an hour or so was almost able to forget the miserable state of her marriage.

Quentin was exerting himself to be charming. It was uphill work. No one had precisely cut him, but Demetra had seen several people anxious to move on when he joined the group with whom they were conversing. At the moment, his charm was turned with full force on Beatrix Thornton, the woman Mama wanted him to marry. Demetra was not sure whether he intended to impress Beatrix—they had known each other for years—or the rest of the company.

Farther down the table, Edwina was also being charming, skillfully dividing her attention between the Earl of Deavers on her left and Mr. Henning on her right. Both men appeared entranced, and Edwina gave no sign that she had any thought to spare for Elliot Marsden. How odd that her brother and sister should be so excessively attractive and yet seem prey to the same brooding discontent. They had always been disgustingly able to make the world go just the way they wanted. Demetra felt a flash of envy. Nursery jealousy, she supposed, and that made her think of Frank and Helen, so she resolutely turned her attention back to the unprepossessing and charming man by her side.

When the ladies later adjourned to the drawing room,

Demetra sought out Sophy, who had been out of her line of vision at the dinner table. "No worse than usual," Sophy whispered, "though there's no one who can hold a candle to Major York. I can't talk, I'm promised to the card tables and I intend to win a great deal of money."

Demetra, who did not have Sophy's devilish skill at cards, evaded a similar fate and took a turn about the room. Her years in Durham had unaccustomed her to the sumptuous meals and the vast amount of sitting that was a part of London life, and for a moment she felt quite homesick. Then she roused herself and went to sit beside Beatrix to learn what Quentin had been saying at the dinner table.

Demetra was not the only one of the family to pay attention to Lady Beatrix. Her mother had had her under observation the entire evening, as was clear from her comments in the carriage going home. "I've told you more than once, Quentin," she said without preamble. "You could do worse. The girl is presentable and has some money."

St. George did not pretend to misunderstand. "I'm quite happy as I am, Mother. And I could not abide a wife I would be obliged to address as Beatrix."

"The name is immaterial, Quentin, and your objection, as you know, is entirely frivolous. You must marry someday. It would do you good to be settled." She did not add that a respectable marriage would help repair his reputation. Lady Buckleigh had watched the progress of her son through the Lievens' drawing room when they first arrived. He had played it well—an unassuming manner, self-deprecating humor, the attentiveness that is the best of all flattery—but she knew there was still much to be done. There was some grudging admiration for what Quentin had done a year ago, but no one in a position of responsibility had publicly condoned his behavior. She felt her son's disgrace keenly and was eager to erase the blot. "Horace?"

Her husband looked up from his corner with a start. "Hmm? Oh. Yes, why not. Look into it." And he turned away and closed his eyes.

"Don't you find her attractive, Quentin?" Edwina asked with the faintest trace of malice.

"Tolerable looks, but not quite in my style."

Lady Buckleigh was roused to sudden fury. "My God, but I am sick to death of the games you children play! Marriage is a duty, not a matter of whim. A clever wife can be the making of you, Quentin. Without one, you're an idle fribble and no one will ever take you seriously. As for you, Edwina"—she paused to take breath—"you're four years out and losing your freshness. Stop whistling for the moon. Settle for a reasonable man, and you can make of him what you will."

After this uncharacteristic outburst, Lady Buckleigh was silent and no one else had anything to say.

Demetra, feeling a nagging guilt about Edwina, went to her room later that night. Her maid had just been dismissed and Edwina was in her nightdress, her thick dark hair tumbling down her back, and a look of utter misery on her face. At Demetra's entrance she stiffened and turned away.

"May I?" Demetra asked. It was strange to feel like a trespasser in a room that had once been hers.

Edwina shrugged and moved to the dressing table, where she sat down and began brushing her hair.

"Here, let me." Demetra took the brush from her sister's hand. "I haven't made things very easy for you, have I?" she said, lifting the soft waves of hair.

"No," her sister said frankly. "Mama wouldn't have been so fierce with me if you hadn't disappointed her. She expected you to marry Tony, and she hated to let a marquis slip through her fingers."

Demetra ran the brush through Edwina's thick hair. "I suppose I should say I'm sorry," she said, "but I can't."

"It wasn't so very bad," Edwina said, "until I realized Mama intended me to marry Tony instead."

"I thought you rather liked the idea. You always admired him."

"I didn't like having to take your leavings." Edwina's voice held a trace of bitterness. "Though in all honesty," she went on, "I wasn't entirely opposed to the idea. I knew I could manage Tony."

Demetra studied her sister's expression in the glass. "Did you mind very much when he left?"

"Not really. No, not at all. Being a marchioness is no guarantee of happiness. But it looks like being in love is no guarantee either."

Demetra paused in her brushing. "If you mean me and Frank," she said, "no, it isn't. Marriage isn't easy, but then, neither is living under Mama's thumb."

She resumed the long, rhythmic strokes, but Edwina pushed her hands aside and turned to look at her. "But it's not the same as at first, is it?"

"Well, of course it's not the same. You couldn't live long in that dizzy state and be fit for anything. It's different, but it's still—it's still nice." Demetra thought this a very paltry word to describe the feel of Frank's hands upon her. "What goes on in bed, I mean," she added, coloring slightly.

"Is it?" Edwina was now frankly curious. "I've always thought that it might be quite horrid."

"Well, you have to *like* the man, or else it would be. And you have to tell him what you find agreeable and what you don't. It takes time, but you shouldn't shy away from marriage on that account."

"I don't. I suppose I could manage that part well enough. It's all the other times."

"Mama would say if you're clever you don't have to see much of a husband the other times."

"And what would you say, Demetra?"

Demetra put down the brush and perched on the nearby bed. "I'd say, marry a poor man and you'll be too busy to worry about whether you're happy or not."

Edwina laughed. "No, thank you. I like my creature comforts."

Demetra drew up her feet under her. "Edwina, have you ever been attached to anyone? Anyone at all?"

Now it was Edwina's turn to color. Her voice remained guarded. "Not really. Except for the gardener's boy when I was nine. There doesn't seem much to choose among them. They're vain or oafish or have nothing to say for themselves or they're clever like Quentin and have the morals of a snake."

"Lord Deavers seems pleasant enough."

"Just tolerable."

"And Mr. Marsden?"

"Oh, more than tolerable. He's not particularly pleasant, but he's clever and not a bore."

"And well connected?"

Edwina stared at her sister. "You haven't heard?"

"Sophy said it was all quite Gothic, but she never explained what that meant."

"He's supposed to be the younger son of Baron Scargill, but he's really the bastard son of Aunt Aurelia's late husband and therefore Tony's half-brother and our cousin. Not that anyone is supposed to know. Papa's quite taken with him, but Mama doesn't like seeing him about so often."

"Wherefore you delight in his company."

"Exactly."

"And does he delight in yours?"

Edwina sighed. "He says everything that is proper and keeps his distance. He's not a man to forget which side his bread is buttered on."

"Ah, now I see. You've not been able to bring him to your feet. It's as good a ploy as any, Edwina, he's piqued your interest. I think Mr. Marsden might be a dangerous man."

"Do you think so?" This was a new idea to Edwina. A wicked light came into her eyes. "Then perhaps I shouldn't give him up."

"On absolutely no account. Men have us at a disadvantage, but where the heart is concerned we can be quite as clever as they."

Demetra hoped this was true. For as she said goodnight and returned to her own room, she was not thinking about Edwina. She was thinking about Frank.

She closed the door of the yellow bedroom behind her and moved to her dressing table, then unfastened the pearl earrings that had been a gift on her eighteenth birthday and placed them carefully in her jewel case. She was not going to ignore Frank's affair. She could never be a complacent wife.

She removed the peacock blue dress with the blond sleeves and hung it carefully in the wardrobe. Frank would have to choose. She knew she was more fit to partner him than Helen Berresford, a milk-and-water woman who didn't deserve a man like Frank. The problem was, did Frank know it? Demetra pulled her nightdress over her head, climbed into bed, and pulled the covers close to hide the emptiness beside her. If Frank were here, she would prove it.

If Frank were here. . . . Demetra sat up and stared into the darkness. Bed was the one place they'd never quarreled. Would that be a way to get her husband back?

When Demetra went up to the nursery the next morning, she found Sophy on the floor building an elaborate structure out of blocks. The children and Mary Rose were not in sight. "They've gone to the kitchen," Sophy said in answer to Demetra's question. "I think it was a matter of currant buns. It's too bad you weren't here earlier. You missed Quentin."

"Quentin? I don't believe it. He's too high-stomached to have anything to do with the nursery, and he doesn't even like children."

"You wouldn't have known it from his behavior this morning. He seemed quite taken with Colin. When I came up he was showing him all the hiding places he used when he was a boy. They went through one of the cupboards and found these." Sophy indicated the blocks, which had reached precarious heights.

The devil. Demetra did not for one minute believe that Quentin was going soft. He must be spying on her. He could not possibly know about the letters, so he must be spying in general. Just to keep his hand in. How dare he use Colin in this way.

Sophy must have read something of this in her face. "Quentin's up to something, isn't he?"

Demetra curled up on a window seat and stared down at the street below. "Just his usual beastly curiosity, I suspect."

"Then why does it bother you so much? Do you have something to hide?"

Hide? Demetra stared at her youngest sister in consternation. Only her quarrel with Frank and what had occasioned it, and the presence of the contessa, and Helen and Frank's infidelity, and the letters which were proof of that infidelity and were now lying concealed beneath the bottom drawer of the chest in the far corner of the room.

"I only asked," Sophy added, "because I thought I should know what to watch out for. Maybe I could help." She lowered her eyes and laid a bridge across two high towers. Despite her care, the towers collapsed and she swept the blocks away in an untidy pile. "I didn't mean to pry."

"Oh, Sophy, it's not that. You can ask me anything you please. There's nothing I can tell you. Quentin doesn't like Frank, he never has, and he'd do him mischief if he could. I've got to keep a step ahead of him."

"It's all right," Sophy said, getting to her feet. "I'll keep an eye on Quentin for you, and I'll see that Lewis does too, but I won't tell him why. I know how to hold my tongue, but maybe it's best if you don't tell me anything."

There was no use insisting that she had nothing to hide, for Sophy would not believe her. Demetra wondered what stories her sister had in her head. They could be no stranger than the truth. And the truth was that it was no longer safe to keep the letters in Buckleigh House, where Quentin's prying eyes and nimble fingers might soon discover them. She resolved to stay in the nursery until she was able to retrieve the letters and move them to a safer place.

But first she had to deal with the children, who ran in and flung themselves upon her, followed by Mary Rose bearing a plate of currant buns. "Daddy's coming to take us driving," Colin announced.

"With two horses," Annie said.

"And I can take the ribbons—"

"And buy us an ice."

"He came last night," Colin explained, "about seven, but he didn't want to bother you."

And small wonder, after that appalling scene on Friday evening. Frank never liked to face her after they'd had a quarrel.

"You can have a bun if you like." Colin held out the plate. "Will you come today?" he added, his voice carefully devoid of any emotion.

Demetra stifled an urge to hug her son. It would be very pleasant to agree, to drive out with her husband and children and watch Colin take the ribbons and share an ice with Annie and pretend that Helen had never come into their lives. But she did not dare leave the letters in the nursery, and she could not bring herself to go driving with Frank while his mistress's letters lay in her reticule. "I'm so sorry," she said, with the bright smile that never deceived her eldest child, "I have some calls to make that can't be put off. But I won't go until Daddy comes."

When Frank came she managed to be very pleasant to her husband. Frank, too, pretended that all was well between them and even succeeded, Demetra thought, in persuading Colin that this was so. When they had gone and Sophy had left the nursery and Mary Rose had been given a few hours of freedom, Demetra pulled out the bottom drawer of the chest in the far corner and picked up the packet of letters. She would take them to Park Street. Frank's house was the one place Quentin would never go.

An hour later she was walking through the rooms with

163

Robbins, examining the progress made by the carpenters and plasterers. A hiding place was not easy to come by. The house was old and offered many possibilities for concealment, but there would be workmen all over the place tomorrow and, save for Robbins, she did not really know the servants. There was the library—it would be only fitting to use Lord Rochester's slim volume—but it was a room Frank used and who knew what freakish impulse would take him to the very books that were keeping her secret.

In the end, she sent Robbins back to his duties and climbed the stairs to the nursery. The painters had finished here, and there was no need for the servants to be in and out. Demetra closed the door carefully, sat down and pulled out the packet of letters. She considered several hiding places, then at last put them in a box at the back of a large cupboard, concealed within a pile of discarded curtains.

She went down a flight of stairs and into the bedroom she had shared with Frank. The bed was an ancient four-poster from which the dust-laden hangings had been stripped. The mattress was old too; they would have to replace it. She smiled. They had managed very well when Frank brought her back to London. She sat down on the bed and stroked the coverlet, wondering if they could manage again this afternoon. Well, of course they could manage, if Frank was agreeable. But what if he was not?

Demetra felt a stir of panic. If she left the house now, she would not have to know. But if she stayed, at least she would learn if there was anything left to save of her marriage.

She decided to wait. She left the bedroom, wondering how to occupy herself until Frank came home. She walked down another flight of stairs and into the drawing room. The workmen had not yet begun here, and the room was much as it had been in old Lord Chester's time. She had thought it ill-designed when she first arrived in Park Street, but today, with a watery sun streaming through the windows, she could see that the room had possibilities. It was well proportioned, but crowded with furniture that had been disposed with no thought to comfort or conversation. Some of the pieces were ugly and would have to be relegated to the attics, and others were in poor repair, but she might make something of the rest. They had more money now, which was a comfort, but they were far from wealthy, and it did not occur to her to think in terms of new furniture. She began to shift tables and chairs.

She was in the process of moving a small ormolu table from its place between two of the windows to a spot by a carved mahogany chair near the fireplace when she heard voices in the hall below and then the sound of someone running up the stairs.

The door was flung open. "Demetra," Frank said, "what the devil are you doing here?"

Chapter 11

"Hullo," Demetra said cheerfully. "Did they enjoy the drive?"

"They seemed to" Frank said, wondering what particular game his wife was now playing. They had not been alone together since their bitter quarrel on Friday evening. She might have come to make peace, but the past few days had taught Frank to be wary of his wife's behavior. He took the table from her hands. "Why don't you call one of the servants to do this?"

"I can't get used to having servants who aren't busy mending the roof or feeding the pigs. Over here, I think. No, the other side. Did Colin take the ribbons? How was he?"

"Yes. And very solemn, but with steady hands. What are you doing here, Demetra?"

"And did Annie get her ice?"

"Two. One went into her lap. You haven't given me an answer."

"I'm trying to think of a plausible one. You haven't shown much willingness to believe anything I say of late," she added, and then was sorry she had done so. She did not want to begin

166

a quarrel.

"Try the truth, Demetra. I'll believe that."

The truth, heavens, yes, but what part of it? "I miss you," she said carefully, but with perfect honesty. She raised gray-green eyes to his.

Of all the answers she might have made, this was one he had not expected. He was bewildered, and he took refuge in anger. "In that case, the remedy is quite obvious."

"Yes, that's what I thought." She had not intended to plunge right into it, but the conversation was not going at all well. "You're so busy, Frank, there's scarcely ever time to talk, or time for anything else for that matter. But I have no engagements this afternoon, and apparently neither do you, and it's Sunday and the workmen aren't here, so it seemed a perfect time."

"A perfect— Demetra, what are you talking about?"

"Oh, Frank, sometimes you are so dense. Bed." There, she had played her hand, too quickly and not at all well. But if she knew Frank, the gamble was worth taking. She stood there, waiting for the familiar smile to break over his face, waiting for him to walk forward and pull her willing body close to his own, waiting for him to sweep her into his arms and carry her up the stairs to their bedchamber. Well, perhaps he wouldn't carry her. They were long past the ardent, impetuous nights of the early years of their marriage. Though when they were reunited after his two months in London, he had been ardent and impetuous enough.

When he made no move toward her, Demetra had another moment of panic. She had been right. It was too late. He no longer wanted her. She fought the temptation to turn away. "Of course, if you don't want to—" she said stiffly, drawing the remnants of her pride about her.

"Demetra, it's the middle of the afternoon."

She felt as if she had been pulled back from a precipice. "Well, I know that." What had gotten into Frank? He had taken her on the hearth rug, in the carriage, and on one

167

memorable hot afternoon, in an open field. "I thought you liked to have a light."

He could not quite believe her. She had left him for her parents' house and refused to return, she would not trust him with her reasons, she had quarreled with him on every occasion, she had made it clear she had no need of him at all. He was coming to fear that their marriage was indeed over. And now this—this extravagant gesture that made a mockery of her behavior the past week. He reached out a hand for her, then let it drop. "We have more important things to do."

"What? What could possibly be more important in a marriage than—"

"We have to talk."

"But that's just it. I can't talk. I mean, I don't want to talk. Not now, when we've been apart for five nights and we have the afternoon ahead of us."

"You aren't making sense, Demetra."

"Sense? Well, I should hope not. There's nothing at all sensible about the way I'm feeling."

He looked down into her upturned face. Her mouth was parted, her eyes glowing. "When you look at me like that, I'm not very sensible myself," he said.

"Well, then."

"You won't come home." It was not a question. He knew that she would not, and he could not reconcile it with what she was now offering.

"Oh, Frank, that has nothing to do with us. Don't you understand? It has nothing to do with now."

He shook his head, his longing for her contending with his anger and pride. "I don't understand anything at all."

She took a step toward him. "I do want you, Frank." She could go no further. The next move would have to be his.

He hesitated, then grinned suddenly. If it was war between them, he was not going to give up an advantage. "Witch," he said. He seized Demetra by the wrist and pulled her out of the drawing room. "Robbins!" he shouted as they came out on the

168

landing. He looked over the balustrade into the hall below.

Robbins came through a baize-covered door at the back of the hall and turned up an inquiring face. "Here, what's the shouting?"

"I am home to no one, do you understand? No one at all."

Robbins grinned and gave Frank a half salute while Frank started up the stairs, drawing Demetra, triumphant, behind him.

Lying on her side within the curve of Frank's body, his arm flung across her and his hand resting companionably on her downy cleft, Demetra allowed herself to drift into that languorous state that is not quite sleep. Whatever differences they had had in the course of their married life, they had learned to pleasure each other. And today their differences had seemed only to heighten the pleasure they took from their coupling. Helen, Quentin, the contessa—there were no problems of any importance, certainly none she could not handle.

Sometime later Frank stirred and murmured against her hair, "Demetra?"

"Hmm?"

"Did you remember to—"

She turned and propped herself on an elbow, clutching the sheet decorously over her breasts, and stared down into the familiar face. "Why Frank, don't you want another child?"

His mouth twitched. "You remembered. And yes, I do."

"Then we'll have to do this again when I forget."

Frank pulled the sheet away. "Demetra, come home."

She drew back. "Well, of course I'll come home, darling. When the workmen are through and the house is fit to live in."

"Don't fob me off with stories of the house and the workmen—"

Demetra leaned down and kissed him gently, her small, neatly formed breasts teasing his skin.

169

As a diversion, it did not work. Frank took her by the shoulders and held her away from him. "Unworthy, Demetra. Why won't you—"

"No questions," she said, her face and voice for once free of guile. She sat up and regarded him steadily. "Not today. Please."

Frank turned on his back, put his hands under his head, and studied her face.

"I do love you," Demetra said.

He reached up and drew her down for another kiss. "No questions," he agreed. "For today."

Demetra tried to ignore the fact that he had not actually said that he loved her. "Frank." Her tangled hair enveloped his face. She traced the curve of his mouth, the line of his chin. She drew her fingers over his chest, the hairs still damp from their lovemaking, rested them on his flat belly, felt his instinctive response. "Frank," she repeated, her voice coaxing. "Let's do it again."

The glow from Sunday afternoon stayed with Demetra long after she returned to Bruton Street, surprising her sisters but not her mother, who wondered if Demetra and Hawksley had managed to reconcile after all. It stayed with her all through the next day and into the evening when Frank called in Bruton Street to look in on Colin and Annie—long since in bed, though not asleep—and escort her to the Braithwood ball.

Two more dresses had arrived that morning from Madame Dessart, a tawny gold satin and a Brazilian corded sarcenet in Pomona green, but Demetra put them both aside for a dress she had brought from Durham, a dark red Scotia silk that Frank had given her on her birthday three years before. "Never wear red, Demetra," her mother used to tell her, "not with your hair," but Demetra had made it up with pride and worn it with confidence. The dress was sadly out of date, with a very high waist, plain short sleeves, a single deep flounce, and a neckline

170

slashed to a deep V front and back, but it was Frank's favorite.

Frank's eyes told her she had made the right decision. He was coming down the stairs from the nursery floor when they met, almost shyly, like new lovers. As she took his arm and they walked down to the ground floor, Demetra debated telling him about her meeting with Major York and her subsequent invitation. In the end, she decided against it. The major was charming but seemed unreliable, and perhaps he would not come after all. There was no point in raising questions that might strain the fragile détente they had built yesterday afternoon.

Frank was almost lighthearted. The sight of Demetra in the dress he had given her, looking like the wife he knew and not at all like a Thane, was immensely reassuring. He was looking forward to dancing with Demetra during the course of the evening and taking her back to Park Street and bedding her when it was over. In the meantime he had to deal with the Contessa Montalto. The bank notes he had obtained that day rested uncomfortably in a coat pocket against the time that he would exchange them for Helen's letters. With luck he could contrive a few moments alone with Helen tonight and be rid of them altogether.

They arrived at the Braithwoods' house in Green Street amid a crush of carriages. The house was lit from the basement to the top story and light poured from the open front door. Frank took firm hold of Demetra's arm, guided her through the knot of onlookers that clustered outside the house, and led her up the steps and into the hall. It was noisy with the sound of voices and laughter, and crowded with milling guests and servants. The heat of bodies and candles and perfume was a sudden contrast to the cool damp air outside. "A crush tonight, Tuttle," Frank said as he relinquished his hat to the butler. "Will there be many more?"

"We hope so, sir," Tuttle said gravely.

Frank grinned and Tuttle nearly smiled in return.

They joined the crowd waiting to ascend the stairs to the

171

reception rooms. Frank kept hold of Demetra's arm. It was their first appearance together at a major entertainment since they had left London five years ago. Frank knew there were lingering questions about what had happened at that time and rumors about a present separation. He was going to see that they were firmly quashed. Whatever their private differences, he and Demetra were a couple.

They stopped on the landing to greet Kenrick and Rowena, then moved on to the drawing room, which was given up to dancing. There was a crowd near the door. Frank steered a path to the edge of the dance floor, where they stopped to watch a vigorous country dance which was then in progress. Several acquaintances greeted them as they passed by, but no one seemed disposed to linger. Frank noted the stares of a trio of women standing on the other side of the room, then the whispered conversation which followed. His lips tightened and he glanced at Demetra, but she did not appear to have noticed.

Before the dance came to an end, Demetra was taken off by Philippa Ashton, and Frank moved into the jade saloon.

"Lord Chester," said Lady Windham, "come and tell us if the Ministers are going to resign. Charles is being diplomatic and he refuses to commit himself."

Charles, Lord Windham grinned. "I told you all I know. The Ministers went to Windsor yesterday to confer with the King."

"I can hardly add more." Frank sat down on a nearby chair, relieved that this group at least did not seem interested in his marriage. "I suspect the Ministers will manage to keep their places. Unfortunately."

"I want to hear more about Lieutenant Flynn's testimony," said Lady Tarrington, a slender woman in a dark green dress. Flynn was the captain of the polacre that had taken the Queen to Jaffa. "I can't believe that some two hundred grown men spent the better part of an afternoon prying into what might or might not have happened in a tent that was on the deck of the polacre and thought of no better questions to ask than the number of yards between the sofa on which the Queen slept

172

and the bed—" She threw up her hands. "Two yards, three yards, what does it matter? Two or three strides would cover it all."

"The problem," said Lady Windham, "is that men have no imagination these days. It wouldn't have been nearly as bad if the men over seventy hadn't been excused from attending the trial. Anyone who lived his life in the last century would understand these things."

"The government," said her husband, "assumed that regular attendance would be too rigorous for their frail constitutions. And," he added, "I have plenty of imagination."

"Or perhaps," said Lady Windham, ignoring this last remark, "they assumed the old men would find the subject matter too exciting."

They all laughed. Frank excused himself a few minutes later. He liked the Windhams and Lady Tarrington, but he was growing tired of hearing about the Queen's sleeping arrangements. His own were all that concerned him at the moment. Whether or not Bergami could see the Queen's bed from his own bed in the adjoining dining room when the Queen slept below, and whether he sat or lay down on the bed under the tent when the Queen slept on deck seemed supremely unimportant. If the Queen chose to lie with a lover, he was sure she would contrive it no matter where her lover was officially bedded.

On the other hand, Frank realized that the location of beds—say, the distance between Bruton Street and Park Street—could get in the way of contriving anything at all. Demetra was making this very difficult. He decided to play cards.

Demetra found him in the card room a half hour later and carried him off for the dance he had promised. They returned to the drawing room, where a quadrille was forming. Demetra was in high spirits, and Frank felt a surge of pride as he took his place opposite her. Two children had not destroyed her light figure, and in her red dress, with the brilliant hair pinned high and tumbling unfashionably down her neck, she made the other women in the room pale into inconsequence.

Frank would have admitted that there were many other handsome women present—the lively Lady Windham and her cousin Lady Tarrington; soft, dark Emily Cowper with her enormous brown eyes; elegant Francesca Scott, who was Rowena's niece; not to mention Rowena herself—but none attracted him as much as his spirited wife.

There was a stir near the door as some new arrivals made their appearance. The Berresfords had arrived and with them the Contessa Montalto. Frank smiled at Helen as the figures of the dance brought them near the door.

"What a striking woman," Demetra said.

"Helen?"

"The Contessa Montalto." Frank thought her voice sounded tart. "Few women can wear that shade of purple without looking a positive hag."

"She's certainly not a hag," Frank said, "but I doubt that the color of her gown has anything to do with it."

Demetra grinned, but continued staring at the contessa. "Berresford has more friends than usual tonight. They all want introductions."

"She's not really in my style," Frank said, as though the matter were of no particular moment. He did not think either of them should be seen taking an interest in the Contessa Montalto.

The Berresfords and their guest had moved down to the end of the room and were now surrounded by a sizable group. The Warwicks were entering the drawing room, followed by a couple Frank did not know and a third man who seemed to be by himself. Frank smiled at Nicholas and his wife. The dance claimed his attention for a moment, but the image of the other couple and the man behind them teased his mind. When the last figure of the quadrille came to an end, he glanced toward the door, seeking the third man. "What the devil?"

He did not realize he had spoken aloud. Demetra took his

arm. "Why, it's Major York," she said. "I didn't think he would come."

"You didn't— Good God, Demetra, what have you done now?"

"I didn't tell you, did I?" Demetra's face was transparently open. "I meant to, Frank, but there seemed to be much more important things to talk about yesterday. He came up and introduced himself—oh, when was it?—Saturday, I think, I was out with Sophy and the children—and I remembered his name, though it's been years since you mentioned it. He said he'd just come to London and hadn't yet been able to find you, and he seemed perfectly respectable and rather lonely, so I mentioned it to Philippa and she must have mentioned it to her mother, who must have sent him a card." They had reached the edge of the dance floor, where they stood watching the next sets form. Demetra opened her fan. "So do go and speak to him, Frank. He did save your life and that should count for something."

"Are you telling me that York accosted you and my children in the street?"

"It wasn't in the street, it was in the park, and he didn't accost me at all. He was most civil and he knew who I was because he'd asked someone—don't look so surprised, Frank, I'm still good-looking enough to attract attention. I'm truly sorry if you don't want the connection, but as usual my tongue ran away with me. I don't see that any harm was done."

Her face was penitent. It could have happened like that. York was determined to get access to the contessa, and he would not have hesitated to use Demetra to do so. But his presence was inconvenient. It was more than inconvenient, it was an outright danger.

"How odd," Demetra said, "he seems to know the contessa."

While they had been talking, Major York had proceeded down the length of the drawing room and was now bowing over the hand of the Contessa Montalto while Lord Berresford glowered at the intruder.

Frank took Demetra by the elbow and led her quickly down the room, intent on separating the two would-be blackmailers. "York," he said, clapping him on the back with a strength that made the other man wince, "this is the last place I'd have expected to find you."

"Hawksley." Ian turned and clasped his friend's outstretched hand. "I was hoping you'd be here."

Frank's grip tightened on the other man's hand. He was about to take York off for a drink when the contessa forestalled him. "Lord Chester," she said, extending an imperious, white-gloved arm, "I thought you had deserted me. Didn't you promise me a dance?"

Frank released Ian and bowed over her hand. Clever woman. The dance would allow them to arrange a time to conclude their business.

But neither had counted on Arthur Berresford. Berresford did not take kindly to interference in his pursuit of beautiful women. And pursuit was clearly in his eyes, as well as concern for his witness. "I don't know what Hawksley has promised you, Contessa," he said, "but you have made a promise to me. The dance is mine."

The contessa gave him a brilliant smile, made a pretty gesture of apology to Frank, and let Lord Berresford lead her away. So much the better. Frank turned to have it out with Ian York. But York was following the other couple onto the dance floor, Demetra at his side.

The next half hour tried Frank's patience sorely. After the dance, Berresford kept a firm hand on the contessa's arm and steered her into the adjoining saloon. There she sat, among a group of five or six gossiping women, while Berresford kept watch behind her chair. Frank dared not approach her, but he wanted to be available in the event she managed to slip away. He was quite certain the contessa would contrive a way for them to meet.

York seemed to have disappeared, probably frustrated by

Berresford's wardership of the contessa. Demetra was still on the dance floor, partnered now by Charles Windham. Windham was a happily married man and safe enough, but Frank longed to ask his wife what York had said to her during their dance. Still, there'd be time for that later, after he had the letters.

Frank waited in the drawing room, strolling along the edge of the dance floor, taking care to remain on the fringe of conversations, keeping always in sight of the adjoining saloon.

At last he saw the contessa turn to say something to Berresford, who then bowed and left the room. Her shawl? A glass of champagne? It would not take her long now.

Frank strolled out of the drawing room and onto the landing. He could see the top of Berresford's head as he descended the stairs. A servant came out of the card room and walked toward the rear stairway. No one else was on the landing when the contessa came by a moment later.

"Lord Chester," she said, looking after the retreating servant. "There is what you call a retiring room here? Up the stairs, is it not?"

Frank nodded and looked down into her lovely dark eyes, now stormy with anger.

The servant had disappeared. "I did not know that you knew Major York," she continued in a low voice.

"I did not bring him, Contessa, he came for you."

"Yes," she said in a fierce rapid undertone, "I knew him before. He is not to be trusted. I want nothing to do with him, do you understand? Nothing at all. He followed me after we met by the reservoir on Friday, but I was clever and lost him. Now he is here again. Keep him away from me."

Two very young women came down the stairs, giggling over some private joke. "I thank you, Lord Chester," the contessa resumed in her normal voice, "I do not understand how you arrange your English houses." She started up the stairs, then turned and leaned over the banister as the young women disappeared. They could hear the voices of the players in the

177

card room. "Lord Berresford takes me down to supper at one," the contessa said, speaking again in that rapid whisper. "But before we go below, I will be obliged to go up the stairs again to retrieve my gloves, which I am going to forget when I go there now. You know the house? Where do we meet?"

A group of men were leaving the card room. "Be sure you turn left at the top of the stairs, Contessa," Frank said in a normal tone. "You'll find someone there to help you." He turned slightly so his back was to the men, who were now on the landing, and lowered his voice. "A stairway for the servants at the back of the house, a plain narrow door. I'll be on the stairs."

The contessa smiled and continued up the stairs. Frank nodded to the men on the landing and consulted his watch. Not much past twelve. There'd be time to deal with Ian York.

It was not difficult to guess where York would be. With Berresford guarding his access to the contessa, he would not try another frontal assault. But he was not a man to let other opportunities slip through his fingers. Frank entered the card room.

York was at the whist table, and he had already amassed a tidy sum. He was clever with cards and seldom had to resort to cheating. Frank watched him for a while, unwilling to break his run. Winning always put York in an expansive mood, and he might then be more amenable to reason. Frank was determined to get him out of the house, but he did not want to create a scene.

When the next hand went against the major, Frank walked up to the table. "Best stop while you're ahead, York." Frank's hand rested lightly on Ian's shoulder, but Ian would not mistake the message. "You'll forgive me, gentlemen? I know you want your revenge, but it's been eight years since I've seen the major. I couldn't get him away from the ladies earlier, and he owes me a few minutes' courtesy, even if he did outrank me."

Ian smiled apologetically at the others and pocketed his

winnings. Then with every appearance of amity the two men left the room.

They came onto the landing in time to see the Contessa Montalto reenter the drawing room. A shawl was around her shoulders and her ungloved hand rested on Lord Berresford's arm. "Downstairs, I think," Frank said, "you'll not get near her again tonight."

"Oh, she'll see me," Ian said with bland certainty.

They pulled aside to let some late arrivals pass them on the stairs, a large man with red hair and a good-humored red face and a slender dark-haired woman with dark pensive eyes. Frank knew them slightly and he nodded. The woman stared with undisguised curiosity at Major York, who favored her with a brilliant smile. She turned away, but when she reached the top of the stairs, she dropped her fan. As her husband bent to retrieve it, she looked back down the stairs where Ian stood, still watching her.

"You're wasting your time, York," Frank said.

"A woman of unassailable virtue?"

"At the moment," Frank said, steering him down the stairs. "She left her husband a few years back, but she returned to him eventually, and they've been quite domestic ever since."

"She has sad eyes. Who is she?"

"Caroline Lamb. George's wife, not William's. Braithwood's a friend of mine, York. Don't play your games with his guests."

"You're getting stiff-rumped, Hawksley."

"Perhaps."

"No need to worry, she's not really my type. Whom did she run off with?"

"Brougham."

"Not the Queen's counsel?"

"The same. He followed her to Geneva and then to Italy."

Ian gave a hoot of laughter.

They had reached the hall. Frank nodded at some acquaintances going into the library, looked around but saw no one else in sight, and opened a door. "In here." Kenrick would

179

not mind if he borrowed his study.

A single light had been left burning on the mantel, but no fire had been laid and the room was cold. "I told you to stay out of this, York. One blackmailer is more than enough."

"Have I interfered?" Ian sounded genuinely hurt. "I'm merely protecting my own interests. The lovely Bianca is a woman who can slip through your fingers." He flung himself in a chair and stared up at Frank. "I'm on your side, you know. I wish no harm to Lady Berresford. Her husband looks a prize ass, and that's punishment enough for any woman."

Frank was inclined to agree, but this was not the time to say so.

"Your problem is the letters," Ian went on. "Mine is Bianca. All I want is my share of the money."

"God rot your soul, York, its's *my* money."

"Yours? You know I wouldn't take your money, Hawksley, but once you've paid off Bianca, the money is hers, and half of it is mine."

"You have a nice conscience." Frank's tone was wry. "Odd. You never used to care if you were plump in the pocket or not."

"I don't. It's a matter of principle. Bianca may have left me for Berresford. I don't like it, but these things have happened before. A woman has to look after herself." Ian leaned forward in his chair. "But no woman is going to cheat me of what is mine."

Frank stared at his friend. In all his months of acquaintance with Ian York, in tavern or brothel or battlefield, he had rarely heard him utter a wholly serious word. This was different. He took the contessa seriously.

Ian was on his feet. "You'll get the letters tonight?"

Frank nodded. "I hope to."

"Then once they're in your possession, you can have no further interest in what lies between us."

Frank wished that were true. But Helen was only part of the problem. There was the contessa's role as a witness—

Brougham planned to put her in the box on Thursday or Friday—and he could not jeopardize that. "It's more than the letters."

Ian eyed Frank speculatively. "It's the trial, isn't it? Berresford has bought her testimony."

Frank returned the look with a level gaze. "That's a harsh way to put it."

Ian grinned. "With Bianca, it's the only way to put it."

Frank's control went. "Get out of here, York. Leave the house, or by God, I'll throw you out."

Ian continued to stare at him. "I think not, Hawksley."

It was not a threat. It was a statement of the position between them. He could not buy York off—he had had trouble enough raising the money for the contessa. He could throw him out, but who knew what dogs this would unleash. Murder would be satisfying, but was hardly an elegant solution. Frank forced himself to unclench his fists.

"I want to make this easy," Ian said. "I seek five minutes with the contessa—no more. I won't make a scene."

Frank knew he had to acquiesce. In his frustration he said the one thing he could still demand. "Keep away from my wife."

Ian looked genuinely surprised. "The delightful Lady Chester?" He shrugged. "As you like."

Frank made a move toward the door, then turned back. York could still give him information. "You followed me to the reservoir on Friday. You followed the contessa when she left me. Where did she go?"

"She told you, did she? I thought she'd seen me. She went north on the Tottenham Court Road, perhaps half a mile. Then she turned—where?—ah, Pancras Street. The house was undistinguished, and I didn't see her come out. Odd place for Bianca to light. I wouldn't have thought it was in Berresford's style."

Frank stiffened. Pancras Street. Someone had mentioned Pancras Street not many days before, but it had had nothing to do with the contessa. Frank had a sudden image of his children. Demetra had taken them to Pancras Street to visit one of her old nursery maids. "York," he said, with sinking certainty, "you didn't just happen to come across my wife in the park."

"Let's say I sought her out," Ian said. "Bianca had moved. I thought Lady Chester would know where."

"You thought Demetra—" Frank could feel the pulse beating in his temples. "Why? Why should she know?"

"Why, because of Pancras Street, of course. She was there. I watched Bianca go into the house and waited for her to come out again. She didn't. It was more than an hour later that the other woman came. She was wearing a dark cloak, but she had glorious hair, you couldn't mistake her. When she came out, I followed her instead. She led me to Bruton Street. Easy enough to make inquiries. I was surprised to learn she was your wife, Hawksley. I thought you lived on Park."

So Demetra had managed to meet the contessa before she was moved to Berresford House. Of course. She must have been the dressmaker whom Pawley said had called the day the contessa disappeared. Demetra had been meddling, wanting to find out what the contessa knew about St. George. And the contessa must have seen her as a heaven-sent way to get out of the house and send her message to Helen.

Frank did not hear Ian leave the room. He paced back and forth, thinking it out. It was Demetra who had taken the contessa to Pancras Street. And then? How much did Demetra know about the letters? Good God. Demetra had approached him near the reservoir only moments after his meeting with the contessa. She must have followed the contessa to her rendezvous. Which meant that she had seen their meeting. Did she know they had been agreeing on blackmail terms?

He had intended to follow the contessa. When Demetra called out to him, he thought she desired his company. And then she fell and twisted her ankle. Had she been faking that as well? What a fool he had been. She had used him. She had used him yesterday afternoon, too, as cruelly as any barrack hack.

Oh, she had not feigned pleasure—he knew her well enough for that—but she had come to him with the deliberate intent of misleading him, of warding off his suspicions. Had she gone beyond protecting her brother? Was she actively assisting him to spy upon the contessa? God in heaven, how far would she go? He did not know his wife anymore.

There must be some desperate logic behind her actions. If he knew, perhaps he would even understand. But Demetra had refused to trust him. She had abused all that was good between them and made a mockery of their lovemaking. He would never forgive her that.

He took another turn around the room, beating his head with his fists. He would have to think about Demetra later. It must be nearly time to go upstairs and meet the contessa. He pulled out his watch. Nearly one. With a preoccupied look he left the study and closed the door behind him. There was no one in the hall save Tuttle, who was closing the door on some early departing guests. Frank turned and made his way to the service stairs at the back of the hall. He could hear voices coming from the kichen apartments below.

Though he was a large man, Frank could move quietly. He ran lightly up the stairs and stationed himself just below the door to the second-floor hall. A sound from above warned him that someone was coming onto the landing. Frank willed his heart to slow and his jaw and fists to relax. The contessa was on time. Thank God for an honest cheat.

Chapter 12

Once Frank was possessed of the letters and the contessa was possessed of the bank notes, further time in each other's company only risked discovery. Frank nodded curtly and started back down the stairs, and the contessa made her way along the second-floor corridor to the main staircase. She had nearly reached the first-floor landing before she realized that someone was waiting for her, leaning against the wall at the base of the stairs, his mustache quite failing to obscure his mocking smile.

She could retreat upstairs to the privacy of the ladies' retiring room. Even Ian would not follow her there. At least, she did not think he would. But he would have to be faced sooner or later, so the contessa continued down the remaining steps and actually smiled at the major—the sort of smile a great lady bestows on an insignificant acquaintance who should be flattered that she deigns to recognize him at all.

"Ah, Major York," she murmured. "I have seen so little of you this evening. You must forgive me, but with so many people present—"

"I understand completely, Contessa. Which is why I must insist that you stroll with me for a few minutes now. I suspect

184

you will not give me another opportunity for private conversation."

The contessa laughed. "How well you know me, Major York." She laid a hand—now gloved—on his proffered arm and they began to stroll along the gallery.

"I believe," Ian murmured conversationally, "that you have just had a meeting with our mutual friend, Baron Chester."

"Perhaps. I have spoken with so many people in the past hour I really cannot say—"

"Cut the line, Bianca," Ian said agreeably. "You've been around Berresford so long you seem to think all men are fools."

"If you are going to insult my friends, Major York, I'm afraid I shall have to excuse myself."

Ian had been determined not to descend to the personal, but now that he was walking beside Bianca, breathing in the heavy scent of her perfume, he found it impossible not to do so. "Not," he said, his voice still low but far more heated, "that I expect absolute fidelity from you. Not that I expect any kind of fidelity. But to be supplanted by a man of that stamp—"

Bianca continued to look in front of her, but her fingers tightened on Ian's arm. "My relations with Lord Berresford are no concern of yours, Major York."

"By God, Bianca—"

"You had best make your case, Major. I can only give you a few more minutes."

Ian stifled another, far stronger oath. "All right," he said. "Let me make this very simple. I believe—I am certain—that you have just come into possession of a large sum of money. As a friend, I felicitate you. However, as the rightful claimant of half that sum, I must look to my own interests—"

"You said," Bianca murmured in a faintly bored voice, "that you were going to make this simple."

"Extremely simple. You, my dear, have two choices. You can give me my half and I will take myself off and leave you to finish whatever other games you are playing—the alternative I strongly recommend—"

"Or?" the contessa inquired curiously.

"Or I shall consider all past obligations of friendship at an end and make it my business to ruin your schemes."

Bianca raised her head and regarded him for a moment. "An interesting threat. I shall be most amused to see how you carry it out. Ah, there is Berresford come to escort me to supper. I do hope you have nothing further to say, Major. I fear Lord Berresford does not like to be kept waiting."

"The latest *on dit* is that the Hawksleys have separated." Emily Cowper, a patroness of Almack's and a powerful Whig hostess, turned inquiring eyes to her childhood friend, Francesca Scott, who was seated beside her on the window seat in an alcove of the jade saloon.

"They hardly gave that impression when they arrived." Francesca settled her skirts of rose Turin gauze over cream satin. "According to Aunt Rowena, Demetra Hawksley has simply gone to stay with her parents for a few days."

"Her Tory parents," Emily said thoughtfully.

The third occupant of the window seat laughed. "Believe me, Emily, Tories can marry Whigs—or the other way round—and everyone can still get on quite charmingly." Harriet, Viscountess Granville, spoke from personal experience, for though her husband was a Tory, she had grown up in one of the strongest of Whig strongholds, Devonshire House.

"Oh, you don't count, Harriet." Emily had known Harriet even longer than she had known Francesca. "Granville's politics are absurdly moderate. He and *your* brother may get on charmingly, but I can hardly see Frank Hawksley and Lord St. George doing the same. Especially after what happened five years ago."

"You mean that business at the by-election?" Harriet asked.

"Granville thought St. George's behavior quite disgraceful. I must say, even putting the best construction on it, it was shockingly careless for Demetra Hawksley to tell her brother that story."

"Are you certain she did tell him?" Francesca asked.

"How else could he have found out?" Emily returned reasonably. "I own I always thought it odd, for Demetra seems too sensible a woman to let something like that slip out, and as for her telling St. George the story *deliberately*—though now that she's gone back to her parents' protection—"

"Their *house*, Emily." Francesca's tone was amused. "Demetra isn't the sort of woman who needs to be protected. I think I could quite like her."

"So do I," Emily agreed. "But one can like all sorts of people without understanding or even approving of them. It's all quite provokingly puzzling."

"If you ask me," Harriet put in, "the really puzzling thing is why any woman would leave Frank Hawksley."

This drew a laugh from her companions. "How very true. Do you know," Emily confided, "I used to quite regret that he seemed so happily married."

Francesca and Harriet, who were both still very much in love with their husbands, turned on Emily, who had long since ceased even a pretense that she was in love with hers. "Emily," said Francesca, half in fun, half not, "you *wouldn't*."

Emily laughed girlishly. "Francesca, when have I *ever* interfered with a happy marriage?"

Before she could answer, Francesca looked up and saw her cousin Philippa making her way across the room in their direction, her arm linked through Demetra's. Fortunately, years in London society had made all three occupants of the window-seat adept at this sort of situation, and by the time Philippa and Demetra reached the alcove, the conversation had become quite unexceptionable.

"I've just been telling Francesca that I think her gown is the color the French are calling *chagrin de la reine d'Angleterre*,"

Emily told the new arrivals.

Demetra smiled in polite amusement. No stranger to London society herself, she was certain that she and Frank had been under discussion only moments before. It was hardly surprising. Though nothing had been said to her face, Demetra knew that she and Frank were the subjects of much speculation this evening—and not merely because of their present separation. The scandal of five years ago had been brought up as well.

And that, Demetra suspected, was why Philippa had made such a point of dragging her to this corner of the room. If Demetra's reputation was to be thoroughly rehabilitated, she needed to win the support of influential women.

"There's a most interesting debate going on in the card room," Philippa said, sitting on a cushioned bench. "One side says that Lieutenant Flynn testified that he saw Bergami lying down on the bed in the tent on the polacre, while the other insists that Flynn merely said he saw Bergami *sitting* on the bed, which is vastly different."

"I don't see why." Demetra settled herself on the bench beside Philippa. "One can do quite as much sitting up as lying down."

The three women on the window-seat looked at Demetra as if seeing her for the first time. Then Harriet smiled, Emily laughed, and Francesca said that Lady Chester had made an excellent point. "Let's hope it doesn't occur to any of the Tories when they examine Lieutenant Flynn."

"I can't speak for all of them," Demetra said, "but I think I can safely say it isn't the sort of question my father will ask."

This frank reference to her father's politics startled the company even more than Demetra's previous remark had done. There was a slight pause. Demetra was not sure of Emily's and Harriet's response, but Francesca regarded her with appreciation. It was she who broke the silence. "Really, the whole trial is becoming sadly commonplace. When the prosecution's witnesses were testifying, we had much more interesting things to discuss than whether someone was sitting up or lying down. Remember the evidence about the condition of the Queen's sheets?"

"Yes," Emily said. "Now that so many of the more disgusting details have proved untrue, the Queen's infamy merely amounts to her having taken a courier for her lover. In fact," Emily continued, languidly wielding a mother-of-pearl fan, "if only the lover had been a gentleman, no one would have any right to object."

"No one?" said Harriet.

"Well, no one but the lover," Emily decided.

"One might hold that her husband had some say in the matter," Harriet pointed out.

"Yes, but the King forfeited that right long since," Demetra said.

"That," said Emily, smiling at Demetra, "is perfectly true, whatever one thinks of the Queen. To be sure, she *has* shown a shocking want of discretion—"

"Oh, if she wanted to be really discreet she should have chosen a lover who was absent—or better yet dead," Harriet decided. "If I didn't adore Granville so much, I'd adopt a dead lover at once. There's nothing like absence and death to make a romance really respectable."

"The only drawback is that it also tends to make romance rather dull," Emily pointed out.

"You can't have it both ways," said Harriet.

"You can try," maintained Emily, who tried very hard and was quite successful.

Emily and Harriet tended to bicker. Philippa intervened hastily, saying that as a novelist she was very grateful that people were *not* more discreet. "For if they were, I'd have nothing to write about."

"And we'd have nothing to gossip about," Francesca added.

"All the same," said Demetra, "perhaps I'm being idiotishly romantic, but I can't help thinking it would be nice if husbands and wives cared for each other enough that there was no need to worry about discretion."

"I don't think that's idiotish at all," said Harriet, who had once claimed that her husband *could make a barren desert smile*. She looked at Demetra with approval.

With that, the last barrier was broken. Whatever these women thought of Demetra's actions in the past, they accepted her in the present. Emily and Harriet had sons who were close to Colin's age. Francesca had a daughter who was just younger than Annie. Their children must play together. Francesca promised to send Demetra a card for her next entertainment. Emily hoped that sometime—if this wretched trial ever ended—the Hawksleys could visit Panshanger, the Cowpers' country estate. Harriet suggested the briefer excursion to her brother's villa at Chiswick. She was sure the children would like the kangaroos.

When the little group at last separated, Demetra turned to Philippa, who had remained uncharacteristically quiet throughout most of the conversation. "Thank you."

"But I did nothing," Philippa protested. "Not that I wasn't prepared to come to your assistance, but you managed capitally on your own."

Demetra laughed and the two women linked arms and made their way back to the drawing room. Demetra surveyed the company, feeling much more at ease than she had on her arrival, and was startled to see Elliot Marsden walking toward them.

Of course there were other Tories present tonight, such as Harriet and her husband. And Edwina had said that, though Marsden was their father's protégé, he allied himself with the more moderate wing of the party. No doubt he was distantly acquainted with the Braithwoods.

But when Philippa extended her hand and said, "Mr. Marsden, I'm so glad you could come," it was not in the manner of one greeting a distant acquaintance. Philippa Ashton and Elliot Marsden were friends. And watching them shake hands, Demetra suddenly wondered if perhaps they were something more. Was that why Marsden had failed to succumb to Edwina? It was a complication Demetra had not foreseen.

"Evening, Marsden." Henry Ashton joined the group. "Good of you to brave an Opposition stronghold. Especially at a time like this."

"On the contrary," said Elliot affably. "In this company I can admit that I'm all for the bill being abandoned."

"Because it now seems the surest way to diffuse the mob. I'm afraid a lot of Whigs would agree with you," Henry said, putting an arm around his wife.

"Emily Cowper for one," Philippa added. "She's quite pleased with Brougham for steering a moderate path and alienating the radicals. Much as I like Emily, her views on the mob are alarmingly—"

"Aristocratic," Henry supplied.

"Exactly." Philippa smiled up at her husband.

That smile answered Demetra's questions about Philippa's relationship with Elliot Marsden. Though these days it was impossible to be sure of anyone's constancy, Demetra was as certain as she could be that Philippa Ashton's heart belonged to no one but her husband.

But there was *something* between Philippa and Marsden. Or there had been once. Henry's behavior bore this out. Demetra did not think it was chance that had brought him to his wife's side shortly after Marsden's arrival. And while Henry spoke to Marsden in friendly tones, there was an undercurrent that was less amicable. Demetra suspected that Henry's feelings toward Marsden were similar to hers toward Helen Berresford. Or to what her feelings had been before she learned that Helen was Frank's mistress. Henry didn't know how lucky he was.

"I hate to interrupt, but if you want a decent table, Philippa, we'd best be going down."

It was the Viscount Granville, Harriet's husband. Lord Granville was a startlingly handsome man, but Henry watched his wife take the viscount's arm with none of the jealousy he displayed toward Marsden.

191

"You'll find Harriet in the saloon, Henry," Granville said, as he and Philippa moved off. "We'll save seats for you, but don't be too long about it."

"The depths to which marriage can bring a man," Elliot remarked, sighing, when he and Demetra had been left alone. "The four of them will wind up sitting at the same table. They might as well be having a quiet family dinner at home."

"Perhaps they wish they were," said Demetra, thinking of dinners at home with Frank.

"Perhaps. May I escort you to your own supper partner, Lady Chester? Or may I hope that you do not yet have one and offer my own services?"

"I don't, Mr. Marsden. And I'd be delighted." Demetra gave him her arm, pleased at the chance to spend time in his company. He was an attractive man, and though it was not a relationship she felt able to bring to his attention, they appeared to be some sort of cousins.

As she and Marsden filled their plates from the buffet in the supper room, Demetra saw that his prediction was true. The Ashtons and the Granvilles were sharing a table with the Windhams, creating a thoroughly domestic scene. Emily Cowper and Francesca Scott were at another table, without their husbands (though Emily's relationship with her supper partner, Lord Palmerston, was almost as long as and a good deal more intimate than her relationship with Lord Cowper). Francesca waved to Demetra and Elliot to join them.

Demetra did not think it was entirely owing to her imagination that the looks she received as she and Elliot moved to the table seemed warmer and that fewer conversations seemed to trail off abruptly as she approached.

Even Francesca's supper partner, Nicholas Warwick, one of the few people who knew of the business with Quentin and the Contessa Montalto, treated her as an old friend. Whatever his suspicions, his public behavior proclaimed his confidence in her. Demetra knew her problems were by no means over, but as she sipped a glass of chilled Barsac, she permitted herself to savor a moment of triumph.

She caught sight of Frank on the opposite side of the room, but he did not seem to see her. Demetra was disappointed, but she took comfort from the fact that he was partnered by Nicholas's clever wife, Livia, and that Helen Berresford was seated some distance away. Demetra gave up trying to catch her husband's eye—really, she was behaving like a lovestruck chit out of the schoolroom, she'd have plenty of opportunity to talk to Frank after the ball—and turned her attention to her companions at the table.

"The Queen says she pities the King for having such foolish advisers," Emily was saying, with a wicked glance at Palmerston, who was the Secretary at War. "She says, if she had wished to get up a thing of this sort, she would have done it better."

Francesca smiled. "She's a droll woman."

"She admits to committing adultery once," Elliot said, "but she says it was with the husband of Mrs. Fitzherbert."

There was general laughter. The King had married Mrs. Fitzherbert some years before he married Queen Caroline. The marriage was considered void as it contravened the Royal Marriage Act, but it had never actually been dissolved.

Demetra sampled the raspberry cream. Mr. Marsden was an entertaining companion, even a flirtatious one, but she suspected this was the way he behaved with most women. She thought she'd glimpsed something stronger when she saw him with Edwina at her mother's soirée, but then there was the matter of his behavior toward Philippa tonight.

It would help if she could get Marsden and Edwina together, away from Mama's supervision. With this aim in mind, Demetra casually mentioned that she and her sisters planned to visit Weyridge's bookshop late the next afternoon. Shortly after four o'clock to be precise. Marsden looked impassive, but Demetra thought he understood.

So much for Edwina. There was still the main business of the evening. Because while, thanks to her newfound friends,

193

people might be forgetting the scandal of five years ago, it would do little good if she could not clear herself of the more recent allegation—and prevent Quentin from making matters worse.

And so far she had learned nothing that would help her with that task. Major York had not set off any explosions. The contessa had not been pleased to see him, but if they spoke at all tonight it would be in private. And if Demetra was seen to pay too close attention to the contessa, it would only confirm the suspicions which Arthur Berresford and Nicholas and Kenrick—yes, and Frank, too—harbored about her.

It was as difficult to get at the contessa now as when she had been in New Cavendish Street. Tonight she was surrounded by crowds, and in private she would see almost no one but the Berresfords.

The Berresfords. Helen Berresford must spend a good deal of time entertaining her Italian guest. And Helen, as Demetra had already noted, was not good at dissembling. Could she know anything that would be of use? Demetra had promised Frank that she would not call at Berresford House, but she had said nothing about avoiding Helen Berresford.

Demetra gave Elliot Marsden a ravishing smile and started to plan an approach to her husband's mistress.

"The man sitting beside Demetra," Frank said, as casually as possible. "I don't think I know him."

Livia Warwick looked across the room. "Oh, that's Elliot Marsden. One of the almost bearable Tories, though he's also Lord Buckleigh's protégé. I expect that's how Demetra met him," she added, and then realized it might have been wiser to leave Frank's in-laws out of the discussion.

"I expect it is," Frank returned coolly. He knew Marsden by name though he had never met him. Hadn't Demetra herself questioned him about Marsden only a few days ago? Yes, the night of Lady Buckleigh's soirée. Something about Marsden as

194

a possible husband for Edwina. But observing the smile Demetra was now giving Marsden, Frank suddenly wondered if her interest could be on her own account rather than her sister's.

At this moment Demetra looked every bit as worldly and elegant and self-assured as Emily Cowper and Francesca Scott. Perhaps that was not surprising. Demetra's family was Tory and the other women's Whig, but all three came from backgrounds of wealth, privilege, and power. It was ironic that Demetra fit in with the frivolity of Whig society in a way Frank could not and did not wish to. Emily Cowper was fiercely loyal to her three brothers. Frank supposed he should be grateful that Demetra only had two.

Livia was observing him with carefully masked sympathy. Frank turned his eyes away from his wife, drained his glass, and asked after the Warwick children.

Helen was not enjoying the ball. First there were Arthur's attentions to the contessa. It was bad enough when he flirted with the woman in the privacy of their home, but when he did so in public it was insupportable. The years had inured Helen to the fact of her husband's infidelities, but not to the flagrant manner in which he conducted them.

And then, just before supper, Frank had asked for a few words with her, steered her into the privacy of an anteroom, and presented her with the remaining letters. She should have been overjoyed. She was overjoyed, of course, but it was impossible to be really happy while the letters remained in her reticule. She was convinced that her guilt must be obvious. Not to Arthur. Arthur was so busy with the contessa that he would probably not even notice if his wife ran through the supper room stark naked, but surely others must see that Lady Berresford was not herself.

Her own worst fears were confirmed when she dropped her reticule on rising from the supper table. Well, not her worst fears, for it did not burst open, and her letters did not scatter all over the floor, but she was persuaded that Johnny Russell must have felt the letters when he bent down to retrieve the fallen reticule. She had returned to the drawing room before it occured to her that even if Lord John knew she was carrying letters he could not possibly be aware of their incriminating contents.

Convinced that if she tried to dance she would drop her reticule again, Helen quickly left the drawing room for the jade saloon. She was standing just within the doorway, debating which of several groups it would be safest to join, when one of the last people she wanted to see appeared at her side.

"Helen! Are you tired of dancing, too? My feet feel positively ghastly, which is a sign of age, I suppose, for I used to be able to outlast the musicians. Do sit down and talk to me for a few minutes, I'd so like a comfortable cose with another sober married woman."

Helen had no desire for a comfortable cose with anyone, and certainly not with Demetra, who had behaved so very oddly at their last encounter, but she was unable to think of an excuse, so she permitted the other woman to take her arm and lead her to a vacant settee.

"There, this is much better," Demetra said, settling her skirts. (Really, Helen thought, that color was a trifle fast, even for a matron.) "Now, you must tell me how the children are getting on. It's been over a year since you last brought them to Durham."

Helen, who had been bracing herself for anything from comments on Frank's calls at Berresford House to actual mention of the letters, blinked in surprise and said that her daughters, all in the country at present, were well. She could not but reflect that Demetra had a son, that Demetra's *first* child had been a son. It was one of the many provoking things about Frank's wife. Still, though Helen had little taste for the messier details of nursery life, she was a fond mother and Demetra's warm interest in the children did her considerable

196

credit in Helen's eyes. Helen realized that in strict propriety she ought to have returned Demetra's call, and she found herself murmuring a disjointed apology.

"Oh, no," Demetra assured her. "Between old friends such social niceties cannot be held to matter. I know how busy you must be with your guest."

Helen had never considered Demetra Hawksley a confidante, but she was longing to voice her vexations about the contessa. "Yes," she admitted, "her arrival has rather thrown the household into a flurry, not that I'm complaining, of course, but servants can be so difficult when their routine is disrupted . . ."

"Precisely," said Demetra, whose servants were accustomed to a household with no routine whatsoever. "I trust the contessa at least brought a maid with her."

"Well, she did, but she dismissed the woman the day after she arrived, and I daresay she had the best of reasons, for it is so hard to find good help and I'm sure foreign servants are worse, only now I am sharing my own maid with her, and of course I could not do otherwise, but there's no denying that it is—awkward." It was one of the things about the contessa's stay which really rankled. Helen was convinced that her hair and gown were not in their customary impeccable state this evening because Minot had been obliged to hurry off and see to the contessa's toilet. One would expect the contessa's appearance to be similarly affected, but even Helen had to admit that the wretched woman was in remarkably good looks. Assuming one's taste ran to overblown brunettes. Unfortunately, Arthur's did.

While Helen brooded on her wrongs, Demetra gloated over the evidence that had just fallen into her lap. The contessa had dismissed her maid. Which meant that if the maid was Quentin's accomplice and the contessa innocent—at least with regard to Quentin's plot—Quentin's power to make mischief had been greatly crippled. But if the contessa herself was Quentin's confederate and the maid had been merely a go-between, the danger remained as great as ever. If only she could be sure.

"There's no denying even the most congenial guest can tire one out," Demetra ventured. "One spends so much time devising entertainments."

Helen nodded. "Fortunately we were able to bring her to the ball this evening, and then we go to the Haymarket tomorrow night. It is the last week in the old theatre, you know, and I hope—"

Demetra did not hear the rest of Helen's speech. She had been wondering how she could invent an excuse to be present at the contessa's next engagement, but there was no need to do so. She was already engaged to attend the Haymarket the next evening. On Friday Quentin had expressed a nostalgic desire to see the old theatre before it closed. He proposed to hire a box and escort his sisters and Lewis. "It's the oddest thing," Sophy had told Demetra later, "for Lewis says Quentin was supposed to go out with a party of friends and I can't think why he would rather spend the evening with us."

Nor could Demetra, at the time. But now it all made sense. By Helen's account, Friday was the day the contessa had dismissed her maid. But the maid could already have known of the theatre party. If she and not the contessa was Quentin's confederate, Quentin might have decided to form his own theatre party in order to spy on the contessa himself. If the contessa herself was his agent, Quentin must want to go to the theatre in order to talk to her. In either event, it appeared her brother was desperate enough or arrogant enough to risk a meeting.

Of the two, Demetra thought arrogance was the likelier explanation. It had always been Quentin's fatal flaw. And in the best tradition of classical drama, his fatal flaw would prove his undoing. His sister would see to that personally.

All in all, Demetra thought as she stood in the Braithwoods' entrance hall an hour later, drawing her black velvet Tyrolese cloak around her shoulders, it had been a most successful evening. She had made considerable strides toward rehabilitating her character, and she had made a discovery about her brother's plans which would, with luck, enable her to rehabilitate it completely. Philippa and Rowena had hugged her when she and Frank took their leave and Kenrick had kissed her cheek. Now Demetra could look forward to spending the remainder of the evening—the remainder of the night—in Frank's company.

The only drawback, Demetra decided, as Tuttle opened the front door, was that Frank was in a strangely preoccupied mood. Odd, for he had been perfectly cheerful when they danced together earlier in the evening. What had disturbed him? Talk about the trial? Or the necessity of facing the Contessa Montalto, whom he knew to be a blackmailer?

Frank had always been moody and Demetra had learned long since not to allow his moods to overset her. She should be able to coax him into a better humor. After all, they had the whole night ahead of them.

But when they had descended the steps to their waiting carriage, Frank curtly instructed Evan to drive to Buckleigh House. Demetra looked at her husband in surprise. No matter how moody he was, she had not expected this. Was he afraid to assume she would go home with him? Did he feel the suggestion should come from her first? Demetra was oddly touched.

"Frank," she said softly, laying a hand on his arm, "it isn't so very late. I thought I could come back to Park Street with you and we could talk for a bit."

Frank looked her full in the face for the first time since they had left the ball. "No, Demetra," he said curtly. "I don't think that's a good idea tonight."

Tonight? What on earth was wrong with tonight? Demetra was puzzled and more than a trifle hurt, but at times like this a light touch was always best. "Well! I think this must be the first time you've ever refused me," she said when they were in the privacy of the carriage. "No, there was the night we were driving home from dinner at the vicarage and I said it was a shame to waste half an hour alone together and you said the road was too rough, but then at least you had an excuse." She waited a moment and, when he made no comment, put her question more bluntly. "What's the matter this time, darling?"

Frank was sitting as far away from his wife as the relatively narrow carriage seat would allow. What hurt more than anything, he decided, was her damnable ability to pretend all was well between them. "Demetra, it's late, I'm tired, it's been a long day."

"Oh, Frank, that's not even very inventive and certainly not believable."

"What you believe or don't believe is, of course, entirely up to you. Did you enjoy the evening?"

"Very much, but at the moment I'm more interested in—"

"You seemed to. Especially during supper."

"Yes, we had a lively table. Mr Marsden is quite clever. Frank—"

"So you still find Marsden of interest?"

"Yes, but—"

"On Edwina's account?"

"Of course on Edwina's account. He certainly wouldn't do for Sophy. Frank, please don't try to change the subject. It's clear something's bothering you. If you don't want to talk about it, I shan't tease you, but I thought perhaps I could help. I am your wife, you know."

That was too much. "You have the oddest way of remembering it only when it suits your purpose!"

Demetra felt as if she had been stung. "I see," she said, her voice cooler. "Evidently tonight it does not suit your purpose to remember that you are my husband."

"No, tonight it most certainly does not."

That was the second time he'd referred specifically to

MORE PASSION AND ADVENTURE AWAIT... YOUR TRIP TO A BIG ADVENTUROUS WORLD BEGINS WHEN YOU ACCEPT YOUR FIRST 4 NOVELS ABSOLUTELY *FREE*
(AN $18.00 VALUE)

Accept your Free gift and start to experience more of the passion and adventure you like in a historical romance novel. Each Zebra novel is filled with proud men, spirited women and tempestuous love that you'll remember long after you turn the last page.

Zebra Historical Romances are the finest novels of their kind. They are written by authors who really know how to weave tales of romance and adventure in the historical settings you love. You'll feel like you've actually gone back in time with the thrilling stories that each Zebra novel offers.

GET YOUR FREE GIFT WITH THE START OF YOUR HOME SUBSCRIPTION

Our readers tell us that these books sell out very fast in book stores and often they miss the newest titles. So Zebra has made arrangements for you to receive the four newest novels published each month.

You'll be guaranteed that you'll never miss a title, and home delivery is so convenient. And to show you just how easy it is to get Zebra Historical Romances, we'll send you your first 4 books absolutely FREE! Our gift to you just for trying our home subscription service.

BIG SAVINGS AND FREE HOME DELIVERY

Each month, you'll receive the four newest titles as soon as they are published. You'll probably receive them even before the bookstores do. What's more, you may preview these exciting novels free for 10 days. If you like them as much as we think you will, just pay the low preferred subscriber's price of just $3.75 each. *You'll save $3.00 each month off the publisher's price.* AND, your savings are even greater because there are never any shipping, handling or other hidden charges—FREE Home Delivery. Of course you can return any shipment within 10 days for full credit, no questions asked. There is no minimum number of books you must buy.

tonight. What was so special about it and why was he so determined not to spend it in her company? A sudden vision flooded her mind, a vision of Frank standing in the Braithwoods' drawing room beside Helen Berresford. It was the only time Demetra had seen them together all evening and she had forced herself not to mind. After all, Frank was going home with her. Only he wasn't. Was it possible that he wasn't because—

Was it possible that she had been wrong to feel so secure after their interlude yesterday afternoon? Was it possible that Frank didn't want her company this evening because he had an assignation with his mistress?

Overcome by fear and anger and hurt, Demetra blurted out, "It's about Helen, isn't it?"

Frank had been staring straight ahead, but at that he swung around, his last remants of hope falling away. "What do you know about Helen?" he said sharply.

"What do you think?" Demetra shot back.

Frank grasped her wrist. "Understand this, Demetra, if anyone—and I mean anyone—does the least thing to hurt Helen Berresford, I won't be answerable for the consequences."

More than his words, the passion in his voice shocked her. "I hadn't realized you cared for her so much."

"She needs me," Frank said shortly, releasing her wrist.

"More than I do?"

He gave a brief, harsh laugh. "Good God, yes."

"I see." Demetra drew the folds of her cloak more closely about her. It was not the first time she had felt her world was collapsing, but it made all the others pale into insignificance. "I think you would have made an excellent actor, Frank. Your insistence that I come home has been most convincing, but I begin to wonder if you want me back at all."

"There are times," said Frank savagely, "when I wonder myself."

The hand that was holding her cloak trembled, but she didn't think Frank could see it in the dark of the carriage. She managed to keep her voice level. "Then perhaps instead of wasting time over trifles such as drawing room chairs, we should be discussing the terms of a separation. A legal one."

Frank stared at her. Despite his last remark, he could not imagine giving her up. He started to protest, but the words stuck in his throat. The Demetra he could not imagine giving up was a figment of his imagination, or at least no longer existed. The Demetra who could calculatingly use him even in the intimacy of their bed, the Demetra who could sacrifice not only his colleagues but the defenseless Helen to her brother's interests, was not a woman with whom he could go on living.

"Then it seems for once we are in agreement," Frank said. "I will speak to our solicitor at the earliest possible opportunity."

Chapter 13

Tuesday, October 10

Frank awoke with a feeling of anguish attributable to his scene with Demetra and a blinding headache attributable to the amount of brandy he had consumed in an effort to put the scene from his mind.

He forced himself to sit up and accepted a cup of coffee from the silent Robbins. The alcohol had done the trick last night. It had very effectively put an end to all conscious thought. Unfortunately the respite was only temporary.

At least the letters were now safely in Helen's possession. Frank felt suddenly cold as he thought of the consequences if the letters had fallen into Demetra's hands and then reached her brother. St. George would not hesitate to use them to hurt Helen and embarrass Berresford. Thank God that problem was off his hands.

He still had to deal with Demetra and St. George's designs on the contessa. Frank's marriage might be damaged beyond repair, but he could at least prevent his wife and her brother from sabotaging the contessa's testimony. He should have confronted Demetra last night. Yet though he would have been quick to accuse anyone else, he had been unable to speak. Somehow it seemed that if he put his suspicions into words, they would become more real.

That had been last night. This morning it was obvious what he must do. As soon as the House adjourned for the day, he would go to Bruton Street, tell Demetra what he knew, and demand an explanation. He doubted that she would give him one, but at least he could make it clear that whatever game she and St. George were playing must come to an end. And then, if there was still time, he would call on his solicitor and discuss the details of a legal separation.

Frank was now shaved, dressed, drinking his third cup of coffee—he could not face solid food—and staring unseeing at the *Morning Chronicle*. He tossed off the last of the coffee and was on the point of leaving his room when Robbins entered and informed him that he had a caller. A lady. He had shown her into the parlor.

A lady? Frank clutched at this fragment of hope. Could it be Demetra, come to say she hadn't meant what she said about a separation, come to confess, to offer an explanation? But that was ridiculous—if Demetra came to Park Street, she would not announce her presence through Robbins. In fact, there was only one lady who would call and not leave her name. What the devil had happened now?

"I know I should not have come," Helen said, when Frank entered the parlor, "and especialluy not so early, but I had to see you before you left for the House. Oh God, Frank, I know this will never come right, Arthur will divorce me and I shall have to go live in a horrid watering place and my family will refuse to see me, except for cousin Mathilda, who will read me horrid moral lectures, and Arthur will forbid me to see the children—not that he cares a straw for them himself, but he will do it to be spiteful—and he will marry again and their stepmother will be odious to them and they will never make good marriages because everyone will be sure that they are as profligate as their mother, who is far *worse* than Queen Caroline!"

Frank slipped an arm about her shoulders. "Easy, Nell." It

was the first time he had called her that in years. He guided her to the sofa and sat down beside her, keeping his arm around her. "What has happened to the letters? Did Berresford find them?"

"That's just it, Frank! I don't know. I haven't the least idea where they are."

"Helen"—Frank made an effort to keep his voice gentle—"are you telling me that you lost the letters after I gave them to you last night?"

"Oh, no, I have the letters you gave me. But they're the wrong ones. That is, the words are the same, but the hand isn't mine. Frank, someone copied them!"

For once Frank was as shocked as Helen. "Are you sure?" he asked automatically.

"Of course, I'm sure. I know you think me a ninnyhammer, but I'm not such a fool as to mistake my own handwriting." She tugged at the clasp on her reticule and pulled it open with such force that several of the letters tumbled onto the worn carpet. Helen seized one and held it out to Frank, her eagerness to prove her point overcoming any embarrasment at showing him the contents.

Frank studied the paper. The writing was feminine in character, and the writer had clearly made some effort to copy Helen's hand, but the most cursory inspection made it clear that Helen spoke the truth. The letter was a forgery.

Frank crushed the paper in his hand and bit back a string of curses. This was not the time for recriminations against anyone, including himself. "You're right. It is a forgery. My apologies for doubting you. And for not taking greater care when I made the purchase. Now please try to be calm and listen because I shall need your help if I'm to recover the originals."

"How?" Helen demanded. "How can you even know where to look? Do you know where to find the blackmailer?"

"That's the easiest part," Frank said cheerfully. Helen had to be told the truth and he thought the bracing approach would be best. "She's in your house. You see—"

"In my—? You mean one of the servants—?"

"No, Helen. Listen. It's not any of your servants. It's the Contessa Montalto."

Helen stared at him. "I might have known," she said with grim satisfaction. "I never *could* like that woman. I shall insist she leave my house at once!"

"You'll do nothing of the kind, not if you want to keep this secret."

"But, Frank, we have to confront her with what we know— that is, I think you should, for—"

"I have every intention of doing so, but not at Berresford House, it's too risky. I must leave for Westminster in a few minutes and I won't be able to get away till late this afternoon. Go home and try to act as if everything is normal. Then, a little before four o'clock, tell the contessa you want to do some shopping and bring her to—" Frank hesitated. "Weyridge's," he decided.

"Weyridge's?" Helen repeated doubtfully.

"Yes." There was a painful irony in the choice, for in the days before their elopement he and Demetra had used the bookstore as a rendezvous.

Demetra. Could she have anything to do with the forged letters? Could the originals have fallen into St. George's hands after all? For a moment Frank was tempted to abandon the trial and go straight to Bruton Street. But absenting himself from the House would only cause more trouble. And it would be wisest to get the contessa's version of events first. Then he would confront his wife.

Demetra awoke from a particularly gruesome nightmare and found herself looking at her youngest sister, who was perched on the edge of the bed.

"I told Lizzie I'd bring in your chocolate," Sophy explained. "I wanted to hear about the ball. I'm sorry if I woke you."

Demetra sat up in bed and realized that the gruesome

nightmare hadn't been a nightmare at all. Frank really had as much as admitted that he was in love with Helen and wanted a legal separation.

"I say," Sophy added, "you look rather ghastly. Did you drink too much champagne last night?"

"Something like that." Demetra summoned up a smile that wasn't too wobbly and reached for the chocolate Sophy had left on her bedside table. She didn't feel like drinking anything, but she could hide behind the cup until she pulled herself together.

"Edwina wants to go out right after lunch," Sophy said, kicking off her shoes and drawing her feet up onto the primrose-flowered quilt, "so we can go to the Burlington Arcade before or after."

"Before or after what?" Demetra looked at Sophy blankly over the rim of the Wedgewood cup.

"Before or after we go to Weyridge's."

Weyridge's. Last night she had told Elliot Marsden they would be there. It had seemed like a good idea at the time. It was still a good idea, only at the moment Demetra was not best suited to steer a couple toward connubial bliss. At the moment, Demetra was not sure she even believed in connubial bliss.

But she mustn't allow her own misfortune to turn her into a cynic. However much of a shambles her marriage had become, she would still rather have had her few happy years with Frank than decades of a passionless marriage of convenience to her cousin Tony. Edwina stood a far better chance of happiness with Elliot Marsden than with the Earl of Deavers. Weyridge's, the site of so many of her early meetings with Frank, was the last place she wanted to go today, but that could not be helped now.

"We'd better go to the Arcade first," Demetra said.

Sophy eyed her sister shrewdly. "I thought you were planning something. Is it about Elliot? I hope so, he's much the best of Edwina's court. Only I don't think Edwina should know you arranged anything, because she does hate to be manipulated—well, so do I—and it might make her willful. If

207

we go to the Arcade first, we should get to Weyridge's about four. Will that do?"

"Admirably."

"Good. Of course, we can't stay out too late, for Quentin's taking us to the theatre tonight."

Where the Contessa Montalto would also be present. It seemed to be a day for rendezvous.

"Hand me my dressing gown, Sophy," Demetra said briskly, "I've a great deal to do."

Mercifully Colin and Annie kept Demetra too busy to think—though she did wish they wouldn't ask quite so many questions about the ball. Shortly after eleven, Stephen informed her that Mrs. Ashton and Lady Francesca Scott had called. Lady Buckleigh was out, but Philippa and Francesca spent half an hour with the Thane sisters. Demetra detected a slight constraint in Edwina's manner toward Philippa, but otherwise the visit was most amicable. At Philippa's request, Mary Rose brought the children down. Colin and Annie behaved beautifully. It was all very gratifying, but though Demetra was grateful for the diversion, now that her marriage was over the question of her acceptance by Whig society seemed almost trivial.

After Philippa and Francesca left, Demetra and Sophy had lunch in the nursery, as had become their custom. Edwina joined them and seemed in good spirits and not in the least willful, which boded well for the meeting at Weyridge's.

As soon as the meal was done, the three sisters left on their shopping expedition, accompanied by Mary Rose, who, Demetra judged, could use an outing without the children. Maggie, one of the housemaids, was looking after Colin and Annie. After nearly two hours in the Burlington Arcade, during which Edwina, not surprisingly, spent an unconscionable amount on a pair of beribboned evening gloves, and Demetra, more surprisingly, was equally extravagant over the purchase of two carved wooden animals at Morel's toyshop, they proceeded to Weyridge's.

In its own way the Picadilly bookstore offered as bewildering an array of delights as the Arcade, but today Demetra's attention was on the shoppers rather than the wares. Seeing no sign of Elliot Marsden in the front room, she at once professed an interest in the books in one of the back chambers and they had just moved through the doorway to this apartment when Sophy exclaimed, in very creditable accents of surprise, "Oh look, there's Mr. Marsden."

Elliot Marsden turned, inclined his head, replaced the book he had been examining, and walked toward the ladies.

"Lady Chester, Lady Edwina, Lady Sophy. What a delightful surprise."

Demetra surveyed him with approval. Sensible man. He knew enough not to mention that she had told him of their visit. "If you'll excuse me," Sophy said (with, Demetra considered, an appalling lack of subtlety), "I want to look for Philippa Davenport's new book—or should I say Philippa Ashton?"

She directed the question to Demetra, but it was Elliot who answered. "I believe she still publishes as Philippa Davenport."

"She very sensibly knows one shouldn't place too much importance on a husband," Edwina said. "Sophy, you can look for the book later. There's something I most particularly want to show Demetra and we shouldn't all desert Mr. Marsden at once."

Without waiting for her sisters to acquiesce, Edwina started across the room. Demetra decided following her was the lesser of two evils.

"I know I've been out for four Seasons," Edwina informed her elder sister in low but fierce tones when they were standing in relative privacy behind a bookshelf, "but I am not so far gone that I need you or anyone else to arrange a rendezvous for me."

Demetra looked up at her sister, suddenly very much aware that Edwina was a good four inches taller. "I'm sorry," she said frankly. "It was a mistake in judgment. Though all I did was tell Mr. Marsden that we meant to be here this afternoon. It was his decision to come."

"There was no need to tell him anything at all. It isn't as if I don't see him. He's at Buckleigh House practically every day."

"I thought you might like a chance to talk without Mama present."

Edwina gave a reluctant smile, but was not to be won over. "He'll think I put you up to it."

"I doubt it. If he knows you at all, he must realize you've never so much as lifted your finger to attach anyone."

"I've never needed to," Edwina said coolly.

"You've never wanted anyone enough to make the effort." While Edwina was mulling this over, Demetra added casually, "Mr. Marsden was at the Braithwoods' last night."

Edwina looked at her sister, her eyes seeming to harden. "I expect Philippa Ashton invited him."

"Are they well acquainted?" Demetra asked.

"You might say so," Edwina said, with studied nonchalance. "He once wanted to marry her."

It was more than Demetra had suspected, and she did not miss the undercurrent of jealousy in her sister's tone. Whether she knew it or not, Edwina cared for Elliot Marsden. Was she afraid that if she made an effort to attach him, she would find he didn't care for her? That was a risk, of course, but if she didn't make the effort, she would never know. She needed something to nudge her into action. Demetra turned and looked across the room. Mr. Marsden was laughing appreciatively at something Sophy was saying to him, while Mary Rose stood a little to one side.

"He's hanging out for a wife then," Demetra said. "Do you think he'd do for Sophy? He's certainly more interesting than the men Mama pushes her way."

Edwina stared at her sister as if she had not heard her aright. "You can't be serious."

"Why not? They're obviously enjoying each other's company."

Edwina looked at the couple with disfavor. "They're completely unsuited. You can't— Demetra, you didn't arrange this meeting on *Sophy's* account, did you?"

"Of course not. But if you aren't willing to expend any energy on him, it seems a pity to let so personable a young man go to waste."

"I have no intention," said Edwina, tightening her grip on her reticule, "of letting him go to waste. Thank you for your assistance, Demetra, but I can handle my affairs for myself."

Demetra watched with satisfaction as Edwina walked purposefully across the room to rejoin Sophy and Elliot. At least something was turning out well.

Absorbed in watching Edwina, Demetra lost track of Mary Rose until the girl suddenly appeared at her side. "Mrs. Hawksley." In times of crisis, Mary Rose invariably forgot her mistress's title. "Don't turn round, but there's a woman standing by the shelves over there, the same woman who—"

But Demetra had already looked around. A couple were standing at the end of a row of shelves. The man had his back to the room and Demetra's view of him was obscured by the woman, who was turned a little to one side. Even with her face shadowed by a deep-brimmed bonnet of blush-colored satin, the Contessa Montalto was unmistakable.

There was no need for alarm. If the contessa had not recognized Demetra as Catherine Newley at their previous meetings, there was no reason she should do so today. It was only when Demetra saw the contessa's eyes focus on Mary Rose that she realized Mary Rose looked no different from the shop assistant who had accompanied Miss Newley. And then the man turned, following the direction of the contessa's gaze.

It was Frank.

*   *   *

211

It had been close to four-thirty when Frank arrived at Weyridge's. He found Helen and the contessa in one of the back rooms and went directly to them, paying no heed to the other customers. His arrival was timely. The contessa did not seem to find the bookstore amusing and Helen appeared to be running out of excuses.

The contessa regarded Frank with amusement. She must think he was having a rendezvous with Helen. Damnable woman. Didn't she realize that if he wanted to meet Helen clandestinely he would have enough sense not to do so under the nose of an acknowledged blackmailer?

"I fear you do not find Weyridge's to your taste, Contessa," Frank said, with every appearance of cordiality.

The contessa shrugged. "I am not a great reader. I much prefer the theatre, where Lord and Lady Berresford are taking me this evening."

"Ah, but you have not been looking at the right books. You must allow me to show you some of my favorites."

The contessa was puzzled—Lord Chester was not behaving like a man who wanted a private interlude with his mistress— but she accepted Frank's arm and permitted him to lead her down a more secluded avenue of shelves. Helen remained where she was, her face a study in anxiety.

When they reached the end of the shelves, Frank's grip on the contessa's arm tightened. "I'll be brief," he said, his voice soft but not at all gentle. "I may have been fool enough to give you the money, but if you don't produce the letters, you can abandon all hope of leaving the country with it."

The contessa stared up at him with a bewilderment he could have sworn was genuine. "But I gave them to you last night."

"You gave me worthless copies. I want the originals."

The contesa continued to look puzzled, but she said quietly, "I hope you do not think me a fool, Lord Chester. Only a fool would try such a thing, knowing she would have no chance to get away before you discovered the trick. I kept my part of the bargain."

Frank was not sure he believed this, but he released her arm. "Did you look at the letters last night?" he demanded.

"There was no time."

"When did you last examine them?"

She gave the question serious thought. "The day I went to— The day I met you in the park."

He saw a sudden speculative light in her eyes. "What?" Frank said sharply.

"I did not bring the letters to my meeting with you. If they were taken, it must have been that afternoon."

"By whom?"

"A woman. She works for a dressmaker. I do not remember her name—"

She broke off suddenly. Frank looked to see what had startled her and found himself staring at Demetra. Before he could think further, the contessa said, "If you want to know where the real letters are, Lord Chester, I suggest you ask your wife."

Demetra considered leaving immediately. But the damage had already been done, and she did not want to interrupt Edwina and Marsden, who were now enjoying a tête-à-tête. Demetra remained where she was and sent Mary Rose off to join Sophy. She was quite alone when Frank reached her side, but he did not look in the least grateful.

"Demetra," Frank said without preamble, "where are they?"

Demetra, who had been expecting a question about her incognito visit to the contessa, looked at him in bewilderment. "Where are what?"

"The letters."

The letters. The contessa must have discovered Hannah's forgery and identified Lady Chester, alias Catherine Newley, as the thief.

"Don't play games with me, Demetra," Frank said when she

213

did not answer immediately. "I told you last night that if you do anything to harm Helen—"

"I haven't done anything to harm your precious Helen," Demetra snapped, though she did remember to snap quietly.

"You've already caused her more anxiety than anyone should have to endure. Where are they?"

Demetra gave him a determined smile. "In Park Street, darling. In the nursery."

Chapter 14

Tuesday, October 10

"What?"

"Don't shout, Frank."

"You're telling me the letters are in the nursery at my house?"

"Yes, in a box of curtains at the back of the large cupboard near the fireplace. They're between the folds."

"My God." Frank turned on his heel and walked away.

Demetra stared after him with dismay. Helen Berresford was standing near the door, and Frank had stopped to talk to her. He was bending over her solicitously, holding her hand, while Helen looked up into his face with her pleading blue eyes. She seemed agitated. And well she might, having a rendezvous with another woman's husband. How *could* Frank have brought his mistress to the very place that had figured so importantly in their own courtship?

Then they were joined by the Contessa Montalto, and the three of them left the bookshop. Demetra had no doubt that the contessa had told her husband all about Miss Newley and how helpful she had been in the matter of the blackmail of Lady Berresford, and how much Miss Newley resembled his own wife. Frank must think her call on the contessa had been on

215

Quentin's behalf. Why else would she do something that looked like an attempt to tamper with a witness?

But he must realize that she had come across Helen's letters by chance. Would he understand why she had taken them, and why, having taken them, she had kept them hidden? She should have explained to him there and then, even though Weyridge's was hardly a safe place to do it. But Frank had been in a temper and she had been angry as well. It was hard to be sensible when you had lost your husband. Would Helen leave her husband to be with Frank? Would Frank want a divorce? Demetra fought back the tears that filled her eyes. The King had certainly made divorce fashionable.

In this confused state of mind, Demetra gathered her sisters and Mary Rose and prepared for the journey home. She settled in a corner of the barouche and looked at Edwina and Sophy. They must have seen something of what had occurred, and it was always best to get one's own explanation in first. "I suppose you saw that Frank was in Weyridge's," she said. "He was being quite disagreeable—it's one of the hazards of married life, though I daresay the trial had something to do with it, the nonsense drives him absolutely wild."

Sophy grinned. "What are you going to do?"

"Why, nothing at all. If there's one thing I've learned in seven years of marriage, it's that moods change. He'll be quite cheerful by morning."

And with that they went on to speak of men and how one is to ever understand them.

It was a horrid mischance that had taken Frank and the contessa to Weyridge's on this particular afternoon, but there was no use dwelling on what had happened. Tonight she intended to learn what was going on between Quentin and the Contessa Montalto.

Much to his sisters' surprise, Quentin hurried them to the theatre so that they actually arrived before the curtain had gone up. This annoyed Edwina, who hated to be rushed over anything. "We're absurdly early," she said, looking with disfavor at the boxes on their tier. Quite half of them were empty.

"It's for Lewis," Quentin said. "Mother's taken him to the opera and some of the more edifying plays, but she never arrives before they're half over. I wanted him to see the entire spectacle." They had left their brother downstairs and could see him now, standing near the front of the pit, staring up at the boxes to watch the new arrivals. "And what could be more conducive to enjoyment than tonight's program—a comedy followed by a farce."

"I wondered at your taste," Edwina said. She looked down at her program, which informed her that *The Heir at Law* was to be followed by something dubiously titled *Valentine and Orson*.

"Should I have waited till tomorrow and taken you to *Hamlet?*"

"Actually, I wonder at your taking us anywhere at all, Quentin. You're being uncommonly agreeable, and it's not like you."

"Ah, well, I'm getting older and I no longer have the energy to be otherwise. Besides, I've been away for several months, and frankly, I'm not quite in good odor. You lend me a certain cachet, Edwina. That wild St. George, settling down at last."

She regarded him with a speculative look. "I see. Beatrix Thornton."

He shuddered. "I hope not. But just in case . . ."

"I don't see why you should worry, Quentin," Sophy said. "A little wildness in a man is always forgiven. And it makes him ever so much more interesting."

"Do you find Quentin interesting?" Edwina asked.

"Of course not, he's my brother. But," Sophy said after a judicious pause, "I daresay I might if I didn't know him."

"Interesting men are all very well when one's young," Demetra remarked. "They would be very tiresome when one's trying to cope with children and servants and the price of wool."

"Oh, Demetra, must I settle for someone dependable and

boring?" Sophy said with a face so melancholy that they all laughed. "It's really quite unfair. If I act to please myself, then I've quite leaped the pale and no one will speak to me. If I act to please Mama, I'm unutterably bored. And if I try to make my life more bearable by seeking out interesting men, I'm told the acquaintance is unsuitable. What's to become of me?"

Edwina seldom paid much attention to her younger sister, but these sentiments echoed her own so precisely that she looked at Sophy with fresh interest. "It's the curse of being female," she said, her mouth twisted in a wry smile. "As the Queen has found out, to her chagrin. If the King had taken a chambermaid—or," she added, with a hard look at her brother, "an opera dancer—no one would have thought the worse of him."

"Hear, hear," Sophy said under her breath.

"And from what I've read," Edwina went on, "she treated her courier Bergami with far more consideration than men ordinarily show for their mistresses." Edwina thought that her brother had been quite unspeakably cruel to pretty little Maria Doddington last year before he left for the Continent. She hoped the girl was faring better with Papa who, rumour had it, had succeeded Quentin in Miss Doddington's bed.

Quentin, who had been standing near the railing scanning the other boxes, turned and faced them. "You see what you've done, Demetra. This was a King's household before you set foot in it."

"It has nothing to do with Demetra," Sophy said hotly, forgetting that her brother rarely said anything he really meant. "It has to do with our sex. Give us credit for having minds of our own."

"Heaven help us," Quentin said with utter sincerity. As a rule he had little trouble with women, but there were those—his mother being foremost among them—for whom he had a healthy respect. "You'd do much better to concentrate on being decorative. Take Edwina. When she's quiet, it's an absolute pleasure to look at her."

Edwina made a rude face, then, lest someone was watching,

hastily raised her fan.

"That's an odious thing to say, Quentin," Sophy said. "Besides, with a face like mine, one has to find other goals to aspire to."

"What's wrong with your face?" Lewis had come into the box in time to hear this last exchange. "I've always thought it a rather nice one."

Sophy, to whom such compliments were rare, was touched by his defense.

But Lewis had other things on his mind than his sister's face. "I say," he said, lowering his voice, "there's the most splendid creature. Over there, in the next box but one. I saw her from down below when she came in. Do you have any idea who she is?"

Sophy, who had not yet learned to be subtle in these things, turned abruptly and stared in the direction Lewis had pointed. "It's Lady Berresford, isn't it?" she asked Demetra. "And the woman who was with her today in Weyridge's."

Till now, Demetra had taken little part in the conversation, content to watch Quentin and wait for the contessa to put in an appearance. She had seen the Berresfords arrive with their guest and had seen the contessa settle with a great flurry in a chair at the front of the box. She was wearing a low-cut gown of rose-colored satin, which showed off her creamy skin, and what appeared to be a remarkably fine rope of pearls. Her hair was dressed high on her head and threaded with more pearls, and she wielded an unusual, large fan made of feathers dyed to match her gown. Helen, in a blue-gray corded silk that draped softly around her graceful figure, seemed pale and insignificant beside her vivid guest.

Quentin must have noticed them, though he gave no sign of having done so. At his brother's words, he glanced idly toward the box and away again. "I commend your taste, Lewis. Lady Berresford is a beautiful woman. So is the other, though she's too terrifyingly robust for my taste. Do you know them, Demetra?"

She could hardly deny it, and the contessa's presence in

London was not a secret. "I know Lady Berresford," she said. "Her family lives in Durham, and we see them occasionally. The dark-haired woman is the Contessa Montalto. I believe she's staying with the Berresfords. They brought her to the Braithwoods' ball last night. I met her there."

"I thought she was foreign," Lewis said. "English girls aren't nearly as exciting."

"Thank you," Edwina murmured under her breath.

"She's Italian, isn't she?" Lewis went on. "I say, do you suppose—"

"Don't be idiotish, Lewis." Sophy did not understand the undercurrents of the conversation, but she sensed that Demetra had been too deliberately casual in her naming of the foreign beauty. "There must be thousands and thousands of people in Italy, and the Queen can't have met them all."

"She must have met this one," Quentin said. "Word is going round the clubs that Brougham is going to call the contessa as soon as he's through with the Royal Navy. Strange, for it's our side that's called most of the Italians. Brougham's been relying on proper Englishmen and women. Still, since you've had the introduction, Demetra, the least you can do is take Lewis round in the interval and present him."

"Oh, I say—" Lewis began, then stopped, his face suffused with color.

"Nonsense, it will be good for you," Quentin insisted. "All you need do is make a proper leg—which you do quite acceptably, by the by—and mumble something incoherent while you look fixedly into the lady's eyes. She'll do the rest. Believe me, I know."

His sisters laughed. "You'd best present Quentin first," Edwina said. "That way Lewis can see how to go on."

Demetra had no desire to be amiable to Helen Berresford, and with half London watching, she did not dare approach the contessa with either of her brothers in tow. "I'll do nothing of the sort," she said. "She seems a pleasant enough woman, and I'm sure she's done nothing to deserve either of you. If you want to scrape an acquaintance, you'll have to do it on your own."

Quentin laughed, but Lewis looked as though he might have taken her seriously and Demetra relented. "You're right, Lewis, she's uncommonly handsome, and Quentin has no right to tease you. For his penance, he'll have to sit by me for the evening. Come, take my place. You can see her quite well from here."

Demetra left her chair at the front of the box and moved to a seat toward the back. The change suited her. She could leave if necessary without attracting notice, and she could keep an eye on Quentin. Her elder brother did not seem pleased by this arrangement, but Lewis was happy. He raised his quizzing glass and ogled the Contessa Montalto quite shamelessly, though with such lack of artifice that his sisters were forced to hide their smiles.

The theatre was rapidly filling up. The lights seemed to burn brighter, though this was perhaps only an effect of the heat and noise generated by the playgoers. Edwina turned her attention to the other boxes and entertained her sisters with the names and pedigrees and habits of the men and women occupying them. The contessa was attracting a good deal of attention, and the Berresfords' box was already crowded with visitors. There was no one else that Demetra recognized until she turned to the other side of the house and saw the Braithwoods entering a box on their tier with Nicholas and Livia Warwick. Kenrick caught Demetra's eye and waved.

Demetra smiled and prayed that neither of the couples would come around during the interval. That was when her brother would act, and she did not want to be distracted.

Sophy—who, like Lewis, had little experience of the theatre—turned her attention to the pit. Both men and women were crowded on the benches below, but the greater number were men and most of these were standing and staring up at the occupants of the boxes. It did not occur to Sophy that she herself might be an object of interest until her eyes

221

were caught by the fixed gaze of a handsome man who acknowledged her with a brilliant smile. She gave a little scream and turned swiftly around. "Demetra, it's he."

Demetra leaned forward and looked over Sophy's shoulder into the pit below. Ian York, the smile still on his face, was looking up at their box.

"Remember," Sophy whispered, "you promised."

"I did nothing of the kind."

"You wouldn't cut him?" Sophy asked in consternation. "You danced with him last night."

"Dancing is different. One isn't obliged to acknowledge a man just because he partnered you on the dance floor. Let alone introduce him to your family."

But it was not in Demetra's nature to cut anyone, so she smiled and bowed slightly to Major York and turned back to her sister.

Quentin had missed none of this byplay. "A friend, Demetra?"

"An acquaintance," she said, as though it was not a matter of great importance. "He knew Frank in the army."

"Do you think he'll come by?" Sophy asked.

"I hope not, but if he does, behave yourself."

"Oh, pooh, I do well enough." Sophy turned around and stared at the door, willing the handsome major to appear. Within a few minutes she was rewarded by a knock at the door. Major York hoped he might have a few words with Lady Chester and begged for the honor of being presented to her friends.

Annoyed, Demetra complied. It would be churlish not to do so and she could not ignore the pleading in Sophy's eyes. Besides, it was difficult to remain angry with the major, whose easy manners and unfailing good humor made him a welcome companion. Quentin, who was sitting back in a dark corner of the box, acknowledged the introduction with no great enthusiasm, but Lewis was polite and Edwina, who had been rather abstracted since her meeting with Elliot Marsden at

222

Weyridge's brightened momentarily. Sophy was entranced and gazed at Major York with open admiration.

Perhaps it was this frank appreciation that led Ian to direct his conversation to the youngest of the Thane sisters. She was not a beauty like Lady Edwina, but she was far livelier and she had an enviable figure.

Demetra decided that Sophy was in no danger, but she was less sure of Major York. Within a matter of minutes, Sophy had elicited a brief account of his life and determined that he was mad for cards. Their pleasure in this discovery of a mutual passion was interrupted when the curtain rose and Sophy's attention was diverted to the stage. Ian settled back on a seat behind her—Demetra could not recall having asked him to remain—crossed his legs and folded his arms. It was only then that she saw his head turn in the direction of the Berresfords' box and knew that he was aware of the contessa's presence.

This was an unforeseen complication. Demetra had determined that Quentin would act during the interval. Major York was very likely to get in the way. She would have to see that Sophy kept him occupied, and if necessary, she would enlist Lewis's help. She stared at the stage, half attending to the problems of Daniel Dowlas's unexpected accession to a barony—had Quentin picked this play on purpose?—and smiled when everyone else laughed, but she was painfully aware of Quentin on her left and the major on her right.

Some forty minutes later she heard the sound of the door opening behind her. Startled, she looked round, but Quentin was still sitting motionless in his corner and York was whispering something in Sophy's ear. She turned and saw Frank standing in the doorway of the box. He was not in evening dress, and his face wore such a look of consternation that she immediately forgot her brother, the major, and the Contessa Montalto. She left the box hastily and went into the corridor to face her husband.

"Frank, it's not the children?" she said, breathless with sudden panic.

He shook his head. "Demetra, they're not there."

"The children aren't there? Frank, what are you—" An elderly gentleman came out of the adjoining box and looked at them curiously before proceeding down the stairs.

"Not the children, Demetra. The letters. You told me they were in the nursery. They aren't there."

The panic subsided, but Demetra felt a sudden surge of anger. How dare he frighten her so. "You idiot!" she said. "You prize idiot! You didn't look. They're in the cupboard, not the one at the end of the room, the one by the fireplace. In a box, under some old curtains or between them, I can't remember, but I put them there on Sunday. You didn't look properly."

"I looked. I tore the nursery apart." He seized her arm. "By God, Demetra, I want some answers. I want to know how you came by those letters and why, but right now I want the letters back. Don't play games with me. It's too late for that."

She was appalled. Beyond Frank's fury, beyond the hurt and bewilderment in his eyes, there was the impossible fact that the letters had been taken. "I don't know," she whispered, "I don't know. Frank, they must be there. The servants? The workmen?"

"No one's seen anyone on the third floor."

"Robbins? He knows everything."

"Oh, God." He let go her arm. "Robbins is in bed with a heavy dose of laudanum. He had a fall and broke his leg. I was going through the nursery for the third time when I heard him scream. He'd tripped on a ladder left by one of the painters— criminal carelessness. I had to go for the surgeon, that's why I missed you in Bruton Street. They told me you were here."

"Oh, Frank." Demetra counted Robbins as a friend. "Is there anything I can do?"

"Tell me about the letters, Demetra."

She heard the sound of laughter from the auditorium. "I'll tell you everything, Frank, but not here, not now. It's nearly the interval. The place will be swarming with people." She had to get him away before Quentin came out. "Kenrick and Rowena are here, round the other side in the third box. Can't you stay there? I'll meet you after the play and we'll go home and talk, I swear it."

They could hear more laughter and applause and the sound of people stirring. "Frank, please. Quentin will come out and Edwina will have all sorts of visitors." Then, before he had time to object, she opened the door and slipped back into the box.

Quentin looked at her curiously, but the others did not seem to have noted her absence. The act was just over and there was a general stirring in the house as people prepared to seek refreshments and pay visits. Lewis said it was a capital play and Quentin was dashed clever to have fixed on it. Sophy, her face glowing, agreed. Even Edwina's mood had lightened.

There was a knock and the door opened and a group of people seemed to burst into the box. "I say, Edwina, how jolly to see you," said the foremost of these, a tall young man with an air of vague amiability. "I had no idea you were coming."

"Hullo, Fordyce." Edwina regarded the Earl of Deavers without enthusiasm. "You know everyone, don't you?"

"Edwina, darling," said a pale blond girl in a depressing shade of green. "My brother's just been sent down and he insists on being presented." She pushed forward a burly young man in a tight-fitting coat and an elaborately tied cravat, who made a self-conscious bow.

There seemed to be three or four other men who had entered the box. Major York had disappeared, and Quentin showed signs of making an imminent departure. Demetra took Sophy's hand and led her into the corridor.

The Haymarket was a small theatre, built on a rectangle rather than the customary horseshoe. Their box was on the left-hand side of the theatre and the corridor behind it led to the broader foyer behind the front boxes. Demetra made for the junction of the corridor and foyer and took up a place against the wall, fanning herself vigorously as though she had

225

been overcome by the heat, and waited for her brother to appear. The Berresfords' box was farther down the corridor and Quentin was unlikely to notice her standing here. And if he did, what was more natural than that she and Sophy should seek a few moments' relief from the crowd of Edwina's admirers.

Demetra had expected Sophy to be out of sorts at the defection of Major York, but her sister seemed quite cheerful. "I'm so glad I met him," she told Demetra. "He's ever so much more entertaining than any of the men I've met since I came out. Now I know that there are men like that in the world, I don't need to settle for anyone dreary. If he comes back, do you suppose I can ask him to call?"

"You'll do nothing of the sort," Demetra said, her eyes on the door to their box. Lewis had just come out and was standing uncertainly, looking in the direction of the Berresfords' box. "Mama would be horrified."

"Oh, I do hope so. Maybe I could arrange a clandestine meeting. That would be an accomplishment. And in my first Season too."

Demetra laughed. "Sophy, you're incorrigible. You've had quite enough experience for one night." She looked around. Frank was nowhere in sight, and for that at least she could be grateful. The doors to the boxes were all open now and the corridor was rapidly filling. Half a dozen men had entered the Berresfords' box and were no doubt keeping the contessa occupied. Quentin had left their own and gone to speak to Lewis. Lewis, his face brightening, moved past his sisters and disappeared into the foyer.

"Quentin must have told him where to find the barques of frailty," Sophy said.

"Sophy, you're not supposed to know about such things." Demetra's voice was amused.

"Oh, Lewis tells me everything. It helps to have the right sort of brother. Mama doesn't tell me anything at all. Demetra," she went on in a lower tone, "you're watching

Quentin, aren't you?"

Demetra looked at her sister in mock despair. "I had hoped no one would notice."

"No one will remark it. As he said about Edwina, when he isn't talking he's quite a pleasure to look at. Why don't we go a little closer?"

As she spoke, the contessa, accompanied by a solicitous Lord Berresford, escaped from her box. Like Demetra, she appeared overcome by the heat. Without seeming to do so, Quentin moved down the corridor toward them. Then he stopped and glanced around, but if he noted his sisters engaged in earnest conversation a little way behind him, he gave it no particular attention.

The contessa raised a hand to her brow in a lovely and dramatic gesture and spoke earnestly to Lord Berresford. Then she turned toward the door of their box as though she would enter it again. Lord Berresford made his way rapidly down the corridor and disappeared around the corner into the foyer. Sent him for lemonade, Demetra thought. The contessa was too clever a woman to tolerate Berresford's company for long.

The contessa turned back to the corridor and began to stroll in Demetra and Sophy's direction. She stopped and attended to a clasp on her bracelet as though it had come loose, and in the process she dropped her fan. Quentin moved forward quickly and retrieved it—there were at least three other men present who would have done the same—and presented it to her with a bow. They exchanged a few words, then Quentin bowed again and withdrew. It could not have taken more than a minute or so, but it was time enough for a message to have been given and received.

Demetra knew with blinding certainty that the two had prior acquaintance and that the contessa had been in her brother's employ from the first. Now was the time to talk to Frank and Kenrick. She turned to make her way toward their box on the other side of the house, but Sophy detained her.

"Demetra, look. Major York seems to know her."

Ian York had appeared out of nowhere and was now talking earnestly with the Contessa Montalto. The contessa did not appear pleased and several times she shook her head. She and the major seemed oblivious of the other people in the corridor.

Sophy, whose curiosity was quite shameless, moved closer to the couple, pulling Demetra with her. *"Va, va,"* they heard the contessa say. *"Basta. Non posso."*

This appeared to anger the major who gripped her upper arm in a threatening gesture. By this time, everyone in the corridor was aware of the argument between the beautiful foreign woman and the handsome man with the mustache. Two or three men whispered among themselves, as though debating whether or not to go to the woman's assistance. Quentin, who was standing not far from Demetra and Sophy, made a move forward. Frank and Kenrick came into the corridor, their eyes seeking out Demetra. And Lord Berresford appeared in the corridor, a glass of lemonade in his hand.

Berresford knew exactly what he should do. "Unhand her, sir!" he called, thrusting the lemonade into the hands of a young man—it was Lewis—who had come into the corridor at the same time. He strode rapidly toward the couple. "How dare you! Madam, are you all right?"

A couple came out of the box nearest the stage, glanced curiously at the tableau, then made their way laughing down the corridor. The men who had debated going to the contessa's assistance turned and conversed among themselves. Lewis looked at the glass of lemonade, then placed it carefully on the floor near the wall and prepared to go to the contessa's rescue. Quentin restrained him. Frank and Kenrick moved past Demetra toward the contessa and York. Demetra saw Frank's face and did not envy York his coming encounter with her husband. As for Demetra and Sophy, neither could have taken their eyes from the scene, no matter how ill-bred their behavior.

Knowing the relation in which the major stood to the contessa and the contessa's apparent unwillingess to have the relationship known, Demetra wondered how that lady would handle her two unwelcome and importunate suitors. Perhaps she would swoon—though it was a drastic gesture, it would serve. But the contessa was not one to use such a weak ploy. "I wish," she said in a dignified manner, "to return to my seat."

"Of course." Berresford bowed as she turned and made her way to the door of the box.

A lock of hair had fallen over the major's brow and his face was red with emotion. He strode toward the box and grasped the contessa's wrist. "Bianca, we are not done."

"Are you mad?"

Berresford pulled him off. "By God, sir, you will answer to me for this insult to the Contessa Montalto."

"The contessa?" Ian laughed, but his voice was bitter. "Bianca has been many things, my lord. But she is not and never has been the Contessa Montalto."

Chapter 15

Tuesday, October 10

The corridor was engulfed in silence. Even Major York appeared startled. Demetra was stunned. For all her speculation about the Contessa Montalto, it had never occured to her that the woman was an imposter.

Frank echoed his wife's thoughts, but this was no time for questions. He and Kenrick exchanged glances and started forward with one accord. Frank meant to leave Kenrick to deal with the contessa while he collared York, but the contessa rushed toward both of them. "Lord Braithwood, Lord Chester, I will not stay here to be made a mockery!"

"There is no need for you to do so, Contessa," Frank said crisply. "But I'm afraid we shall have to talk."

"You stay out of this, Hawksley." Berresford strode to their side. "The contessa has already endured enough."

"The mortification—" the contessa began, gesturing wildly and dropping both her fan and her reticule in the process.

Kenrick retrieved the fallen objects, while Arthur reiterated that it was none of Frank's affair.

"Unfortunately," said Kenrick, returning the fan and reticule to the contessa, "it is all of our affair. The contessa wishes to return home. I suggest you take her there. Frank and

Nicholas and I will join you shortly."

"I'll have a word with York first," Frank said, but even as he spoke he realized Ian was no longer standing where he had been when he confronted the contessa. Frank swung around, his eyes searching the corridor, but Kenrick stated the obvious. "The major seems to have made himself scarce."

Frank stared hard at the contessa. He was certain she had deliberately diverted their attention so Ian could make good his escape. For once her interests accorded with York's. Ian didn't wish to face questions and the contessa didn't wish to face the answers he would give. The contessa, whom Berresford was now tenderly escorting back to the box, seemed impervious to Frank's regard.

"If I've judged the major rightly," Kenrick said, "there will be little chance of finding him now. We'd best collect Nicholas and tell Rowena and Livia why we're deserting them in the middle of the play."

Though he wanted nothing more than to go after York and throttle the truth out of him, Frank knew Kenrick was right. He followed his friend back down the corridor, barely noticing Demetra and Sophy as he moved past them.

The corridor, which had grown silent at Major York's accusation, was becoming noisy once again. Curious heads poked out of the open box doors. Someone asked if there had been an accident and someone else offered to go for a doctor. Edwina emerged from the Thanes' box and joined her sisters.

Demetra hadn't been able to overhear all of the conversation among Frank, Kenrick, Arthur, and the contessa, but she had heard enough to realize that they meant to adjourn to Berresford House immediately. If she wanted to tell them about Quentin, she must do so at once. Demetra murmured an excuse and started after her husband, but she had taken only a step when a hand closed about her wrist.

Quentin, whom Demetra had last seen leaning against the wall on the opposite side of the corridor, surveying the scene with idle interest, was suddenly beside her, the expression of

231

concern in his eyes belied by his firm hold on her wrist.

"Lewis," he said to his younger brother who had followed him, "you are about to be charged with a manly duty. Demetra has the headache. I am taking her home—"

"Don't be idiotish, Quentin," Demetra said, pulling away from his grip. "I never have the headache."

"You do tonight. I know you won't be so foolish as to deny it." Quentin maintained his hold. She could have escaped, but only by creating a scene. Though she hated giving in to Quentin, it would be best to learn what she could about his plans for the remainder of the evening.

"But I see no reason why the rest of you should miss the play and supper," Quentin was saying. "We'll send the carriage back for you. Lewis, at seventeen you should be more than capable of escorting your sisters from the theatre to Mivart's and back to Buckleigh House."

Lewis appeared pleased, but Edwina, who hated Quentin's high-handedness, said, "Now that you mention it, I have a touch of the headache myself. It must be something about the air in here."

"Yes," said Sophy, "I feel it as well. Perhaps we should all go home."

Demetra looked at her sisters with gratitude and appreciation. But she could handle Quentin better on her own. "No," she said, "you must see the end of the play. I insist. Are you ready, Quen?"

The brother and sister left the Haymarket in silence, but when they were settled in the carriage, Demetra said, "Now that we're away from prying ears, would it be too much to ask for an explanation?"

She had no hope of a real answer, but after a slight pause, Quentin said, "Of course. I hope your headache is better, 'Metra. We have rather a long evening ahead of us."

Demetra turned her head sharply. Quentin was leaning back in his corner of the carriage, his face lost in the shadows. She had expected him to return her to Buckleigh House and then make some excuse to go out again, and she had been debating whether it would be better to follow or to go to the Berresfords' and lay her story before Frank and his colleagues. But those plans depended on her brother acting in a reasonably straightforward manner. It had been a mistake to think he would do anything of the kind. "Quentin," Demetra said, "where are we going?"

"Buckleigh House first," her brother returned cheerfully. "We have to send the carriage back to the Haymarket for Lewis and the girls. I'll have one of the smaller carriages made ready. Hunter can drive it. I'd as lief not bring any of the servants along, but the fellow has been in my service since I was at Cambridge and I think he can be trusted not to talk."

"Not to talk about what?"

"Our visit to Berresford House."

"And why," said Demetra, though she had a fairly shrewd notion of the answer, "are we going to Berresford House?"

Their carriage passed beneath a street lamp and she had a brief view of her brother's face. She knew that look. Quentin had worn it from nursery days, whenever he managed to best her. "To collect Bianca, of course. The woman you and the rest of London think of as the Contessa Montalto. Come, 'Metra, if you're half as intelligent as I think you are, you must realize that I can't leave her in that nest of Whigs after Major York's denunciation. Berresford may be fool enough to believe Bianca's story, but Braithwood and Warwick and even your husband have more sense. They're going to ask a lot of questions. They may even take Bianca to see the Queen. And when the esteemed Caroline says that this woman certainly isn't the Contessa Montalto, there's no telling what Bianca may say to save her face. She's likely to turn around and confess the whole, which would make things most uncomfortable for me. I was certain you'd have worked all that out by now."

"What on earth makes you think I'm in the least interested?" Demetra demanded, with genuine curiosity.

"Oh, I see. You're wondering if you gave yourself away. You didn't, if it's any consolation. Bianca told me."

Damnation. She should have foreseen this. "When she dropped her fan this evening, I suppose," Demetra said sweetly.

"You saw that?" There was, Demetra noted with satisfaction, genuine surprise in Quentin's voice. "She didn't have a chance to say a great deal, merely that Lady Chester had been following her. I don't think she even knows you're my sister. But once I heard that much, it wasn't difficult to guess the rest. And to think I believed you returned to Bruton Street because your marriage had soured. I should have known it was too much to hope you'd actually leave Hawksley."

"Yes," said Demetra, "you should." She tucked a stray curl into place. "How long have you known the contessa?"

Quentin laughed. "Still ferreting out the facts, sister mine? Give over, Demetra. You've been very clever, but the game's changed and now we're going to play by my rules for a bit."

For a man whose plans were collaspsing about him, Quentin sounded remarkably calm. "Well put, Quen. But you're hardly in a position to set the rules."

"On the contrary. I just haven't played all my cards. You see, I recently visited your house—you're right, it is in appalling condition, you can hardly be blamed for leaving—and happened across some very interesting letters. I hate to be the one to disillusion you, but your husband is having an affair with Helen Berresford."

The carriage made a sharp turn. Demetra clutched the strap more tightly than was necessary. She should have guessed the moment Frank told her the letters were missing, but she had refused to believe it could come to this. It is a very lowering thing to find you have underestimated your younger brother. Demetra started to ask when the contessa had told him about the letters, but she realized that Quentin probably knew nothing of the contessa's involvement. He must assume that Frank had hidden the letters in Park Street. She would have to

234

feel her way carefully.

"Would it be too much to ask what you were doing in my house?"

"I took Colin."

"You did *what?*"

"He wanted to collect his wagon."

"So help me, Quentin," Demetra said, anger taking over, "if you as much as go near my children again—"

"I think your outrage is misdirected, 'Metra. I said your husband—"

"Is having an affair with Helen Berresford." Demetra stifled her anger. "I've know for some time."

"Have you?" Quentin sounded surprised again. "I know women claim to have an instinct about these things, but I never pictured you as the sort to be a complacent wife."

"That's my business. If I already know and don't care, why on earth should the fact of the letters persuade me to help you?"

"Because if you don't help me, I shall send the letters to Arthur Berresford. Or make them public. Yes, I think that would be best. More damage all round."

Demetra felt as if she were listening to a stranger. She had thought of Quentin as a clever, malicious boy whose games might inadvertently prove explosive. He was certainly capable of setting off an explosion, but now she realized that if he did so, it would be a calculated effort. "Perhaps I'm not as complacent as I sound," Demetra suggested. "Perhaps I'd like to see Frank and Lady Berresford suffer."

"Oh no, Demetra. You dissemble well, but not that well. You're still head over heels in love with your unsuitable and unfaithful husband. Don't try to deny it."

"And if I do as you ask?" She refused to let him see her desperation. "What guarantee do I have that you won't make the letters public in any case?"

"My word as a gentleman."

Demetra laughed shortly. "Quentin, if I ever thought you

merited the title, you've certainly disqualified yourself in the past quarter hour."

"If you were a man," said Quentin idly, "I'd call you out for that. Let me put it this way. If you *don't* do as I ask, you may be certain I *will* make the letters public."

Demetra drew a breath. "What do you want me to do?"

"I knew you'd see sense. You always had a pragmatic streak. Comes from Mother, I expect, she knows when to cut her losses. After we change carriages, we'll drive to St. James's Square and pull up near Berresford House. I doubt I could get past the doorstep, but they'll hardly deny you. While you're in the house, you will contrive to get a message to Bianca. She's to meet us in the square as soon as possible."

"How the devil," Demetra demanded, "do I come up with an excuse for calling on Helen Berresford at this hour, let alone manage to see the contessa?"

"That I leave to your ingenuity. I have every faith in you."

It was nearly nine-thirty when they reached St. James's Square. Late for a social call, but not absolutely beyond the pale. After being wished the best of luck by her brother, Demetra climbed the steps of Berresford House alone. The door was opened by a footman who looked no more than twenty and whose expression indicated that he knew Stirring Events were taking place under his roof this evening. He assumed Lady Chester had called to see her husband. Demetra made haste to disabuse him of this notion. The last thing she wanted was a confrontation with Frank. She had called, she explained with her most disarming smile, because she had found a ring in the corridor at the Haymarket, and she believed it belonged to the Contessa Montalto.

At the mention of the contessa, the footman grew wary. Both the contessa and Lady Berresford had retired, but if Lady Chester would wait for a few minutes, he would inform his mistress of her visit.

Demetra, who had not expected to be taken straight to the contessa, acquiesced with a smile. As she had hoped, the footman did not leave her to wait on the ground floor. No doubt he wanted her well away from the gentlemen's conference. Demetra had glimpsed a light under a door which probably led to the library, and as she climbed the stairs, she glanced down and saw a second footman hurrying in that direction with a tray bearing sandwiches and coffee.

The first footman conducted Demetra to an anteroom. She waited a few moments, then rose and eased the door open a crack in time to see the footman start up the next flight of stairs to his mistress's apartments. Thanks to Quentin, who had had the information from the contessa's maid, Demetra knew that the contessa was lodged in a suite on the first floor. Helen would take several minutes to make herself presentable before she came down to greet her guest. With luck, there would be enough time.

As soon as the footman had disappeared from view, Demetra slipped into the hall and made her way toward the south wing. She located the contessa's suite without difficulty, but paused before the three imposing doors. She knocked at one and received no answer. When she tried the second, it opened almost at once.

Demetra had been prepared to face one of the Berresfords' maids, but she found herself looking directly at the woman who claimed to be the Contessa Montalto.

"There's no time for explanations," Demetra said quickly. "I have a letter for you." She produced the note which Quentin had scribbled while they changed carriages at Buckleigh House. The contessa glanced at the handwriting, then looked at Demetra in surprise. But she knew better than to waste time on questions. She nodded quickly and shut the door.

Her mission completed, Demetra hurried back into the main block of the house. She felt a momentary thrill of excitement at having managed the job so neatly, but then remembered that she had just helped her brother thwart her husband and his friends. Sobered, Demetra moved into the corridor which led back to the anteroom.

"Demetra"

Helen had appeared on the stairs and was looking down at her guest in surprise.

"Hullo, Helen," Demetra said brightly. "I hope you haven't been looking for me. I just slipped out to the convenience."

Helen's brows drew together, but that was probably owing to the indelicacy of the reference rather than to any suspicion that Demetra was lying. Demetra waited until Helen had descended the stairs, then followed her hostess back into the anteroom. She wondered if Frank had told Helen she had taken the letters, and decided he had not done so. Helen seemed troubled, but not on account of her visitor.

"Thomas said something about a ring which belongs to the contessa," Helen said when they were seated.

"Yes, I found it in the corridor at the Haymarket," Demetra explained, reaching inside her reticule and abstracting the ring the contessa had given to Catherine Newly. Demetra had been carrying it with her ever since, thinking it might be of use, though not quite in this way.

Helen took it and stared at it dully. "I don't like to disturb her this evening, but I'll ask her tomorrow. Thank you," she added, almost as an afterthought.

"It was no trouble at all," Demetra returned, studying her rival. Helen had exchanged the dress she'd worn to the theatre for a dressing gown of puce broché velvet. The color and the elaborate cut quite overpowered her pale, delicate features, but in it, her fair hair brushed loose over her shoulders, Helen looked more fragile and helpless than ever. Perhaps Frank was right. She did need him more than Demetra did. Was that what Frank wanted, someone defenseless and clinging, without the spirit to stand up to him? That did not sound like Demetra's Frank. But perhaps he wasn't her Frank anymore.

"I'll go then," Demetra said, giving herself a mental shake. "I'm sorry to trouble you so late in the evening."

"It was no trouble," Helen returned mechanically. "Would

238

you like some refreshment before you leave?"

Demetra almost smiled as she declined the offer. How great a crisis would it take for Helen to forgo the social forms? Helen rang for the footman to see her guest out and the two women made desultory conversation until Helen said suddenly. "Surely the play isn't over yet?"

Demetra summoned up another bright smile. "I daresay it isn't. I had the headache and left early."

Helen nodded, then frowned, and no doubt would have said, *But if you have the headache, why did you call on me?*, had the footman not made a fortuitous entrance. Five minutes later, Demetra was back in the carriage and able to tell her brother that his message had been delivered.

"I knew you could manage," was the cordial reply. "Pity the war's been over so long, you'd have made a capital spy. Though I suppose self-respecting radicals would have caviled at spying on the French, wouldn't they?"

"I've done as you asked, Quen," Demetra said levelly. "When do I get the letters?"

"Don't be so impatient, 'Metra. There's still a great deal of work to be done."

"What sort of work?"

"You'll see," Quentin said comfortably.

Chapter 16

Tuesday, October 10

Helen returned to her room in a state of considerable agitation. She did not understand what was going on and no one had seen fit to tell her. It was bad enough to have to escort that appalling woman out in public and pretend that one was the greatest of friends, all the time knowing that she was the vilest of creatures and held the power of one's future in her hands. It was bad enough to sit by her and inhale her heavy perfume—it made Helen quite sick—and watch one's husband staring down into her shamelessly exposed bosom, contemplating sin—if he had not already sinned with the contessa, as Helen was sure he had if the woman had given him the least encouragement. But then to be subjected to that crude outburst of hysteria at the theatre while all her friends wondered what was going on, to have her husband tell her abruptly that they were going home, without a word of explanation and as though it were somehow all her fault. . . .

Helen paced the room in an agony of anger and uncertainty. If only she knew what had happened to the letters. This afternoon at Weyridge's, Frank had taken her hand and said, "It's all right, Helen," in a way she would have called patronizing if it hadn't been Frank. And then he had told her he

240

knew where the letters were and she was not to worry. How could she not worry? He had explained nothing at all. No one, Helen thought bitterly, ever told her anything. Not her family, who behaved as though Arthur's notorious reputation with women did not exist, not her friends, who assured her that she was fortunate to marry so handsome and virile a man, and certainly not her husband. Was it any wonder she was driven to Gareth's arms?

Helen sat down at her dressing table and put her head on her arms. But the tears would not come. She sat up and stared at her reflection in the mirror, holding the candle high to study her face. Were those the beginnings of lines at the corners of her eyes? Perhaps, but they were hardly noticeable, and her skin was still flawless. Her hair had scarcely darkened, and her waist was nearly as small as it had been when she married Arthur. Even after three children. Men admired her. Women looked at her with envy. Arthur should count himself fortunate in his wife. But he seemed hardly aware of her existence, and he spoke to her only to criticize. When he visited her bed, he scarcely took the trouble to woo her. Arthur had become a perfunctory lover. If it were not for those damning letters and the horrid danger they represented, she would be tempted to break her marriage vows again.

And then the tears came, a few brief tears of self-pity and exasperation. Helen wiped them away and applied a faint dusting of powder. Very well. She was tired of having other people act for her. The contessa must know where the letters were. She would go to her now, tonight, and have it out.

Helen stood up, and then sat down abruptly. The contessa would probably refuse to see her. She had not said one word on the way home. If Helen insisted on being admitted, the contessa was likely to create a scene and then Arthur might hear and she would not be able to talk to her at all.

Helen clenched her fists and beat on the table in an agony of frustration. Then she saw the ring. She had carried it back with her after her interview with Demetra and thrown it on the dressing table. She picked it up and weighed it in her hand. It was a heavy thing, with an intricately worked gold band and a large red stone that might be a ruby. The contessa was a greedy woman. She would want it back.

With an air of sudden resolve, Helen closed her hand around the ring and, her step firm and her back erect, swept out of the room.

The London residence of Lord and Lady Berresford stood on the west side of St. James's Square, just north of King Street, which ran between St. James's Street and the square. It was not much past ten and lights were still visible on the first and second floors of the house and in the front room on the right-hand side of the ground floor. The carriage had pulled up just south of King Street so that its occupants had a clear view of the house. There was still a good deal of traffic in the square and the carriage was not likely to excite much curiosity. Its two occupants were scarcely visible to the passers-by.

Demetra sat in a corner of the carriage, her dark mantle wrapped tightly against the chill of the evening, its hood covering her bright hair. She would not look at Quentin, though she knew he was staring at her with that air of arrogant amusement which had been so tiresome during the years of her growing up and which now seemed positively dangerous. Nor would she give him the satisfaction of asking questions he would refuse to answer.

They were waiting for the contessa, but it was likely to be a long wait. In a house as large as the Berresfords', there were always servants hanging about the halls. The contessa's departure would not go unremarked and would certainly be reported to Lord Berresford at once. She would have to wait until the visitors had left and the family had gone to bed and all the lights had been turned down.

Demetra pulled her cloak more tightly about her and schooled herself to patience. Beside her, Quentin was absolutely still. It was a skill he had cultivated when he was young, and it led people to think he was cleverer than he was. Inconsequentially, she thought of Beatrix Thornton and wondered what kind of hell he would make for her if he could be persuaded to offer and Beatrix was foolish enough to accept. Something like the bleak place that Helen Berresford must inhabit. And who then would be Beatrix's Frank?

Demetra felt a tingling behind her eyes that told her she was close to tears. Willing them away, she straightened in her seat and stared out the window. A woman was crossing King Street, the hood of her cloak drawn up to cover her hair. The lights were still on in the house. She had underestimated the contessa.

Quentin saw her too and was out of the carriage in an instant. The contessa was carrying a jewel case as well as a reticule and two larger bags. St. George settled her and her belongings beside Demetra and was about to climb in after her when the contessa forestalled him. "No," she said, "you must go back to the house. I threw a traveling bag out the window, but it was too heavy for me to carry. Go through the garden. It is simple."

"No." Quentin's manner was decisive. "You do not need—"

"*Cielo!* Is it not enough I must leave my trunks? Send him." She gestured toward the coachman seated on the box outside.

Quentin hesitated, then shrugged his shoulders and told Hunter to stand down. The two men walked toward King Street together, then Hunter went on alone while Quentin stayed to watch his progress.

"So," Demetra said, "you are not the Contessa Montalto."

"So," the other woman replied amicably, "you are not Miss Catherine Newley." She threw back her hood and smiled.

Demetra could not help smiling back. This was not a woman to be beaten by circumstance.

"I think perhaps you should return my ring," the contessa went on. "Now that Miss Newley has no need for it."

"Oh, but I've just given it to Lady Berresford."

The contessa stiffened. "To return to you," Demetra said. "You dropped it in the corridor tonight. I think you were too preoccupied with Major York to notice."

The contessa threw back her head and laughed. "*Ah, quel bello diablo.*" And then she screamed, because that handsome devil, a smile on his face, had flung open the door and reached into the carriage to grasp her arm.

"Bianca, my distraction, you'd leave without me?"

"You fool!" Her anger was uppermost now. She pulled away but he did not release her arm. "You fool. You've ruined everything."

"Leave us," Demetra said. "It's not safe—"

Ian turned startled eyes to Demetra. He had not been aware that the contessa had a companion. But he had no chance to respond. While the woman stared in surprise and consternation, Major York was pulled roughly from the carriage and flung against the railing fronting the nearby house. Before he could recover his balance, he was plucked from the railing and given a well-aimed blow which left him lying flat on his back in the middle of the sidewalk.

The contessa leaned out of the carriage. "You've hurt him," she said, alarm and accusation in her voice.

"Only for a moment." Quentin picked Ian up under the arms and dragged him nearer the railing, where his presence would be less noticeable. "He's breathing," he said to the contessa, who was showing signs of leaving the carriage. "Stay where you are." He stood there, a gentleman hovering over a friend who was deeply in his cups, until Hunter returned, weighed down by a large traveling bag, which he threw up onto the box. Quentin entered the coach and sat down across from the two women. "Bianca," he said. "I think you know Lady Chester. She happens to be my sister. Demetra, may I present Madame Falconetti."

The two women said nothing. Quentin rapped on the roof and Hunter turned the carriage into King Street.

"Where do you take me?" Bianca demanded.

"We stop briefly at my house," Quentin informed her. "I must return the carriage—it belongs to my mother—and hire another one. Lady Chester will see to your needs. My parents are out, as are my other sisters and my brother. I'll draw off the servants before you enter. No one will know you are there. Demetra is clever and will arrange it."

"I see. And then? What have you in mind for me then?"

"Dover, I think. Dover and a swift packet to France. Your usefulness here is at an end, Bianca. It has not gone the way I had hoped, but we must take the cards as they are played."

"I see. I am an inconvenience."

Quentin looked at her sharply. "You're a delightful woman, Bianca, but—"

"I will not go."

"I beg your pardon?"

"I said, I will not go."

He had not expected opposition. "You have little choice."

"No. That is not quite right. I received your note, and it told me you are frightened, and for a time I lost my head. But now I have it again, thank you. They will not make me a witness, but they will want to know what I have to say, and how it is that I came to England with Lord Berresford. You dare not abduct me, Lord St. George. So I think I will stay."

Quentin took a deep breath and regarded his opponent. "What is it you want, Bianca?"

"What I was promised," she said, beating her fist on the seat. "What is mine. You were to give me money for going to Lord Berresford, for going to England, for doing what we talked of in this House of Lords. You told me Lord Berresford would also give me money. But I have nothing, I tell you, nothing. I will not leave."

"I gave you money in Paris."

"Bah! For a few necessary trifles. It is gone."

"You will have your money, Bianca. I will send it after you."

"No, I will see it first. The money you promised. The money

Lord Berresford promised. If I do not have it from you, I will go to Lord Berresford and tell him everything."

"If you go to him, you will have nothing at all."

Bianca smiled. "I will have satisfaction. It is worth a great deal."

Quentin was silent. After a moment he said, "How much?"

"Three thousand pounds," she said without hesitation.

He sat up abruptly. "Good God, that's more than my yearly allowance."

Bianca shrugged.

Quentin sat back and regarded his guest thoughtfully. "Demetra," he said at last, "we have a problem."

"We?"

He ignored her. "I cannot raise the money Madame Falconetti needs immediately. It will take two or three days. We can hardly conceal her in your bedroom for two or three days."

"Take her to Cranford," Demetra said. Cranford was a small house belonging to Quentin, about an hour out of London.

"I think not." He was silent for a time. Demetra had enjoyed seeing Quentin bested by the contessa, but she did not trust the look in her brother's eyes.

"Your husband has a house in Surrey, doesn't he?" Quentin said. "Near Epsom, I believe."

"No, Quentin," she said with a confidence she did not feel. "It's Frank's house. I can't use it."

She might not have spoken. "You've been there, haven't you? The servants know you?"

They had driven down the Sunday after her arrival in London, she and Frank and Colin and Annie. It had been a happy day. What a beast Quentin was. If anything went wrong, if the spurious contessa was discovered, it could only discredit Frank.

"I think that will do, Bianca," he said. "There will not be much company, but you will be quiet there. My sister and I will drive you down tonight." And he leaned back in his seat looking as though this was what he had wanted all along.

The four men in the library had been arguing for the past hour. "The man is a jealous suitor," Arthur Berresford said for the fourth time. "She wanted nothing to do with him, and he turned on her in revenge. You know what these Latins are like."

"He's Irish," Frank said. He was weary of Berresford and his posturing.

"It's the same thing." Berresford drained his glass. He had been drinking steadily since he returned home and his words were beginning to slur. He set the glass down carefully and looked at his three companions. "What I do not understand, what I fail to comprehend, is why we should be expected to take the word of a vagrant soldier"—here he looked hard at Frank, who had admitted acquaintance with Ian York—"against that of the Contessa Montalto."

Because, Frank wanted to scream, she's an unscrupulous woman who came to England to blackmail your wife. Because York once saved my life and in this case I believe his story. But he could say none of this, so he slid farther down into his chair and contemplated the dregs of coffee in his cup.

Kenrick leaned forward. "He called her Bianca, and she didn't correct him. Is that the contessa's given name?"

"I have no idea," Arthur said. "The matter never came up, and it's not the sort of thing one asks a lady."

Nicholas stood up. He too was growing tired of Berresford. "The thing is, we can't take the chance that it might be true. That she might not be the Contessa Montalto."

Arthur dismissed him with a shrug. Warwick was a man of some substance, a friend of Brougham and also close to Holland, but he sat in the Commons and Arthur did not feel obliged to take him seriously. "I'll tell you what I think happened," he said. He had had a new thought and was pleased by it. "St. George put him up to it."

247

"Why St. George?" Kenrick looked at him sharply.

"He was seen in Wardour Street, wasn't he? And he was at the theatre tonight. He's been trying to get at the contessa. But since we keep her close, he had to try another tack. If he couldn't suborn her, he'd discredit her."

"Ingenious." Unlike his two colleagues, Kenrick was a model of patience. And he did not want to alienate Berresford.

Frank put down his cup and got to his feet. "Yes. But it doesn't alter the situation. Nicholas is right, we can't take the chance that the woman is an imposter."

Arthur took a step forward. He was shorter than Frank, but he had the arrogance of a man who has been blessed from birth with fortune and good looks. He did not like to be crossed. "It's a monstrous accusation, Hawksley."

"Agreed." Kenrick, too, got to his feet. "Nevertheless, we must be sure. St. George may or may not be involved in this, but he was there tonight, and he heard it. He'll tell his father, and you can be sure the prosecution will make much of it in cross-examination." He looked round the group. "We need proof that the woman is who she claims to be. The Queen would recognize the real contessa. We'll take her to the Queen."

"She'll be outraged that we thought it necessary," Arthur said. "Oh, very well."

Kenrick pulled out his watch. "Nicholas and I will call on Her Majesty tomorrow morning and arrange it. It's too late to do anything tonight. And we'll have to tell Brougham to delay the contessa's testimony. We don't want her in the box until we're sure. I think it best if she doesn't leave the house, Berresford."

"Arthur?"

The four men looked around as the soft voice cut into their conversation. Helen stood framed in the doorway, her face unusually pale. She was still wearing her dressing gown.

"Can't you see I'm busy," Arthur barked. He was as upset by her attire as by her intrusion into his private business.

"Yes, I know." She gathered strength and closed the door behind her. "It's important, Arthur. I went to the contessa's room and she wasn't there. She's gone."

"Don't be a fool! She's probably gone to the— Or to look for a book. She's somewhere about."

"I'm not a fool, Arthur." Helen's voice was now strong and composed. "She's not where you said, I looked there. And if she'd wanted a book, she'd have had to come here, wouldn't she? Her jewel case is missing, and her dark cloak, and some other things—well, you wouldn't understand, but things a woman would need. She's left the house."

For the the first time in many long months, Helen had her husband's undivided attention.

There was a stunned silence in the room. Then Arthur threw open the door and ran up the stairs. Nicholas was close behind him. Kenrick looked at Frank. "It's as good as a confession, isn't it? We may be luckier than we know." He started for the door, then looked back. "I'd best keep an eye on them. Stay here with Lady Berresford."

When he had gone, Helen's composure vanished and she began to tremble. "Frank, it wasn't my fault, I swear it."

"Of course it wasn't your fault, Helen. She'd been found out."

"Found out? Oh, my God, the letters!"

"The letters?" He was puzzled. "This has nothing to do with the letters—" He broke off. "Don't you know?"

"Why should I know, Frank? Arthur never tells me anything. No one ever tells me anything. No one—"

She would have gone on with the litany of her complaints, but Frank interrupted. "Listen carefully, Helen. Tonight Major York—you remember him, he was at the Braithwoods'—Major York accosted the contessa in the corridor outside your box and accused her of not being the Contessa Montalto. York disappeared before we could question him, but now it seems likely that he was right. We don't know why she was playing this charade. It may have been only to come to

249

England to approach you, or it may be more complicated than that. I'm sure that money is involved. But I don't think she'll come near you again."

"But the letters?"

"I don't think she has the letters."

Her eyes were wide with bewilderment. "Then—"

"I'll get them, Helen, I promise. Now, sit down and tell me what happened."

"Nothing happened. We were at the theatre and there seemed to be a dreadful commotion in the corridor—you were there, you must have heard—and then the contessa came back into the box looking stormy and talking wildly in Italian, and Arthur followed her and told me the contessa was ill and we were leaving at once, in that peremptory way of his, and he hurried us out of the theatre. Arthur didn't speak to me all the way home. And then that woman swept upstairs without a word to me and Arthur said he was having visitors and I should go to my room. So I did."

"And then? Why did you go to the contessa's room?"

"To talk with her. To beg her to tell me what had happened to the letters. Oh, and to return the ring."

"The ring?"

"Yes." She opened her palm and displayed the ring which she had been clutching ever since she left her room. "She dropped it in the corridor, and Demetra came by to return it."

"Demetra?"

"Don't yell at me, Frank. Everyone yells at me. She found it in the corridor of the theatre after the contessa left, and she thought it might be valuable so she brought it here. Which was very thoughtful, considering she had the headache and left the theatre just after we did, though I don't think it was really necessary. It's a vulgar piece of jewelry and I'm sure the stone is not real. Here, take it."

She held the ring out as though it would burn her. Frank took it from her hand and studied it. It was certainly not Demetra's ring, but he doubted that it had been dropped by the contessa. His wife's visit and the contessa's disappearance could not be unrelated. "What else did Demetra do, Helen? Where did she go?"

"She didn't go anywhere at all. When I came downstairs she was in the hall. She said she'd been to the—you know. And then we went into the anteroom and she gave me the ring. She didn't want coffee or tea, she only stayed a few minutes. Why do you ask?"

Frank gave a warning shake of his head and slipped the ring into his pocket just as Kenrick reentered the room.

"I'm afraid you were right, Lady Berresford," Kenrick said. "Your husband is questioning the servants now, and in his present mood . . ." There was a note of pity in his voice.

"Of course. If Arthur asks for me—though I don't think he will, he never does—tell him I've gone to bed."

They watched her leave the room, a slender, graceful figure in a velvet dressing gown with a touch of dignified sadness in her bearing. But Frank could not spare much pity for Helen. He had to see Demetra, and at once, though he could not tell even Kenrick why. "You won't need me here," he said. "I'm going after York."

His thoughts filled with anger and despair, Frank left the house. He could not remember at first where he had left his carriage. He looked around, forcing himself to think, and saw a dark mass near the railing just beyond King Street. He would have ignored it, but it was unexpected, so it might have something to do with his wife and the Contessa Montalto. With those women, anything was possible.

He walked toward the railing and looked down. The mass was the figure of a man sprawled inelegantly on the ground. He turned him over and saw without surprise that the man was Ian York.

Ian was just returning to consciousness. He moaned softly and tried to move his head. "Easy, old chap." Frank knelt beside him and ran practiced fingers over the back of his skull. "You're going to have the devil of a head. Do you think you

251

can get up? I'll bring the carriage round."

When Frank returned, Ian was sitting on the curb, cursing fluently in three languages. "I just wanted her back," he said as Frank hoisted him into his curricle. "Hang the money. It didn't matter." He leaned forward, his head in his hands.

"You rather spoiled things for her tonight."

Ian looked up. "Why? Didn't Berresford want her without a title? No, there's more to it. They were going to use her in the trial. This will create a holy stink."

Frank sprang into the curricle. "Why didn't you tell me she wasn't the Contessa Montalto?"

"I didn't want to spoil her game."

"You knew she was going to be a witness?"

"No, not at first." Ian felt the back of his head. A large lump had been raised when he hit the sidewalk. "I thought she'd run off with a wealthy lover. When I got to London and heard the rumors, I suspected it was more than that." Ian leaned back, resting his head gingerly against the squabs. "You should thank me. Bianca can't be trusted even on oath. Funny, though. I didn't think she'd be mixed up in something like this. Your wife, I mean. Such a pretty little thing. Why do you suppose he wanted her?"

"Who?" Frank barked.

"The viscount. What's his name? George, St. George. She said he was her brother. He's the one who laid me out. Bianca was already in the carriage. With Lady Chester." He glanced up at Frank. "No mistake there, Hawksley. It was your wife."

Frank had known it, but this was bitter confirmation. Demetra must have left the theatre with St. George. She had made an excuse to call on Helen, but it was the contessa she had wanted to see. St. George wanted the contessa to escape, and Demetra had helped him.

"Listen, York," he said, trying to work it through. "The contessa—what's her name, by the way?"

"Falconetti."

"Madame Falconetti wasn't found by Berresford in Paris.

She found him. She was intended to find him. You're right, it's about the trial. She was the perfect Italian witness—titled, wealthy—"

Ian snorted.

"—a lady. Berresford was taken in. He was full of his own cleverness when he brought her back. And she seemed all right to us. Even now the others don't know about the letters. She was to testify this week, until your performance tonight put a stop to that. She might have tried to brazen it out, but St. George wanted to get her away. He has no reason to do so— Madame Falconetti can only be an embarrassment to the Queen's defense, and he's a King's man—no reason, unless he put her up to the whole business in the first place and he's afraid that she'll expose him."

Ian shook his head as though to clear it. "St. George sent her to Berresford?"

Frank nodded. "I think so. Perhaps she was to change her testimony on the stand. Perhaps she was to be denounced as an imposter. Either way, it would make mischief for our side."

"Then St. George knew her before?"

"He'd been on the Continent for some months. Most recently in Paris."

"Paris!" Ian spat the word out. "I hate the French. I spent eight days in a filthy cell and couldn't get a message to a damned Englishman in all that time. A mistake, they told me. So sorry for the inconvenience. Or— Or maybe it wasn't a mistake," he added slowly. "Could St. George have arranged that?"

Frank shrugged. "I'm not much acquainted with my brother-in-law. But from what I've heard of him, yes, he could have."

"I'll pay him out for that," Ian said, "see if I don't."

Frank set the horses in motion. "I'll drive you to your lodgings. A night's sleep and you'll be all right."

Ian frowned. "Thought the man looked familiar. Can't remember where . . ." He lapsed into silence.

253

Frank was not inclined to further talk. He dropped Ian at the Black Horse and turned his carriage toward Bruton Street. He had no idea where his wife might be—halfway to Dover, perhaps—but she would have to return sometime and he was going to be there to meet her.

Manningtree, who had been waiting for the family to return, opened the door and greeted him without surprise. Lord Chester was now a frequent visitor. Lady Chester, he said, was at home, and if Lord Chester would wait, he would inform her of his arrival.

But that was unnecessary. Demetra was already halfway down the stairs, as though she had been waiting for him.

Frank strode to the foot of the stairs and looked up into the familiar face. He felt a stab of pain. "Demetra," he said, echoing the words he had used four days before, "we have to talk. Now."

Chapter 17

Tuesday, October 10

"Of course, Frank. Come into the front parlor. I believe there's a fire laid."

Demetra's voice was composed. She had been expecting this scene. No matter how late the hour, she was certain Frank would come to Bruton Street and demand an explanation about the letters as soon as he left Berresford House. She had been watching from an upstairs window and had hurried down to intercept him. With the fraudulent Contessa Montalto at present drinking tea in the yellow bedroom, Demetra was not about to let Frank beyond the ground floor. She continued down the stairs while Frank stared fixedly at her, his face a chilling mask.

The tension-filled silence was abruptly shattered by the sound of the doorbell. Demetra started and uttered a silent prayer that it wasn't Quentin, and even Frank looked round involuntarily, as the imperturbable Manningtree opened the door.

"Hullo, Manningtree," said Sophy cheerfully, stepping into the house. "Demetra, we've had the most— Oh, Lord Chester, I didn't realize you were here."

"Are *you* here, Chester?" Lewis walked into the house behind

255

Edwina, who had followed Sophy. "I say, it's a pity both you and Demetra had to leave before the end of the play. It was capital fun. I daresay the farce would have been too, only Edwina insisted we go on to supper—"

"I hardly think they're interested in a catalogue of our evening, Lewis." Edwina was standing motionless while Manningtree removed her swansdown-trimmed cloak. "Good evening, Lord Chester."

"Lady Edwina." Frank inclined his head briefly.

"Don't be so stuffy, Eddy." Lewis was feeling very grand. "He's our brother-in-law, ain't he? Actually, it was a good thing we left early, because when we got to Mivarts—"

'Demetra," Sophy interrupted, concern suffusing her face, "nothing's wrong with Colin and Annie, is it?"

"No, of course not," Demetra descended the remaining steps, all smiles. "Frank just came by to discuss something with me. We were about to go into the parlor, so if you'll excuse us—"

"If there's no crisis," said Lewis, "care to come into the library and have a drink, Chester? There's some very tolerable brandy."

"Don't be so pretentious, Lewis." Edwina moved toward Demetra. "You don't even like brandy."

"How do you know?" Lewis demanded.

"You got sick the last time you—"

"It's very good of you to offer, Thane," Frank intervened (with, Demetra thought, surprising kindness), "but I'm afraid I'm in rather a hurry. Some other time perhaps. Demetra—"

This time Demetra and Frank managed to take two steps across the inlaid marble floor before the doorbell rang again. Demetra considered making a bolt for the parlor, but before she could do so, Manningtree opened the door to admit her parents.

Lady Buckleigh surveyed the crowd and immediately picked out the one person who did not belong there. "Lord Chester," said the countess, in accents of unfailing patience, "I wish you

256

would make up your mind about your place of residence. If you must call at such very odd hours I can direct the servants to make up a room for you."

"My apologies, Lady Buckleigh, I—"

"No need to apologize to me, I'm not *your* mother. We're delighted to see you, of course, aren't we, Horace?"

Demetra looked from her husband to her father. She could still vividly recall that horrible scene seven years ago when Frank informed Papa that he was too late to stop their runaway marriage. Though the two men must have seen each other in the House of Lords, they had not spoken since.

"Sir," said Frank.

"Hawksley." Buckleigh returned Frank's nod.

Considering their past history it was a remarkably amicable exchange, and at another time Demetra would have been pleased. At the moment she was preoccupied with extricating Frank from her family before Quentin returned home. She started to make her excuses, but was forestalled by her mother, who had noticed an absence from the throng. "Where," Lady Buckleigh demanded, "is Quentin?"

"He left the theatre early to bring Demetra home," Lewis explained. "She had the headache."

"Demetra? Nonsense," said Lady Buckleigh, "Demetra never has the headache."

"How very true," said Frank, looking at his wife.

"I escorted Sophy and Edwina to supper," Lewis added proudly.

"That does not," said Lady Buckleigh, ignoring her younger son's remark, "explain Quentin's present whereabouts."

"No." Frank was still looking at Demetra. "It doesn't."

"He went out again after he brought me home," Demetra explained with perfect truth.

"Well, I call that shabby!" said Sophy. "Leaving you to spend the evening alone."

"Preferable to spending it with Quentin if you ask me." Edwina stifled a yawn.

"No one," said their mother, "is asking either of you anything. I don't at all understand what is going on this evening and I'm not sure I wish to. Horace, aren't you going to offer Lord Chester a drink?"

"I don't need you to tell me how to go on, Catherine," Buckleigh said testily. "Care for a drink, Hawksley? I've some very tolerable brandy."

"Thank you, sir, no. Demetra and I—"

"Frank and I are going to talk," Demetra said. "Now."

But the "now" was drowned out by the doorbell. And this time, Demetra knew with dismaying certainty, there was only one person it could be.

"My word," said Quentin, handing his hat to Manningtree. "Decided to have a family party, Mother?"

"I have decided," Lady Buckleigh informed him, "not to ask questions."

"Splendid idea. Headache better, 'Metra?"

"Much. If everyone will excuse us, Frank and I have things to discuss."

"Just a minute." This time the opposition came from, of all people, Frank himself. "St. George, I think you should come with us."

"Nonsense, Frank," Demetra said sharply. "This is between you and me. There's no need to involve Quentin."

"That," said Frank, his eyes now focused on the viscount, "is a point of debate. St. George?"

"For once," said Quentin, "I am quite happy to oblige you, Hawksley. Shall we?"

"For an intelligent man," said Demetra, when the three of them were behind the closed parlor door, "you can be apallingly idiotish, Frank. Mama and Papa might not wonder that you and I want to talk at this hour, but you and I and Quentin? They'll know something's afoot."

"Do you always talk to him like this?" Quentin asked curiously, disposing himself in the most comfortable chair in the room. "I'm surprised your marriage lasted as long as it did.

258

I should think even a radical would want a reasonably submissive wife."

"Oh, shut up, Quen," said Demetra.

"There's nothing wrong with the way she talks," snapped Frank. "I'm in no mood for clever remarks and I don't give a damn about what your parents think, Demetra. I want answers."

St. George shifted his position, draping one leg across the ebony-inlaid chair arm. "Better give us the questions then, hadn't you, Hawksley?"

"Where," said Frank, striding to the center of the room, "is the supposed Contessa Montalto?"

Demetra and St. George regarded him with identical expressions of polite incomprehension. Frank had never thought they resembled each other, but looking at the two of them ranged against him, he wondered how he could have been so blind. They were both very much Thanes.

"Why at Berresford House, I assume," Demetra said. "Isn't that where the Berresfords took her when they left the theatre?"

"Don't trifle with me, Demetra. Ian York saw all three of you before St. George knocked him senseless."

"And naturally," St. George murmured, "you would take the word of a scoundrel like York over that of your wife."

"At the moment," said Frank, "I consider you and Demetra rather less trustworthy than—than—"

"Napoleon?" St. George suggested derisively.

"Among others."

"Oh, come, Frank," Demetra said seating herself in a Trafalgar chair, "you can do better than that. At the moment you're much angrier with us than you ever were with the poor Emperor. You always said if only the government would—"

"Demetra, we aren't discussing international relations."

"We are now," said St. George, idly swinging his foot against the leg of his chair. "So you went about defending Boney, did you, Hawksley?"

259

"Whatever his faults, the man was more honorable than some I could name."

St. George sprang to his feet. "See here, Hawksley, if you imagine I'll sit tamely by while you claim that Corsican upstart is more honorable than a Thane—"

"Oh, for heaven's sake," said Demetra, stepping between them. "If the two of you want to waste the evening on a ridiculous quarrel, I suppose I can't stop you, but I thought we all had more important things to do."

"A point," Quentin acknowledged, his stance relaxing somewhat. "But let it be noted that I yield only at the entreaty of a lady. You were saying, Hawksley?" he asked, returning to his chair. "Before Demetra dragged in Bonaparte?"

"You know perfectly well what I was saying. I should add that Lady Berresford told me Demetra called on her this evening with a most improbable story—"

"What's improbable about it?" Demetra demanded. "I'm not the one who dropped the ring."

"And that she was wandering about the house—"

"I went to the convenience."

"Really, 'Metra," Quentin murmured, "if Mother could hear you."

"Are you going to tell me what happened, or do I have to choke it out of St. George's lying throat?"

"You wouldn't," said the viscount comfortably. "Not in front of Demetra."

"Don't be too sure."

At least they had the sense not to offer further protestations of innocence. "You see—" Demetra began.

"Leave it, Hawksley," St. George advised, and though the words were addressed to Frank, Quentin's gaze flickered in Demetra's direction. "If you have any brains at all—and I have to admit that you do—you must realize you're well rid of the contessa. No one—with the possible exception of Arthur Berresford—can really want to find her."

"What Quentin means is—" Demetra said.

"Thank you, Demetra. But unlike Hawksley, I do like my women submissive. I advise you to stay out of this."

"When I know the contessa's whereabouts," Frank said, looking at St. George, "I'll be the judge of whether or not I want to find her."

"As you wish, old fellow. But you aren't going to discover her whereabouts."

"No?" said Frank softly.

"No." St. George raised his eyes above Frank's head and contemplated the elaborate frieze over the chimney glass. "Because if you make any attempt to do so, if you interfere in the smallest way, Demetra and I will make Helen Berresford's letters public."

He should have seen it coming. But Frank felt as if he had been slapped in the face. Or stabbed in the back. He looked at Demetra, seeking some sign of denial, some hint of explanation, but her face was a complete blank.

"I had not thought you would stoop so low." His voice was bitter. "But then, as I've learned tonight, you are far more like your brother than I ever imagined."

Without another word, he turned and left the room.

"That," said Demetra, when the parlor door had closed behind her husband, "was pure malice, Quen."

"A simple matter of self-preservation."

"You didn't have to make it sound as if I'm a party to your blackmail scheme!"

"Well, in a manner of speaking you are."

"Only because you blackmailed me into it."

"Exactly. Clever of me, wasn't it?" He rose and walked toward the chimney glass.

"If you were trying to destroy my marriage," Demetra informed him, "You are going to be disappointed."

"Now why," said Quentin, turning and smiling at her, "would I try to do a think like that? You and Hawksley are managing so very adroitly on your own."

He turned back to the mirror. Demetra stared at him, her

loathing intensified by her helplessness. "You really are a bastard, Quen."

"Oh, I don't think so," said Quentin, adjusting his cravat. "I don't think even Lewis and Sophy are. Mother's a strong-minded woman, but she's very particular about the family line. Shouldn't you be getting back to our guest?"

"That sounds preferable to further time in your company."

It was not a very satisfactory parting shot, particularly as Quentin merely replied, "I'll let you know when it's safe for us to leave."

The hall was now empty and Demetra was able to escape upstairs without facing her family or even Manningtree. Suddenly she felt overcome by exhaustion. She opened the door to the yellow bedroom and found the contessa—Bianca, rather—seated at her dressing table, examining the contents of her jewel box.

"Go ahead by all means," Demetra said cordially. "You'll forgive me if I count my jewels before we leave."

Bianca laughed, set down a topaz necklace, and turned to look at St. George's sister. "Frankly, Lady Chester, none of your jewels is fine enough to tempt me."

Demetra could not help smiling. "I didn't have a great deal of jewelry when I left home," she explained, quite as if she was talking to Philippa Ashton. "And Frank never could afford to buy me anything expensive."

"You love him very much." It was a statement, not a question.

"Of course." Demetra did not have the energy to deny it. She dropped down on the edge of the bed, kicked off her satin slippers, and studied her visitor. "Do you love Major York?"

"Ian? Of course."

Demetra had not expected such a categorical answer. "Then why are you running away from him?" she demanded.

Bianca eyed Demetra shrewdly. "Why are you running away from your husband?"

"That's different, I— Aren't you worried?" Demetra asked,

turning the conversation away from Frank. "You'll leave England before long and—"

"Oh, Ian will find me." Bianca sounded completely secure. "He always does. One must be practical and take care of business, and one must not expect that one's own interests will always be the same as one's lover's. I think we are in somewhat the same situation in that regard, are we not?"

"I suppose you could say that," Demetra admitted, drawing her feet up onto the quilt.

"Well then. I am confident and so should you be."

"It's not quite the same. Major York isn't having an affair with Lady Berresford."

"That," Bianca acknowledged, "is true. She is not at all in Ian's style. Still, a woman such as Lady Berresford—beautiful, but no spirit. It should not be difficult to win your husband back."

"If he really loves her," Demetra said, wrapping her arms around her legs and resting her chin on her knees, "I'm not sure I want him back."

"Ah. That is different, and something you must decide for yourself. Tell me, purely as a matter of curiosity, what did you do with the letters?"

"The letters?" Demetra raised her head and looked at Bianca, half a dozen different lies hovering on her lips. But what was wrong with the truth? It would be a relief to tell someone. "I hid them. In Frank's and my house. I thought they'd be safe there. But I underestimated my brother."

"The viscount? He found them?" Bianca's back straightened and her magnificent eyes narrowed. "I begin to see. He threatens to expose the letters and so you are obliged to assist him with my escape. Oh, I am not a fool," she added, in response to Demetra's look of surprise. "I see that you do not wish to help him. Your brother is not a very pleasant man, is he?"

"That," said Demetra, "is a gross understatement. You didn't tell him about the letters, did you?"

"And risk this sort of interference? Of couse not. Does he know that I—"

"No. He thinks Frank hid them in our house."

"That is something. Still, it is most unfortunate."

"It isn't your problem. Frank paid you for the letters, didn't he?"

"Certainly," Bianca admitted. "But I do not like people who interfere in this high—how do you say it?"

"High-handed," supplied Demetra. "That describes Quentin to perfection. From childhood. Only then I got the better of him. Sometimes. I even helped him out of scrapes. I never thought—"

She was interrupted by a knock. Both women stiffened, expecting St. George, but the voice that followed was Edwina's.

"Demetra? Are you awake? May I come in for a few minutes? There's something I need to talk to you about."

Demetra hesitated. In all fairness, having arranged the meeting with Elliot Marsden this afternoon, she owed it to Edwina to listen to her problems. She could not let her sister in, of course, but she could go to Edwina's room. Except that then she might be gone when Quentin returned. The thought of disrupting her brother's plans was momentarily satisfying, but reflection told her it would not be wise.

"I'm half asleep, Eddy," she said, yawning loudly. "We'll talk in the morning. Right after breakfast. Or before if you like. I promise."

Bianca looked speculatively at Demetra. "A man?" she asked.

"A man," said Demetra.

"Sophy? Sophy, wake up!"

Sophy opened her eyes and stared about her in confusion, then sat bolt upright, suddenly wide awake. "Lewis? What is it? What's happened? Is someone ill?"

"No. That is I don't think so. It's the Contessa Montalto."

264

"Oh, for heaven's sake." Sophy plopped back against the pillows. "I know how spooney boys can get—well, girls too—and I can understand your wanting to talk about her, but did you have to wake me up in the middle of the night to do it?"

"Sh! Keep your voice down—"

"Why should I—"

"This is secret. It's not just talk. She's here!"

"Who is?"

"The contessa!"

Sophy stared at him suspiciously. "Lewis, did you have some of the brandy after all?"

"No, of course not, it makes me sick. She's here, I tell you. Or at least she was. In Demetra's room."

"In Demetra's room?"

"That's what I said. I was walking past Demetra's door and I smelled her scent—the contessa's I mean, I'd recognize it anywhere—"

"Oh, is that all." Sophy was disappointed. "I thought perhaps something really exciting was happening. Demetra probably spilled her perfume."

"And so," Lewis continued, "I hid in the alcove, behind the curtains, and before long Quentin came down the corridor and knocked at Demetra's door, and Demetra came out with the contessa. They were wearing cloaks or pelisses or something"—Lewis was not a careful observer of feminine fashions—"and they talked in whispers which I couldn't understand, and then they went down the stairs. Sophy, you don't suppose Quentin and Demetra have kidnapped the contessa, do you?"

"Of course not." Sophy was frowning. "She doesn't look the sort of woman who gets kidnapped."

"But you believe me?"

"Oh, I believe you. Quentin's up to something."

"Demetra is too."

Sophy continued to frown. "Demetra's been suspicious of Quentin ever since she came home. She wouldn't tell me what it was about, but I promised that you and I would keep an eye on him."

"You did what? You never said anything to me about it."

"Why do you think I suggested you go to White's with Quentin yesterday?"

Lewis thought, with indignation, of how his sister had manipulated his engagements in the past few days. "I say, Sophy, you might have told me—"

"Put that candle down, Lewis, you're dripping wax all over the bed. Demetra was watching Quentin earlier tonight."

"Watching him?" Lewis set the candle down on the bedside table.

"Yes, at the theatre, during the interval. Just before all that fuss with the contessa and Major York. And then Quentin made her pretend she had the headache and leave early—"

"I didn't know she was pretending."

"I know you didn't, you were too busy being grand, but it was plain as a pikestaff to the rest of us. Lewis, if Demetra was helping Quentin with the contessa, I don't think it was because she wanted to."

"Then why did she do it?"

"Because Quentin made her. You know how he is."

Lewis considered this a moment. "He's always been very decent to me."

Sophy gave a most unladylike snort. "You mean now that you're almost a man he thinks it's his duty to show you how to go on. And it suits his purpose to do so. Quentin never does anything that doesn't suit his purpose. He's one of the most autocratic people I know."

"No, he's not, he's—"

"Oh, he's subtle about it, I'll give him that. But he's a genius at getting people to do what he wants. Think about it."

Lewis admired Quentin, but he was closer to Sophy than to any of his other siblings. He thought back over nursery and schoolroom days. Quen could be rather high-handed. All the same— "All the same," Lewis said, "he couldn't push Demetra around like she was—"

"Like she was you or me," Sophy concluded for him. "Which is why something must be really wrong."

"What?"

"I don't know, but I'm certain she's in trouble."

"Then let's ask her about it when she gets back from wherever she and Quen and the contessa are going. I want to know if the contessa is all right. Maybe they both need help."

"Lewis, I know you're itching to rescue a fair maiden from deadly peril, but Demetra and the contessa aren't in deadly peril. They aren't even maidens."

"What do you mean they aren't— Oh, I see." Lewis blushed. "Well, I still say we should ask Demetra."

"She won't tell us anything. And if they are in trouble, there's not much we can do on our own."

Lewis looked at Sophy in surprise. "You're not saying we should ignore the whole thing?"

"Of course not."

"But if we don't talk to Demetra and you don't think we can do anything on our own—" Lewis was struck by an awful thought. "Sophy, if you're going to suggest we ask *Mama*—"

"Good heavens no! Credit me with some sense. But there is one person we can talk to. Someone who doesn't like Quentin and who knows more about the contessa than we do. Someone who will certainly want to help Demetra."

"Who?" Lewis demanded.

Sophy was no longer frowning. "Lord Chester," she said.

Chapter 18

Shortly before eight-thirty the next morning, Frank drew up his curricle in Bruton street, still weighing his desire to see his children against the possibility of encountering Demetra or St. George.

Colin and Annie won the battle. He was damned if he'd let Demetra and St. George disrupt his children's lives. Besides, Frank acknowledged as he sprang down from the curricle and tossed the reins to Evan, at the moment he needed his children as much, if not more, than they needed him.

He found the entrance hall and staircase blessedly free of Thanes, and when he reached the nursery he was relieved to discover only Mary Rose and the children. Colin and Annie were sitting on a hearth rug, a pack of cards spread out between them.

"Daddy!" Annie sprang up, but she did not run to her father as was her wont. "You didn't come yesterday," she informed him, short legs firmly planted, hands on her hips. "Not at all."

"I know." Frank smiled at Mary Rose, who was at the table, mending one of Annie's dresses, and walked to the hearth rug. "I'm sorry," he said, dropping down beside the children. "I should at least have sent you a message."

"Yes." Annie, still standing, refused to give ground.

"It's all right," Colin said. "Was it something about the Queen?"

"Partly." Frank tried to be honest with his children. "Am I forgiven?"

"Of course," Colin said promptly. "You'd have come if you could."

Annie was less easily persuaded. "Not happen again?" she suggested.

"I can't promise that," Frank told her, "but I can promise to send you word if it does. All right?"

Annie considered the offer gravely for a moment, then nodded, a smile breaking across her face. "We're playing faro," she informed her father by way of forgiveness.

"Faro?" Frank was not sure he had understood.

"Aunt Sophy taught us," Colin explained. "I'm not sure we're doing it right, but we make up the things we don't understand."

"Look." Annie reached down and picked up a carved wooden horse. Now that she had forgiven her father, she was eager to share all her news. "Mummy bought her in the Burl'ton 'Cade yesterday."

Yesterday. In addition to quarreling with him at Weyridge's and conniving with her brother at the theatre and sneaking the false contessa out of Berresford House, Demetra had found time to buy presents for the children. It was oddly comforting. "What's her name?" Frank asked.

"Caroline." Annie plopped down on the rug, Caroline in her lap. She was back to normal.

The same could not be said for Colin, who was unusually quiet. There were drawbacks to having sensitive, intelligent children. The boy was aware of far more than was good for him. Or for his parents. Frank suddenly wondered what would happen to the children when he and Demetra formally separated. Children frequently remained with their fathers in such situations, but Frank knew that Demetra would fight him tooth and nail if he tried to take Colin and Annie away from her. And even if he could, would he really separate her from the children? On the other hand, was he prepared to give them up himself?

"What did your mother bring you?" Frank asked Colin.

"A giraffe." Colin reached behind him and handed the giraffe to his father with a smile which, Frank suspected, was an attempt to reassure his parent, rather than an expression of childish joy. Frank took the giraffe, thinking that Demetra had given more thought to the children than he had this past week. And that reminded him of something else he'd neglected to do.

"I'm sorry, old chap," Frank said. "I've forgotten your wagon." When Frank had gone up to see his children before the Braithwoods' ball, Colin had asked his father to bring the wagon the next time he visited.

"That's all right," Colin said. "I got it myself."

Himself? When had Colin been in Park Street? Demetra hadn't been there since Sunday. Or had she? "When did your mother take you to Park Street?" Frank asked.

"Mummy didn't." Frank recognized Colin's expression. It meant he would rather not say what he was about to say because he was unsure of the response. "Uncle Quentin did."

Frank stiffened, an instinctive response to hearing his loathsome brother-in-law referred to as "uncle." Then the rest of Colin's statement registered. "St. Ge—your uncle took you to Park Street?"

"Yesterday." Colin's solemn face told Frank the boy knew perfectly well that his father and uncle were far from friends. "He came up to the nursery after lunch, when Mummy was out, and he was asking about our toys and when I said something about the wagon, he said why didn't we go get it."

"I stayed here," Annie put in, making it clear she recognized this as an injustice. "Uncle 'Tin likes Colin better. Because he's a boy," she added, repeating something she'd heard Aunt Sophy say.

"I'm sorry, sir," Mary Rose said. "I was out with Lady

Chester. One of the housemaids was minding the children."

"It's all right." Frank smiled his reassurance at the girl. He thought of the shocked expression on Demetra's face when he told her the letters weren't in the nursery. In that instant he could have sworn she was genuinely surprised. And perhaps she had been. It was too much of a coincidence that St. George had been poking about the nursery on Tuesday afternoon and Tuesday night the letters were in his possession. If Demetra was wholly in her brother's confidence, there would have been no need for him to make the trip to Park Street. St. George must have found the letters on his own. Whatever else Demetra was capable of, she had not stooped to blackmail.

"Daddy?" Annie tugged at his sleeve. "Play faro with us?"

Frank grinned.

"Chester!" As Frank came down the stairs, his younger brother-in-law jumped up from a bench on the first-floor landing. "Thank goodness. We need to talk to you. It may be a matter of the greatest urgency."

"Don't be so theatrical, Lewis," advised Sophy, who had been sitting beside him. "I know you need to get to the House, Lord Chester, but this won't take long. And even though Lewis sounds like something out of a bad novel, he's actually telling the truth. It may be urgent."

Frank did himself great credit in the eyes of his young in-laws by not protesting or asking questions. Sophy led the way to the old sitting room, where she said the words Frank had been both hoping for and dreading.

"It's about Demetra. We think she's in trouble. Yesterday—"

"I say," Lewis cut in, "whose story is this?"

"Both of ours. Let me tell my part first then you can tell yours."

"But mine's the most—"

"I think," said Frank, "that we'd best start at the beginning.

271

Whose part comes first?"

"Mine," said Sophy firmly. "At the theatre last night." She fixed Frank with a level and refreshingly direct gaze. "Demetra was watching Quentin during the interval—she told me so—and we saw the contessa drop her fan and Quentin pick it up and return it to her. They exchanged a few words. And then Major York went up to the contessa and—well, you know the rest. Except that after you'd gone back to your box, Quentin forced Demetra to leave the theatre."

"*Forced* her to?"

"Now who's sounding theatrical?" Lewis muttered.

"I don't mean he held a pistol to her head. But he announced that she had the headache and insisted on taking her home at once. And he had hold of her wrist. Anyone who was paying the slightest attention"—Sophy glanced at her brother—"would have seen how it was. And it was odd, because normally Demetra wouldn't let Quentin push her around. And then later—oh, all right Lewis, you can talk now."

"Later," Lewis said, very much on his dignity, "after you'd gone home, I was in the corridor outside Demetra's room and I was sure I could smell the contessa's perfume." He hesitated, his cheeks reddening. "I'd seen her at the theatre, you know."

"Of course," Frank said kindly. "And she uses rather a lot of scent."

"Yes. And I was—well, curious—so I waited in an alcove and I saw Quentin come and knock at Demetra's door and Demetra and the contessa come out and the three of them leave together. Sir, do you think the contessa—"

"Bother the contessa," Sophy interrupted. "The thing is, Lord Chester, at the theatre Demetra was spying on Quentin—that's what it was, even if we were in a corridor full of people—and a few hours later she was helping him sneak the contessa out of the house. I don't know what happened in between, but I'd be willing to bet my dowry—if I could get my hands on it—that Quentin blackmailed her somehow."

Blackmail. Frank stared into his sister-in-law's young but far

272

from childish face. It fit with Colin's story. St. George had found the letters when he went to Park Street with Colin on Tuesday afternoon. And Tuesday night he had dragged Demetra away from the Haymarket and threatened to use the letters if she did not help him.

But would such a threat have any effect on Demetra? She wouldn't care about Helen. She didn't even like Helen. On the other hand, Frank's Demetra, who might not be a figment of his imagination after all, would not sit by and see another woman ruined.

"Lord Chester?" It was Lewis. "Do you think the contessa is all right?"

"The contessa? I'm sure she is. She can take care of herself."

"So can Demetra," said Sophy. "But now I think she could use some help."

"I think," said Frank, as if this was a singularly wonderful circumstance, which in a way it was, "that you may be right."

"Then what can we do?" Lewis asked. "Where do you think the contessa is? Should we—"

"No," said Frank firmly. "I don't know where the contessa is"—he did not add that he was under threat from their brother if he made any effort to find out—"and there's nothing you can do. Yet. Except," he added, as both Lewis and Sophy started to protest, "to be alert and let me know if you discover more."

"Should we say anything to Demetra?" Sophy asked.

"No," Frank decided after a moment. "Don't mention this to anyone." He needed time to think before he approached his wife. Demetra had not turned against him entirely, but much was still unexplained. Why had she taken the letters? Why hadn't she returned them? Did she think she couldn't do so without exposing her efforts to help her brother? And how far was she committed to rescuing St. George? Thank God for Ian York. At least St. George's plot with the contessa had been thwarted. Frank looked from Sophy's determined face to

273

Lewis's eager one. "All this is assuming that you trust me. Do you?"

"Of course," Sophy said, without hesitation. "You're Demetra's husband."

Frank smiled wryly.

"Demetra? Are you still asleep? I need to talk to you, it's urgent."

Edwina was standing by Demetra's bed, and even half awake, Demetra knew that her sister's temper was at the boiling point. According to Sophy, Edwina rarely had tantrums these days, but this morning seemed to be an exception. Demetra recalled that her sister had wanted to talk to her last night and that she'd put Edwina off till morning, but something else, something quite drastic, must have happened in the interim.

"What?" Demetra said.

"I've been offered for."

Demetra sat up, pushing the hair out of her eyes. "Well, it can't be the first time that's happened."

Edwina gave a short, mirthless laugh. "Mama seems to think it may be the last."

"Then Mama's a good deal less intelligent than I credited. Did she say so?"

"She said if I was fool enough to think I could count on another earl coming along, she washed her hands of me."

"The offer came from Lord Deavers?"

"He as much as said so last night at the theatre, that's why I wanted to talk to you when I got back. Then he called this morning, before Papa left for the House."

"And Papa gave his consent?"

"Provided I'm willing," Edwina said grimly. "He asked Deavers to dinner tonight. Somewhere between the soup and the pudding my future will be settled." Too restless to stand still, Edwina walked to her sister's dressing table. "If you knew the mortification of being told you're at your last prayers," she said, picking up Demetra's comb and hitting it against her other hand for emphasis, "of being ordered about as if—"

"I do know," Demetra said quietly. "Mama once made a very similar speech to me about marrying Tony."

Edwina looked at her sister in surprise, a sign that Sophy had been right. In the old days, Edwina's bursts of temper allowed thought for no one but herself. "What did you do?"

"Threw some things in a valise, slipped out of the house, turned up on Frank's doorstep, and said, *I'm yours if you want me.*" And being a gentleman, he couldn't refuse. If it had been left to Frank, Demetra wondered for the first time, would he have proposed?

Edwina looked thoughtful. "Do you think that would work?"

"Do I think what would work?"

"Turning up on his doorstep?"

"Whose doorstep."

"Whose do you think?"

"I don't think such a drastic remedy is called for. Sit down. Let's talk about this sensibly. I know how Mama puts you out of temper. She has precisely the same effect on me—you'd think we'd be used to her by now, wouldn't you?—but what she wants or doesn't want isn't the issue. What do you want?"

Edwina returned the comb to the dressing table and sat on the edge of her sister's bed. "I think you knew the answer to that before I did."

"I have yet to hear you say it."

"All right," said Edwina, part amused, part defiant, and part, Demetra realized with surprise, self-conscious. "I want to marry Elliot Marsden. I don't know much about love, but I think I'm in love with him. I think I've been in love with him since I saw him stand up to Tony more than a year ago, even though I didn't realize it until yesterday afternoon at Weyridge's."

"Good," said Demetra. "This makes things much easier."

"Does it?" Edwina, the epitome of self-assurance, looked

more than a little doubtful. "There's no indication that he's in love with me."

"He came to Weyridge's yesterday. He wouldn't have done that if he wasn't interested."

"Yes, but he didn't respond to my hints. And don't say I was being too subtle. Elliot Marsden may be a lot of things, but he's not stupid." Edwina pulled a loose thread from the blond ruffle at her wrist. "He may very well still be in love with Philippa Davenport. If so, I'm not sure I want to marry him, even if he'll have me."

If he really loves her, I'm not sure I want him back, Demetra had told Bianca last night. Had Frank still been in love with Helen the night Demetra turned up on his doorstep seven years ago? If Edwina married Elliot, would she, too, be doomed to a marriage haunted by her husband's old love?

"Tell me one thing, Edwina. If you knew you couldn't have Elliot, would you accept Deavers?"

"I don't know," Edwina said frankly. "What do you think I should do?"

"What I think is immaterial. The point is, you should have a chance to see Elliot before you have to make your decision about Lord Deavers."

"But I have to decide by tonight."

"Exactly. What time is it?"

"Past ten I should think."

"Ten!" How could she have slept so long? But then it had been past four when she and Quentin returned from Epsom. "No time to be lost then." Demetra pushed back the bedclothes and swung her legs to the floor. "Could you be a love and pick me out a dress? Something suitable for calling on a single gentleman."

"We're going to call on Elliot?"

"I know it would be better for you to go alone, but we must give some heed to the proprieties."

"He may be in his law chambers."

"Then we'll go there." Demetra was kneeling before a

mahogany and satinwood chest of drawers.

"No wonder Mama called you a terror. I don't think I've ever fully appreciated you, Demetra."

"Sisters rarely appreciate each other." Demetra tossed a chemise over her shoulder.

"I suppose not. Will this do?"

Edwina held up a dress of willow green Egyptian cloth, trimmed with plaitings of cream-colored satin.

"Fine. There's a ruff somewhere that goes with it. It's called a Catherine de Medici or something."

"Marguerite de Valois," said the knowledgable Edwina, laying the dress out on the bed. "This is the one Madame Dessart wanted to trim with pink satin rosettes, isn't it? What a good thing you stood up to her. I enjoyed that. It was rather like countermanding Mama. Demetra," Edwina exclaimed, suddenly dismayed, "You don't suppose I want to marry Elliot just to spite Mama, do you?"

"Of course not, any more than I married Frank for that reason," Demetra said, and then wished she hadn't mentioned her husband. Fortunately Edwina was preoccupied with her own dilemma. Demetra turned the conversation back to their immediate plans. By the time she had dressed and pinned her hair into a semblance of order, they had decided to begin with a visit to the breakfast parlor. No adventure, Demetra insisted, romantic or otherwise, should be embarked upon on an empty stomach. Besides, there was always the chance that Elliot would call, as he sometimes did, to leave papers for their father. If he had not put in an appearance by eleven, they would take more drastic action.

Fortunately, when the sisters reached the hall, they found Elliot accepting his hat from Stephen. He was on the point of departure, but Demetra insisted he come into the breakfast parlor for a cup of coffee.

Though he agreed with only a token demur, Demetra could understand her sister's frustration. It was difficult, if not impossible, to discern any difference between the way Elliot

277

looked at Edwina and the way he looked at Demetra or even at Stephen. Edwina certainly needed time alone with him. They would have to get him away from Buckleigh House.

"It's a beautiful day, isn't it?" Demetra, who had scarcely glanced out the window since she'd gotten up, smiled and handed Elliot a cup of coffee. "It would be a shame to spend it indoors. Edwina and I were thinking of taking my children for a drive in the country. Could we persuade you to come with us?"

Elliot appeared startled. "That's very kind of you, Lady Chester, but I'm afraid I must decline. I am a working man."

"Doesn't your work go faster if you leave it for a few hours? I always found that to be true when we lived in Durham, and I had enough to keep me busy twenty-four hours a day."

Elliot hesitated. Demetra could almost see him weighing the costs and benefits of the choice. To her disappointment, he did not look at Edwina as he debated the decision, but whatever his motivation, he at last agreed to make one of the party.

"Splendid." Demetra sipped her coffee. "I thought we might go to Cranford. We have a house there, you know. Well, actually it's our brother's house now, but Edwina and I played there as children and I'd like my children to see it."

An odd expression seemed to cross Elliot's face at the mention of Cranford, but it was quickly masked, so Demetra gave it a little thought. The grounds of Cranford would allow Edwina and Elliot to stroll together in privacy, and Demetra had her own reasons for wanting to visit Quentin's house. She thought it very likely that he had hidden the letters there.

Despite her brother's threats, Demetra had no intention of abandoning the letters. There were risks in searching for them, she acknowledged as she went up to the nursery to get Colin and Annie, but she had no illusions that Quentin would return the letters once Bianca was safely out of the country. He might make them public there and then or he might keep them as a permanent hold over Demetra, Frank, and Helen Berresford. Both alternatives were equally insupportable.

Quentin had left Bruton Street early this morning. Demetra wondered briefly how he planned to raise the exorbitant sum Bianca had demanded. She should be grateful he hadn't insisted she help him with that as well. Lady Buckleigh had also gone out and Sophy and Lewis were riding, so Demetra was able to order a carriage and assemble her party without hindrance.

The drive to Cranford proved awkward. Edwina's customary social facility had quite deserted her and even Elliot was unusually quiet. Demetra was not sure if this was due to Edwina or to the fact that he was not used to being in the presence of small children. She decided they were both best left to their own thoughts, and spent most of the journey answering questions from Colin and Annie.

It was difficult not to make comparisons with her even more awkward journey to and from Epsom only a few hours before. Edwina had prevented Demetra from thinking about that journey this morning. Now she wondered if they would really be able to keep Bianca's presence at Chester Priory a secret. Demetra had told the servants there that Bianca was a dear friend of hers who was leaving her husband and needed a place to remain for a few days, and that the greatest secrecy was required. She did not even wish Lord Chester to know, for if there was any scandal he must not be involved. She had introduced Quentin as Bianca's solicitor, so he would have an excuse to return to the Priory when he brought Bianca the money. Provided all went smoothly—which, considering the way things had gone thus far, was a dubious proposition at best—the story should answer.

Demetra was relieved when they finally reached Cranford and she could abandon thought for action. She had not seen the house for seven years, but it was much as she remembered: the rectangular red brick facade, the evenly spaced windows, the white pillars flanking the front door. She rang for admittance.

"The Luscombes must be out," Edwina said, when several

minutes had passed with no response. "It's probably market day or something. Is the door open?"

It was, and there was no reason for them not to enter. They were, after all, family (two hours ago Demetra would have vehemently denied that she could ever be grateful for her relationship to Quentin). The Luscombes, the couple who looked after Cranford, did indeed appear to be out, which suited Demetra very well.

"I want to show Colin and Annie the house," she said, "but there's no need for Mr. Marsden to be bored by my childhood reminiscences."

"Would you care to walk in the garden, Elliot?" Edwina asked.

Elliot smiled politely. "That would be delightful, Lady Edwina."

Demetra watched them leave with a touch of anxiety. But she had done all she could. The matter was now in Edwina's hands.

For the whole of the interminable drive from Bruton Street and even before they left London, Edwina had pondered the problem of getting Elliot Marsden to declare his feelings for her. But she had not arrived at any clear plan of action. She had carefully chosen a Marie Stuart bonnet of black velvet lined with pale lilac silk, and she knew she was in her best looks. But then, she was very seldom not in her best looks, and beauty was not what it took to catch Elliot's interest. Only look at his pursuit of Philippa Davenport last year.

Thinking of Philippa reminded Edwina of another difficulty. Cranford was an unfortunate setting for this scene, for it was here that Philippa had refused Elliot's offer of marriage.

Edwina stole a glance at Elliot as they descended the terrace steps. She wondered if he was remembering that earlier visit and, if so, how painful a memory it was. As usual, his expression told her nothing at all.

They wandered about the grounds for some minutes, exchanging desultory commonplaces. At last Edwina threw caution to the wind and plunged ahead.

"Do you think I would make a good countess?"

"I think there is very little you could not do well if you put your mind to it, Lady Edwina," Elliot returned politely.

Edwina regarded him with exasperation. "It's no wonder you're such a success in politics. You know how to answer a question without saying anything at all."

"Thank you, Lady Edwina."

"And I wish you would not call me Lady Edwina when we are private. I've been calling you Elliot for months."

"So I've noticed."

They took two more steps without speaking. "I wasn't talking in generalities, you know," Edwina said. "About being a countess. Lord Deavers has asked me to marry him."

"My felicitations." Elliot didn't miss a beat.

"They aren't in order yet. I haven't given him an answer."

"I see."

Edwina stopped and looked up at him. "Do you?" she demanded.

Elliot released her arm and turned to face her. They had walked down a gentle slope and were standing on the edge of some shrubbery. There was a painted iron bench conveniently near. "I think," he said, "that we had best sit down."

"I'm quite comfortable as I am, thank you," Edwina replied tartly.

"As you wish." Elliot walked to the bench and stood with his arms resting on its back, his hands clasped together. "You must know that I cannot afford to support a wife."

"I thought," Edwina retorted, "that we were talking about my matrimonial future, not yours."

He shot her a brief, mocking smile. "Unfair, my girl. If you expect me to understand your hints, you must return the favor and understand mine."

"I wasn't asking if you could support a wife. I was asking if

281

you wanted one."

The pause before he answered seemed interminable. "Edwina, you don't need me to tell you that you're a beautiful woman."

"No," she said coolly. "I don't."

"A man would have to be blind or a fool not to find you desirable. I don't think of myself as either."

Edwina's hands clenched on the soft cashmere folds of her pelisse. "And is that all?"

"Isn't it enough of an admission for one afternoon?"

"For God's sake, Elliot, it hasn't been easy for me to say any of this. You owe me an answer. *Is that all?*"

Elliot was looking at the shrubbery. "No," he said shortly. "It isn't."

It was not the most romantic of declarations, but Edwina felt a dizzying rush of joy. "Well then?" she demanded.

"I told you, I can't afford to support a wife."

"Elliot, this is no time to be practical. Aren't you even going to kiss me?"

He looked at her and smiled, but remained where he was standing. "I don't think that would be wise."

"Why not?"

"Because I might lose my head. I might even ask you to marry me."

"That's the general idea."

"Edwina, your father is an earl."

"And yours was a marquis." Edwina slipped onto the bench and leaned toward him, at her most beguiling.

"Who never publicly acknowledged me and who left me with no more than a modest competence."

Edwina drew back. "Are you still in love with her?" she demanded.

"Am I still in love with whom?"

"Philippa Davenport, of course. Do you mean there've been others since?"

"No. To both questions."

"Are you sure?"

Elliot looked down at the lovely face framed by the black velvet bonnet. Edwina's blue eyes had darkened to indigo. "I won't deny that Philippa meant a great deal to me. She was the first woman I—"

"The first woman you loved?"

"Yes." Elliot sounded almost surprised, "I suppose she was. In that sense of the word. She was the first woman I asked to marry me. But we never would have suited. She's much happier with Ashton."

"The question," said Edwina, "is would you be happier with me?"

"You must know that I was never indifferent to you, even before Philippa refused me. Though I didn't bargain on letting things go this far. You're a devilish inconvenient woman for me to love, Edwina Thane. But if you doubt my feeling for you—"

"No!" Edwina was afraid she would lose him altogether. "But you didn't have a qualm about disparity of fortune when you proposed to Philippa, yet when it comes to marrying me—"

"The problem isn't disparity of fortune. It's the prospect of no fortune at all. Philippa's family wouldn't have cut us off without a shilling."

"And you think mine would?"

"What do you think?"

Edwina lifted her chin. "I always get my own way. In the end."

"That's nonsense." Elliot's voice was suddenly rough. "Your father feels some responsibility toward me for his late brother-in-law's sake. He may even like me. But he doesn't see me as a candidate for his daughter's hand and you know it. And as for your mother—"

"If you really loved me," Edwina said with conviction, "none of that would matter."

"Meaning if I really loved you I wouldn't care for your

comfort? You wouldn't like being poor any more than I would. Probably less."

"How on earth can you know that?"

"I know you better than you think, my sweet."

Edwina brightened at the endearment, but said, "You can't expect me to wait for you indefinitely."

"I'm not asking you to."

"Then you're telling me to *accept* Deavers?"

"I can't make your decision for you."

"You are the most odious man!" Edwina rose, intending to return to the house, but she made one last attempt. "Frank didn't worry about such things when he married Demetra."

"And seven years later, would you call them happy?" Elliot inquired.

Edwina was unable to answer.

Annie stared around the unfamilar entrance hall. "Our house?" she inquired. In the past fortnight, she had been shown two strange houses which suddenly belonged to her parents.

Demetra shook her head. "No, darling. It belongs to Uncle Quentin."

"Oh." Annie's expression indicated her opinion of Uncle Quentin.

"But I spent a lot of time here when I was young," Demetra said quickly. "And so did Aunt Edwina and Aunt Sophy and Uncle Lewis. Come, I'll show you."

Fortunately Cranford was not a large house. Demetra and the children wandered through the study and the library, finding plenty of opportunity to look in and underneath and on top of things. Annie decided the house was quite interesting, even if it did belong to Uncle Quentin. While she was engrossed with the carved lions by the library fireplace, Colin tugged at his mother's sleeve. "What are we looking for, Mummy?"

Demetra turned from the map cabinet she had been examining and met her son's solemn gaze. "Papers. Don't talk about it, but if you see anything, show me."

Colin nodded. Demetra found it was much easier to search with his help. They moved on to the drawing room—which now housed a billiard table, how like Quentin—and the dining room, but though Colin produced several papers for his mother's inspection, they met with no success.

Undaunted, Demetra led the way upstairs to the bedrooms. They started with a room at the front of the house which was reserved for guests. The chests of drawers, dressing table, and wardrobe offered numerous places to search and Demetra and Colin fell to with enthusiasm.

But Annie was growing tired of this game. The novelty had worn off, and the house seemed no different from the bewildering number of other houses she had been in recently. She wandered back into the corridor. There were several other doors and one of them, she noticed, was ajar. Annie pushed it open and found herself looking into another bedroom. A woman was standing by the window. A pretty woman, with soft, pale curls, dressed in something white and frilly.

Delighted to have found a diversion, Annie ran forward, then stopped in the middle of the room and stood looking up at the stranger. "What's your name?" she demanded.

Chapter 19

The young woman had been standing near the windows, watching the man and woman who were strolling in the garden at the back of the house. Now she turned startled eyes on the small girl who stood before her.

"What's your name?" the small girl repeated.

The young woman smiled and crouched down so their eyes were on a level. "Anna. They call me Annina."

The girl considered this. "That's my name." She looked at the woman a moment longer, then turned and ran out of the room.

The young woman stood up. She had been disarmed by the child, but she could hear the voice of a strange woman. It seemed to come from the bedroom down the hall. She moved swiftly to the window and looked down. No, the woman in the black bonnet was still there. So this was someone else. She moved toward the door, then realized it had no lock. There did not seem to be any place to hide, and the other woman was now in the corridor. Annina clenched her hands, shut her eyes, and murmured a hasty prayer to Our Lady.

It was in this attitude that Demetra found her. She hastened to reassure the trembling woman. "I'm so sorry. We didn't mean to frighten you, but Luscombe isn't about so there was no one to announce us. We didn't realize there was anyone else in the house."

Annina opened her eyes. The woman in the doorway—she was not so very much older than herself—seemed friendly. She had a nose that turned up and freckles on her face and hair of a color Annina had not seen before. It shone like copper, and it fell around her face in a mass of ringlets. The small girl was hanging on her skirt and a serious-faced young boy stood on her other side as though ready to take to his fists in her defense. Annina smiled at the notion that she could be considered a threat to anyone. "Please," she said, forming the unfamiliar words with care, "I do not know who it is that comes. I think perhaps you are—" She could not find the word. "*Un ladro*," she whispered.

Demetra did not understand the word, but the intent was clear. Thieves indeed. No wonder the young woman looked as though she would jump out of her skin. "I assure you, we weren't trespassing," she said. "I used to play here when I was young. I'm Demetra Hawksley, Lord St. George's sister. There's another sister outside, Lady Edwina." She felt a tug at her skirt. "My daughter Annie. And my son Colin."

There was another tug. Her daughter pointed. "Annie too."

The young woman relaxed. "Not Annie. Annina. It is very much the same."

Colin looked up at his mother. "May I see the other rooms?"

Demetra nodded. Colin might as well continue the search. She could hardly do so herself under the eyes of—what was she? Quentin's latest mistress? Quentin had been back in England less than a month. She would not have expected him to find and install one at Cranford so quickly. But this woman was clearly foreign, so perhaps he had brought her with him. She was very much Quentin's type—fair-skinned, small-boned, with shining fair hair framing a delicate face. No wonder he was reluctant to come to the point with Beatrix Thornton.

287

Annina was delighted with her visitor. Quentin did not come often and she had been lonely here at Cranford. Besides, she had been longing to meet Quentin's family, and now here were two of his sisters come to pay a call. Perhaps Quentin had sent them? No, for then they would have known of her presence. She wondered if he would be angry that she talked to them. He was so very, very insistent that she talk to no one at all. But she could not say, I cannot talk with you, go away. So she invited Mrs. Hawksley to come downstairs and take some tea, and only when she reached the bottom of the stairs did she remember that Mrs. Luscombe was away for the afternoon too.

"Never mind," Demetra said. "I've not forgotten how to brew tea, and I'm sure I can manage." With Annie in her arms, she led Annina into the kitchen.

Demetra was puzzled by the woman who called herself Annina. She had been frightened by the arrival of visitors, yet she seemed reassured by the fact that the visitors were members of her lover's family. That was not the behavior expected of a *fille de joie*. But that was just it, Annina did not seem to be one of her brother's usual ladybirds. Quentin appeared to have seduced a girl of good family.

Demetra set about making tea while Annina sat nearby and Annie sat on her lap, playing with her soft blond curls. But if Demetra hoped the domestic setting would be productive of confidences, she was disappointed. Annina said that she came from a small town in the province of Viterbo, just north of Rome. She was vague about her acquaintance with Quentin and would say nothing at all about their present relationship, save that he came to Cranford infrequently. It was too much to hope that Quentin had told her anything about the Contessa Montalto or about Helen Berresford's letters.

They had tea in the dining room, which overlooked the rear garden. Colin came running downstairs to join them, but Edwina and Elliot were still outside, intent, it seemed, on some private quarrel. Then Elliot walked off in the direction of the

288

stables and Edwina came toward the house with a look of mingled anger and dismay on her lovely face.

"I think it's time we were going," she said as she walked into the dining room.

Annie pointed to her new friend with the yellow hair. "'Nina."

Only then did Edwina become aware of Annina's presence. She saw a young woman of fragile beauty who looked almost exactly like Maria Doddington, the opera dancer Quentin had been keeping the year before. Seeing the terms that Demetra had established between them, Edwina schooled her features and allowed herself to be presented.

Annina was delighted by the acquaintance. "Lady Edwina," she said, as though the name gave her pleasure, "would you be so kind as to take a cup of tea?"

Frank folded his arms and shifted his position on the hard bench, forcing his attention back to the man who was speaking. It was Lieutenant Hownam's second day in the witness-box. The lieutenant had joined the Queen's suite in 1815 and accompanied her on her journey to the East. Today he had been examined by both Queen's and King's counsel and then subjected to further interrogation by the peers. The questions ranged back and forth over time, covering the Queen's behavior from Como to Jerusalem.

Frank had heard it all before. Yes, the *dami dimi* was danced aboard the polacre, but no, it was not indecent, *any more than in the Spanish bolero, or the Negro dance.* Yes, Her Highness took part in theatricals at the Villa d'Este, but no, he could not recall who played Columbine to Bergami's Harlequin. The lieutenant thought Her Highness had performed the part of an automaton, *a woman that could wind up anything.* (The remark caused laughter throughout the House, and even Frank smiled.) Yes, Bergami may have slept in the same tent as the Princess aboard the polacre, but no, Hownam did not find it at all improper. For Her Highness's safety it was necessary that someone should sleep in the tent with her. The lieutenant was pressed repeatedly on this point. The Earl of Limerick wanted to know how Hownam would feel if Mrs. Hownam were to sleep in a tent with a male person. The lieutenant doggedly refused to answer. *Every man*, he said, *looks at his wife without making any comparison or exception.*

Every man, Frank thought wryly, thinks his own wife is different. Or hopes she is. The House adjourned in considerable noise and confusion. The shorthand writer complained that he had been unable to hear what was being said. When Frank walked out the door at four o'clock, his head was throbbing. He could bear to talk to no one. He dismissed his carriage and began the long walk home, hoping the exercise and fresh air would diminish both his headache and his temper. So what did it matter if the Queen entertained farmer's daughters or played at blindman's buff or performed upon a private stage? Demetra had done as much, and he never had cause to accuse her of infidelity. At least, not until they came to London.

He shook his head to rid himself of these thoughts and turned down Great George Street. He would cut through St. James's Park and then Green Park and avoid his colleagues, who were now making for their clubs to drink and argue and talk in wearying detail about what had and had not been said that day.

By the time he reached Park Street the throbbing in his head was almost gone. The new footman let him in (Robbins was still confined to his room) and informed him in hushed tones that he had a visitor—a lady—waiting for him in the parlor. Frank stifled a groan. It had to be Helen.

She had been pacing back and forth in front of the fireplace and she looked up, startled, at his entrance. "I've done it, Frank." She clapped her hands over her lips. "Oh, God. You've got to help me."

This was more than Helen's usual hysteria. Had she given up

hope that he would recover her letters? Had she told her husband? "Done what, Helen?"

She stared at him in surprise. "Why, left Arthur, of course. What else could I do? What other choice did I have?"

A muscle twitched in her cheek, and he saw that she was shivering. "You'd better sit down."

"I don't want to sit down. It's no use trying to calm me, Frank, I'm angry and I don't want to be calm." She began to pace about the room. "It's not the letters. Not just the letters, though they're bad enough, and if he doesn't decide to divorce me he'll make my life a living hell, though it hardly seems it could get any worse, but I'm sure Arthur will contrive something." She caught her breath and began again. "I think you know what kind of husband Arthur has been. Even on our wedding journey he was looking at other women, though I'm sure it was no more than looking, for I know he spent all his nights with me. But we hadn't been back in London six months before I was hearing the most horrid sort of talk, and then he began a perfectly reckless flirtation with Amelia Langford and even I could hardly ignore it. It wouldn't have been so bad if he'd taken an actress or an opera dancer for his mistress, or even one of the servants, though I would have drawn the line at Minot, that sort of thing is so unsettling and I couldn't have trusted her with my hair, but he insisted on forming liaisons with women who were supposed to be my friends. . . ."

"Helen—"

She stopped her pacing and sat on the edge of a chair, jumped up, then sat down again. "Even you must remember Georgina Nelliston. It started the year before you left London and went on for the longest time and of course everyone talked about it. If Georgina hadn't made such a dreadful scene at Warwick House when Arthur took her stepdaughter down to supper, he'd be in her bed still, though I've always thought Georgina really wanted an excuse to break it off. Arthur was dreadfully upset and for weeks he had the most beastly temper, which is quite unfair because whoever's fault it was, it certainly wasn't mine."

She stopped. Tears welled in her eyes, enlarging them and making their blue depths luminous. "Arthur always blames me when things don't go his way. Last night he said it was my fault that the Contessa Montalto had run off. He stormed into my room and accused me of not looking after the woman—the woman he was trying to make his mistress." A tear fell and with an impatient gesture she brushed it away. "Don't tell me to go back, Frank. I can't live with him any longer."

Frank sat down suddenly, trying to conceal his shock. Berresford was a vain, insensitive, and stupid man who seldom thought beyond his own pleasure, but Helen was a compliant woman with great respect for social forms. It had never occurred to Frank that she could be driven to leave her husband. "Do you want to go to Bewdley?" he said, playing for time. "Or to your parents?"

"Of course I don't want to go to my parents. My father doesn't understand these things and my mother will be furious and there's no one to talk to except you and Demetra and you aren't there anymore. And not Bewdley. It's Arthur's house, and that's where he'll expect to find me. I tell you, Frank, I have to get away, completely away. I can't think what I'm to do when I'm near him."

"You can't stay here," he began, alarmed by the direction she was taking.

"Well, of course I can't stay here. I may be leaving my husband, but I have no intention of being called an abandoned woman. I thought maybe a hotel, or an inn somewhere, quiet and out of the way. You must know."

He shook his head. "Friends."

"Do be sensible, Frank. Do you want the story all over London by morning? I have no friends who aren't Arthur's friends as well."

"I'll have to think. . . . When do you want to go? Tomorrow?"

"Frank, haven't you been listening to me at all? I've already

292

gone. I sent Minot off to visit her sister in Gravesend. I know Gravesend is a strange place for a French maid, but her real name is Mabel, though she's quite clever enough to have come from Paris. I packed a small bag, I took what money I could find, and I came here so you could tell me where I am to sleep tonight." Her voice began to rise. She fumbled with her reticule and gloves and stood up. "If you can't help me, Frank, I'll just have to fend for myself. I'll go to a hotel for tonight, and tomorrow I'll take the stage to—to anywhere."

By this time Frank was on his feet as well. "It's out of the question. Respectable women don't go to hotels alone. Arthur might tolerate an episode of adultery, but he would never forgive you that."

She cried out as though she had been struck.

"I'm sorry, Helen, but that's what it's called. It's a legal term. In ordinary language, it's called love, as in your case, or lust and vanity, as in your husband's. I pray that you work something out with Berresford so you don't have to put it to the legal test. I've heard enough about adultery these past weeks to sicken my mind and soul."

"You think me a fool, don't you?" Two spots of color had come into her normally pale face. "I don't care, I won't do what you say. All my life I've done what other people say, and it's *my* soul that's been sickened. So don't tell me to go back to Arthur." She said nothing more. There was a pathetic dignity in her manner and a look of bleak determination in her eyes.

Frank was startled by her newfound assertiveness. "All right, Helen." His voice was now brisk and matter-of-fact. "Get your things. I'm taking you down to Epsom."

"Epsom?"

"My uncle left me a house near there. Not too large, no close neighbors, three or four servants to look after things, a gardener, and a stable boy. It will be quiet, and you'll be able to think things over." He picked up her pelisse and held it for her. "Does Arthur know you've gone?"

"I left him a note. He'll get it when he comes home. If he

293

comes home." Her voice was bitter.

"What did you tell him?"

"That his behavior last night was inexcusable and I was going away."

"Did you say where you were going?"

"No. And I certainly didn't say that I was coming to you. Give me credit for some common sense, Frank."

He smiled down at her in relief. "Oh, I do, Nell." How like Helen not to make her intentions clear. Berresford would understand a quarrel and a temporary separation. He would not read her note as a complete break. There was time then to work something out. Time to talk to Demetra, time to learn how to retrieve the letters from St. George. As for Helen, a day or two at Chester Priory and the isolation and absence of her husband might induce her to think about a reconciliation.

But by the time they drew up at Chester Priory some two hours later, he knew this hope was vain. In a strange reversal of their customary roles, Frank persisted in urging caution. Helen, carried on a floodtide of fury, refused to think about reputation and duty and what might happen tomorrow. Frank was exasperated by her unwillingness to look at consequences. A woman thrown off by her husband would be shunned. Helen did not have the resources to cope with social ostracism, and she had no money of her own. But Helen would consider none of this. Even appeals to the fate of her children brought only a momentary wavering in her resolution. She would never abide under the same roof with Arthur Berresford again.

Frank was relieved when the carriage at last pulled up at Chester Priory. It was eight o'clock and already dark, but there were lights in the windows. Too many lights for the few servants they kept. Puzzled, Frank jumped down from the carriage and ran up the front steps. What kind of revels were they keeping in his absence?

Whatever his servants were about, it was sufficiently absorbing for them to keep him cooling his heels on the doorstep. Frank's temper rose. When the door was opened at last, the dismay on the face of Morton, the elderly man who had served his uncle for thirty or more years, told Frank that his surmises were correct.

"Lord Chester," Morton said in a quavering voice.

"Lord Chester," Frank agreed. "Are you going to admit me into my own house? What the devil is going on?"

Morton bowed and flung the door wide. "We didn't expect you, sir. Pray come in. Have you come for the night?"

"Yes. I mean no. I return to London tonight, but I've brought a guest who will be staying for a day or two." He lowered his voice. "See here, Morton, this is a matter of some delicacy. The lady has left her—her relations, and does not want to be found. Her presence is to be kept quite secret. By everyone."

Morton stared at his new master as though he had not properly heard him. "Another one?"

"Another what?"

"Frank?" Helen's voice came from the carriage window. "Frank, it's cold, am I to be kept waiting?"

The problem of his servants' odd behavior would have to wait. Frank returned to the carriage and handed Helen down, then led her into the square hall of Chester Priory. "Morton," he said, "this is Mrs. Cameron. She is to be treated with every consideration. Young Betty can attend to her. Make up the best chamber and see that there's a proper fire."

"But—" the old man began.

"We'll require some dinner as soon as possible. Something cold will do. And bring me a bottle of claret."

Morton made a move toward the stairs, but Frank forestalled him. "We'll see ourselves up. Tell them in the kitchen."

Morton hesitated, then shrugged helplessly, and moved toward the servants quarters. Frank turned to offer Helen his arm, but she stiffened and drew away. "Frank, how could you! I will not stay under the same roof as that woman!"

Stunned, Frank followed the direction of his gaze. The Contessa Montalto—the quondam Contessa Montalto—stood on the landing, regarding them with the eyes of a householder who has just experienced an unwarranted intrusion.

Bianca was the first to recover. Taking in the situation at a glance, she ran downstairs and seized Helen's hands. "*Povera donna!* You have left your husband, is it not so? Bah, he is a man of the most sublime stupidity. Only a woman with the temper of an angel could have put up with him for these many years. How you must have suffered!"

Helen could not believe this outpouring of sympathy from a woman she had at once envied, despised, and feared. She wanted to slap her face. She wanted to run away. She had an overwhelming impulse to put her head on that capacious bosom and be comforted. She did none of these. Pulling her hands away and covering her face, she burst into tears.

The contessa put an arm around her. "Come, we will go into the dining room. You have had a long journey, you are tired, you must rest. I will give you a glass of wine and you will feel better. We will have some dinner together, and then, if you like, we can talk."

Neither woman had paid the slightest attention to Frank. He was left quite speechless by the encounter, but as the two women moved off toward the dining room, he muttered a soldier's oath of surpassing vulgarity. Then he strode after them. By God, it was *his* house.

When he reached the dining room, Helen was sitting in a chair that had been pulled away from the table and the contessa was bathing her eyes and forehead with a dampened napkin. The table, Frank noted, had been set for two, but this oddity was forgotten in his urgent need for information.

"Contessa—" he began, "Madame—what the devil am I to call you?"

She looked up at him, her enormous dark eyes alight with amusement. "Falconetti. Signora or Madame, as you prefer. It is my real name." She put down the napkin and poured a glass of wine, which she offered to the unresisting Helen.

"And might I be allowed to ask, Madame Falconetti," he said

with elaborate courtesy—he was keeping tight rein on his temper—"just what you are doing in my house?"

She poured a second glass of wine and offered it to him. Frank took it and swallowed half its contents without thinking. "Well?"

She had now poured a glass for herself. "But of course you wish to know," she said in a tone that might be used to appease an angry child. "I was brought here last night by Lady Chester. And by her brother, the Viscount St. George," she added hastily, noting the thunderous expression on Frank's face. "I do not think Lady Chester wished it, but she"—here Bianca glanced at Helen—"she felt obliged to do as he wished. St. George, you see, owes me some money, and I must wait for it before I leave England. And here it is quiet and I will inconvenience nobody." She shrugged. "Nobody but you and Lady Berresford. I am very sorry."

St. George. He might have known. If St. George returned and saw Helen— But St. George already had the letters, and Helen could scarcely be further damaged by being seen at Chester Priory. Frank swallowed the last of his wine. When the House rose tomorrow he would return to Epsom. Perhaps by then Helen would be willing to go back to her husband. And if she was not, he would make some other arrangements.

In the meantime, what was he to do with this Madame Falconetti, who had extorted money from Helen and was now offering her comfort? And what was he to do with Helen? Her tears had ceased, but she was staring at the other woman in utter bewilderment. Frank poured himself a second glass of wine. Perhaps after another bottle and some dinner he would be able to cope with the two of them.

"Bianca," said a voice from the doorway, "when the devil are we going to dine?"

Helen gave a small shriek of dismay. "Frank," she said in an accusing voice, "you told me we would be alone."

"Oh, Lord," said Ian York, meeting Frank's eyes. "Did you come here to— I say, I am sorry, I had no idea . . ."

Ian's moment of confusion did not last long. He walked to the table and poured a glass of wine, then raised the bottle and studied it judiciously. "We'd best have another one. You're both staying for dinner, aren't you?"

Frank stared at him in outrage. "I'm staying. You aren't."

"But I say, I haven't dined." Ian was genuinely aggrieved.

"Go back to the inn, Ian," Bianca said. "They will take care of you there. They can—what is it you say here?—do you a chop. Now leave, leave." She made a shooing motion with her hands. "We have woman talk here and you will be in the way."

"What about Hawksley?"

"I can't send him away. It is his house. Go now, you can come tomorrow, but do not come too early."

Ian would have protested again, but the look in her eyes told him it was useless. With a bow to Helen and a sketchy salute to Frank, he turned on his heels and left the room.

Frank folded his arms. "Now, Madame Falconetti."

"Yes, yes, I am sorry, but I had forgotten he was here."

If she had forgotten, Madame Falconetti was indeed a remarkable woman. She was not wearing her customary jewels and her hair had been disarranged and hastily repinned. York, too, had shown signs of a hasty toilet. Frank had no doubt about how they had been spending the time before his arrival.

"He came to Bruton Street last night and watched the house," Bianca went on. "He followed me down here, then today he came to call. I was very angry because of what he had done and I would not see him, but—" She made a gesture of helplessness. "It is tedious here and there is no one to talk to. What would you have me do? How else am I to spend the afternoon?"

Frank burst into laughter.

Helen looked from him to Bianca. "You mean— Oh, I see. Well, I think it's a very good thing I came, Madame Falconetti. I know you don't require a chaperone, but the presence of another woman— Frank, I really think I would like another glass of wine."

At this moment Morton came into the room cradling a bottle in his arms. "The claret, m'lord. But it needs decanting."

"See to it. And serve dinner as soon as you may. We're sharp-set."

The old man looked around. "There will be three for dinner?"

"Yes. No. Lay places for four."

Helen looked up. "Frank, no!"

"Why not? He already knows we're here. And the presence of another woman— We'll keep the conversation general, and I'll take him away with me when I leave." He flung open the door and strode into the hall. He could hear Helen begin to laugh.

Ian, cloaked and hatted, was just coming down the stairs. "I'm leaving," he said when he saw Frank looking up at him.

"I can't send a guest away hungry, York. Dine with us first. No questions, either side." Frank grinned. "I'm not sure I'll get through dinner otherwise."

"I do wish you hadn't asked Mr. Marsden to dine with us again, Horace." Lady Buckleigh inspected herself once more in the glass. "You'd think he was one of the family."

"So he is," Lord Buckleigh reminded her.

Lady Buckleigh looked pained. She had summoned her husband to her dressing room because she had something particular to say to him and she did not like this reference to her late brother-in-law's irregular behavior. "Particularly when we have other guests."

"We have some things to discuss later," Lord Buckleigh said. "And I wanted at least one intelligent man to talk with."

"Deavers dines with us tonight."

"Exactly."

Lady Buckleigh suppressed the retort that rose to her lips. It was never wise to stray from the point at hand. "He's going to make Edwina an offer."

"So he told me. Is Edwina going to accept him?"

"Edwina is going to be sensible. At least I pray she is going to be sensible. The girl can't stay unwed indefinitely. She attracts more than her share of admiration, but a few more years and all she'll attract is pitying looks. That's why I wish you hadn't invited Marsden."

"Marsden? What's Marsden to do with this?" Lord Buckleigh stared at his wife. "You don't mean— Rot. He would never dream of looking so high."

"Nonetheless, he distracts her." Lady Buckleigh rose and prepared to leave the room. "I expect your support in this, Horace."

Lord Buckleigh shrugged and returned to his room. His wife proceeded to the drawing room.

Except for Quentin, all of the children were present, as well as the two guests. Lady Buckleigh sat down at some distance from the others and considered her second daughter. What Horace thought of his future son-in-law was of little moment. Marriage was a woman's business. Unfortunately, Edwina was showing a similar lack of enthusiasm for Lord Deavers. It was hard to see why. He had regular features, dark blue eyes, and a good head of silky light-brown hair. He was faultlessly dressed and would one day be a marquis. He was almost as good a catch as Tony, who had already inherited his father's title, and if Deavers was not as devastatingly handsome, his temper was much sweeter.

Edwina's objection could not then be to his person. It must be marriage in general that gave her pause. Lady Buckleigh wondered if her daughter was afraid of its physical side. Perhaps she should have a talk with her. Or better, ask Demetra to do so. After all, it was Demetra's indecent enthusiasm for that aspect of the married state that had led to her impulsive elopement.

There was, of course, another explanation, which Lady Buckleigh forced herself to consider. Edwina had shown some interest in Elliot Marsden's company, but it was likely that she did so because she knew it annoyed her mother. Unlike Demetra, Edwina had a healthy respect for social position and the Thane name, and an alliance with the bastard son of Lady Buckleigh's late brother-in-law would do little for either.

Edwina was quite aware of her mother's expectations, but at the moment these were of less concern to her than the unsatisfactory nature of her earlier interview with Elliot. She knew now that she had attached him, but this gratifying intelligence was negated by the ungratifying knowledge that he valued his career more than he desired her person. She had not been pleased by her father's dinner invitation to Elliot, and since he entered the drawing room, she had carefully avoided his eye. Unfortunately, he also seemed to be avoiding hers. After a polite and distant greeting, he had gone to sit by Sophy and Lewis. They were talking now with something approaching enthusiasm and were the only people in the room who did not seem out of sorts. Roused to anger, Edwina turned to Lord Deavers and set herself to be charming. This byplay was not lost on Demetra, who had known from the time they left Cranford that matters between her sister and Elliot had not been resolved.

"Ah, good evening, good evening." Lord Buckleigh entered the room, bringing a welcome aura of vigor and purpose. "Deavers. Marsden, glad you could come. Where's St. George?"

"I'm sure he'll be with us shortly," Lady Buckleigh said. "He knows we dine at eight." She was annoyed with her eldest son, for she valued punctuality, but she could not rid herself of the habit of excusing his actions.

Lord Buckleigh drew out his watch. "It's near that now."

"Ring the bell, Lewis," Lady Buckleigh said. There was an uncomfortable silence, broken by Manningtree's entrance. "Put dinner back by a quarter hour," she told him. "We're waiting for St. George."

The butler nodded and withdrew. Lord Buckleigh made an inarticulate sound.

"I detest having people join the table late, Horace. But we'll not wait beyond that time."

Conversation resumed after a fashion, but it was with some relief that the occupants of the drawing room greeted the errant St. George when he arrived some ten minutes later. He seemed quite pleased with himself and clearly had a matter of import to communicate. A bit of vicious gossip, thought Edwina. A rousing good story, thought Lewis. Something about Brougham or the Queen, thought his father.

Quentin did not apologize for his tardiness. He nodded to Deavers, ignored Marsden, and made a perfunctory bow to his mother. Then he took up a stand in front of the fireplace and waited until he had everyone's attention. "Before we go down, I have some news," he said. "It will hardly come as a surprise, but I trust it will be welcome. I've just been with the Thorntons. Beatrix and I are betrothed."

Lady Buckleigh uttered a profound sigh and visibly relaxed. Lord Buckleigh gave an approving nod.

"Oh, I say, Quentin—" Lewis stopped, not at all sure how he felt about this change in his brother's status.

"It's perfectly splendid," Sophy said. Marriage, she was sure, could do nothing but improve her eldest brother.

"How very enterprising of you, Quentin," Demetra said. So that was how her brother was raising the money to pay off Madame Falconetti.

Quentin strolled toward Edwina. "No congratulations, Eddy?"

"Oh, I do congratulate you. It took a lot of courage."

"Perhaps it will give you some of the same." He glanced at Deavers, who colored slightly and looked away.

"I have my own sort of courage, Quen." Edwina glanced at Elliot, who said nothing at all.

Manningtree entered and announced dinner. As the company rose to go downstairs, talking with more animation than they had since they arrived in the drawing room, Quentin drew Lord Buckleigh aside. "I don't like to bring up matters of business in the evening, Father, but there *is* going to be a change in my circumstances. Perhaps after dinner we can talk."

Chapter 20

Though the rest of her life remained in chaos, Demetra's sleep pattern had returned to normal. She woke at her customary early hour, paid a visit to the nursery, then descended to the breakfast parlor in search of coffee. Noting the sole occupant of this apartment, she hesitated on the threshold.

"It's all right," said Quentin, not looking up from the paper, "I'm about to leave. You can breakfast in peace."

"Suit yourself." Demetra had been considering retreat but now that he had seen her she was determined to hold her ground.

"I am. I have a full day ahead of me. You'll be pleased to know that your unwelcome guest will be gone from Chester Priory by this afternoon."

"Papa gave you the money that quickly?" Demetra wasn't in the habit of eating a large breakfast but she filled her plate with care, just to show Quentin she wasn't intimidated.

"Oh, yes. He was remarkably decent about it. Said he was happy to settle up my debts now that I'd taken a step toward settling down. Edwina was a tremendous help by being fool enough to refuse Deavers. Not that Father thinks much of

304

Deavers, but having Mother tell him Edwina has no sense of family duty didn't hurt my case any."

"Efficient, Quen. But wasn't it rather drastic to sacrifice yourself on the matrimonial altar?"

"I'd have married someone sooner or later. Beatrix isn't a bad choice."

"Rather strong-willed for you, I'd have thought." Demetra recalled the fragile young woman she'd met at Cranford. "She'll be just like Mama in a few years," she added, and had the satisfaction of seeing a look of doubt cross her brother's face. But before either of them could pursue the subject, Stephen entered the breakfast parlor bearing a letter addressed to Lady Chester.

Demetra recognized the handwriting at once. She had seen it often enough in the months since Frank's uncle's death, when they had been deluged with correspondence about the Chester estate. Instead of retreating to her room, she opened the letter at the table. Like it or not, she might have to share the contents with Quentin.

"Bad news?" Quentin inquired, when Stephen had withdrawn.

"Unfortunately you're going to have to know about this." Demetra folded the letter. "It's from Morton."

"Morton?"

"The steward at Chester Priory." Demetra's voice was devoid of any emotion. "If you'll recall, I told him I didn't want Frank to know about Madame Falconetti's presence at the Priory in case there was a scandal. He's written to tell me that Frank found out anyway."

Quentin's eyes narrowed. "How?"

"He arrived there last night."

"He what?"

"With a lady," Demetra added steadily. "Who also wishes to remain unnamed."

Quentin stared at his sister for a moment, then flung back his head and began to laugh. "So Hawksley has removed his

305

chère amie to Chester Priory. Still feeling like the loyal wife, 'Metra?"

"My only concern," Demetra said, "is whether or not you consider this a breach of our agreement."

"That would be most unsportsmanlike, wouldn't it? Hawksley clearly went to the Priory for his own purposes."

"Then you'll hold to your side of the bargain?"

"Provided neither he—nor you—interferes further. Yes. I'm in an agreeable mood this morning." Quentin pushed back his chair and rose. "If you'll excuse me, I have a pressing appointment with my banker."

"Oh, hullo, Sophy." Lewis looked up with relief as his sister entered the library. "Have you come to rescue me from the Greeks? Jolly good of you. I say," he added, looking at her more closely, "what have you been up to?"

"Listening at keyholes."

"Well, I call that shabby," exclaimed the aggrieved Lewis. "I thought we were going to talk before we tried anything like that."

"I didn't plan it," Sophy said, walking to the desk at which Lewis was sitting. "I was going into breakfast, only the door was ajar and I heard Quentin and Demetra talking so I thought I'd stay and listen for a bit. You'd have done the same."

"I suppose so. Oh, all right, yes, I would have. Did you learn anything?" He studied her face. "You did, didn't you?"

"Yes, but don't look so excited. This is serious."

"Of course it's serious. I keep trying to tell you the contessa may be in danger—"

"That's what I mean, Lewis." Sophy pushed aside the books her brother was supposed to be studying and perched on the edge of the desk. "This isn't exciting and it's certainly not romantic. It's beastly."

"What is?" Lewis demanded, with justifiable impatience.

"Lord Chester has a mistress."

Lewis looked disappointed. "Is that all?"

"*All?*" Sophy said, with such vehemence that a copy of Herodotus clattered to the floor.

"Most men have mistresses," Lewis pointed out, picking up the book. "Father does."

"That's different. Papa isn't in love with Mama. More important, Mama isn't in love with Papa. I don't think she ever was."

"Well, maybe Demetra isn't in love with Hawksley. They've been married for years."

"Don't be a dunderhead, Lewis. Haven't you seen the way she looks at him?"

"I—"

"Take my word for it."

"Are you sure she minds?"

Sophy regarded her brother with exasperation. "How would you feel if you had a wife and you found out she had a lover?"

"That's different."

"Not that different."

Lewis considered for a moment. He did not go so far as to acknowledge the truth of Sophy's claim, but he did not argue the point either. "Why was Demetra talking to Quentin about Chester's mistress?" he asked instead, bracing his feet on the front of the desk and tilting his chair onto its back legs.

"I don't know." Sophy relaxed a little. "The first thing I heard was Quentin saying something like, *So your husband's taken his chère amie to Chester Priory.*"

"Chester Priory?"

"It's their house in Surrey, the one Frank inherited from his uncle."

"I know. But dash it, Sophy, a married man isn't supposed to install his mistress in his own house. Do you suppose Hawksley couldn't afford to engage lodgings for her?"

"I haven't the slightest idea, but at least this way we can go talk to her."

"*Talk* to her?" Lewis's chair crashed to the floor. "Sophy, you can't talk to a common trollop—"

"I doubt she's that, I think Lord Chester's taste would be more sophisticated. Of course I have to talk to her. How else am I to persuade her to give him up? Unless you think it would be better to talk to Lord Chester?"

"No!" said Lewis forcefully. "Sophy—you wouldn't."

"Well, I own it seems awkward. That's why I'd rather start with the mistress. Are you coming with me or not?"

"I thought we were trying to rescue the contessa."

"You're trying to rescue the contessa. I'm trying to rescue Demetra. It just turns out that her problems are more complicated than I thought."

"Didn't Demetra and Quentin say anything about the contessa at all?"

"No, just something about a bargain. Then Quentin started walking toward the door and I ducked in here. Are you coming to Chester Priory or would you rather spend the day studying Greek?"

That settled it. Lewis stood up and slammed shut the book he had been reading. Any adventure was better than Greek.

After Quentin left the breakfast parlor, Demetra walked to the fireplace and mechanically fed Morton's note to the flames. Then, ignoring her untouched plate and half-empty cup, she returned to her room, flung herself on her bed, and for the first time since the whole wretched business had begun, burst into tears.

Edwina found her there ten minutes later. Demetra did not know anyone had come into the room until she felt a hand on her shoulder and heard her sister's voice saying, "Demetra? What is it? What's the matter?"

Demetra hiccupped, rolled onto her back, and half sat up.

"You don't want to know."

"Try me. I'm sick of my own problems, I'd much rather hear about yours. Here," Edwina added, pulling out her handkerchief.

Demetra took the handkerchief and wiped her eyes. It was an amazing relief to talk to someone sympathetic. Still, she had absolutely no intention of telling her sister the truth and was very nearly as surprised as Edwina when she found herself blurting out, "Frank's having an affair."

Edwina's beautiful eyes widened. She was a sophisticated young woman. She knew that her father kept a mistress and she knew that the men and women of their set frequently indulged themselves outside of marriage. But she had thought Frank and Demetra were different. Was this the reward for flying in the face of parental authority and marrying the man of one's choice?

"Are you sure?" Edwina asked. "I mean, did Frank admit it?"

"No, but I've seen the wretched woman's letters."

"You know who it is?"

"Unfortunately."

"And you've seen her letters?"

Demetra hesitated, dismayed by how much she had already disclosed. "It's complicated," she said, sitting up properly, as if that would help marshal her thoughts. "Tell me what Mama said to you last night. Was it dreadful?"

"I deserve better than that, Demetra. If you don't want to talk about it, say so, but don't try and change the subject."

Edwina looked genuinely hurt. Demetra bit her lip. Her usually self-absorbed sister was showing real concern and she repaid Edwina by brushing aside her interest. "I'm sorry, Eddy," Demetra said, laying a hand over her sister's, "it's just that—"

"You're afraid I'll tell tales? No, it's all right. I understand if you don't want to talk."

Oh, no, Demetra thought, you don't understand at all. The problem was that her desire to talk was suddenly overmastering. After telling so many different stories to so many different people, it would be wonderful to share the truth. Not that Edwina could do anything to help—

Or could she? Demetra twined a stray lock of hair around her finger. She had run out of places to look for the letters. But Edwina, who had spent far more time in Quentin's company these past years might have some ideas of her own.

Characteristically, once Demetra reached a decision she plunged straight ahead, with no time for second thoughts. "I do want to talk," she said. "More important, I need help and I hope to goodness you can give it to me."

Edwina nodded, though she did not see precisely what she could do about her brother-in-law's infidelity.

"I told you it was complicated," Demetra said. "It has to do with why I came to Buckleigh House. No," she added quickly, "that wasn't because of Frank's affair. It was—I suppose you could say it was because of Quentin."

"It's amazing," Edwina said without surprise, "how many things turn out to be because of Quentin. What's he up to now?"

Demetra told her the story, starting with Nicholas Warwick's sighting of Quentin in Wardour Street and ending with the letter she had received that morning, telling her that Frank had brought a woman to Chester Priory.

Edwina listened in silence. "Demetra," she said, when her sister had finished, "I know you don't want to talk about this, but how were the letters addressed? I mean, was his whole name on them, or just *Frank?*"

"Neither, actually." Demetra had more important things to think about than Helen Berresford's epistolary style.

"So she only used his initial? *Dearest F.?* Any number of men could be called that—Frederick and Felix and Ferdinand and Fabian—even Fordyce."

"Actually," Demetra said, "she didn't even use his initial, but it's obvious—"

"You mean she just wrote *My beloved darling* or something like that?"

"Something like that."

"Then maybe I'm the one who's being blind, but how can you possibly know the letters were written to Frank?"

Demetra looked at her sister blankly. "I saw Frank discussing blackmail terms with Madame Falconetti."

"I'm not questioning that. But does it mean he's Lady Berresford's lover? Think, Demetra. What would you do if you received a blackmail letter? No, that's silly, you'd meet the blackmailer of course. But Helen Berresford sounds a thoroughly insipid sort of woman—"

"She is. So she sent her lover to deal with the blackmailer instead."

"Not necessarily. Perhaps the lover's still abroad. If she couldn't call on him, she'd have to turn to someone in London."

Edwina saw a flicker of hope in her sister's eyes, but it was quickly suppressed. In the tone of one who will not allow herself to hope, Demetra said, "If there's nothing clandestine between them, why go to Frank? There must be dozens of people she could have asked—"

"Must there? I don't think she'd have gone to another woman, and most of the men she knows must be friends of her husband."

"She has family in London." Demetra sounded almost defensive. "Lady Pembroke is her aunt."

Edwina regarded her sister with exasperation. "Use your head, Demetra. Would you tell Aunt Aurelia about something like this? It's not the sort of thing one tells an aunt."

Demetra returned Edwina's look and fought down a wave of exhilaration. Edwina was right. It was not the sort of thing one told an aunt. But a childhood companion, who had rescued

Helen from scrapes long before she saw him in a romantic light— It made sense. Except— With a sinking heart, Demetra remembered their conversation on the way home from the Braithwoods' ball.

"Yes," she said flatly, "I could almost believe it. Except that Frank as much as admitted they were lovers."

"What did he say?"

"It was after we left the Braithwoods' on Monday. Frank and I had—well, we'd been getting on rather better, only all of a sudden he was dreadfully distant. He wouldn't tell me what was the matter, so I said, *It's about Helen, isn't it?* And he didn't even try to deny it. He just asked what I knew about Helen. I said, *What do you think?* or something and he warned me that if Helen was hurt he wouldn't answer for the consequences. I've never seen Frank so fierce."

"Well, of course he was fierce, you idiot. He must have been afraid you knew about the letters."

"But—" Demetra faltered. Could simple concern for Helen's marriage and reputation account for Frank's attitude toward his old love? "I suppose it's possible," Demetra said cautiously. "But even if they aren't lovers, I'll never be sure how Frank feels about her. And about me. I'll never be sure which of us he'd have chosen if Helen hadn't married another man. I never have been sure, but until all this happened, I didn't realize how much it mattered."

Edwina traced the outline of a flower on the quilt. "I asked Elliot about Philippa yesterday. He claims he's gotten over his feeling for her, but I'll never know how he'd have felt about me if he could have had her. I used to think that I couldn't live with that, the possibility that I was second choice. And yet it's not as simple as first and second choice, is it? Look at the Granvilles. He was her aunt's lover for years and yet they're one of the happiest couples I know."

Demetra frowned. Edwina had a point. Hers was not a unique problem. Nicholas and Livia Warwick had both been married before. So had Rowena Braithwood and Francesca Scott. In fact, Francesca's first husband, Demetra recalled from talk at the ball, had been the best friend of her second.

"It must be easier for Mr. Ashton," Edwina said. "At least he knows Philippa chose him and not Elliot."

Demetra thought of Henry Ashton's manner toward Elliot Marsden. "I'm not sure it is," she said. Yet despite this, his marriage appeared happy and secure. As did the Granvilles', the Warwicks', the Braithwoods', and the Scotts'. But knowing that did not diminish the jealous thoughts which had tormented her this past week. She had much to think about. After the letters were recovered. She said so and asked if Edwina had any idea where Quentin might have hidden them.

Edwina considered. "At his mistress's?"

"She's at Cranford. We met her yesterday, remember."

"He might have more than one."

Demetra regarded her with appreciation. "What an excellent idea, I never thought of that. Of course he hasn't been back in England much more than a fortnight—"

"Perhaps he brought her with him."

"He brought the one at Cranford with him. She's quite definitely Italian."

Edwina leaned back against the bedpost. "Do you think she knows about Madame Falconetti?"

"I'm not sure. It's one of the things that's bothering me. I wish I knew exactly what Quentin was doing."

"But you do know. And he's been stopped from doing it. He may have the letters, but he can't do anything to disrupt the trial now that Madame Falconetti has been exposed."

"No. So I don't understand why he's so disgustingly cheerful."

"Putting a good face on it?"

"Quentin?" Demetra said in disbelief. "He hates to lose."

Edwina acknowledged the truth of this and the two sisters sat in silence for a time. "What happened to Madame

Falconetti's maid?" Edwina said suddenly. "If she was taking messages to Quentin, why would Madame Falconetti dismiss her?"

"She must have felt the maid couldn't be trusted."

"It's a pity we can't find her." Edwina stretched her arms above her head and pushed the heavy waves of dark hair back from her face. "We could use her story as counter-blackmail."

Demetra smiled. "I'm sure Quen's managed to get her out of the country. Unless— Oh, Lord!"

"What?"

"He didn't send her out of the country," Demetra said, her voice carefully calm. "She's at Cranford."

"You mean Quentin has her waiting on his mistress?"

"No, I mean she is his mistress. At least, she's the woman called Annina whom we assumed was Quentin's mistress. I thought there was something odd about her, but I didn't realize it until you did that with your hair. You look quite different with it pulled back. Hair can change a person. Annina must have worn a wig when she was posing as the maid—very dark and severe, with braids. It made her look years older and not nearly so fragile, but I'm certain she's the same woman."

"But why? Why disguise her? And why suddenly move her to Cranford?"

"The maid was dismissed just after Madame Falconetti moved to Berresford House. I don't think Quentin wanted too many people to get a close look at Annina."

"But Lord Berresford and Mr. Warwick had already seen her."

"Berresford doesn't pay much attention to servants and Nicholas only saw her briefly. She was out when Kenrick and Frank met the contessa. I expect that was deliberate. At Berresford House she would have had to mingle with the other servants all day. Perhaps Quentin didn't want anyone to connect Annina with the contessa's maid when she reappeared in the future."

314

"Reappeared as what?" Edwina gasped, struck by a sudden thought. "Demetra, you don't suppose Quentin *married* her, do you?"

Demetra looked at her sister.

"No," Edwina agreed, "he wouldn't. But then why all this secrecy— Demetra? What is it?"

Demetra had begun to laugh, not joyfully but with a kind of desperation. "I know who she is. Who she has to be. It's the only answer that makes any sense."

"Who?"

Demetra sobered. "The Contessa Montalto."

Edwina stared at her sister. "But," she said, "if Quentin's had the real Contessa Montalto under his protection all along, why not simply take her to the Tories and have her testify? Why go through the charade with Madame Falconetti?"

"I imagine," said Demetra, piecing the story together, "because whatever Annina has to say about the Queen isn't very damaging."

Edwina snorted. "Quentin wouldn't let that stop him. He'd have her tell lies."

"But he might have been afraid that Annina couldn't stand up under Brougham's cross-examination. You've seen her. No, this was much more clever. The Whigs put Madame Falconetti in the witness box and Annina appears to denounce her as an imposter. No wonder Quentin's been so cheerful. He can still put most of his plan into effect."

"He can?" Edwina was not as well versed as her sister in the nuances of the trial.

"Lord Berresford has put it about that the contessa was suddenly called back to the Continent and cannot testify. He hasn't admitted that she was an imposter. If the real contessa appears now, how do you think it will make the Whigs look?"

"They can say Madame Falconetti tricked them."

"They can, but I doubt many people will believe it. At best, it will be embarrassing. At worst it could ruin careers, Frank's

315

included. It's fiendishly clever."

"It's pure Quentin," Edwina agreed. "So you must be right."

"I'm sure I'm right." Demetra jumped off the bed. "There's no time to be lost."

"What about the letters?"

"I'll have to take my chances. This is more important." Demetra was pulling a pelisse from the wardrobe. "Do you want to come with me?"

"Where?" Edwina asked.

"Cranford," said Demetra.

Chapter 21

Helen woke with the sense that something was amiss. To her surprise, she had slept unusually well. No doubt that was from the unaccustomed amount of wine she had taken at dinner. She also had a slight headache, and that, too, she attributed to the wine. It had been, she thought, the strangest dinner party she had ever attended. It was not the first time she had sat at table with the woman who had called herself the Contessa Montalto, but it was the first time since she had learned that the woman was not a contessa nor anything else in the least respectable. And from his conversation, the man who was her lover was not much better, though he was undeniably handsome and claimed friendship with Frank. Major York had told some very funny stories, which grew funnier as the evening progressed, and they had all stayed around the table after dinner was over, laughing immoderately, until Frank had at last taken him away and she and Madame Falconetti had gone upstairs to bed.

She sat up and looked around the unfamiliar room, wondering if she should ring for help and, if she rang, if anyone would come. She had seen no servants the night before save for the man called Morton and Betty, a sweet-faced girl of no more

317

than sixteen who had helped her into her nightdress. Betty had said she did not sleep in the house. But if she did not, she had returned that morning, for it was Betty who opened her door a moment later and told her that although the other lady, being a foreigner and strange in her ways, took coffee when she woke, she was sure Mrs. Cameron would like a nice cup of tea.

Helen propped the pillows behind her and drew up her knees and sipped the hot brew gratefully. Already her headache had lessened, but she still had the nagging feeling that something was amiss. Arthur. By now Arthur would have read her note. What would he do? For that matter, what was she to do? It had all been very clear the day before when she had made her decision to leave him. It had been very clear during her flight from London when she had explained to Frank exactly why no other course of action was possible. But what happened from today forward was not clear at all. Helen considered the alternatives open to her. As a result of these reflections she was seized with a very hollow feeling in the pit of her stomach and was forced to forgo her usual second cup of tea.

But though Helen felt frightened and bewildered, she was not without resources. She had, after all, lived with Arthur for the past eleven years and she had managed his house very well indeed. She dressed herself with care and went down to the dining room, where she rang for Morton and ordered toast and a fresh pot of tea. Then she occupied herself by exploring the house. And at last she returned to her room for a shawl and went outside to walk in the garden. She was there when Bianca found her some two hours later.

Helen was still in two minds about Madame Falconetti, but she was growing tired of her own company and she had not been able to resolve on a course of action about her future. So she accepted the other woman's proposal that they walk as far as the home farm which was some half-mile distant. "Unless," Helen said with a trace of malice, "you are expecting Major York."

"I am not expecting Major York. I told him last night to stay in Epsom until he hears from me. I think you and I need to talk."

"I don't think there's any need for that at all," Helen said with some stiffness in her manner, though talk was what she was longing to do.

"Yes," said the other woman as though she had not heard her, "about your husband and Lord Chester and Gareth Lovell."

"Gareth!" Helen stopped and turned around as though she had been stung. "You know Gareth?"

"But of course I know Gareth. How do you think I got the letters that you wrote to him?"

Helen stared at her in horror. The careful edifice of a deathless romance that had sustained her through the past year crumbled away into nothingness. "He gave them to you?" she whispered.

Bianca immediately saw her mistake. "No, no, he did not give them to me. He did not even show them to me. But he talked about you—not by name, of course. He was desolated that you had had to part. And he talked about your letters."

Helen had no doubt at all how Gareth had come to discuss her letters with Madame Falconetti and where that discussion had taken place. Dear God, how many others had he spoken to in this way? She felt an intense bitterness toward her former love. Desolated indeed. He had been quick enough to seek consolation.

Helen walked on, fighting back tears and indignation. What could she have expected of Gareth? He had wanted her to run away with him and she had refused. Should he have stayed celibate all his life? Better a woman like this, who could have meant nothing, than another like herself. Helen felt she was very rapidly acquiring some much needed wisdom about the world.

"So you stole the letters," she said.

"I? No, I did not do that. Major York took them one evening when Mr. Lovell was calling on me."

319

"Major York?" Helen stopped once more. Of course, Frank had said there were two blackmailers. "Then he was part of this too." She had liked Ian York, but no one, it seemed, could be trusted.

"In a manner of speaking. We have had some disagreement, but that is neither here nor there."

"But did he tell Major York— How did you know who—"

"You are not to worry. Your Gareth was not indiscreet. Ian rescued him from the card tables, and he was grateful. He was also lonely, and he wanted to talk about his hopeless passion for a woman who was married. He told Ian about his travels and the different people he had met. When we saw the letters, it was not difficult to guess who Helen must be."

Bianca began walking again and drew Helen along with her. "That is not important now. Listen to me, Lady Berresford. I was married once, and like your husband, my husband was unkind. Worse. He was a beast, but no matter. He left me, and I was without friends, without family, without money. How was I to live? I am a woman, I have youth, I have beauty. I can be a servant, or I can be as I am. Do not judge me."

Helen knew about women like Madame Falconetti and she despised them, but this woman she could not help liking. How was it possible to like a woman who had attempted to extort money for letters that were not hers. Who had actually done so and given the wrong letters in exchange, and to make it worse it was Frank's money, and though of course she would pay him back, she had no idea how she would manage it as she had left most of her jewels at Berresford House.

"I tell you this," Bianca went on, ignoring Helen's evident agitation, "because you must think what it is you do when you leave your husband. You think you are safe because you have found a lover, but a lover, you understand, is not for all time."

Helen, thinking of the past, nodded. "How true."

"You do not have money of your own? Then what will you do when it is over? I do not think you can live like me, so you must return to your family"—Helen shuddered—"or you must return to your husband."

"Never!" The word rang out sharp and clear in the brisk morning air.

They walked on a few moments in silence, their eyes drawn to the thatched roof of the farm house ahead, a thin spiral of smoke rising from its chimney. Helen felt some further explanation was called for. "I can no longer live as I have done."

Bianca laughed. "But of course you cannot live as you have done. You must live to suit yourself. You have married a man who is rich and well-looking and does not beat you. He does not, does he?" she added in an anxious tone, as though fearing her judgment of the man had been in error.

Helen shook her head.

"Do you love him?" That would be an unfortunate complication.

It was not a question to which Helen had given much thought. She had been inordinately pleased when Arthur had offered for her. She had wanted his admiration and good opinion, but as for love— "No," she said. It was a liberating thought. "No, I don't love Arthur. I don't even like him very much."

"That makes it easier. Think now. What is so very terrible about your marriage? So your husband is stupid? Good. That gives you more scope to be clever. So he neglects you for other women? That gives you time to find your own pleasure. You do not need to run away. You have a house and money and position. Yes, and you have beauty, Lady Berresford. You can live as you please. You need only be discreet. And if you find that you still desire your husband's attention, assure him that you do not and his vanity will do the rest."

No one had ever talked to Helen like this, not even her mother. Especially not her mother. Of course she could not follow such cynical advice. It did violence to everything she had ever been taught. But . . . Helen turned it over in her mind and looked at it again.

Bianca urged her case. "Such men can be managed, Lady Berresford. In this you have the advantage over him."

A small smile broke across Helen's face. She had never seen her relationship with Arthur in quite this way. Then she remembered that there was one way at least in which the advantage was not with her. "The letters," she said. "What if Arthur sees the letters?"

"If he says a word about the letters, you will laugh in his face and tell him they are none of his affair."

"I couldn't," Helen said with desperate certainty. "Madame Falconetti, where are they? Who has them? How can I get them back?"

"The question," Bianca said, "is not how to get them back. The question is how to make them harmless. If you cannot laugh them off, we will find another way. It is a problem, yes, but a problem that can be overcome."

Madame Falconetti was a persuasive woman. Helen almost believed her.

The landau that Lewis had commandeered that morning, fervently hoping his mother would not require it before their return, pulled up at an inn on the outskirts of Epsom. Sanders, the groom whom Lewis had persuaded to drive them, descended to inquire the way to Chester Priory. Lewis and Sophy had no clear idea of what they would do when they reached there, but they were agreed on one thing. The woman must be induced to break off her relationship with Frank Hawksley.

The identity of this woman had been a matter of considerable speculation, but since neither of them knew Hawksley well nor moved in his particular circles, they finally gave it up. Sophy said that, whoever she was, she must have some remarkable assets, for no one would lightly leave Demetra. Lewis insisted that such a liaison was to be expected,

322

and in any case it was Demetra who had left Chester. Still, if his sister was unhappy about the arrangement, he would do his best to bring it to an end.

They had now left Epsom behind and were traveling along a road that wound gently through pasture land, the water of a small stream keeping pace with their horses. There was a farm house ahead, and some half-mile beyond, the stones of Chester Priory, half obscured by ivy, could be seen through the trees. His attention on this building, Lewis did not see what was in the nearer distance until Sophy leaned out of the window and pointed to the road beyond the farm house. "Lewis, look. That must be the woman."

There were, in fact, two women. They had not expected this. A maid, perhaps? Or a companion? It seemed almost too respectable. Lewis wondered whether he should stop and what on earth he was to say if he did. He had envisioned a quiet talk with one of the servants, suitably tipped, of course, which would disclose the evidence of shame with which he would confront the errant woman. But two fashionably dressed ladies, out for a morning stroll?

He decided to go on to the house. As the carriage drew near, the two women stepped aside to let it pass. Lewis glanced at them to acknowlege the gesture. "It's she!" he said, letting down the window so he could see more clearly.

"Who?" Sophy asked.

"The contessa. Quentin must have brought her here. I suppose it was Demetra's idea."

"Demetra? She never would."

"You think Chester found her and brought her here?"

"I don't know." Sophy signaled Sanders to stop the carriage and it came to an abrupt halt.

"There are two of them. The other one looks familiar."

Sophy leaned over his shoulder. "It's Lady Berresford. I wonder which one is Chester's mistress?"

Lewis turned on her in horror. "He wouldn't have two?"

"Don't be an idiot. Get out, we'll have to talk to them."

Lewis tumbled out of the carriage and walked toward the women. "Contessa, my lady," he began, and then realized that he had been presented to neither woman and should not properly be speaking to them at all.

Sophy had no such qualms. "How very fortunate," she said as she joined her brother. "We're going to Chester Priory and we weren't sure there'd be anyone there to talk to. I'm Sophy Thane, Lady Chester's sister, and this is our brother Lewis." Lewis, his face reddening, made an awkward bow.

Bianca looked at the young man with an amused smile. "Then you must walk back to the house with us, Sophy and Lewis Thane, and take some refreshment. Your man can take the carriage to the stable. Straight ahead," she told Sanders, "then to the right after you pass the pillars."

Helen was silent as they returned to the house. What demon had decreed that two more persons should know of her flight to Chester Priory with Frank Hawksley? But Bianca, chatting amiably with Sophy, knew that it was no demon. The only question was who—St. George, Lady Chester, or Lady Chester's husband? Bianca did not like games in which she was kept in ignorance, and she set herself to find out who had sent these children after her or after Lady Berresford, and why. But first she needed to calm them, for the boy was much too stiff and the girl talked far too much and Lady Berresford showed a distressing return to her former timidity.

When they reached the house, Bianca called for Morton and ordered a cold collation and wine, and they sat around the dining room table pretending that this was a social call and wasn't it nice, after all, to make new acquaintances.

It was a parody, Helen thought, of last night's dinner. The wine—which she never took in the middle of the day, how had she let herself be persuaded?—warmed her and made her feel that the presence of the young Thanes was not after all such a great danger, and in any case Madame Falconetti would find a way to protect her.

Lewis drank somewhat more than was good for him. He nursed a secret fear that it was the magnificent contessa who would turn out to be his brother-in-law's mistress. Beside her, the pale Lady Berresford dimmed to insignificance. If he were Chester, he knew which woman he would have installed at Chester Priory.

Sophy drank little at all, but her appetite was good and she ate steadily, content to watch the two women who were her hostesses and try to come to some decision between them. The contessa was more likely to be the woman they were seeking. It was very like Quentin to force Demetra to house her husband's mistress. But Sophy thought her brother-in-law's taste would not run to someone quite as obvious as the contessa. Neither would it run to someone quite as tame and respectable as Lady Berresford. Still, respectable women did have lovers, and there had been—hadn't there?—some talk about an early acquaintance between them.

It was no use. She could not decide, and neither woman offered any clue. Even her introduction of Frank Hawksley's name failed to bring a telltale blush or perceptible agitation of manner to either woman. Sophy was beginning to contemplate a frontal attack when the contessa brought the matter up herself.

"Now," she said suddenly, "I think you must tell us what it is that makes you two charming young people drive all the way from London to visit a house where you do not expect to find anybody at all."

Lewis choked on his wine and sputtered something about escaping from his studies and a fine day for a drive, but Sophy cut him off. "Of course we owe you an explanation," she said without any trace of self-consciousness or apology. "We heard that Lord Chester had brought a lady to Chester Priory. We want to talk with her."

This was not what either of the women had expected. "But

why?" Bianca asked. "Surely that is Lord Chester's business." She had some glimmering of what they were about, but she was playing for time.

"Not when it concerns Lord Chester's wife."

"It has nothing to do with Lord Chester's wife," Helen said, thereby giving herself away.

"An interesting argument," Bianca murmured.

But Sophy held firm. "Our only concern is for our sister's happiness. We don't want to see her marriage destroyed."

"*Her* marriage?" Helen stared at Sophy in bewilderment. It was her own marriage that had come to an end.

"I know there are women who don't mind these things particularly, but Demetra's not like that. She'd be terribly hurt."

"You mean Frank has mistresses too?" Helen looked incredulous. She turned to Bianca. "Don't tell me you—"

"Certainly not," Bianca said firmly. "But—you mean you are not—"

"Not what?" Helen stared at the other woman.

"How strange. I am not usually wrong about these things. When you came last night, I naturally assumed that you—"

"That I— With Frank? Whatever gave you such a ridiculous idea? There is no one, no one at all."

"*Che peccato,*" Bianca said.

"Then you and Lord Chester—" Sophy said.

"Of course not."

Sophy turned to Bianca. "And you and Lord Chester—"

"Regrettably, no."

"Oh, I'm so glad!" Sophy threw herself back in the chair with relief. Quentin was wrong. She might have known. But then, what were Lady Berresford and the contessa doing at Chester Priory? "I do apologize," she said hastily. "We'd heard, you see, that he brought down a woman who was—"

"He brought me down," Helen said. She grew defensive. "Frank is my friend, I've known him all my life. How could you

326

possibly think, how could anyone think— Oh, my God!" Helen suddenly realized why Demetra had called on her last Friday.

In the silence that followed this outburst, the four occupants of the dining room could hear the sound of hoofbeats and the creak of carriage wheels. "Frank?" Helen said.

"No, he'll be at the House." This was from Lewis.

Bianca rose hastily. "I know who it is. Quick. Go upstairs. You must not be seen." She shepherded them out of the dining room and watched as Helen led Sophy and Lewis up the stairs. "Morton," she said as the butler appeared in answer to the summons from the front door, "if that is my solicitor, bring him to me in the library. You may offer him some wine. There is no need to mention the presence of the others."

Morton nodded at the imperious woman who had taken to ordering the household—nothing like this would have happened in the late Lord Chester's time—and went to admit Mrs. Long's solicitor.

When Quentin was ushered into the library a few moments later, he found Bianca standing disconsolate by one of the windows. "What, not at the books, Bianca? I was sure the treasures of Chester Priory would keep you enthralled for days."

"Bah, there is nothing here worth reading." She indicated the half-dozen books that had been pulled from the shelves and strewn on the table that occupied the center of the room— Bianca was nothing if not careful. "I do not like the country. I am bored."

Quentin laid down his hat and gloves. "A pity. I would have thought the other lady would provide some company."

Bianca glanced at him sharply but said nothing.

"As you wish," he said. He remained silent while Morton reentered the room with a decanter and glasses; then he dismissed the man with a gesture. "Take a glass of wine with me, Bianca, a valedictory to our ill-fated enterprise." He was,

327

she thought, surprisingly pleased with himself. "I've brought your money, and you shall soon be quit of this depressing country."

He withdrew an envelope and laid it on the table. Bianca picked it up and proceeded to count its contents. "Satisfactory," she said.

"I should think so." He did not add that it was more than she had any right to expect. With his newly gained wealth he was in a charitable mood. "I dropped my groom in Epsom. He's to hire a carriage and drive you straight to Dover. You'll be on the road half the night, but there'll be lodging when you arrive and you can get an early packet for France. He'll see you on it."

"Every thought for my comfort." Her tone was mocking.

He looked at her sharply. "Very well, stop on the way if you must. Hunter will stay with you until you sail. Expect him within the hour. I'm for London." With a quick salute he swallowed the rest of his wine, picked up his hat and gloves, and left the house.

Bianca picked up the envelope and walked slowly up the stairs, conscious of a rising resentment. True, she had the money, but she did not like the viscount's arrogant assumption that she could be sent back and forth at his bidding. She was not at all sure that she was ready to leave England, and she was not at all sure what she wanted to do about Ian. Then there was the problem of the letters, for which she felt some responsibility, letters which might prevent Lady Berresford from acting on the very sensible advice she had given her that morning, letters which, according to Lady Chester, were now in the hands of the Viscount St. George. She had a shrewd idea of the games he was playing with those letters. They could hurt Lady Berresford, and they could hurt Lady Chester as well. Bianca was learning to dislike St. George. It would give her a great deal of satisfaction to thwart him on this point.

Bianca stepped into her room and concealed the envelope in a pocket which she wore under her skirt. Then she smoothed her dress and went in search of the others.

They had retreated to the bedchamber occupied by Lady Berresford. Bianca found them there in animated conference. "I'm going to London," Helen announced as the other woman entered the room. "Mr. Thane and Lady Sophy will drive me. I must see Lady Chester, you see," she went on, as though she were deserting her companion and needed to explain herself, "I cannot bear that she should think such lies about me and Fr—her husband. And after that, well, after that I will go home." Her resolution faltered and she crossed the room to stand before Bianca. "Come with me, please do."

It was all that was needed for Bianca to reach a decision. She embraced Helen and promised that she would not desert her. "I need only a quarter hour," she said. "Lady Sophy, you will help Lady Berresford. Mr. Thane, you must bring round the carriage, but first you must wait while I write a letter."

Lewis followed her down to the library, where she found ink and paper and hastily scribbled a note to Ian, bidding him meet her back in London at Buckleigh House in Bruton Street. "Here," she said, handing Lewis the sealed letter, "give this to the boy in the stable and tell him to deliver it to Major York at the Rose and Thistle in Epsom. Give him money to do so—you have money? Good, it is imperative that this letter reaches Major York at once."

Like their younger sister and brother, Demetra and Edwina arrived at Cranford with no very clear idea of how they were to carry out the mission that had brought them from London. It was one thing to conclude that the gentle young woman who had dandled Annie on her knee was engaged in a plot to embarrass the political party that Demetra called her own. It was another to induce the young woman to admit it, and still another to persuade her to come forward and tell her story.

Edwina was convinced that the girl who called herself

Annina was Quentin's mistress, no matter what else she might be. "I know his type."

Demetra was not so sure. Annina had appeared to be a carefully brought up young woman and, Quentin's type or no, he would not risk the larger game for a fleeting diversion.

In either event, Annina seemed genuinely pleased by their arrival. She led them into the dining room and ordered tea and sandwiches for her guests. Luscombe, normally of a dour and complaining disposition, was observed to smile as he left the room. Demetra had always been a favorite and he had not seen her in the past seven years.

It is not easy to raise awkward questions when one is sitting over a meal. Demetra ate fish paste and cucumber sandwiches —she was really very hungry—and drank tea and let Edwina carry the burden of the conversation. But when the refreshments were done, she set down her cup and plunged into the matter.

"Annina—I'm sorry, I don't know your last name—"

"Vaselli."

"Miss Vaselli—"

"No, no, it is *signora*, how do you say, madame. I am a widow."

"Madame Vaselli. But are you not also known as the Contessa Montalto?"

The girl looked stunned, and then frightened. "I am Madame Vaselli," she said in a small voice.

Unconsciously Demetra adopted the soothing tone she used with the children when they were upset. "Of course. You do not wish to use your title here." She nodded to Edwina, who rose and stepped behind Annina's chair. With a swift movement she swept the loose blonde curls away from Annina's face, exposing the delicate and somewhat angular face beneath. Then she dropped her hands, leaving Annina quivering in fear and outrage.

"I was sure of it," Demetra said under her breath. Then, in a more normal tone, "I do not understand why you allowed another woman to use your title. I do not understand why you put on a black wig and traveled as her maid. Or is this woman truly the Contessa Montalto while you, Madame Vaselli, are nothing more than a servant?"

It was a brutal way to put it, but it was effective. "No!" Annina burst out. "I am no servant, not to such a woman as that. My husband was the Conte Montalto, it is an old family and it goes back many, many years. Ask anyone in Viterbo."

"Oh, I'm so glad," Demetra said, cheerfully flinging Madam Falconetti's reputation away, "I could not believe that she was a real contessa. Tell me about your home." And she proceeded to draw forth from Annina an increasingly lyrical description of Viterbo, which she missed most dreadfully, and an accounting of her life with her late husband, which she did not miss at all. He was an old man, Annina said, and was not fond of company, so they visited rarely and scarcely entertained at all. Though once, she confided, the woman who was now Queen of England had stopped for the night, owing to an accident to her carriage, along with the man who called himself Bergami and several other people of her retinue.

"I've never seen her," Demetra admitted with what she hoped was an expression of envy at the other's good fortune. "What was she like?"

"Oh, a coarse woman, but good tempered, you understand. My husband did not like her and told me to stay away. He said she was a bad woman, but he would not tell me why."

"But you didn't stay away, did you?" Demetra asked. "You saw something, or St. George persuaded you that you did. Is that why he brought you to England?"

Annina looked uncomfortable and refused to say any more. "He wants you to tell about it, doesn't he?" Demetra went on. "Before all the lords and bishops of England, and the archbishops too. You must be very sure of what you saw before you go before these people and swear before God that what you say is the truth."

Annina nervously fingered the gold chain round her neck

331

which ended, Demetra was sure, in a cross.

"Why would you want to do that, Madame Vaselli? Why would you come all the way to England to say something about a woman you scarcely knew? What did he promise you? Was it money?"

Annina jumped to her feet. "Money? You think I take money?" She was breathing hard. "I come to be with Quentin. He is to be my husband. And you"—she looked at them in turn—"you are to be my sisters." Then she sat down abruptly, put her head on her arms, and burst into tears.

"But he can't marry you," Edwina said in a matter-of-fact voice. "He's going to marry Beatrix Thornton."

Annina sat up as though she had been jerked back by a string. "Marry— No!" she cried. "No, you lie, you lie! He promised me, I tell you, he promised me!" She beat the table with her fists, and her pale face grew red with fury.

Demetra was appalled by what she had done. No, she was appalled by what Quentin had done, for it would have come to this sooner or later.

Edwina, who had been prone to hysterical fits as a child, was not in the least dismayed. She stood up and poured a glass of water, debated dashing it into Annina's face, then offered it to her instead. "Here, drink this," she said. Her voice was not at all unkind. "I know it's a dreadful shock, but Quentin's behavior does take people that way."

The water, or perhaps it was Edwina's calm tone, helped Annina bring herself under control. She set the glass down carefully and wiped her eyes. She was paler than ever. "I will never believe it," she asserted, "never."

"Nonetheless, it's true," Edwina said. "Yesterday he visited Lady Beatrix and asked her to be his wife. Then he went to her father and asked his permission. He told us about it last night."

Demetra could not bear the look of misery on the young woman's face, but she could not draw back now, not when they were so near success. "What our brother did was very, very wrong, Annina. Everything he did. Come to London with us.

332

Tell your story to my friends."

Annina shook her head.

"We'll take you to our mother first. She'll tell you it is true."

Annina hesitated. A mother, particularly of one's intended husband, carried real authority. She stood up and looked down on them. "Very well," she said, "I will come. To your house. But I will not talk to anyone until I talk to Quentin." And with a dignity neither of the others could muster, she left the room.

A half hour after the departure of the guests at Chester Priory, Ian York rode up on a roan hack that was the best the Rose and Thistle had to offer. Bianca had told him to stay away till he was sent for, but by God, it was well past midday and he had had no word. She might pretend to be annoyed by his arrival, but he had no doubt of his welcome. Not after yesterday. Even Lady Berresford had not seemed averse to his company.

So Ian was perhaps not to be blamed for failing to understand what Morton told him. "They've gone out? How? Where?"

"In a carriage driven by a Mr. Thane."

"You mean the Viscount St. George?"

"I don't know any viscount, sir. This was a very young man. He had his sister with him. She was young, too, but a very well-developed girl, if you know what I mean."

That young cub, Lewis Thane? And Lady Sophy? Whatever brought them to Chester Priory? "When do you expect them back?"

"I don't think they are coming back." Morton devoutly hoped this was true. "It was just after Madame Falconetti had a visit from her solicitor. She packed all her bags. She seemed in a fearsome hurry. She said they were going to London."

So. He had been tricked once more. Tricked and cheated. Bianca had been paid off and had left him to cool his heels in

333

Surrey. He had actually believed her promises of love and fidelity. No, not fidelity, one did not ask that of Bianca. But she had promised to return to the Continent with him, to let him live with her on the munificence of the English.

A cold wave of fury swept him. He would not be mocked. She had gone to London with young Thane? Then it was at the Thanes' that he would find her.

Chapter 22

Thursday, October 12

It was nearly three when Demetra and Edwina returned to Bruton Street with the second Contessa Montalto. Annina had not spoken a word on the journey to London, but once inside the house she looked round the hall and then addressed the footman. "Where is the Viscount St. George?"

"Lord St. George is not at home, madam," said Stephen, startled at being addressed in this peremptory tone by a guest. He looked to Lady Edwina for guidance.

"Let us know as soon as he returns," Edwina said. "We'll be in my dressing room. Oh, and Stephen, we'd like tea. Have a tray sent up." She put her arm around the now unresisting Annina and led her up the stairs. Demetra went to the library and scribbled a hasty note to her husband. *Frank, I have information. It's urgent. Come to Bruton Street as soon as the House rises. Bring Kenrick.* There, that was all she could do for the moment. She returned to the hall and told Stephen to see that the note was delivered to Lord Chester immediately. Then she ran up the stairs to join Edwina.

During the next hour, Annina went from sullen silence to tears to hysterical rage. Then Demetra had the happy thought of sending for Mary Rose and the children, and Annina, to

335

Demetra's relief, became composed and even cheerful. When Stephen came in half an hour later, Annina was sitting with Annie on her lap, watching Colin's efforts to write under his Aunt Edwina's tutelage. Stephen informed Lady Chester that her husband and Lord Braithwood had arrived and were waiting for her in the old sitting room. Demetra left the dressing room quietly and ran down to the floor below.

"I'm sorry to send for you this way," she said as she entered the sitting room, "but I have something of the greatest urgency to tell you." Both men looked suitably grave, but there was something more in Frank's eyes. Not wanting to deal with this yet, she addressed herself to Kenrick. "I have a young woman upstairs—please sit down, this is a rather long story and excessively complicated—there is a young woman who calls herself the Contessa Montalto. I found her at Cranford, a house owned by my brother, St. George. I think she is the contessa—at least she appears to be Italian, and it seems too much to expect that there would be two imposters. She came to England as Madame Falconetti's maid, and when the contessa —that is, the woman we all thought was the contessa—was moved to Berresford House, my brother moved her—that is, the other contessa—to Cranford."

The two men exchanged startled looks. "St. George is playing a more devious game than we thought," Frank said.

"Oh, Quentin is nothing if not devious, but he has been rather cleverer about this than I gave him credit for, and I do blame myself for not seeing it at once. It was only when I saw that he was not the least bit crestfallen after the first contessa was exposed that I thought there must be something more."

Kenrick leaned forward. "It was your brother who arranged for Madame Falconetti to meet Lord Berresford?"

"Yes. Or put her in the way of making his acquaintance. Before I knew she was an imposter, I thought—you must have thought so too—that Quentin was simply trying to suborn a defense witness, to get her to change her testimony on the stand. But now I think he planned to expose her as a fraud

336

when she testified for the Queen. It would be much more effective that way."

"Which," Frank said, "would make it look as though the defense had bribed her to pose as the Contessa Montalto and give false testimony about a conversation with the Queen, a conversation that could never have taken place. We were talking about bribery today," he added for Demetra's benefit. "There's evidence that both the workmen at the Villa d'Este and the Queen's servants were suborned by the King's agents. The defense is bound to recall Rastelli—after he left the Queen's service, he was employed by the Milan Commission— and that will shake the prosecution's case to its core." He turned to Kenrick. "But if it's suggested that the defense is also bribing witnesses . . ."

Kenrick nodded. He did not need to have it spelled out.

"It's rather worse than that, Frank," Demetra said. "The Whigs can argue that they were tricked by Madame Falconetti, but there will be all sorts of whispers. Anyone who had seen both Annina—that's the woman upstairs—and Madame Falconetti would realize that one could not possibly be mistaken for the other. The Queen would have known Madame Falconetti was an imposter. Madame Falconetti could only have succeeded in her charade if the Queen was a party to the deception. And if the Queen was, Berresford and the rest of you must have been as well. It would damage the Queen's case, if it did not destroy it altogether. And it wouldn't do your reputations any good either."

"Your brother's a resourceful man, Demetra," Kenrick said after a moment. "What does he intend to do now?"

"I can only guess, of course. But I think he'll offer Annina as a witness for the prosecution—can they bring forward another one now? If not, he could have her tell her story to one of the newspapers. Whatever it is, it won't be creditable to the Queen. And the prosecution will be able to say whatever they like about Brougham's plan to use Madame Falconetti as a witness because Quentin intends to get Madame Falconetti out of the country as soon as possible, and the defense won't be able to bring her forward to contradict it."

"I see." Kenrick was thoughtful.

Frank, noting the mixture of anxiety and excitement in his wife's eyes, knew there was more. "You've been meddling, Demetra. With what result?"

"That's just it. With none at all, I'm afraid. I'd hoped I could persuade Annina to come forward and tell the real story—I've put this all together from bits and pieces of things she told me—but I doubt she'd even talk to you, though she seems calm enough at the moment now that Annie is there."

"You took that woman to see the children?"

"No, I brought them to see her. Annie can have a very calming effect, Frank, though in the ordinary way of things you wouldn't think it. But they became quite good friends when they met at Cranford."

Frank started to speak, but Kenrick brought the discussion back to the point at hand. "How did you get her here, Demetra?"

"She wanted to see Quentin. She says he's going to marry her, but he won't, of course, because he's going to marry Beatrix Thornton. Annina thinks we're lying about it, but when she learns we aren't, I think she'll be willing to tell you everything. Only she won't do anything until she speaks to Quentin, and I'm afraid once she does he'll be able to talk her round. I'm sorry I haven't worked it all out, Kenrick, but I wanted you to know as soon as possible."

"Demetra," Frank said, "how sure are you that Annina is the real contessa?"

"Almost as sure as Lord Berresford was that Madame Falconetti was the real one. I suppose that means not sure at all."

Kenrick rose with an air of decision. "That much at least can be cleared up. She'll have to see the Queen."

"The Queen? But she can't. I mean, she won't. She refuses to leave the house until she sees Quentin."

"Then I shall have to bring the Queen here." Kenrick picked up his hat and moved toward the door. "I do hope your mother won't mind."

After Kenrick's departure, Demetra could think of nothing more to say. Frank regarded his wife with mingled affection and exasperation. She had used their quarrel as an excuse to run off to her parents' house so she could spy on St. George. She had never intended to help her brother, she had suspected him from the beginning. Why in the name of heaven hadn't she told him so? "We're in your debt, Demetra," he said. That was certainly true. If she was right, she had saved their entire case. "But I fail to see why you found it necessary to involve the children."

"Oh, but I didn't. Not today, that is. I took them to Cranford yesterday. It was because of Edwina, but I don't think I'd better tell you about that now. And because of the letters. I thought Quentin might have hidden them there and I wanted to look for them, and I must say the children were a great help, at least Colin was a great help, though in the end we didn't find a thing. Except the other Contessa Montalto, of course, and Annie found her, so the trip wasn't a complete waste."

But Frank wasn't listening. Through the long day of testimony about where and when and in what company the Queen had taken her baths aboard the polacre, and whether or not Her Royal Highness's legs had swelled as a result of the voyage from Jaffa to Syracuse, and whether or not there were fig leaves on the statues of Adam and Eve that stood in the grotto at the Villa d'Este, to say nothing of the testimony of an army man about the dancing of the dami-dimi in Calcutta and the presence of ladies at such a performance (the bishop's wife had been present, as well as the bishop), Frank had had little time to think of Helen Berresford and her letters. Now Demetra recalled them forcibly to mind. He struck his forehead. "Oh, my God."

"I know, Frank, it's dangerous for Helen, but what Quentin is doing with Annina is even more dangerous. I couldn't not speak out. But about the letters. Listen. I have an idea."

Before she could say more, Stephen was at the door to inform her that she had another caller. The caller was too impatient to wait to be announced. Lord Berresford shoved the footman aside and lunged into the room. "Lady Chester, what the devil have you done with my wife?"

"See here, Berresford—" Frank began.

"Your wife?" Demetra asked at the same time. "Why would I know anything about your wife?"

"You called on her Tuesday night."

"I did."

"And she left the next day." Arthur had been too intent on his grievance to think much of what he was saying, but this sounded thin even to his ears. "You must have said something to upset her."

It had been a long day. Demetra's despair on learning that Frank had taken Helen to Chester Priory, the sudden kindling of hope that he had taken her as a friend and not a lover, the headlong journey to Cranford and the equally hasty return, the hours spent trying to cajole and control Annina, the outpouring of her discovery to Kenrick and Frank, all made Lord Berresford's problem seem utterly inane. Demetra stifled an hysterical impulse to laugh. "I assure you, Lord Berresford, I said nothing of the kind. And if you have had the misfortune to mislay your wife, then I suggest you look to your own behavior rather than that of her friends."

It was an insulting statement. Arthur would never have tolerated it from a man, but he could not round on a woman of his own class. In his mounting rage he did the only thing possible. He turned on Frank.

He opened his mouth to speak, then closed it abruptly. In his haste to leave the room, Stephen had neglected to close the door and Arthur could hear clearly the voices of new arrivals in the hall outside.

"Demetra, I'm so glad you're here."

340

Arthur turned and saw a tall and well-developed young girl standing in the doorway.

"Oh, hullo, Lord Chester," Sophy added, "I'm glad you're here, too." She glanced with inquiry at the third occupant of the room.

"Lord Berresford," Demetra said, hastening over the introduction. "My sister, Lady Sophia Thane. Lord Berresford is looking for his wife. You haven't come across her, have you?"

Sophy did not understand the tangle of relationships among the Hawksleys and the Berresfords, and she was unsure of how much she should say. "As a matter of fact," she began cautiously, "she's just called. She wants to see you, Demetra."

"I knew it," Arthur said, and made for the door.

Sophy moved into the room and stopped his progress. "If you'll wait a moment, Lord Berresford." She turned and called, "Bring the ladies into the sitting room, Lewis. Everyone's in here."

Helen was the first to enter. "Demetra," she began, "there's something I must—" Then she realized that Frank was also in the room. She stopped in embarrassment, which quickly turned to astonishment as she saw that her husband was in the room as well. "Arthur, what on earth are you doing here?"

He came up to her. "Where have you been, Helen? Why are you here?"

"We are calling on Lady Chester, Lord Berresford."

The deep, faintly accented voice would have told Arthur the woman's identity had he not already recognized her perfume. He whirled around. "You?"

"Why not? Surely I, too, may call on Lady Chester. Didn't I meet her in your own house?"

That reminded Arthur of his other grievances. "Where have you been? Why did you leave? Are you or are you not the Contessa Montalto?"

"Sir!" Lewis stepped forward to defend his lady's honor.

Arthur neither saw nor heard him. "And what am I to do

with your trunks?"

"How thoughtful of you, Berresford, to think of my trunks." Bianca laid a hand on his arm. "My plans are uncertain, but I will let you know." Arthur sputtered, then smiled sheepishly. "Unless you wish me to return to your house? But no, I do not think that would be wise, do you? There have been too many questions raised, and we cannot proceed as we intended. It is a great pity." And she looked at him with such palpable regret in her large dark eyes that Arthur forgot he had intended to repeat his question about whether or not she was the Contessa Montalto.

Lewis hovered nearby, harboring unfamiliar jealous thoughts, until Sophy drew him away and told him to stop being such a looby, a remark that escalated into a low-voiced wrangle.

Helen meanwhile took advantage of her husband's preoccupation to speak once more to Demetra. "It's most urgent," she said with unaccustomed insistence. "Isn't there someplace we can be private?" She turned to Frank, who was doing his own hovering. "If you want to be of help, take Arthur away or make him go home. I can't deal with him now."

Demetra had no desire to hear Helen's incoherent ramblings. "Of course, Helen," she said, "but this isn't really the best time—"

"I didn't know you had guests, Demetra." Lady Buckleigh stood in the doorway, regarding the odd collection of people her daughter had assembled. Lady Buckleigh was distantly acquainted with the Berresfords, though they did not move in the same circles and it would not have occurred to her to invite them to her home. The dark, foreign-looking woman who was wearing entirely too much scent she had never seen before.

Demetra wished her mother at the ends of the earth, but she could not ignore her. "I believe you know the Berresfords, Mama, but I don't think you have met Madame Falconetti. My mother, Countess Buckleigh."

Lady Buckleigh inclined her head a scant two inches.

342

"She's the Contessa Montalto." Lewis had come forward to stand near his mother. He had hoped to make the introduction himself.

"Madame Falconetti." Bianca hastened to correct him, leaving it open whether the title was unwarranted or she did not choose to claim it. She returned Lady Buckleigh's salute to the exact fraction of an inch.

"Lady Beatrix Thornton." Lady Buckleigh indicated the young woman who had appeared at her side. "Beatrix, this is Madame Falconetti."

Beatrix's acknowledgment was even chillier.

"Lord Berresford is just going," Demetra said, eager to draw attention away from Bianca.

Arthur had no intention of going without his wife or without an explanation from the woman who now called herself Madame Falconetti. He took Helen's arm possessively. "Go home and wait for me."

Helen pulled away. "I need to talk to Demetra, Arthur. You go."

"I need to talk to the contessa."

Lady Buckleigh watched this unseemly behavior with distaste. "Since your guests do not seem to know whether they wish to go or stay, Demetra, I think it would be advisable to give them something to do until they make up their minds. I suggest you adjourn to the small drawing room. I will ring for tea. Tea, I have always found, has a civilizing effect." She glanced around the entire group, not omitting her younger children and her son-in-law. Then she turned and swept out of the room.

It did not occur to the rest of those present to dispute her request. It had something of the air of a royal command. Helen left the room first, eager to apologize to Lady Buckleigh for the intrusion into her house, though she had no intention of leaving it until she and Demetra had cleared up the matter of Frank's infidelity. Arthur went where Helen went, and Bianca followed them both, to protect Helen against her husband.

Lewis naturally followed Bianca, which left Sophy to take Frank's arm. "I've always found," she said in a confiding tone, "that it is wise to follow Mama in small things. That way one can be free to disregard her when it really matters."

Lady Beatrix would have followed her future mother-in-law, but Demetra detained her. "The truth is," Demetra said when they were at last alone, "I have something to tell you, and it is not at all pleasant."

Beatrix raised her pale, perfectly arched brows. She had known the Thane family for years, but she had never been friendly with Demetra, whom she considered an impulsive girl with ill-placed enthusiasms and a penchant for dramatic statements. She preferred Edwina, who was nearer her own age and who knew the forms and how to get her way despite them. Still, Demetra would also be her sister-in-law, so she answered her with some attempt at good-humor. "You don't need to hesitate to tell me anything, Demetra. I'm not at all missish."

"Yes, of course you aren't. It's one of the things I've always liked about you." It was perhaps the only thing she liked about Beatrix Thornton, but this was no time for that kind of honesty. "It's about Quentin."

Beatrix had suspected it would be something about Quentin, but despite herself she stiffened. Her voice remained cool. "Then you'd better tell me, hadn't you?"

Demetra hesitated, but saw no way to put the matter delicately. "There's a woman."

"With a man like Quentin, I suppose there might be." Beatrix adjusted her shawl, a heavily fringed white cashmere bordered in blue, as though to take comfort from its warmth. "I must confess I had rather expected him to put such things aside, at least for a decent interval. I suppose," she went on— Lady Beatrix was not stupid—"she's making trouble."

"Yes," Demetra said, "but—"

"Then that's Quentin's problem. He can pay her off. In fact, I shall insist that he do so."

"It's not quite that simple, Beatrix, and I don't think money is what Annina has in mind."

"Annina?"

"Yes, she's Italian."

"How quaint." Beatrix's lips narrowed in an unattractive line.

"Quentin was responsible for bringing her here, and I'm not at all sure she's willing to go back. Not unless I can convince her that Quentin is truly betrothed to another woman."

Beatrix looked affronted. "Which he certainly is. And everyone would know it, if Quentin hadn't insisted on keeping back the announcement until the trial is over." Beatrix was not pleased on this point.

It was clear to Demetra why Quentin had postponed the announcement. Annina would never testify if she knew he was betrothed to another woman. "I thought perhaps if you would talk to her—"

"Oh, I'll talk to her. When can you arrange it?"

Demetra smiled in relief. "At once. We have her upstairs in Edwina's dressing room. She's been demanding to see Quentin, but he's only likely to dig himself in deeper, and I didn't want to go to Mama."

Beatrix realized that this was her first opportunity to wield her power within the family. "There's no need to bother Lady Buckleigh. I'll take care of it myself."

When they reached the dressing room, they found Colin and Annie on the floor, listening with wide appreciative eyes while Mary Rose told them a story that sounded suspiciously like an expurgated version of *The Sorceress of Montillo*. Demetra hoped that Mary Rose had been discreet when she came to the part about the Moorish harem. Annina was following the story with avid interest, and even Edwina appeared amused. It was a moment before they were aware that Demetra and Lady Beatrix had entered the room.

"Mummy!" Annie ran to Demetra and threw her arms around her knees.

Demetra picked up her daughter and handed her to Mary

345

Rose. "Take the children upstairs. It must be nearly time for their dinner." She tousled Colin's hair as he walked past on his way to the door. "Find someone to sit with them," she added quietly, "then come back here. We may need you."

Beatrix stood apart from the others, her back erect, her face expressionless, waiting for Demetra to clear away the detritus of children and nursemaid. She ignored Edwina's offer of a chair and kept her glance fixed on the stranger who must be the woman Demetra had called Annina. Aware of the scrutiny and then of who the other woman must be, Annina rose to face her.

"Lady Beatrix Thornton," Edwina murmured—the contessa, after all, had the higher rank. "Beatrix, may I present Anna Vaselli."

Beatrix, intent on inspecting the other woman, gave no sign that she was aware of the slight. The two were very much alike and yet vastly different. Beatrix was taller, but they were both blond, with pale skin, clear blue eyes, and finely drawn features. Both would be accounted beautiful women. Annina, however, was more delicately made. There was a greater play of feeling upon her face and a greater pliancy in her body. She was dressed in a long-sleeved, high-necked gown in a shade of pale lavender that accentuated the appearance of fragility, and her hair, which she had loosened so that it tumbled about her shoulders in shining waves, made her appear younger than her actual years. Beatrix's hair was coiled high on her head, and her dress—a blue lustring cut to show her admirable figure—lent vivid color to her face and intensified the blue of her eyes. She was, carriage, dress, and hair attested, a woman of consequence.

Annina stood her ground. "Lady Edwina and Lady Chester say that you are betrothed to their brother, the Viscount St. George. Is this true?"

Beatrix did not like being called to account by a woman of this class and could not keep the distaste from her face. "It is true."

"I think that it is not. The Viscount St. George is betrothed

346

to me."

Beatrix's face went white. The fool! He had promised her marriage. She fought down her anger. This was the first test she must pass if she was to become Quentin's wife. "My poor girl," she said, her tone making it clear that she pitied the stupid little wretch, "surely you do not believe— No, it is evident that you do. St. George asked for my hand yesterday, and I accepted him. My father has given his consent. The betrothal will be announced as soon as this deplorable trial is over, and we will be married before the year is out."

"Ha! I knew it." The scorn was evident in Annina's voice. "I am betrothed to St. George for many weeks now, in Viterbo it happened, and he brought me to England so we can be married from his family's home, except that we, too, wait until the trial is at an end. So, Lady Beatrix, I think I have the earlier claim, and you are not betrothed to anyone at all." She tossed her head in a gesture of supreme assurance.

Demetra and Edwina had moved aside to let the scene play out. Now their eyes met. This was a side of Annina they had not seen before.

Beatrix colored, but her calm did not desert her. "I do not doubt that Quentin has made you his mistress. You are not the first creature to grace his bed, and I am sure he has paid you well for your efforts. But if you think that gives you any claim—"

"Money! You think I take money to come to England? You insult me. You insult Quentin. You do not know him at all."

"I have known Quentin most of my life, and I know him very well indeed." Beatrix had few illusions about her husband-to-be, but she had decided to become his wife the day that she met him and she had not once since wavered in that determination. "Quentin may have filled your head with all kinds of nonsense. He may have led you to believe that his intentions were serious. But I tell you this, Miss Vaselli, and you had best believe it because it is true. The Viscount St. George may couple with a shop girl or an opera dancer, but he will never marry her."

Annina looked as though she had been struck. Her breath came in quick gasps, and her normally light voice rose to an alarming pitch. "I do not come from a shop! I do not dance! I am the Contessa Montalto, and I have friends who will avenge me!" She stopped, her bosom rising and falling with the quick intake of her breath. She drew herself up with great dignity. "I swear by the Virgin that it is so."

Beatrix stared at her in disbelief. Then she turned for confirmation to her future sisters-in-law. Edwina shrugged. "We thought you should know."

Beatrix had a great respect for titles—she would become a viscountess when she married Quentin, and though his father was disgustingly healthy, she had hopes of becoming a countess herself one day. An affair with a woman of no particular class did not matter. An affair with a titled lady was more serious. The woman might have some real claim upon him. No. Quentin could not be that careless. She could not be a real contessa. And even if she were, titles were so common in that country—didn't that courier Bergami's sister call herself a contessa?—that they meant nothing at all.

Shaken, uncertain, but determined to fight it out, Beatrix took refuge in denial. "I do not believe it. I will not believe it. Never. Not unless I hear it from Quentin's own lips." And with something between a sob and an exclamation of anger, she turned away and ran out of the room.

Chapter 23

Demetra had said she had an idea about how to handle the letters, but Frank could not be easy on this score. When St. George returned home and discovered his sister had spoiled his plans, he must not find Arthur Berresford under his roof. As Lady Buckleigh's oddly assorted guests arranged themselves in the small drawing room, Frank drew Helen to one side. "This is no place for you, Nell," he said, without preamble. "Take Berresford and go home. I'll explain later."

"I can't, Frank." Helen's voice was surprisingly firm.

"Why not?"

Helen colored. "That is between me and Demetra. It's no concern of yours."

"Damn it, Helen, I am concerned," he insisted in a fierce undertone, but Helen was already moving off toward the rose damask sofa on which Lady Buckleigh was seated. Why the devil was it so urgent that she talk to Demetra? Bianca might be able to tell him, but she had also settled herself beside Lady Buckleigh, probably to avoid unpleasant questions from Berresford. Berresford was hovering behind the sofa, unwilling to question either Bianca or his wife in Lady Buckleigh's presence. That left the two youngest Thanes, who were holding a fierce conversation by the fireplace, some distance down the room.

"How much," asked Frank, joining them, "do you two know about all this?"

"Almost nothing," Lewis said with regret. "We just brought Lady Berresford and the contes—Madame Falconetti to London."

"You did what?"

"We brought them to London. From Chester Priory," said Lewis, quite heedless of the way his sister was glaring at him.

"I see. And what, may I ask, took you to Chester Priory?"

'Oh." Lewis began to see the pitfalls in this line of questioning. "Well, you see—it was Sophy's idea."

"Yes?" Frank transferred his gaze to his sister-in-law.

"Lewis was tired of his books," Sophy said brightly, "and we felt like a drive and Demetra had told us what a lovely house you have in Epsom—which is perfectly true, Chester Priory has the most romantic air—so we drove down and found Lady Berresford and Madame Falconetti and they were very kind and asked us to stay for luncheon, which was quite delightful, so when they said they were planning to return to London, of course we offered them seats in our carriage."

"You sound," Frank informed her, "exactly like your sister. I don't believe a word of it."

"But a lot of it is true," Sophy said indignantly.

"See here, Hawksley." Intent on their conversation, none of the trio had noticed the approach of Arthur Berresford. "We need to talk."

"We certainly do," Frank agreed, with an affability that momentarily threw the other man off his guard. "Sophy, Lewis, pray excuse us for a few moments. Try to come up with a more plausible story in my absence. Berresford." Frank started toward the windows on the other side of the room.

"More plausible story about what?" Berresford demanded, following him.

"Family joke. Berresford, take the advice of a married man.

Go home."

Berresford laughed shortly. "You're hardly in a position to advise married men just now, Hawksley."

"Perhaps. Nevertheless, go home. Helen has some maggot in her head about talking to Demetra, but she'll follow you before long, I'm sure of it."

"I don't need you to tell me how to deal with my wife," Berresford snapped, realizing he'd been diverted from his original intention. "I want to know what the Contessa Montalto—I mean Madame whatever she's calling herself—is doing here."

"I haven't the faintest idea," Frank said truthfully.

"Damn it, man, she's in your wife's house!"

"At which she arrived in the company of your wife."

Berresford glared at him. "Helen left Berresford House yesterday." He hated to admit it.

"Demetra left Park Street over a week ago," Frank returned, "as you just were kind enough to point out."

"By God, Hawksley—" Berresford brought his hand down for emphasis. Frank caught him by the arm, seconds before he would have smashed his fist onto the marble top of a pier table. Berresford looked at the other man in outrage. Frank jerked his head toward Sophy and Lewis. Berresford removed his arm from Frank's grasp and smoothed his sleeve with what dignity he could muster. "I mean it, Hawksley. If you've had anything to do with hiding my wife or my witness— Was she working for St. George?"

"Helen?" Frank looked at him in mock astonishment.

"Madame Falconetti, of course."

"I don't know. Why don't you ask her?"

Arthur, who had been trying to do just that, gave Frank a look of disgust and marched back toward the far end of the room. Frank followed, wondering what his mother-in-law would do if he forcibly removed Berresford from her house.

"Madame Falconetti," said Arthur, his exasperation not quite overcoming his manners, "there are some things we must

351

discuss. I beg you to give me a few moments of your time."

"Things?" Bianca turned and looked innocently up at Berresford over the back of the sofa. "What things, Lord Berresford?"

"I think you take my meaning, madam."

"No, I assure you. But then I have a shocking memory. Have we some business to discuss?"

"You know perfectly well—" Berresford stopped, uncomfortably aware that there were a number of eyes upon him.

"Do sit down, Lord Berresford," Lady Buckleigh suggested. "It must be quite apparent that Madame Falconetti does not desire a private conversation."

Arthur Berresford had not been spoken to in that tone since his grandmother's death when he was still at Harrow. He swallowed.

"You oughtn't to scowl so, Arthur," Helen said in tones of wifely concern. "You know it always gives you the headache."

It was questionable how much longer Berresford's good manners would have held out, but at this point the door opened and he ceased to be the center of attention.

Demetra and Lady Beatrix? Frank wondered. Or, please God no, St. George?

It was neither. "Mr. Marsden, my lady," Stephen announced.

If Elliot was curious about what the Earl and Countess of Berresford, not to mention the Contessa Montalto, who had supposedly been called back to her homeland, were doing at Buckleigh House, he gave no sign of it. In fact he seemed somewhat abstracted. Once Lady Buckleigh had performed the introductions, he apologized for intruding. "I called to see Lady Edwina. Is she at home?"

Lady Buckleigh did not appear pleased by this information. "I do not," she said, "know precisely where Edwina is at present. I should perhaps warn you that all my children are behaving most unpredictably today. Perhaps you would care to return tomorrow?"

"Thank you," said Elliot, "I'll wait."

Arthur had returned to a state of something approaching calm. He stationed himself in a chair near his wife and Madame Falconetti. If he could not talk to them, at least he could keep them within view.

Frank once again wandered toward the fireplace, hoping for further conversation with Sophy and Lewis, but instead he found himself standing by Elliot Marsden.

"I must compliment you," Elliot said, unexpectedly. "You have a powerful speaking style. And a very enterprising wife."

A few days ago, Frank's feelings toward Marsden had been far from cordial, but now that Demetra's behavior was explained, he found that his jealousy had ended as quickly as it had begun. Marsden said he'd called to see Edwina. And judging from the look on his face, it was going to be more than a social call. Demetra had been interested in him on her sister's account, just as she had said. Anyone not blinded by hurt and anger would have seen that from the outset. Frank smiled. "Thank you. Though I'm afraid I can't take credit for the latter."

"You had the sense to marry her." Elliot glanced down the room at Lady Buckleigh, then said more softly, "It can't have been easy at first."

Frank looked at the other man in surprise, but somehow in the midst of all this confusion it did not seem odd to be discussing his personal life with a man he scarcely knew. After all, it appeared they were going to be brothers-in-law. "It wasn't. I wish I could say it got easier with time—"

"But it didn't?" The question was not an idle one.

Frank hesitated. Demetra was once again on speaking terms with her family, and though he'd sworn it would never happen, he was as well. He scarcely knew Edwina, but he genuinely liked Sophy and Lewis and he even had a certain grudging respect for Lady Buckleigh.

"That's not entirely true," Frank said. "But I'd never call it simple."

"Is it worth it?"

Frank's mouth curved into another smile. "Oh, yes."

Elliot's face lightened. "That's what I thought."

"Lady Buckleigh!"

The cry ripped through the room, putting a period to all conversation. Heedless of her audience, Lady Beatrix marched across the drawing room to her prospective mother-in-law. "I want to see Quentin."

The company, most of whom did not know of Beatrix and Quentin's engagement, looked at her in astonishment. Even Lady Buckleigh was momentarily nonplussed. "My dear Beatrix," she said, staring up at her son's usually decorous fiancée, "what has happened?"

"That is between Quentin and me, ma'am. I will not trouble you with this—this matter—until he is here to answer for himself."

She sat down and stared straight in front of her, hands tightly clenched, lips compressed. Frank did not stay to see more. Demetra and Edwina had quietly followed Beatrix into the room and were standing near the door. Frank went to his wife's side.

"Did it work?" he murmured.

"Not exactly as I hoped. Now they both insist on seeing Quentin."

"Edwina," said Elliot, who had followed Frank to the door, "come outside with me for a moment. There's something I must say to you."

"I can't, Elliot." Edwina was looking across the room at Beatrix. "Not until Quentin gets back. Demetra, do you think we should—"

"Demetra," Sophy suddenly appeared at her sister's side, "what have you been saying to Beatrix? Did you tell her that Quentin—"

"Demetra," Lewis was close behind Sophy, "if this is anything to do with the con—Madame Falconetti, I think I should—"

"Demetra," Helen joined the group, Bianca at her side, "I

354

must speak with you. Is there somewhere we can—?"

"Helen," Berresford lost no time in following his wife and Madame Falconetti, "I forbid you to leave this room. Lady Chester has already done enough damage."

"Arthur!" Helen rounded on him with an outrage that surprised everyone. "That is monstrous! Demetra has done nothing, and you have no right to speak of what you do not know about."

Arthur stood speechless at his wife's uncharacteristic outburst.

"Edwina," Elliot persisted, "if you'll only listen for a moment—"

"Do be quiet, Elliot, this is important."

"So is this," he said urgently. "It's about yesterday. I need to explain—"

"You needn't explain anything. You made your views perfectly clear."

"But you don't understand—"

"I understand all too well, and I have no wish to discuss the matter again, Mr. Marsden." Edwina took a step away from Elliot, and was nearly hit in the face as the door from the corridor opened once again. Elliot steadied her. The astonished Stephen took in the crowd standing practically in the doorway. As he paused, the gentleman behind him strode into the room without waiting for an announcement, pushed his way through the crowd, and seized hold of Bianca's arm. "Viper! Did you think you could give me the slip so easily?"

"Oh," said Sophy, quite delighted, "Major York."

"You!" Arthur Berresford stared in fury at the man whose denunciation of the putative Contessa Montalto had begun all his problems. "You, sir, have a great deal to answer for!"

"Not half so much as this woman does," Ian said grimly, his eyes trained on Bianca. "Well, madam?"

"Pray let go of my arm, Ian, you are crushing my sleeve. I do not understand why you are so perturbed. I told you in my note—"

"By God, Bianca, do you think anything you might have said

355

could possibly excuse—"

"York." Frank placed a firm hand on Ian's shoulder. "It appears you and Madame Falconetti have private matters to discuss. I'm sure my wife's family would be happy to put one of the smaller reception rooms at your disposal."

"Just a minute," said Berresford. "Neither of these people is going anywhere until I hear some explanations."

"Seems to me you're making a lot of demands about who can go where, Berresford," Lewis said, "considering this isn't your house."

"It makes no difference." Bianca had taken advantage of Frank's intervention to remove her arm from Ian's grasp. "I have no intention of leaving the room for the present. Major York may do as he pleases."

"Major York," said Frank, his hand tightening on Ian's shoulder, "is going to depart at once unless he can behave in a manner suitable to Lady Buckleigh's drawing room."

"But he hasn't done anything worse than the rest of us," Sophy protested.

"Tell me one thing, Bianca," Ian said, his voice softer, but no less intense, "when you sent me away from the priory last night, did you already intend—"

"I demand—what priory?" said Arthur.

"Did you already intend to give me the slip?"

"What priory?" Arthur repeated.

"It's a common name for houses," Sophy said. "I can think of dozens. Morford and Longman and Storningham—"

"Wait a minute." Arthur turned to Frank. "Isn't your—"

"Major York," Demetra stepped forward with authority, "you have not yet been presented to my mother. Pray forgive my shocking manners." She took his free arm and drew him across the room. Ian began to protest, but Demetra was already saying, "Mama, Beatrix, we have another caller. Major York, a very old friend of Frank's. Indeed, were it not for him, Frank would very likely not be alive today, so we all owe him our warmest gratitude. Major York, this is my mother, the Countess Buckleigh, and this is Lady Beatrix Thornton."

Whatever his other concerns, Major York knew what to do when presented to a lady. He swept Lady Buckleigh and Beatrix a more than creditable bow. Lady Buckleigh, whose attempts to question Beatrix had been meeting with an exasperating lack of success, surveyed him with faint interest and said that of course she was glad to receive any friend of her son-in-law.

But while Demetra's ploy had prevented Major York from making any more awkward statements, it had not stopped Arthur Berresford from asking awkward questions.

"Hawksley," said Berresford, paying scant attention to the introductions taking place on the other side of the room, "you have a house called Chester Priory."

"I have," Frank returned coolly. "What of it?"

"Your friend York says Madame Falconetti was there yesterday."

"I think you misunderstood, Berresford. York said Madame Falconetti was at a place he called the priory. And as Lady Sophy has just pointed out, many houses are called—"

"Very clever, Hawksley, but I do not believe in coincidence. Were you at Chester Priory?" he demanded, turning on Bianca.

Bianca shrugged. "The names of your English houses all sound alike to me. So unimaginative. In Italy—"

"I am not interested in Italy, madam. Did you—"

"I think," said Sophy, "that you had better step aside, Lord Berresford."

"What?"

"Jason is trying to come in with the tea," Sophy explained.

Tea, Lady Buckleigh had said, has a civilizing effect. For once, Demetra was grateful that her mother's words proved true. It would have been ill mannered to refuse refreshment, so the company clustered around the Pembroke table while Lady Buckleigh poured and Demetra, Edwina, and Sophy handed around the cups. And with a teacup in hand, exasperation and anger were more difficult to express. It was not exactly a congenial atmosphere, but Lady Buckleigh's talents were equal to far worse.

"Tell me, Major York," she said as she poured, "are you connected with Sir Theodore and Lady York in Essex?"

"I believe there may be some connection, ma'am," he said, his eyes straying impatiently to Bianca, "but it is quite distant. I come from the Irish branch of the family."

"Ah. I'm afraid I am not acquainted with them."

"What did you think of the play on Tuesday night, Major York?" said Sophy, who thought that perhaps he would prefer not to talk about his family. "Wasn't it amusing?"

"Vastly, though unfortunately I had to leave before the end. How did it turn out?"

"Oh, it was entirely satisfactory. Dick let his great fortune as Lord Duberly's son go to his head and he turned his back on Cecily, but then he repented and said he would marry her anyway. And then it turned out that Henry—old Lord Duberly's son—hadn't drowned at all—"

"He'd been shipwrecked and rescued by friendly Indians," Lewis put in.

"And he came back just in time to rescue Caroline, whose last two hundred pounds had been stolen by a thieving banker—"

"Only Cecily's brother Zekiel won twenty thousand pounds in a lottery, and he was going to give some of it to help Caroline—"

"But since Caroline was going to marry Henry, he was going to give it to Cecily instead, because Dick was no longer the son of a lord—"

"And Daniel Dowlas, who thought he was Lord Duberly, had to go back to being a chandler in Gosport—"

"But Henry said he would make provision for them," Sophy concluded. "So you see, everyone was called back to his proper place in life, except that a great deal of money was spread around."

"Except for Doctor Pangloss, who got nothing at all."

Ian laughed. "You're too young to be a cynic, Lady Sophy."

"I'm not a cynic. Card players are hopelessly optimistic."

358

"Then I must suspect you of radical views."

"Oh, I do hope so. I would hate to think like everybody else."

"Has Hawksley been corrupting you?"

"No, I thought of it myself."

Lady Buckleigh decided enough was enough and was about to intervene, when Beatrix brought the scene to an end. She rose suddenly and uttered a single word in tones of anger and reproach. "Quentin!"

"Hullo, Beatrix," Quentin said from the doorway—how long, Demetra wondered, had he been standing there? "I didn't realize you were entertaining this afternoon, Mother."

"I wish to speak with you," Beatrix informed him. "At once."

"Certainly, Beatrix," Quentin said affably as he advanced into the room, "though I really ought to pay my respects first. I don't believe I have the honor—"

"Quentin!"

This time the exclamation came from behind him. Before the startled eyes of Lady Buckleigh's guests, a small whirlwind of lavender skirts and golden hair rushed into the room and seized Quentin by the arm. If Demetra had had any lingering doubts about how formidable an adversary her brother was, in that moment he put them to rest. "Annina," Quentin said, with a smile of utter charm, "how delightful to see you. I didn't know you were acquainted with my family."

"Quentin," said Annina, looking at Lady Beatrix, "are you betrothed to this lady?"

"Quentin," said Beatrix, glaring at Annina, "are you betrothed to that lady?"

Quentin looked from one woman to the other. "Mother," he inquired, "do you think I might have a cup of tea?"

Chapter 24

Lady Buckleigh ignored her son's request. There was a problem here, but it was not one to be discussed before these ill-assorted people. "I do not believe I have met the young woman, St. George. Pray present her."

"I'm so sorry," Quentin said with a rueful smile of apology. "I assumed you were already acquainted. Mother, may I present Madame Anna Vaselli. We met when I was in Paris. Annina, my mother, Countess Buckleigh."

Annina had dreamed of the day she would be presented to Quentin's mother, but she had not expected it to happen in the presence of a rival. She acknowledged the introduction briefly, then turned to Quentin. "There are things you must explain to me," she said in an urgent undertone.

Beatrix had no difficulty hearing this remark. "There are things you must explain to both of us."

"Beatrix, sit down," Lady Buckleigh said. "I cannot carry on a conversation when I have to crane my neck. Madame Vaselli, come sit beside me. Quentin, ring for a fresh pot of tea."

The two women remained standing, but Quentin hastened to obey his mother. Then he went to Demetra and took her roughly by the arm. "You have much to explain to me," he said, glancing at Bianca and the man he had last seen lying unconscious in St. James's Square, "but that can wait." He pulled her toward the group at the tea table. "Annina, I don't think you know my sister, Lady Chester. She would like to show you the house."

It was a command. Demetra would have followed it if she could, but Annina was not to be swayed. "I have met Lady Chester and I do not want to talk to her. I do not want to see your house until you show it to me yourself. I have that right, Quentin. Tell this woman I have that right."

"Annina, you're overwrought." His voice was soothing, as though he were speaking to a fretting child. "Come into the next room and we will talk."

"I am not overwrought. I am angry. We will talk now and here, in front of your mother and your sisters and this woman who says you are to be her husband. In the sight of God, did you ask her to be your wife?"

"He did!" Beatrix exclaimed.

"He certainly said that he did," Lady Buckleigh added.

"No, I must hear it from Quentin."

"Not here," he whispered, glancing around the room. The others had withdrawn to a decent distance from this family scene, but he knew their indifference was feigned.

Lady Buckleigh looked with distaste at the flushed, disheveled young woman before her. The town was full of Italians of dubious pedigree—the exotic Madame Falconetti had some connection with the Berresfords, but then the Whigs were always careless in drawing the line—and this woman was no doubt one of them. "I don't know what right you have to make such a demand, Madame Vaselli. It certainly should not be made in the drawing room. You will come upstairs with me." She rose, certain that she could get rid of the greedy girl once she had her alone. It was very tiresome of Quentin to become involved in these tawdry affairs.

"He has promised to marry me," Annina insisted. There

were tears of frustration in her eyes. "Deny it, Quentin, deny it if you dare."

Lady Buckleigh was not moved. "I have no doubt you thought he said something of the kind. Quentin has always been imprecise in his use of language. Come with me, my dear."

"No! Quentin must come too."

"And I." Beatrix was determined that nothing be settled without her. "You mustn't believe anything this woman says, ma'am. She calls herself a contessa. She's an imposter."

Annina looked coldly at the other woman. "Tell them, Quentin."

There was an expectant silence, not only among the group at the tea table but throughout the entire room.

"Quentin?" His mother's voice held a note of warning.

Quentin seemed to rouse himself from a fit of abstraction. "Of course." He smiled at his mother. "Madame Vaselli is the Contessa Montalto."

Demetra could not but admire her brother. He had answered neither woman's accusation and had told their mother nothing at all except Annina's name.

"Damnation!" Arthur had overheard the last few statements, as had everyone else in the room.

"She's tricked him," Beatrix murmured.

Lady Buckleigh's face went blank. If the Vaselli woman was gently born, then the matter was serious indeed. She took Annina's arm and turned her toward the door. "Quentin, come with us. Beatrix, you will remain here until I send for you. Demetra, see to your guests."

But Arthur was not about to let the viscount escape. He had been stunned by St. George's revelation and had no intention of postponing an explanation. "Forgive me, madam. I must have a word with your son."

Lady Buckleigh gave him a withering look. The man was presumptuous, even if he was an earl. "Not now, Berresford. I require him."

"As do I. This is a political matter, ma'am, and must take precedence over family concerns." He turned to Quentin. "I was under the impression, sir, that I had met the Contessa Montalto in Paris and had brought her to London. This woman." He turned and extended a hand toward Madame Falconetti, who was standing near the fireplace, watching him with amusement. "You met this woman"—he pointed to Annina—"in Paris, and you claim she is the Contessa Montalto. I suppose you brought her to London."

"No." Annina was anxious to set the record straight. "We meet in Viterbo and I go with him to Paris. I come to England with you."

"I don't care how you came to— With me?"

"Yes. I am Marta."

"Marta?"

"My maid, Berresford." Bianca came forward slowly and stood by Arthur, so close that he was enveloped by her perfume.

"Your maid—" Arthur began to think the more extreme Whigs were right to call the Tories madmen. "Who is the Contessa Montalto?" he demanded. "Who is the imposter? Or are they both frauds?"

"How dare he?" Lewis whispered to Sophy. He still believed Madame Falconetti was the real Contessa Montalto.

"I can speak only for myself," Bianca said. "I am not the Contessa Montalto, I am Madame Falconetti. I have deceived you, yes, I admit it. A pity, but you understand, it was necessary."

Lewis's face fell. She was such a beautiful, such a desirable woman, and he would have championed her against all accusation.

Arthur felt some of the same regret, but it was quickly swamped by his awareness that he had been played for a fool. "Why? Why did you do it? What did you hope to gain?"

"You must not ask such questions, Berresford. They are no business of yours." Bianca turned her back on him and walked away.

Arthur looked after her in outrage. Balked of the explanation due him, he rounded on St. George. "You're not innocent in this affair, sir. What do you have to do with this woman?"

Quentin's voice was contemptuous. "You presume, Berresford."

"Berresford! Good God, what are you doing here?" Lord Buckleigh had returned home, intent on speaking with his wife, and was told he would find her in the small drawing room. His eye lit on his son-in-law. "Hawksley. I might have known." He looked around the room, noting the exotic dark-haired woman, the handsome man with the mustache who stood by her side, and the slender woman whose blond hair tumbled about her shoulders. Everyone was standing, looking expectantly at his eldest son. He turned to his wife. "I wasn't aware this was one of your afternoons, Catherine."

"Demetra is entertaining. Horace, we have a problem. This is Madame Vaselli, who may or may not be the Contessa Montalto. Come to the sitting room with us. Quentin. Beatrix, you had better come with us as well."

Lord Buckleigh looked with pleasure at the fragile young woman before him. He shared his son's taste in women, and Madame Vaselli was a splendid example of the type. "Lord Buckleigh," he said, making amends for his wife's shameful introduction. "I am honored, madam."

"You are Quentin's father? Thank God, you must hear me and do me justice. No one will believe me, and Quentin will say nothing." She turned to St. George in desperate appeal. "Why will you say nothing, Quentin?"

Quentin looked around. Berresford was hovering nearby and Hawksley was standing near him. On his other side stood his mother and Beatrix. "It's rather difficult to say anything at all in this crowd, Annina. Come into the next room and we can talk."

"No. We'll all go." Beatrix was not about to be fobbed off by her intended husband. She turned to Lord Buckleigh. "This woman refuses to believe that Quentin and I are betrothed. Am I or am I not betrothed to your son?"

Startled by this question, Lord Buckleigh turned away from the pleasant sight of Madame Vaselli, who might or not be the Contessa Montalto. He began to have some notion of the quagmire in which his son was struggling. "I have every reason to believe so, ma'am. He told me so himself."

"Then he is not a man of honor," Annina said, "and he has dishonored me."

Arthur broke away from Frank, who had placed a restraining hand on his shoulder. "See here, Buckleigh, there's something deuced peculiar going on. The Contessa Montalto is over there"—he indicated the exotic woman Lord Buckleigh had noted earlier—"only now she says she isn't, but she's a devilish woman and a liar and I don't know whether or not to believe her. St. George says this woman"—he pointed to Madame Vaselli—"is the Contessa Montalto, but if the other woman is a fraud, then this one is likely to be a fraud too. And if the other woman isn't a fraud, then of course this one has to be. Your son's involved with one of them and I have reason to believe he's involved with both—"

Lady Beatrix made a wordless sound of dismay.

"Quentin, you didn't!" Lewis had no illusions about his brother's behavior toward women and thought none the worse of him for it, but he was outraged that Quentin could have betrayed Madame Falconetti as well.

"That's enough, Berresford." Lord Buckleigh's face was red, which with him was a clear sign of anger. "My son's behavior is no concern of yours."

"But the Contessa Montalto's is. I brought her to England to testify for the Queen."

"You brought Madame Vaselli to England?"

"No, the other Contessa Montalto."

"But you told me she's not the contessa."

"That's just it. She's not. Or she says she's not. But in Paris

365

she said she was. We met by chance, but I think there was no chance about it. I think your son arranged it, knowing she wasn't the contessa. If he didn't know her then, he tried to get to know her in London, but in that case he thought she was."

"Was what?" Lord Buckleigh had the sense that he was rapidly losing command, and his color heightened alarmingly.

"It's very simple, Papa." Sophy stepped forward and began a patient explanation, ignoring the hot-tempered interruptions of both her father and Lord Berresford.

Seeing that Berresford could not be contained, Frank turned his attention to St. George. The viscount was trying to get Annina out of the room, but the young woman stood her ground. St. George abandoned the effort and moved toward the door. Frank was there to intercept him. "I think you'd better remain, St. George. We mean to have the story, and from the look of things, your father does too."

"I warned you, Hawksley."

Frank knew he was talking about the letters, but he welcomed the confrontation. It had to come sooner or later. Helen would be in constant danger if he did not have it out with St. George, and Frank thought he saw his way clear to protect her. "So you did."

"Quentin," said Lady Buckleigh in a voice that brooked no disobedience, "come here."

While everyone's attention was on St. George, Helen insisted that Demetra accompany her to the other end of the room. "It's important," she insisted. "I must tell you before someone else does, and I don't want him to hear it."

"Your husband?" Demetra felt a sudden constriction in her chest. Had she been wrong to think the letters were not written to Frank? Was Helen about to confess to the affair?

"No, Frank. He'd be so embarrassed, and I'm sure it never crossed his mind, but everybody else seems to believe it's true. I can't think why, for I'm sure neither of us has given any cause. Arthur and Frank have never really liked each other, and he's dreadfully hotheaded."

"Frank?" Demetra kept her tone light.

"No, Arthur. Though as I remember, Frank is hotheaded too. That's one of the reasons I left him, left Arthur I mean. I thought he was bedding the contessa—Madame Falconetti—under my own roof, and then he blamed me because she left the house. I couldn't stay with him after that, and who else was I to go to but Frank? He's the only friend I have." She hesitated over her next words. "I couldn't come to you, could I, Demetra? We've never seemed to like each other very well."

Demetra would never have been able to describe their relationship so clearly. She looked at Helen with growing respect. "I was jealous because Frank had loved you," Demetra admitted and waited, heart beating wildly, to see what Helen would say next.

Helen looked at her in surprise. "I was jealous because you were happy in your marriage and I was not. Demetra, did you really think that Frank and I—you know, that there was something between us?"

"Yes, for a while." It was a relief to be able to breathe again. "Then Edwina told me I was a blind idiot and I began to think she was right. There isn't anything, is there?" Demetra said, still not quite able to believe it. "There never has been?"

"Not since we were young, before he joined up, and even then we never—not that he didn't want to, but then men always do, and of course I couldn't. I've been faithful to Arthur, though he's not been faithful to me, not from the very beginning. There was only Gareth, but that was a long time ago." Helen turned away, distressed less by the memory of Gareth Lovell than by the fact that she could no longer clearly recall his face.

Demetra was exultant. It had not been Frank in Paris. What a fool she had been to doubt him. Even the feelings he might still harbor for Helen suddenly seemed inconsequential. She was Frank's wife, the mother of his children. He loved her, he needed her, he—He did not trust her. Demetra's exaltation ended abruptly. The trouble between them was far older than

367

her suspicions about Frank and Helen. The unraveling of her brother's plot should do much to restore Frank's faith in her. But it would not alter the fact that he had not trusted her to begin with.

"Demetra?" Helen said anxiously. "Do you mind? I know I should not have agreed, but—"

"Mind what?" Demetra realized that she had not been attending to what Helen was telling her.

"That I let Frank take me to Epsom. I thought I would go to a hotel, but Frank said I mustn't, and it was late, so in the end he took me to Chester Priory. The contessa was there, the woman I thought was the contessa, and Major York, who turns out to be an old friend of Frank's. Madame Falconetti and Major York—well, you know." Helen colored.

Demetra nodded. She knew very well.

"I hated her, Demetra, but I don't now. I've never known a woman like her. Then your brother and sister came to Epsom to save Frank from making a fool of himself with the woman he had brought to Chester Priory, only they didn't know whether the other woman was me or the contessa. Well, when I finally understood what they were about, I had to come back and tell you."

Demetra was touched. "You were running away and you came back so I wouldn't be unhappy?"

"Well, partly." Helen was not willing to take credit for so noble an action. "Madame Falconetti has convinced me that I should go back to Arthur. I really don't have any other choice, do I, for I have no money and I couldn't bear to return to my family, but I'm going back on my own terms. I'm never going to let him frighten me again." Helen was not as resolute as she sounded, for the letters were an ever-present threat, but she would not let herself think of that now.

Demetra was puzzled. Why had Madame Falconetti come back with Helen? She must have the money from Quentin by now, and Quentin wanted her out of the country. She would have no reason to stay, and surely she courted some danger by doing so. "Helen," she said, "why did Madame Falconetti come back to London?"

"To see me through," Helen said. "She's kindness itself."

It was a preposterous explanation and Demetra could not believe it. Nor could Ian, who had just been told the same thing by Bianca.

"I am telling you the truth," Bianca insisted, controlling her fury at his pigheadedness. "I am sorry for the little Berresford woman, I feel responsible. If it were not for me, she would not now be in this trouble with her husband. I must see her through."

"You took money from her."

"Ah, that is business. This is from the heart, of which I think you have none or else you would understand."

"I understand you well enough." His voice was bitter. "I left you in Choisy to get some money and you ran away to Paris with St. George. Was it your idea to have me rot in prison for a week while my papers were lost and my letters went unanswered?"

"Ian, no."

"Why no message for me, Bianca, when I finally got out of prison and went back to Choisy for you? Had you met Berresford by that time? Had you decided he offered you even more than you were getting out of St. George? Did you have something more permanent in mind? You can still get round Berresford, Bianca. Despite what you've done, he'd be happy to keep you."

"You fool. You are angry because you did not wait for my note this afternoon. How often must I say I sent it? Ask Lewis Thane. He carried it for me."

Ian wavered. The mention of the Thane boy had a ring of truth. "Then come away with me now, Bianca. We'll be in trouble if we stay."

"No, not until it is finished here."

He could not understand her stubbornness. "It's Berresford, isn't it?"

369

She looked at him in exasperation. "Oh, *caro*, do you know me so little? Do you think that overgrown child is any match for you?"

Those who had met Madame Falconetti would have been surprised by the look of tenderness on her face, but no one was paying them any heed. Most of the room's occupants were standing near the tea table, where Sophy, Beatrix, Annina, and Arthur were contending for Lord Buckleigh's attention with growing passion. Demetra and Helen were still at the other end of the room. A third couple had sought privacy by the windows.

Edwina had had no desire to talk to Elliot. He had admitted that he loved her, but he did not love her enough, and that was somehow worse than outright rejection. She had no intention of settling for the admiration and friendship that was all he had to offer and that he now seemed eager to resume.

But Elliot was importunate. "If you do not hear me at once," he informed her, under cover of the hubbub occasioned by her father's arrival, "I will go to your father and swear that you have compromised me."

"Elliot, this is no time to be clever."

"I'm in deadly earnest, Edwina. Say the word and I'll go to Lord Buckleigh."

"You couldn't make yourself heard," she said crossly. Beyond her anger with the man, she was furious that she should be drawn away from what was quite the most interesting thing to happen in her family since Quentin's disgrace the year before. "I won't leave the room," she told him, "but I'll give you five minutes, no more."

"Five minutes should suffice," said Elliot. "I admit the attractions of your brother's matrimonial future," he continued, when they had walked farther down the room, "but I think you'd be more interested in your own."

"You have nothing to say about my future, Elliot, and no right to talk to me about it."

"I have at least the right of a friend."

"No longer. Friendship between us is impossible."

"Did you accept Deavers?"

His eyes were intent on her, and she was forced to turn her own away. "Why should it matter to you?" She began to walk off, but he held her by the arm, his fingers pressing into her flesh. "Oh, very well." She pulled away and rubbed her arm where he had touched her. "I did not. But I may. And don't tell me he's not good enough for me, Elliot, because that has nothing to say to it."

He relaxed then, and his mouth broke into a crooked smile. "Oh, but it does. He's not nearly good enough, Edwina. I am. You'd better marry me."

She looked in his face to see if he was mocking her. She could not be sure. "We've had this conversation before. It will be ten years before you can properly afford a wife. I won't give you those ten years."

"I'm not asking you to give me ten years. Not even ten days, if we can get a special license. Marry me now."

He could not be serious. She would laugh if she weren't so angry. She did not know how to respond to him, and her uncertainty was mirrored in her face.

"I'm in earnest, Edwina. Let me say it now. It won't be easy. We'll live in lodgings, perhaps a small house. There won't be many servants, there won't be much money for clothes or entertaining. I don't know how you'll spend your days. I work hard, I won't be with you often. It's a receipt for disaster, but I'll risk it. I'm not going to let you settle for Deavers. I love you too much to lose you."

She believed him then, and the wonder of it kept her silent. She should refuse him, of course. She knew that they would quarrel, that there would be a thousand times she would regret it, but when it came to the point, she could not send Elliot out of her life. Edwina could not remember when she had been so flooded with happiness. She flung her arms around his neck and sought his mouth, molding herself to his body as his arms came around her.

It was not a chaste embrace and it caught the eye of one of the group standing around Lord Buckleigh. With an oath, St. George strode across the room toward the oblivious couple. "Marsden, take your bloody hands off my sister."

Lady Buckleigh was occupied with the teapot which Jason had brought in a few minutes earlier, but these words caught her attention. She did not tolerate unseemly language in her drawing room. Nor did she tolerate unseemly behavior. "Edwina," she said, "come here."

The couple had broken apart, but Edwina clasped Elliot's hand to make sure that it remained around her waist. "No, Mama, I don't think I will."

"Oh, good for you, Edwina," Demetra murmured.

Lady Buckleigh moved forward to confront her daughter. She was followed by her husband, who stared at Elliot in disbelief. "I had thought better of you, Marsden."

"I'm sorry, sir." Lord Buckleigh was not a man to attract affection, but Elliot genuinely liked the older man. "I expect nothing from you. I can't keep her well, but by God, I'm going to keep her."

St. George raised his fists in a threatening gesture. "You filthy bastard!"

It was a statement of fact, but Elliot did not like this reference to his birth. He pushed Edwina behind him and moved forward.

The door to the drawing room was thrown open and Stephen appeared, trembling with unaccustomed excitement. "My lord, my lady," he said, his voice squeaking on the last syllable, "the Queen."

Chapter 25

Thursday, October 12

Whatever Caroline of Brunswick had or had not done in the past twenty years, there was only one possible response to the arrival of the Queen of England. With varying degrees of grace, the group in the small drawing room bowed and curtsied to their sovereign's wife.

Her Majesty, never one to stand on ceremony, swiftly gestured for them to rise. It was the first chance many of the company had had to observe Caroline since her return from the Continent.

"I say," Lewis mouthed into Sophy's ear, "she doesn't look very royal."

"They never do," Sophy returned, thinking that it was nice to see someone whose bosom was even more ample than hers.

Caroline was certainly a striking woman. She had an abundance of black curls, which Lady Buckleigh, who had known Her Majesty in her younger days, knew were not her own. Her eyebrows, Helen noted, were very definitely painted and her cheeks had certainly been rouged. She wore a sober gown of gray silk with a high ruff (a poor choice, Edwina thought, for a woman with such a short neck) and a hat surmounted by a profusion of ostrich feathers (which helped

373

to balance Her Majesty's less than slender form). But despite the hair and the clothes and the paint, her features appeared rather delicate. Demetra thought she had a nice face.

"I apologize for intruding on you, Lady Buckleigh," the Queen said in her accented English, "especially when you are entertaining. But Lord Braithwood"—she nodded to Kenrick, who was standing by the door—"has informed me that a friend of mine is in the house. Anna, my dear, I had no idea you were in England. Have you come to testify about me?"

Annina looked extremely confused, but she warmed to the kindness in the Queen's voice. "Yes," she murmured, eyes downcast.

"And what," Caroline inquired with friendly interest, "are you to testify about?"

Annina looked down the room at Quentin, lifted her chin, and turned back to the Queen. "Lord St. George wants me to tell lies about you. But," she concluded with emphasis, "I am not going to do it."

"Well then," said the Queen, "that makes everything all right, doesn't it?"

Annina seemed unsure how to answer this remark, and in the ensuing silence, Arthur Berresford was unable to contain himself.

"Forgive me, Your Majesty," he said, "but—is this lady the Contessa Montalto?"

The Queen surveyed him calmly and almost, it seemed, with amusement. "Certainly she is, Lord Berresford."

"By Jupiter!" Lewis exclaimed involuntarily. "Now you'll have to marry her, Quen."

Annina turned to the man whom she had been so determined to claim only a few minutes before. "Marry me?" she said fiercely. "Do you imagine I would ever agree to marry him?"

Queen Caroline looked from Annina to St. George with interest. "He is certainly more attractive than your first husband," she observed, "but if you feel so strongly about the matter, of course you must not marry him. Come"—she extended a hand to the younger woman—"you shall tell me all about it. I am sure Lady Buckleigh will excuse us."

Pointedly ignoring Quentin, Annina took the Queen's proffered hand and the two women walked to a sofa at the far end of the room. The company stood in silence during this progress, but once the Queen and Annina had settled and begun a low-voiced conversation in Italian, Lord Buckleigh rounded on his son.

"It seems you have a good deal to explain, St. George. I suggest you start. Now."

"Horace." Lady Buckleigh appeared less angry than her husband. "This is a family matter. It would be best—"

"Oh, no, Lady Buckleigh." Berresford strode toward the center of the room, where the Thane family were still gathered. "I have an interest in this and I demand that your son give an accounting of his actions."

"Certainly, Berresford." Though St. George was quite pale, he did not give the appearance of a man who has been cornered. "But before I do so, perhaps you would care to have a look at these."

After taking the letters from Park Street, St. George had left them in the one place he was sure Demetra could not go: White's. He had been there this afternoon when Hunter came to tell him Madame Falconetti had disappeared from Chester Priory. Suspecting trouble, St. George had thought it prudent to retrieve the letters before he left the club. Now he reached inside his exquisitely cut coat and withdrew a packet of papers.

Berresford declined to take them. "I will not be fobbed off, St. George. Once and for all—"

"I have no intention of fobbing you off, Berresford. I think you will find these papers of the greatest interest. I found them," the viscount added deliberately, "in Hawksley's house."

"What's this? What the devil were you doing in Hawksley's house?" Buckleigh demanded.

"Taking my nephew to look for his wagon."

"You took Colin on an outing?" Lewis was indredulous. "Have to do better than that, Quen."

"Quentin," Lady Beatrix had joined the group, "how you can have a care for anyone's papers at a time like—"

"Read them, Berresford," St. George said softly.

"Arthur, no, you mustn't!" Helen rushed to her husband's side. "They're private!"

Arthur stared at his wife in bewilderment.

"Berresford." Frank stepped forward. "This is rather awkward—"

"Yes," St. George murmured, "I should think it would be."

"It's no secret from you or my wife that Helen and I were once attached to each other. I am afraid that my brother-in-law has come across some letters which Helen wrote to me at that time. Perhaps it was overly sentimental to keep them all these years, but that does not give St. George the right to remove them from my house."

It was, Demetra thought, a much more convincing story than the one she had been going to use. She would have felt quite confident had she not read the letters, which Frank had obviously not done. For if he had, he would know that a reference to Paris made it highly improbable that the letters concerned Frank and Helen's youthful romance.

"Very clever, Hawksley," said Quentin, who obviously had read them all, "but if you examine the papers I think you will find—"

"Oh, Frank, they can't be those letters," Demetra exclaimed. "I threw them out years ago. I'm afraid I had a burst of jealousy, which was quite absurd, for if there'd been anything for me to be jealous about you'd have noticed that the letters were missing before now. These must be the letters you told me about, Helen, the ones you wrote to your husband and never sent."

As she spoke, St. George opened one of the letters and pressed it into Berresford's hand. Berresford glanced down at it. "It's a love letter!" he exclaimed in disbelief.

"Of course it is," Demetra said. "What other sort of letter would Helen write to you?"

On the face of it, this was perfectly logical, but there was something, Berresford felt, vaguely wrong with Lady Chester's explanation. He turned to his wife. "Helen, is this true?"

"I—"

Oh, Helen, do try to be sensible for once, Demetra thought.

"Yes, Arthur, it is true," said Lady Berresford, faintly but clearly.

"She is embarrassed to speak of it." Demetra came to the rescue of the bewildered Helen. "It was when she returned from Paris last autumn. You were still abroad and Helen missed you quite dreadfully. Only a few days ago she told me how she wrote to you almost every night and how she was too embarrassed to send the letters, just as she is too embarrassed to speak of them now. It is the oddest thing, you know, but such sentiments between a husband and wife are not thought at all fashionable."

"While between people who are not married they are considered the height of sophistication," said Edwina, who was still holding Elliot's hand. "Only look at all the fuss everyone makes over *Les Liaisons Dangereuse*."

"Well, but that's different," Sophy could not help pointing out. "It's not about love, it's about—"

"Sophy!" Lady Buckleigh had not entirely lost her powers of command.

"—all those other things," Sophy concluded blithely.

"I think," St. George said to Arthur, "that you had best ask your wife—or my sister, since she seems to be giving most of the explanations—how the letters came to be in Park Street."

"You only have my brother's word for it that they did," Demetra told Arthur. "And you've seen how reliable Quentin's word is."

"But he must have gotten hold of them somehow," Arthur protested.

"To be sure. He had them from me," Bianca announced.

"You!" Arthur wheeled round on the woman who had already been far more trouble than she was worth.

"I took them with me when I left Berresford House," Bianca explained calmly. "I thought I might need something—how do you say it?—something with which to bargain."

"To what?"

"Bargain. You may say it was wrong of me, but I was a defenseless woman, alone in a foreign land. I had to protect myself somehow. Only when St. George left me at—left me in the country, I discovered that the letters were missing. I sent for Lady Berresford so I could explain."

"Explain that you had stolen her letters?"

"Explain that her letters had fallen into the hands of a man I knew to be most unscrupulous."

"And you went?" Arthur demanded of his wife.

"Well, naturally, Arthur." Helen was beginning to enter into the spirit of the thing. "What else was I to do when I received an urgent summons from the Contessa Montalto begging me to join her? You said I was to treat her like a sister."

"But she's not the Contessa Montalto!"

"You didn't tell me that, Arthur. You never tell me anything."

"You said nothing of this in the letter you left for me."

"Of course I didn't. You told me that everything about the contessa—that is, about Madame Falconetti—was to be most secret. Naturally I wouldn't write it in a letter which any of the servants might have read and which I daresay some of them did, for I have always suspected—"

"Perhaps," St. George interjected, "you should ask your wife exactly where she and Madame Falconetti spent the night."

Arthur glanced at the viscount with some annoyance. He was not fond of having words put in his mouth—his political colleagues tried to do it far too often. Still, he did want to know where Helen had been. "Well?" he asked his wife. "Where were you?"

"At Chester Priory."

"But you said—"

Demetra decided it was time to step in again. "She said nothing about where she had or had not been. And you mustn't glare at Frank like that, he knew nothing about it." She laid special emphasis on this last, for Frank's benefit. "I took Madame Falconetti to Chester Priory."

"And why did you do that, 'Metra?" Quentin asked with great interest.

"Because you forced me to, Quen. Surely you haven't forgotten."

"I knew it!" Sophy exclaimed. "You are a beast, Quentin!"

"Sophia!" Lord Buckleigh stepped into the fray. "Exactly what are you accusing Quentin of doing, Demetra?"

"Blackmailing me, Papa. After he helped Madame Falconetti escape from Berresford House—"

"Escape from Berresford House?" Buckleigh repeated.

"There was no need for her to do so," Arthur said stiffly.

"There was every need," Bianca maintained.

"I told you she was in trouble," Lewis whispered to Sophy.

"After they left Berresford House," Demetra continued, "Quentin brought Madame Falconetti to Bruton Street. He must have stolen the letters from her then, for he used them to force me to hide her at Chester Priory."

"Naturally you were filled with alarm at the sight of letters which Lady Berresford had written to her own husband." Quentin almost seemed to be enjoying himself.

"I was alarmed," Demetra explained to Arthur, "because I was fool enough to believe the story Quentin is now trying to foist on you. He told me Helen had written the letters to Frank."

"Demetra!" Frank stared at his wife. "How could you possibly think—"

"I know, darling, it was the most idiotish mistake and I'm sure Lord Berresford is much too sensible to fall into the same trap. But Helen has just explained it all to me. You see why she was so eager to speak with me, Lord Berresford. Naturally such a misunderstanding had to be cleared up as quickly as possible."

"If I didn't—coerce—you into helping me until after Madame Falconetti left Berresford House," Quentin said dulcetly, "what on earth were you doing there earlier that same evening, 'Metra?"

"Returning the ring, of course."

"What ring?" Berresford latched on to the mention of a tangible object.

"The one Madame Falconetti dropped at the Haymarket," Demetra explained. "I gave it to Helen."

"And Helen gave it to me, later that same evening." Frank reached into his pocket. "Here it is."

"How thoughtful of you to keep it, Lord Chester." Bianca moved forward and took the ring from Frank's hand. "I'm so glad to have it returned."

Quentin looked from Demetra to Frank to Helen to Bianca with sardonic amusement. "Bravo," he said. "That's the most entertaining tissue of lies since *School for Scandal*. Don't tell me you believe a word of it, Berresford."

"I think," said Demetra, "that if you will only reflect for a moment, Lord Berresford, you will see the truth of my story. I know you will think carefully, for you must realize how great the consequences could be."

Arthur was not sure he understood Lady Chester's story, let alone believed it. St. George had a point. It all sounded dashed odd. On the other hand— Lady Chester also had a point. If he believed the version of events St. George was hinting at, he faced scandal, perhaps even divorce. True, he would be the injured party, but that was not a role for which Berresford had much liking.

"St. George," said Arthur, "I don't know exactly what it is you've been implying about my wife, but I demand that you retract it at once."

380

Quentin regarded him with something approaching contempt. "You disappoint me, Berresford. I had not expected a fellow Cambridge man to be so easily duped."

"Cambridge!" Ian exclaimed. "By God, that's it!"

"What is 'it,' Ian?" Bianca asked.

"I knew I'd seen St. George before. It was in Cambridge. I didn't think much of him then either."

"Very interesting," said Arthur, "but—"

"When?" Frank demanded, so suddenly and so sharply that Demetra looked at him in surprise.

"Hawksley," Arthur protested, "this is no time—"

"Wait a minute, Berresford, this may be important, I want you to hear it. You too, Kenrick." Elliot had been right about Frank. He had the knack of achieving silence in the most unruly Parliamentary debate and it proved equally effective in Lady Buckleigh's equally contentious drawing room. "When did you see St. George in Cambridge, York?"

"Must have been '14," Ian decided after a moment. "While Boney was still on Elba. I was on furlough, on my way to show my face at the ancestral estate, and I stopped off in Cambridge to see my younger brother. He's the scholarly one," he added for the benefit of the company. "In orders now. Don't know how he stands it, though I suppose it's not a bad life if you can stomach the reading matter."

"Where did you encounter St. George?" Frank persisted.

"Some tavern or other—can't remember the name now. Full of undergraduates, of course. There was a card room in back. I joined a faro game and St. George was at the table."

"Did he win?" Sophy prided herself on always being able to best Quentin at cards.

"Later, Sophy," said Frank, his eyes on Ian. "You spoke to him?"

"Certainly. We were both at the table half the night. I had a devilish bad run of luck. Had to borrow off my brother just to make it on to Ireland."

"What did you talk about?"

"Lord, Hawksley, I don't remember. What does it matter now?"

"Did you tell war stories?"

"I suppose so. What else did one talk about in '14?"

"Did you by any chance mention Captain Rowland?"

"It was six years ago, I tell you, I can't possibly— Good God," Ian exclaimed softly.

Demetra, suddenly realizing the significance of the discussion, drew in her breath.

"Well?" Frank insisted.

"I don't know how you remembered it," Ian said. "*I* haven't thought of it in years. But I did talk about Rowland."

"You're sure?"

"Oh, yes. St. George asked a devil of a lot of questions. Didn't you?" he concluded, turning on the viscount.

St. George returned the look, his face a complete blank.

"I doubt he'll admit to it," Frank said. "But he had his reasons for asking those questions. He later used the story to ruin Rowland in a by-election. There was some speculation about how he came by the information, but the mystery is now solved."

"Conclusively." Kenrick spoke up for the first time and smiled at Demetra.

"Assuming you believe York's word," Quentin observed.

"Between York's word and yours," said Arthur, "there can be no contest. And speaking of your word, I don't believe you have yet—"

But no one paid him any heed. The gentle murmur of Italian at the end of the room had ceased and the Queen was saying, quite loudly and in English, "What have we here?"

Demetra turned. The double doors from the gold drawing room were partly open and her son and daughter were peering through them curiously. Demetra started forward, but Frank's hand closed on her arm. The Queen smiled warmly and

382

gestured for the young Hawksleys to approach. Annie ran to her at once. Colin glanced down the room at his parents. Frank nodded and Colin followed his sister more slowly.

Annie stared fearlessly up at the Queen. "What's your name?"

The Queen leaned forward, bending to the children's level. "Caroline."

"I'm Annie. This is Colin. And this," said Annie, holding out her wooden horse, "is Caroline, too."

"Mary Rose had gone to see about their dinner," Demetra explained, "and they came out in the hall and heard the servants talking about the Queen. So they decided to come down and meet her."

"It's a mercy they did," said Frank. "The Queen loves children. And there's nothing like children and royalty to put a damper on a tense situation."

They were once again alone in the old sitting room. After Colin and Annie's intervention, St. George had at last been prevailed upon to return the letters to Helen and offer her a resonable apology. This done, Buckleigh had taken his son off, assuring Arthur, Frank, and Kenrick that St. George would give a full explanation on the morrow. (It was, Edwina murmured to Elliot later during an interval between kisses, remarkably like the scene following Quentin's disgrace a year ago.)

Berresford was reasonably mollified. When Helen reminded him that they were engaged to attend the Marchfield rout, the couple took their leave. Bianca and Ian also left, with remarkable discretion, to the disappointment of the two youngest Thanes and the relief of most of the others. After a brief word with Frank and Demetra, Kenrick also departed, escorting the Queen and Annina, whom Her Majesty had invited to be her guest.

383

Lord Buckleigh was now closeted with Quentin in the study. They had probably been joined by Lady Buckleigh, if she was not still in her dressing room with Beatrix. Edwina and Elliot had slipped off somewhere together, and Sophy and Lewis were consoling themselves for the departure of Ian and Bianca by entertaining the children.

"I think we have a fairly accurate picture now," Frank said. "We'll talk to the contessa tomorrow—the real contessa—and we'll see what sort of story St. George comes up with. By this time it ought to have some resemblance to the truth. I—we—owe you our thanks, Demetra."

"Besting Quentin was reward enough," Demetra said, but her voice sounded unusually subdued.

They regarded each other in silence for a few moments, Frank leaning against the wall by the door, Demetra sitting on a small chair on the opposite side of the room. "I suppose," Frank said, in a tone of detached interest, "that you had your reasons for not telling me the truth from the beginning."

"If I had done so, would you have believed me?" Demetra asked quietly, but with a glint in her eyes that was anything but subdued.

"I wouldn't—"

"You wouldn't have wanted me to move to Buckleigh House. If I hadn't done so, how could I have found out what Quentin was up to?"

"A point," Frank conceded. "But later, when you took Madame Falconetti to Pancras Street—yes, I know about that, York saw you, never mind the details. The point is, even after you had proof you didn't tell me."

"I didn't have proof, only circumstantial evidence, and I was going to tell you, only—"

"You might at least," Frank continued, all vestiges of detachment gone, "have told me about the letters. I paid our money—"

"I might have known it was ours," Demetra exclaimed, springing to her feet. "Why couldn't Helen buy back her

384

own letters?"

"Helen only has what Berresford gives her. I had to help her."

"So you paid our money—"

"For the contessa's copies, while all the time the originals were safely in my own house."

"How was I to know you'd be fool enough to pay for the letters without verifying the handwriting?"

"How the hell could I verify the handwriting? It was pitch black on the stairs and— Oh, the devil. At least you can't deny that you came to Park Street on Sunday with the express intention of getting me into bed so you could—"

"Of course I meant to get you into bed. I had to do something to get you back."

"Get me back? You're the one who left me. Why on earth were you worried about getting me back?"

"Because I thought you were having an affair with Helen," Demetra said patiently.

"You thought *what?*" Frank stared at his wife as though she had gone mad.

"I thought Helen had written the letters to you. I said so just now in the drawing room."

"I assumed that was for Berresford's benefit." Frank was still astonished. "Good God, Demetra, how could you possibly think such a thing?"

"It wasn't so hard. I saw the note Madame Falconetti sent to Helen. And you were the one who came in response to it."

"Of course I was. There wasn't anyone else Helen could turn to."

"I understand that now, Frank, but I didn't think that way at the time. And then you were suddenly so cold on the way home from the Braithwoods'—"

"I should think I was cold. I'd just learned that my wife had been paying clandestine visits to Pancras Street in the company of the woman I thought was the Contessa Montalto."

"But I didn't know that. I assumed it was because of Helen.

385

And when I asked you if it was, you said she needed you more than I did—"

"That may still be true."

"And you got furiously angry—"

"Because I thought you knew about the letters."

"Which I did. But not in the way you thought."

They were silent once again, still on their respective sides of the room. "So it's been a series of misunderstandings," said Frank, "all the way back to the business about Captain Rowland."

Demetra looked at him but did not answer.

"Only it's not just a misunderstanding, is it?" said Frank softly.

"You didn't trust me." The hurt in Demetra's voice was palpable. "You don't trust me. You thought I told St. George about Captain Rowland. No matter how much I denied it, you never believed me, not completely. If Major York hadn't conveniently come up with an explanation, I expect you'd still be wondering. How could you possibly think I would betray your secrets to anyone, let alone Quentin?"

"How could you possibly think I would have an affair with anyone, let alone Helen?"

Demetra blinked in surprise. "But that's—that's different."

"Is it?"

"Of course it is. You really did love Helen, once."

"You really did care about St. George, once. Lewis says you were always getting him out of scrapes."

"When we were children. I would never help the man Quentin has become."

"And I would never have an affair with the woman Helen has become."

"That's not fair, Frank! There's no comparison between the two situations," Demetra said, moving impatiently across the room. "They're totally different. They're—" She stopped and stared unseeing at a watercolor of the Thane sisters which hung beside the fireplace. Were the situations so very different? She had condemned Frank with astonishing speed and without a great deal of evidence. Yes, but at the time it had all seemed so clear. Had it been that way for Frank as well?

"Are you saying I've been as much of a fool as you?" Demetra demanded, turning back to her husband.

"You could put it that way."

"I'm sorry."

"So am I."

She carefully adjusted her lace collar. "There's no guarantee that either of us won't be foolish in the future."

"No," he agreed.

Demetra sighed. "It isn't easy being married, is it?"

Frank grinned. "That's what I told Marsden earlier this afternoon."

"Marsden asked you about marriage?"

"I expect he was thinking of his future with Edwina. I admitted marriage was difficult and he wanted to know if it was worth it."

"What did you tell him?"

Frank's eyes glinted with amusement and something stronger. "What do you think?"

Still confused and uncertain, Demetra contemplated the pattern on the carpet with apparent interest.

"Demetra," Frank said.

She looked up expectantly.

"I have to be getting home. I have dinner guests."

"You have what?" Demetra said.

"I asked York and Madame Falconetti to dinner. It seemed the least I could do. They were both remarkably helpful this afternoon."

"They aren't going back to the Continent then?"

"Not just yet."

"And where," Demetra inquired, "are they staying while they remain in London?"

Frank shifted his weight. "In Park street. Don't look like that, Demetra, the workmen have been doing wonders. At least

387

one of the spare bedrooms is in remarkably good repair and I
don't think two will be required."

"You might have asked me."

"Do you disapprove?"

"I think it's a splendid idea. That's not the point. It's *our*
house."

"Is it?"

Demetra was silent, lowering her gaze to the carpet once
more. Frank watched her for a moment, then crossed the room
in three strides and grasped her by the shoulders. "Confound
it, Demetra, you know that I love you. Please come home."

Demetra looked up at him, her eyes full of laughter though
to her own surprise she found that she was on the verge of
tears. "Of course I'll come home, darling. I always said I
would."

Her arms slid around him and he lowered his head to hers in
a kiss that was surprisingly urgent. They could not have said
which was stronger, their relief or their desire. They clung to
each other, afraid to separate. Neither of them could quite
believe that everything had at last come out right.

It was Demetra who made the first move. "Frank," she
murmured when she was finally able to speak, "shouldn't
we—"

"No," said Frank, taking her face between his hands. "I
don't want to talk."

"You don't?" Demetra's voice was incredulous. "Frank
Hawksley, for the past ten days you've insisted—"

The words were lost in his kiss. Demetra gave it up without
further protest. Frank was right. At the moment some things
were much more important than conversation.

"Let's get the children and Mary Rose and leave at once,"
Frank said at last, his lips against her hair. "You can—" He
raised his head. "What the devil's that?"

"Someone's at the door."

"That's impossible."

"Nevertheless. Let me go, Frank."

"Don't answer it." Frank's face was inches from hers.

"It might be important."

"After this afternoon, nothing more could possibly—"

"Lady Chester?" Stephen's voice came from the corridor.

"Yes, Stephen," said Demetra, twisting her head away from Frank and controlling a sudden desire to giggle. "Come in."

Stephen barely suppressed a grin when he entered the sitting room and saw Lady Chester standing in the circle of her husband's arm. He'd bet Jason a crown that her ladyship would return to Lord Chester within the month.

"Forgive me, my lady, my lord, but there's a caller below." Frank groaned.

"Another one?" Demetra asked.

At that Stephen did grin. "Yes, my lady. A Mr. Gareth Lovell. He asked for Lord Chester."

Frank frowned. "That's odd, I don't know any— Good God," he exclaimed, his eyes meeting Demetra's in startled comprehension, *"Gareth?"*

Epilogue

Friday, November 10

Demetra turned away from the window with a sigh. "No sign of them."

"They could be another hour yet." Rowena Braithwood was a model of calm. One would never guess that the House might be deciding Queen Caroline's fate at this very moment. "They have the rest of the speeches to get through before they can vote. More tea, anyone?"

Philippa shot Demetra a look of sympathy. "I do hate waiting. Only think how anxious the Queen must be."

Demetra returned to the small group sitting around the fireplace in Rowena's elegant saloon. It was difficult to believe that the trial might at last be coming to an end. Since Queen Caroline's visit to Buckleigh House four weeks ago, Demetra was more on Her Majesty's side than ever. "Do you think the Government will really abandon the bill after this vote?" she asked.

"They will if they have any sense," said Francesca Scott. "But that hardly answers the question."

Harriet Granville accepted a fresh cup of tea from Rowena. "Lord Liverpool says if the majority against the Queen is large enough, he'll send the bill on to the Commons."

"It will never pass the Commons," Livia Warwick said with conviction. "Even the King seems to realize that."

"It would be much the best thing for the Government if the bill was abandoned," said Harriet, whose brother-in-law, Lord Harrowby, was in the Cabinet. "Lord Castlereagh was booed at Covent Garden on Wednesday. It was *Twelfth Night* and the audience went quite wild at the line, *To thy defense make what thou canst of it.*"

Philippa bent down to pet Hermia. She wished her baby, asleep upstairs, would awaken. At least that would give her something to do. "I can't believe Emily picked this of all times to go to Brighton. She's missing out on all the excitement."

"She manages to keep up with the news," said Francesca. "I had a letter from her this morning. She says she's shocked beyond measure by the Queen's protest."

Demetra looked at Francesca in surprise. Emily Cowper did not seem the sort of woman who shocked easily. In any case, Demetra did not see what was so shocking about the formal protest against the trial which the Queen had sent to the House of Lords a few days ago.

"Emily thinks it wicked and unprincipled for her to swear she is guiltless of the charges when she cannot possibly be innocent," Francesca explained.

"That doesn't sound much like Emily," said Livia. "I thought she'd decided the Queen had a perfect right to a lover as long as she chose one of decent birth."

"It was the apparent lie that bothered her, she wasn't saying the Queen didn't have a right to a lover. Emily thinks a woman can reconcile infidelity with her conscience."

"How?" Philippa asked, intrigued by this notion.

Francesca smiled. "By recognizing that the real sinner is the man who forced her to do it."

"Her lover or her husband?" Demetra asked.

"Emily wasn't clear on that point, but I think in the Queen's case it would be the husband."

Harriet snorted. "In Emily's case it would have to be the

391

husband too. She couldn't very well blame all her lovers. Has she told Peter Cowper the blame is his?"

"I doubt it," said Rowena, handing around a plate of sandwiches. "Emily has a good grasp of diplomacy."

"Well, I'm sure the Queen would have taken her marriage vows more seriously if the King had been more serious about his," Demetra said.

"Hear, hear," said Philippa, so enthusiastically that Hermia woke up long enough to bark an accompaniment.

"That's quite true." Harriet selected a bread-and-butter sandwich. "Though I do think Denman went a bit far when he compared the King's treatment of the Queen to Nero's treatment of Octavia."

"Oh, but if he hadn't, we wouldn't have the fun of calling Carlton House *Nero's Hotel*," Philippa said.

"Well," said Kenrick, when he and the five other husbands walked into the saloon a few moments later to find their wives laughing, "we thought you'd be desperate for news, but I see you're enjoying yourselves so much we needn't have hurried."

The laughter stopped abruptly. The women turned. Six pairs of eyes were fixed on the six men.

"They've dropped the bill, haven't they?" said Rowena.

"Devil take it," Frank exclaimed, "you've ruined the scene. We've been rehearsing our dramatic announcement all the way from Westminster."

"Ruined nothing," said Demetra, leaning forward eagerly. "What was the vote? How did the Queen take it? We want details."

"Well," said Frank, sauntering into the room, "first Morley said it would be contrary to the spirit of English justice to infer the Queen's guilt from such questionable evidence as the prosecution had brought forward, and then Bedford made a speech about how the whole proceeding was derogatory to—"

"The vote, Frank," Demetra said.

"I'm coming to that. It was past one before strangers were ordered to withdraw—"

"Leaving us commoners to cool our heels outside," Henry put in.

"And nearly another half hour before the division," said Granville, dropping down on the sofa beside his wife.

"And what was the division?" Harriet was nearly as impatient as Demetra.

"The Government still had a majority, of course," Kenrick began.

"That was expected," Philippa said. "How much of a majority?"

The gentlemen exchanged glances. "Three times three," said Frank.

"Nine?" Demetra exclaimed. It was even lower than expected.

"Nine," said Nicholas. "Creevey's fairly shouting it in the streets."

"The Opposition made the most unbecoming display of glee after the division," Granville said with a grin.

"A lot of Tories voted with us," Kenrick retorted. "Including the Right Honorable Viscount Granville."

"That's nothing," said the Right Honorable Viscount. "My arch-Tory brother Stafford voted against the bill too. I don't know if his wife will ever forgive him. Harrowby didn't vote at all, and he's in the Cabinet."

"Liverpool said if the majority had been higher he would have felt it his duty to send the bill to the Commons," Frank said, picking up the thread of the story, "but as it was, he thought it best to proceed no further."

"And the Queen?" Demetra asked. "Was she there? How did she take it?"

"She was there," said Frank, "but I'm not sure how she took it. She said nothing and her face looked a complete blank. She left almost at once."

"The crowds in the street are jubilant," said Francesca's husband, Gerry Scott. "Though the Government should be thanking God the bill's been got rid of."

393

"The Ministers will keep their places?" Philippa asked.

"There may be some reshuffling, but the Government isn't going to fall," Nicholas said.

"And the mob will cease to protest now that they've lost their figurehead," said Henry. "We can all stop worrying that there'll be a revolution tomorrow."

"More's the pity," said Frank.

"There are still some matters to be decided." Granville, a skilled diplomat, declined to enter into a debate on the need for reform. "But we'll adjourn for a time."

"That," said Harriet, "is the best news of all. When can we leave for the country? I'm longing to see my children."

The conversation continued for an hour or so more, plans for the recess mixed with further details of the day's proceedings and speculation about the next moves of Government, Opposition, King, Queen, and populace. Harriet and Granville, who were expecting guests, were the first to leave. The Warwicks and the Scotts followed. Frank and Demetra and Philippa and Henry stayed to dine with the Braithwoods, and the discussion contined over the dinner table.

"I saw the Contessa Montalto at the Windhams' last night," Rowena said, when the meal was at an end and they were lingering in the dining room. "The Berresfords brought her. She's utterly charming. I don't know why you described her as a frightened rabbit, Demetra. She's a spirited little thing and quite an accomplished flirt."

Demetra was moved to protest. "I never called her a rabbit. But she was frightened when I met her. I suspect standing up to my brother was a liberating experience."

"It seems odd for the Berresfords to have taken a second contessa into their home," Rowena went on. "Though it appears that this time it was Helen's idea. The contessa couldn't have stayed with the Queen indefinitely, and I suspect Helen enjoys the companionship."

"Speaking of contessas," Kenrick said, "have you heard

anything about Madame Falconetti?"

Frank leaned back in his chair and stretched his legs. "She's still in Paris, I imagine. That's where they intended to go when I packed them off."

Kenrick sighed. "I find it hard to believe she went so quietly. Even with St. George's confession, she was an embarrassment to us. She might even have tried her hand at blackmail."

Frank smiled and shook his head. Bianca had left with four thousand pounds of his money, and according to Demetra, three thousand from St. George, but he could not share this story with Kenrick and the others. "She knew it would be awkward for us, and Major York was eager to go."

"I was surprised they left together." Philippa looked at Frank in inquiry. "Kenrick said Major York was the one who denounced her."

"It was a lovers' quarrel," Demetra said. "They made it all up when they met in Bruton Street, the day the Queen came to call."

Frank thought of his own lovers' quarrel. "I hope they've learned something from it. I like York."

Demetra sat up very straight. "I like Madame Falconetti, and if you'd admit it, Frank, you do too. Even Helen Berresford likes Madame Falconetti, and she has more cause to think badly of her than anyone."

"I would think it's difficult to be perfectly charitable toward your husband's mistress," Rowena said, "though it's been known to happen. They managed very well at Devonshire House. I suppose it's because the women had so much in common. In addition to the duke, I mean."

Demetra would not let this pass. "But Madame Falconetti wasn't Berresford's mistress. It's quite a tribute to her good sense, which in this case triumphed over her greed."

Henry set down his wineglass. "Was she so very greedy?"

Demetra saw that she was getting into dangerous waters. "Well, she must have been, else why would she have let Quentin persuade her to come to England and engage in that ridiculous charade?"

"Not ridiculous," Kenrick said. "Dangerous. Though at least it's made Berresford cautious, and that's to be applauded."

"While his wife is throwing caution to the wind. I've never seen a woman so changed," Philippa said. "She ignored her husband the entire evening at the Windhams', she flirted with at least three young men, and I actually heard her laugh."

Henry turned to his wife. "See here, are you arguing for inconstancy in women?"

"Oh, I'm for constancy in both sexes," Philippa assured him.

"Lord Rochester to the contrary," Demetra added.

The others laughed. "With the edifying example of our sovereign," Rowena said, "it's a wonder anyone marries at all. Though that doesn't seem to have deterred your sister, Demetra. I understand she marries next month." Rowena glanced at her daughter.

Philippa took up the challenge. "I'm delighted Elliot is getting married. It helps to relieve my guilt for turning him down last year."

"She means," Henry said, "it helps to moderate my jealousy. Now if only your other suitor would find himself a wife . . ."

"Oh, I daresay Anthony will find someone abroad." Philippa reached for her husband's hand.

"Perhaps," Henry acknowledged. "The Americans are easily impressed, and he is a marquis."

Demetra started. A marquis? America? "You mean Philippa and my cousin Tony—"

Henry grinned. "Of course he was quite out of his depth."

"If Tony was courting Philippa, he has more sense than I gave him credit for." Demetra looked at Henry with sympathy. She had only had Helen to deal with. Tony and Elliot were a formidable combination.

"Do your parents approve of your sister's marriage?"

Philippa asked.

Demetra shrugged, remembering the weeks of protest and recriminations and threats. "There was little else they could do, short of a complete break. They don't want to lose Edwina, and Papa, oddly, doesn't want to lose Elliot. And with Quentin's wedding so near—he marries Beatrix Thornton in January—Mama didn't have the energy to fight it any longer. She's been so distracted she even agreed to let Sophy stay with us for a time after Edwina is married."

"Demetra's subverted one sister," Frank said. "Now she's determined to subvert the other."

"I'm not sure I like your choice of words, Frank, but if you mean that I want to get Sophy away from the stultifying atmosphere of Bruton Street, that's exactly what I intend. Now if I can only get Lewis to come to us as well . . ."

Kenrick smiled. "You're a successful meddler, Demetra, but keep your sister away from men like Major York."

"Sophy is too sensible a girl to have her heart broken by a man like Major York."

"No girl is too sensible to have her heart broken," Rowena said.

Demetra looked around the table. Kenrick, Henry, and her own Frank. "Then I shall have to enlist your help to find her a man with scrupulous morals and irreproachable opinions." And an equable temper and perfect trust in his wife, she added to herself. But no, a hot temper could be lived with, and trust could not be given, it had to be won.

Rowena rang for coffee and they sat around the table, reluctant to break the bond of amity that linked them, till Philippa was called upstairs to her baby. Frank and Demetra at last rose to take their leave. "You didn't bring your carriage," Kenrick said. "Take one of ours."

"It's not far," Frank returned. "We can walk."

"Nonsense." Rowena moved to the bell rope. "It's much too cold, and Demetra's slippers aren't fit for walking. I'll have Porter bring round the barouche."

Twenty minutes later, Frank and Demetra settled into the luxurious interior of Rowena's carriage, a rug over their legs to ward off the chill of the night. Demetra leaned close to the warmth of her husband. "It seems hours since I've had you to myself."

Frank pulled away and she sat up in surprise. "Now what's the matter?" she asked.

"This." He pulled an envelope from his coat pocket and handed it to her.

She took it reluctantly. "Frank, if this is another blackmail attempt . . ."

He grinned. "Go on. Open it."

The envelope was thickly padded. She reached in and drew out a wad of paper. Bank notes, she could tell by the feel of them.

Frank signaled the driver and Porter brought the carriage to a halt near a street lamp. Demetra stared at the notes for confirmation, then began to count them. Five hundred, a thousand— She looked up at her husband in astonishment. "Frank, it's four thousand pounds." She handed the notes back to him. "It *is* about blackmail, isn't it? It's the money you paid for the letters. Is it from Helen?"

Frank shook his head. Helen had asked him for help in selling her jewels, but he had refused. He could not take her money. "Not Helen," he said, his eyes alight with amusement. "Gareth. Gareth Lovell."

"Gareth? But how on earth—"

"He caught me today outside the House." Frank grinned, thinking of the afternoon four weeks ago when Lovell had tracked him down at Bruton Street. Lovell had just returned to London and was desperate to see Helen, but he hadn't dared approach her at home. He'd asked Frank, whom he knew to be her friend, to take a message to her. "Helen has refused to see him," Frank went on, "but last night he cornered her at the Windhams' and she couldn't escape."

"What did she tell him?"

"Everything."

"You mean the letters?"

"Yes. The boy was shocked to the core. More than anything by the fact that she knew about his liaison with Bianca. Helen, it seems, was very kind and, I suspect, rather condescending. There could, of course, be nothing further between them—she hasn't forgiven him Bianca—but she trusted him to do the honorable thing. Fortunately, the young cub is plump in the pocket, and he went straight to his banker and then to me."

Demetra fell back against the squabs in helpless laughter. "Oh, Frank, it's so—"

Frank replaced the envelope in his pocket and signaled the driver to go on. "So what?" he asked as he drew her against his shoulder.

"So complete. Full circle. All the untidy ends cleared away." She drew back and looked up at him. "Frank, do you realize that if Major York hadn't been playing cards that night in Siena, none of this would have happened?"

"If York hadn't been playing cards that night in Cambridge, Rowland would have been elected and things would never have gone wrong between us."

"We'd have found something to quarrel about. But it's all right now." She rested her head against his chest and his arm tightened around her.

"Mmm." Frank slipped his other hand under the rug.

Demetra reached beneath the rug to clasp his hand, but it had found other occupation.

"Frank, what on earth are you doing?"

"It seems a shame to waste the time," he said, "and it's a remarkably smooth road."

She drew away from him abruptly, trying to hide her laughter. "Not here, Frank! It's not even our carriage. For heaven's sake, can't you wait?"

Historical Note

The King never got a divorce. The Cabinet refused the Queen's request for a palace, and she stayed at Brandenburgh House at Hammersmith with an allowance of 50,000 pounds a year. Her public support dwindled and the King's popularity grew.

George IV was crowned on July 19, 1821. Caroline was not crowned with him. She was refused admission to the Coronation at Westminster Abbey and to the Coronation banquet at Westminster Hall.

Caroline died less than three weeks later, having burned her diary and forgiven her enemies. George IV lived on until 1830. Bergami died in Pesaro, Italy, in 1841.

The Tories retained control of the government until 1830. When the Whigs returned to power, Henry Brougham became Lord Chancellor.

Information about the proceedings in the House of Lords comes from the transcript of the trial given in *Dolby's Parliamentary Register, 1820*. Other contemporary sources include the *Morning Chronicle*, the letters of Emily Cowper, Thomas Creevey, Harriet Granville, and Dorothea de Lieven, and the journal of Harriet Arbuthnot.

Dorothea de Lieven did give a dinner on October 7, and *The Heir at Law* was performed at the Theatre Royal, Haymarket, on October 10.